COLTON BY
MARRIAGE

BY
MARIE FERRARELLA

AND

COVERT AGENT'S
VIRGIN AFFAIR

BY
LINDA CONRAD

MILLS
BOON

Dear Reader,

Welcome to *The Coltons of Montana!* Prepare for total immersion in the events of Honey Creek, Montana, a small town dominated by three diverse families: the Coltons, branches of which have appeared in previous miniseries; the Walshes, owners of a famous brewery and keepers of a secret that is about to explode; and the Kelleys, owners of a famous barbeque steakhouse chain.

In this story, I focus on Duke Colton, a stoic rancher of few words who just happens to be related to the current sitting President of the United States, Joe Colton (a man readers met in the last Coltons series) and Susan Kelley, the perpetually optimistic girl-next-door who runs the catering side of her father's restaurant. Oh, did I happen to mention there's also the second murder of a man who was killed fifteen years ago?

Interested? Well then, come along for a wild ride.

As ever, I thank you for reading and from the bottom of my heart, I wish you someone to love who loves you back.

All the best,

Marie Ferrarella

COLTON BY MARRIAGE

BY
MARIE FERRARELLA

First published in Great Britain 2011
Harlequin Mills & Boon Limited,
Eton House, 18-24 Paradise Road, Richmond, Surrey TW9 1SR

COLTON BY MARRIAGE © Harlequin Books S.A. 2010

Special thanks and acknowledgment to Marie Ferrarella for her contribution to the Coltons of Montana mini-series.

ISBN: 978 0 263 88508 8

46-0211

Harlequin Mills & Boon policy is to use papers that are natural, renewable and recyclable products and made from wood grown in sustainable forests. The logging and manufacturing processes conform to the legal environmental regulations of the country of origin.

Printed and bound in Spain
by Litografia Rosés S.A., Barcelona

USA TODAY bestselling and RITA Award-winning author **Marie Ferrarella** has written almost two hundred books for Silhouette and Harlequin, some under the name of Marie Nicole. Her romances are beloved by fans worldwide. Visit her website at www.marieferrarella.com.

To Bonnie G. Smith.
Thank you for having
such a wonderful daughter.

Prologue

"It's here, Sheriff." Unable to contain his excitement, Boyd Arnold all but hopped up and down as he pointed toward the murky body of water. "I saw it right here, in the creek, when Blackie ran into the water and I chased him out."

Blackie was what Boyd called his black Labrador retriever. Naming the dog Blackie had been the only unimaginative thing Boyd had ever done. Aside from that one example of dullness, the small-time rancher had an incredibly healthy imagination.

Some people claimed that it was a mite *too* healthy. At one time or another, Boyd had sworn he'd seen a ghost crossing his field, watched in awe as a UFO landed near Honey Creek, the body of water that the town had been named after, and now he was claiming to have seen a dead body in that very same creek.

As the town's recently elected sheriff, thirty-three-year-old Wes Colton would have liked just to have dismissed Boyd's newest tall tale as another figment of the man's overworked imagination. But, *because* he was the recently elected sheriff of Honey Creek, he couldn't. He was too new at the job to point to a gut feeling about things and so he was legally bound to check out each and every story involving wrongdoing no matter how improbable or wild it sounded.

Dead bodies were not the norm in Honey Creek. Most likely someone had dumped a mannequin in the creek in order to play a trick on the gullible Boyd. He hadn't put a name to the so-called body when he'd come running into the office earlier, tripping over his tongue as if it had grown to three times its size as he tried to say what it was he saw.

"Was it a woman, Boyd?" Wes asked now, trying to find the humor in the situation, although, he had to admit, between the heat and the humidity, his sense of humor was in extremely short supply today. Local opinion had it that a woman of the inflatable variety would be the only way Boyd would be able to find any female companionship at all.

Wes would have much rather been in his air-conditioned office, going over paperwork—something he usually disliked and a lot of which the last sheriff had left as payback for Wes winning the post away from him—than facing the prospect of walking through the water searching for a nonexistent body.

"I think it was a man. Tell the truth, Sheriff, I didn't stick around long enough to find out. Never can tell when you might come across one of them zombie types, or those body-snatchers, you know."

Wes looked at him. Boyd's eyes were all but bulging out. The man was actually serious. He shook his head. "Boyd, you want my advice? You've got to stop renting those old horror movies. You've got a vivid enough imagination as it is."

"This wasn't my imagination, Sheriff," Boyd insisted stubbornly with feeling. "This was a real live dead person."

Wes didn't bother pointing out the blatant contradiction in terms. Instead, he stood at the edge of the creek and looked around.

There was nothing but the sound of mosquitoes settling in for an afternoon feed.

A lot of mosquitoes, judging by the sound of it.

It was going to be a miserable summer, Wes thought. Just as he began to turn toward Boyd to tell the rancher that he must have been mistaken about the location of this "body," something caught Wes's eye.

Flies.

An inordinate number of flies.

Mosquitoes weren't making that noise, it was flies.

Flies tended to swarm around rotting meat and waste. Most likely it was the latter, but Wes had a strong feeling that he wasn't going to be free of Boyd until he at least checked out what the insects were swarming around.

"There, Sheriff, look there," Boyd cried excitedly, pointing to something that appeared to be three-quarters submerged in the creek.

Something that had attracted the huge number of flies.

There was no way around not getting his newly cleaned uniform dirty, Wes thought. Resigning himself to the unpleasant ordeal, Honey Creek's newly minted sheriff waded in.

Annoyance vanished as he drew closer to what the flies were laying claim to.

"Damn, but I think you're right, Boyd. That *does* look like a body," Wes declared. Forgetting about his uniform, he went in deeper. Whatever it was was only a few feet away.

"See, I told you!" Boyd crowed, happy to be vindicated. He was grinning from ear to ear like a little kid on Christmas morning. His expression was in sharp contrast to the sheriff's. The latter had become deadly serious.

It appeared to be a dead body all right. Did it belong to some vagrant who'd been passing through when he'd arbitrarily picked Honey Creek to die?

Or had someone dumped a body here from one of the neighboring towns? And if so, which one?

Bracing himself, Wes turned the body over so that he could view the face before he dragged the corpse out.

When he flipped the dead man over, his breath stopped in his lungs. The man had a single bullet in the middle of his forehead and he was missing half his face.

But the other half could still be made out.

At the same moment, unable to stay back, Boyd peered over his shoulder. The rancher's eyes grew huge and he cried out, "It's Mark Walsh!" No sooner was the name out of his mouth than questions and contradictions occurred to Boyd. "But he's dead." Confused, Boyd stared at Wes, waiting for him to say something that made sense out of this. "How can he look that fresh? He's been dead fifteen years!"

"Apparently Walsh wasn't as dead as we thought he was," Wes told him.

It was extremely difficult for Wes to maintain his decorum, not to mention an even voice, when all he could think of was that finally, after all these years, his brother was going to get out of jail.

Because Damien Colton had been convicted of a murder that had never happened.

Until now.

Chapter 1

Duke Colton didn't know what made him look in that direction, but once he did, he couldn't look away. Even though he wanted to.

Moreover, he wanted to keep walking. To pretend that he hadn't seen her, especially not like that.

Susan Kelley's head was still down, her short, dark-blond hair almost acting like a curtain, and she seemed oblivious to the world around her as she sat on the bench to the side of the hospital entrance, tears sliding down her flawless cheeks.

Duke reasoned that it would have been very easy either to turn on his heel and walk in another direction, or just to pick up speed, look straight ahead and get the hell out of there before the Kelley girl looked up.

Especially since she seemed so withdrawn and lost to the world.

He'd be doing her a favor, Duke told himself, if he just

ignored this pretty heart-wrenching display of sadness. Nobody liked looking this vulnerable. God knew that he wouldn't.

Not that he would actually cry in public—or private for that matter. When he came right down to it, Duke was fairly certain that he *couldn't* cry, period. No matter what the situation was.

Hell, he'd pretty much been the last word in stoic. But then, he thought, he'd had to be, seeing as how things hadn't exactly gone all that well in his life—or his family's life—up to this point.

Every instinct he had told Duke he should be moving fast, getting out of Susan's range of vision. Now. Yet it was as if his feet had been dipped in some kind of super-strong glue.

He couldn't make them move.

He was lingering. Why, he couldn't even begin to speculate. It wasn't as though he was one of those people who was bolstered by other people's displays of unhappiness. He'd never believed in that old adage about misery loving company. When he came right down to it, he'd never had much use for misery, his own or anybody else's. For the most part, he liked keeping a low profile and staying out of the way.

And he sure as hell had no idea what to do when confronted with a woman's tears—other than running for the hills, face averted and feigning ignorance of the occurrence. He'd never lay claim to being one of those guys who knew what to say in a regular situation, much less one where he was front-row center to a woman's tear-stained face.

But this was Susan.

Susan Kelley. He'd watched Susan grow up from an awkward little girl to an outgoing, bright-eyed and bushy-tailed little charmer who somehow managed to be completely oblivious to the fact that she was as beautiful as all get out.

Susan was the one who cheered people up. She never cried. Not that he was much of an expert on what Susan did or didn't do. He just heard things. The way a man survived was to keep his eyes and his ears open, and his mouth shut.

Ever since his twin brother Damien was hauled off to jail because everyone in town believed he had killed Mark Walsh, Duke saw little to no reason to socialize with the people in Honey Creek. And Walsh was no angel. Most people had hated him. The truth of it was, if ever someone had deserved being killed, it was Walsh. Mark Walsh was nasty, bad-tempered and he cheated on his wife every opportunity he got. And Walsh and Damien had had words, hot words, over Walsh's daughter, Lucy.

Even so, Damien hadn't killed him.

Duke frowned as, for a moment, fifteen years melted away. He remembered watching the prison bars slam, separating him from Damien. He didn't know who had killed that evil-tempered waste of human flesh, but he would have bet his life that it wasn't Damien.

Now, like a magnet, his green eyes were riveted to Susan.

Damn it, what was she crying about?

He blew out an impatient breath. A woman who was that shaken up about something shouldn't be sitting by herself like that. Someone should be with her, saying something. He didn't know what, but *something*. Something comforting.

Duke looked around, hoping to ease his conscience—and not feel guilty about his desire to get away—by seeing someone approaching the sobbing little blonde.

There was no one.

She was sitting by herself, as alone as he'd ever seen anyone on this earth. As alone as *he* felt a great deal of the time.

Damn it, he didn't want to be in this position. Didn't want to have to go over.

What was the matter with him?

He didn't owe her anything. Why couldn't he just go? Go and put this scene of vulnerability behind him? He wasn't her keeper.

Or her friend.

Susan pressed her lips together to hold back another sob. She hadn't meant to break down like this. She'd managed to hold herself together all this time, through all the visits, all the dark days. Hold herself together even when she'd silently admitted, more than once, that one conclusion was inevitable. Miranda was going to die.

Die even though she was only twenty-five years old, just like her. Twenty-five, with all of life standing right before her to run through, the way a young child would run barefoot through a field of spring daisies, with enthusiasm and joy, tickled by the very act.

Instead, six months ago Miranda had heard those most dreadful of words, *You have cancer,* and they had turned out to be a death sentence rather than a battlefield she could somehow fight her way through.

Now that she'd started, Susan couldn't seem to stop crying. Sobs wracked her body.

She and Miranda were friends—best friends. It felt as if they'd been friends forever, but it only amounted to a tiny bit more than five years. Five years that had gone by in the blink of an eye.

God knows she'd tried very, very hard to be brave for Miranda. Though it got harder and harder, she'd put on a brave face every time she'd walked into Miranda's line of vision. A line of vision that grew progressively smaller and smaller in range until finally, it had been reduced to the confines of a hospital room.

The room where Miranda had died just a few minutes ago.

That was when the dam she'd been struggling to keep intact had burst.

Walking quickly, she'd made it out of Miranda's room and somehow, she'd even made it out of the hospital. But the trip from the outer doors to the parking lot where she'd left her car, that was something she just couldn't manage dry-eyed.

So instead of crossing the length of the parking lot, sobbing and drawing unwanted attention to herself, Susan had retreated to the bench off to the side of the entrance, an afterthought for people who just wanted to collect themselves before entering the tall building or rest before they attempted the drive home.

But she wasn't collecting herself, she was falling apart. Sobbing as if her heart was breaking.

Because it was.

It wasn't fair.

It wasn't fair to die so young, wasn't fair to have to endure the kind of pain Miranda had had just before she'd surrendered, giving up the valiant struggle once and for all.

Her chest hurt as the sobs continued to escape.

Susan knew that on some level, crying like this was selfish of her. After all, it wasn't as if she was alone. She had her family—large, sprawling, friendly and noisy, they were there for her. The youngest of six, she had four sisters and a brother, all of whom she loved dearly and got along with decently now that they were all grown.

The same could be said about her parents, although there were times when her mother's overly loud laments about dying before she ever saw one viable grandchild did get under her skin a little. Nonetheless, she was one of the lucky ones. She had people in her life, people to turn to.

So why did she feel so alone, so lonely? Was grief causing her to lose touch with reality? She *knew* that if she picked up the phone and called one of them, they'd be at her side as quickly as possible.

As would Linc.

She and Lincoln Hayes had grown up together. He'd been her friend for years. Longer than Miranda had actually been. But even so, having him here, having *any* of them here right now, at this moment, just wouldn't take away this awful feeling of overwhelming sorrow and loss.

She supposed she felt this way because she was not only mourning the loss of a dear, wonderful friend, mourning the loss of Miranda's life, she was also, at bottom, mourning the loss of her own childhood. Because Death had stolen away her own innocence. Death had ushered in an overwhelming darkness that had never been there before.

Nothing was every going to be the same again.

And Susan knew without being told that for a long time to come, she was going reach for the phone, beginning calls she wouldn't complete, driven by a desire to share things with someone she couldn't share anything with any longer.

God, she was going to miss Miranda. Miss sharing secrets and laughing and talking until the wee hours of the morning.

More tears came. She felt drained and still they came.

Susan lost track of time.

She had no idea how long she'd been sitting on that bench, sobbing like that. All she knew was that she felt almost completely dehydrated. Like a sponge that had been wrung out.

She should get up and go home before everyone began to wonder what had happened to her. She had a wedding to cater tomorrow. Or maybe it was a birthday party. She couldn't remember. But there was work to do, menus to arrange.

And God knew she didn't want to worry her parents. She'd told them that she was only leaving for an hour or so. Since she worked at the family restaurant and still lived at home, or at least, in the guesthouse on the estate, her parents kept closer track of her than they might have had she been out somewhere on her own.

Her fault.

Everything was her fault, Susan thought, upbraiding herself.

If she'd insisted that Miranda go see the doctor when her friend had started feeling sick and began complaining of bouts of nausea coupled with pain, maybe Miranda would still be alive today instead of...

Susan exhaled a shaky breath.

What was the point? Going over the terrain again wouldn't change anything. It wouldn't bring Miranda back. Miranda was gone and life had suddenly taken on a more temporary, fragile bearing. There was no more "forever" on the horizon. Infinity had become finite.

Susan glanced up abruptly, feeling as if she was being watched. When she raised her eyes, she was more than slightly prepared to see Linc looking back at her. It wouldn't be that unusual for him to come looking for her if he thought she wasn't where she was supposed to be. He'd appointed himself her keeper and while she really did value his friendship, there was a part of her that was beginning to feel smothered by his continuous closeness.

But when she looked up, it wasn't Linc's eyes looking back at her. Nor were they eyes belonging to some passing stranger whose attention had been momentarily captured by the sight of a woman sobbing her heart out.

The eyes she was looking up into were green.

Intensely green, even with all that distance between them. Green eyes she couldn't fathom, Susan thought. The expression on the man's face, however, was not a mystery. It was frowning. In disapproval for her semi-public display of grief?

Or was it just in judgment of her?

Duke was wearing something a little more intense than his usual frown. Try as she might, Susan couldn't recall the brooding rancher with the aura of raw sexuality about him ever really smiling. It was actually hard even to summon a memory of the man that contained a neutral expression on his face.

It seemed to her that Duke always appeared to be annoyed. More than annoyed, a good deal of the time he looked angry. Not that she could really blame him. He was angry at his twin for having done what he'd done and bringing dishonor to the family name.

Or, at least that was what she assumed his scowl and anger were all about.

Embarrassed at being observed, Susan quickly wiped away her tears with the back of her hand. She had no tissues or handkerchief with her, although she knew she should have had the presence of mind to bring one or the other with her, given the situation she knew she might be facing.

Maybe she hadn't because she'd secretly hoped that if she didn't bring either a handkerchief or tissues, there wouldn't be anything to cry about.

For a moment, she was almost positive that Duke was going to turn and walk away, his look of what was now beginning to resemble abject disgust remaining on his face.

But then, instead of walking away, he began walking toward her.

Her stomach fluttered ever so slightly. Susan straightened her shoulders and sat up a little more rigidly. For some unknown reason, she could feel her mouth going dry.

Probably because you're completely dehydrated. How much water do you think you've got left in you?

She would have risen to her feet and started to walk away if she could have, but her legs felt oddly weak and disjointed, as if they didn't quite belong to her. Susan was actually afraid that if she tried to stand up, her knees would give way beneath her and she would collapse back onto the bench. Then Duke would *really* look contemptuously at her, and she didn't think she was up to that.

Not that it should matter to her *what* Duke Colton thought, or didn't think, of her, she silently told herself in the next breath. She just didn't want to look like a complete idiot, that was all. Her nose was probably already red and her eyes had to be exceedingly puffy by now.

Crossing to her, still not uttering a single word in acknowledgment of her present state or even so much as a greeting, Duke abruptly shoved his hand into his pocket, extracted something and held it out to her.

Susan blinked. Duke was holding out a surprisingly neatly folded white handkerchief.

When she made no move to take it from him, he all but growled, "Here, you seem to need this a lot more than I do."

Embarrassment colored her cheeks, making her complexion entirely pink at this point. "No, that's all right," she sniffed, again vainly trying to brush away what amounted to a sheet's worth of tears with the back of her hand.

"Take it." This time he did growl and it was an unmistakable command that left no room for refusal or even wavering debate.

Sniffing again, Susan took the handkerchief from him and murmured a barely audible, "Thank you."

He said nothing for a moment, only watched her as she slid the material along first one cheek and then the other, drying the tear stains from her skin.

When she stopped, he coaxed her on further, saying, "You can blow your nose with it. It won't rip. I've used it myself. Not this time," he corrected uncomfortably. "It's been washed since then."

A glimmer of a smile of amusement flittered across her lips. Susan couldn't begin to explain why, but she felt better. A lot better. As if the pain that had been growing inside of her had suddenly abated and begun shrinking back down to a manageable size.

She was about to say something to him about his kindness and about his riding to the rescue—something that seemed to suit his tall, dark, closed-mouth demeanor—when she heard someone calling out her name.

Linc. She'd know his voice anywhere. Even when it had an impatient edge to it.

The next moment, Linc was next to her, enveloping her in a hug. Without meaning to, she felt herself stiffening. She didn't want to be hugged. She didn't want to be pitied or treated like some fragile child who'd been bruised and needed protection.

If he noticed her reaction, Linc gave no indication that it registered. Instead, leaving the embrace, he slipped his arm around her shoulders, still offering protection.

"There you are, Susan. Everyone's worried about you," he said, as if he was part of her family. "I came to bring you home," he announced a bit louder than he needed to. And then his voice took on an affectionate, scolding tone. "I told you that you shouldn't have come here without me." Still holding her to him, he brushed aside a tear that she must have missed. "C'mon, honey, let's get you out of here."

A while back, she'd allowed their friendship to drift toward something more. But it had been a mistake. She didn't feel *that* way about Linc. She'd tried to let him down gently, to let him know politely that it was his friendship she valued, that there was never going to be anything else between them. But Linc seemed not to get the message. He seemed very comfortable with the notion of taking control of her life.

She found herself chafing against that notion and feeling restless.

He was being rude and completely ignoring Duke, she thought. Duke might not care, but *she* did.

Susan turned to say something to the rancher, to thank him for his handkerchief and his thoughtfulness, but when she looked where he'd just been, he was gone.

He'd left without saying another word to her.

The next moment, Linc was ushering her away, leading her toward the parking lot. She heard him talking to her, saying something about how relieved he was, or words to that effect.

But her mind was elsewhere.

Chapter 2

"You really shouldn't try to face these kinds of things alone, Susan," Linc quietly chided her as he guided Susan to his car. Once beside the shiny silver convertible, he stopped walking. "I'm here for you, you know that. And I'll *always* be here for you," he told her with firm enthusiasm.

"Yes, I know that." Fidgeting inside, Susan looked around the lot, trying to remember where she'd parked her own car. Linc meant well, but she really wanted to be by herself right now. "And I appreciate everything you're trying to do, Linc, but—"

Her voice trailed off for a moment. How did she tell him that he was crowding her without sounding as if she was being completely ungrateful? He was only trying to be kind, to second-guess her needs, she knew all that. But despite all that, despite his good intentions and her understanding, it still felt as if he was sucking up all the oxygen around her and she just couldn't put up with that right now.

Maybe later, when things settled down and fell into place she could appreciate Linc for what he was trying to do, but right now, she felt as if she desperately needed her space, needed to somehow make peace with this sorrow that kept insisting on finding her no matter which way she turned.

Linc opened the passenger door, but she continued to stand there, scanning the lot. He frowned. "What are you looking for?"

"My car." Even as she said it, Susan spotted her silver-blue four-door sedan. She breathed a sigh of relief.

He opened the passenger door wider, silently insisting that she get inside. "You're not up to driving, Susan. I'll take you home."

Her eyes met his. Susan did her best to keep her voice on an even keel, even though her temper felt suddenly very brittle.

"Don't tell me what I can or can't do, Linc. I can drive. I *want* to drive my car," she told him with emphasis.

He pantomimed pressing something down with both hands. Her temper? Was that what he was insinuating? She felt her temper flaring.

"Don't get hysterical, Susan," he warned.

The words, not to mention the action, were tantamount to waving a red flag in front of her. If the words were meant to subdue her, they achieved the exact opposite effect.

"I am *not* hysterical, Linc," she informed him firmly, "I just want to be alone for a while."

"You didn't look very alone a couple of minutes ago."

For a moment she thought he was going to pout, then abruptly his expression changed, as if he'd suddenly come up with an answer that satisfied him. "Was he bothering you?"

Susan stared at Linc, confused and wondering how he'd come to that kind of conclusion. Based on what? "Who?" she wanted to know.

"That Colton guy. You know who I mean. His brother killed Lucy Walsh's father," he said impatiently, trying to remember the man's name. "Duke," he finally recalled, then asked again as he peered at her face, "Was he bothering you?"

She felt as if Linc was suddenly interrogating her. Not only that, but she felt rather defensive for Duke, although she really hadn't a clue as to why. She'd had a crush on him when she was a teenager, but that was years in the past.

Still, he'd stopped and given her a handkerchief when he didn't have to.

"No, what makes you say that?"

Linc's shoulders rose and fell in a spasmodic shrug. "Well, you just said you wanted to be alone, and when I found you, he was in your face—"

Susan was quick to interrupt him. Linc had a tendency to get carried away. "He wasn't in my face, Linc. He hardly said a whole sentence."

Linc's expression told her that it hadn't looked that way from where he was standing. "Then he was just staring at you?"

Susan didn't like the tone that Linc was taking with her. He was invading her private space, going where he had no business venturing. He was her friend, not her father or her husband. And even then he wouldn't have the right to act this way.

"In part," she finally said. "Look, he saw I was crying and he gave me his handkerchief. No questions, nothing, just his handkerchief."

Linc snorted. "Lucky for you he didn't try strangling you with it."

It was a blatant reference to one of the theories surrounding Mark Walsh's death. The county coroner had said that it appeared Mark Walsh had been strangled, among other things, before his face was bashed in, the latter being the final blow that had ushered death in.

Susan just wanted to get away, to mourn her best friend's passing in peace, not be subjected to this cross-examination that Linc seemed determined to conduct. She lifted her chin stubbornly. "Duke's not Damien," she pointed out.

The look on Linc's face was contemptuous, both of her statement and of the man it concerned.

"I dunno about that. They say that twins have an unnatural connection. Maybe he's *just* like his brother." Linc drew himself up, squaring his shoulders before issuing a warning. "I don't want you talking to Duke Colton or having anything to do with him."

For a second, even with the emotional pain she was trying to deal with, Susan could feel her temper *really* flaring. Linc was making noises like a possessive *boyfriend*, and that was the last thing on earth she needed or wanted right now. "Linc, it's not your place to tell me what to do or not do."

Realizing the tactical error he'd just committed,

Linc tried to backtrack as quickly as he could and still save face.

"Sure it is," he insisted. "I care about you, Susan. I care about what happens to you. We don't know what these Coltons are really capable of," he warned. "And I'd never forgive myself if anything happened to you because I didn't say something."

Did Linc really think she was so clueless that she needed guidance? That she was so naive that she was incapable of taking charge of her own life? From out of nowhere a wave of resentment surged within her. She struggled to tamp it down.

She was just upset, Susan told herself. And Linc did mean well, even if he could come across as overbearing at times.

It took effort, but she managed to force a smile to her lips. "I'll be all right, Linc. Don't worry so much. And I'm still driving myself home," she added in case he thought he'd talked her out of that.

She could see that Linc didn't like her refusing his help, but he made no protest and merely nodded his head. She was about to breathe a sigh of relief when Linc unexpectedly added, "All right, I'll follow you."

Susan opened her mouth to tell him that he really didn't have to put himself out like that, but she had a feeling that she'd just be wasting her breath, and she was in no mood to argue.

Maybe she was being unfair. Another woman would have been thrilled to have someone voluntarily offer to all but wrap her in cotton and watch over her like this. There was a part of her that thought she'd be thrilled, as well. But now, coming face to face with it, she found it almost suffocating. All she wanted to do was run away.

Maybe she was overreacting, making too much of what was, at bottom, an act of kindness. But if she was overreacting, she did have a really good excuse. Someone she loved dearly had just died and blown a hole in her world, and it was going to take a while to come to terms with that.

Rather than prolong this no-win debate, Susan nodded. "All right, I'll see you at the house." With that, she turned and walked quickly over to where she'd parked her vehicle.

Duke watched the tall, slim, attractive young blonde make her way through the parking lot. More to the point, she was walking away from that annoying prissy little friend of hers.

Lincoln Hayes.

Now, there was a stalker in the making if he ever saw one, Duke judged. He wondered if Susan was aware of that, of what that Linc character was capable of.

Not his affair, Duke told himself in the next moment. The perky little girl with the swollen eyes was her own person. There was no reason for him to be hovering in the background like some wayward dark cloud on the horizon, watching over her. She might look like the naive girl next door, but he had a feeling that when push came to shove, Susan Kelley was a lot stronger, character-wise, than she appeared.

A fact, he had a feeling, that wouldn't exactly please Lincoln Hayes.

And even if she could be pushed around by the likes

of Hayes, what was that to him? Why did he feel this need to make sure she was all right? The girl had his handkerchief and he wanted it back. Eventually. There was absolutely no other reason to pay attention to her, to her comings and goings and to whether that spineless jellyfish, Hayes, actually turned out to be a stalker.

Annoyed with himself, with the fact that he wasn't leaving, Duke watched as Susan crossed to the extreme right side of the lot and got into her car, a neat little sedan that would have been all but useless on his own ranch. It wouldn't have been able to haul much, other than Susan and some of her skinny friends.

Her sedan came to life. Another minute and she was driving off the lot.

Rubbing his hands on the back of his jeans, Duke got into the cab of his beat-up dark-blue pickup and drove away.

"Have you been crying?"

Bonnie Gene Kelley fired the question, fueled by concern, the moment her daughter walked into the rear of Kelley's Cookhouse, the restaurant that she and her husband Donald ran and had turned into a nation-wide chain.

Seeing for herself that the answer to her question was yes, Bonnie Gene quickly crossed to her youngest child and immediately immersed herself in Susan's life. "Did you and that boy get into an argument?" she wanted to know.

Ever eager for one of her children to finally make her a grandmother, the way all her friends' children had, Bonnie Gene fanned every fire that potentially had an iron in it. In Susan's case, that iron had a name: Lincoln Hayes.

Lincoln wouldn't have been her first choice, or even her second one. Bonnie Gene liked her men more manly, the way her Donald was—or had been before the good life had managed to fatten him up. But Linc was here and he was crazy about Susan. Her daughter could do a lot worse than marry the boy, she supposed.

But if he made Susan cry, then all bets were off. She absolutely wouldn't stand for someone who could wound her youngest born to the extent of making her cry. Sophisticated and worldly—as worldly as anyone could be, given that they were living in a place like Honey Creek, Montana—her maternal claws would immediately emerge, razor-sharp and ready, whenever one of her children was hurt, physically or emotionally.

"No, Mother," Susan replied evenly, wishing she'd waited before walking into work, "we didn't get into an argument."

Part of her just wanted to dash up to her room and shut the door, the other part wanted to be enfolded in her mother's arms and be told that everything was still all right. That the sun still rose in the east and set in the west and everything in between was just fine.

Except that it wasn't. And she needed to grow up and face that.

"Is Miranda worse?" her father asked sympathetically, coming out of the large storage room where they kept the supplies and foodstuffs that were being used that day. He pushed the unlit cigar in his mouth over to the side with his tongue in order to sound more intelligible.

Focusing on her husband for a moment, Bonnie Gene allowed an annoyed huff to escape her lips. She marched over to him, plucked the cigar out of his mouth and made a dramatic show of dropping it into the uncovered trash basket in the corner. It was an ongoing tug of war between them. Donald Kelley seemed to possess an endless supply of cigars and Bonnie Gene apparently possessed an endless supply of patience as she removed and threw away each one she saw him put into his mouth.

Susan had long since stopped thinking that her father actually intended to smoke any of these cigars. In her opinion, he just enjoyed baiting her mother.

But today Susan didn't care about the game or whether her father actually smoked the "wretched things" as her mother called them. All of that had been rendered meaningless, at least for now. Her friend was dead and she was never going to see Miranda again. Her heart hurt.

"Miranda's gone," Susan said in small, quiet voice, answering her father's question.

"Gone?" he echoed. "Gone where?" When his wife gave him a sharp look, a light seemed to go on in his head and Donald realized what Susan had just told him. "Oh. *Gone*." A chagrined expression washed over his face as he came over to his youngest child. "Susan, sweetie, I'm so sorry," he told her. The squat, burly man embraced her, a feat that had been a great deal easier in the days before his gut had grown to the size that it had.

Coming between them, Bonnie gently removed Susan

from Donald's grasp, turned the girl toward her and hugged her daughter closely.

For a moment, nothing was said. The other people in the kitchen, employees who had helped make the original restaurant the success that it was, went about their business, deliberately giving their employers and their daughter privacy until such time as they were invited to take part in whatever it was that was happening.

Still holding Susan to her chest and stroking her hair, the way she used to when she had been a little girl, Bonnie Gene said gently, "Susan, you knew this day was coming."

She had. Deep down, she had, but that didn't mean that she hadn't still hoped—fervently prayed—that it wouldn't. That a miracle would intervene.

"I know," Susan said, struggling again to regain control over her emotions, "it's just that it came too soon."

"It always comes too soon," Bonnie Gene told her daughter with the voice of experience. "No matter how long it takes to get here."

Bonnie Gene had no doubt that if Donald were to die before she did it wouldn't matter whether they'd been together for the past hundred years. It would still be too soon and she would still be bargaining with God to give her "just a little more time" with the man she loved.

"She's in a better place now, kiddo," Susan's father told her, giving her back a comforting, albeit awkward pat. "She's not hurting anymore."

Bonnie Gene looked at her husband, a flicker of impatience in her light-brown eyes. She tossed her head, sending her dark-brown hair over her shoulder. "Everyone always says that," she said dismissively.

"Don't make it any less true," Donald told her stubbornly, pausing to fish the cigar out of the trash. He brushed it off with his fingers, as if the cursory action would send any germs scattering.

Bonnie Gene's eyes narrowed as she looked at her husband over her daughter's shoulder. "You put that in your mouth, Donald Kelley," she hissed, "and you're a dead man."

Donald weighed his options. He knew his wife was passionate about him not smoking, and she seemed to be on a personal crusade these days against his beloved cigars. With a loud sigh, Donald allowed the cigar to fall from his fingers, landing back in the trash. There were plenty more cigars in the house—and a few of them stashed in various out-of-the-way places. Places that Bonnie Gene hadn't been able to find yet. He could wait.

The rear door opened and closed for a second time. All three Kelleys turned to see Linc walk in. He was accompanied by a blast of hot July air. It was like an oven outside. A hot, sticky, moist oven.

"I must have caught every red light from the hospital to the restaurant," Linc complained, addressing his words to the world at large.

Bonnie Gene felt her daughter stiffen the moment she heard Linc's voice. The reaction was not wasted on her. Her mother's instincts instantly kicked in.

Releasing Susan, she approached her daughter's self-appointed shadow. "Linc, I was wondering if you could do me a favor."

It was no secret that Linc was eager to score any brownie points with the senior Kelleys that he could. "Anything, Mrs. Kelley."

"The linen service forgot to send over five of our tablecloths. Be a dear and run over to Albert's Linens and get them." Taking the latest receipt and a note she'd hastily jotted down less than an hour ago, she handed both to Lincoln. "Nita at the service is already waiting for someone to come for them. Just show her these," she instructed.

Lincoln glanced at the receipt and the note, looking somewhat torn about the assignment he'd been given. It was obvious that he'd hoped that whatever it was that Susan's mother wanted done could be done on the premises and near Susan.

But then he nodded and promised, "I'll be right back." He looked at Susan, possibly hoping that she would offer to come with him, but she didn't. With a suppressed sigh and a forced smile, he turned on his heel and walked out of the kitchen through the same door he'd come in.

Susan looked at her mother. It completely amazed her how the woman who could drive her so absolutely crazy when the subject of marriage and babies came up could still somehow be so very intuitive.

She flashed her mother a relieved smile. "Thanks, Mom."

Bonnie Gene's eyes crinkled as she smiled with pleasure. "That's what I'm here for, honey. That's what I'm here for."

"Here for what?" Mystified, Donald looked first at his wife then at his daughter, trying to understand what had just happened. "And thanks for what?"

But rather than answer him, his wife and his daughter had gone off in completely opposite directions, leaving him to ponder his own questions as he scratched the thick, short white hair on his head. The action unintentionally drew his attention to the fact that his haircut, courtesy of his wife whom he insisted be the only one to cut his hair, was sadly lopsided. Again.

Though she'd been cutting his hair ever since they had gotten married all those years ago—originally out of necessity, now out of his need for a sense of tradition—Bonnie Gene had never managed to get the hang of cutting it evenly.

Donald didn't mind. He rather liked the way the uneven haircut made him look. He thought it made him appear rakish. Like the bad boy he'd never had time to be. And because he was who he was, the owner of a national chain of restaurants, no one ever attempted to tell him any differently.

Glancing over his shoulder in the direction that his wife had gone—to the front of the restaurant, undoubtedly to rub elbows with the customers—Donald quickly dipped into the trash basket and retrieved his cigar for a second time. This time, he didn't bother going through the motions of dusting it off. Instead, he just slipped it into his pants pocket.

With a satisfied smile, Donald assumed a deliberately innocent expression. Hands shoved into his pockets—his left protectively covering the cigar—he began to whistle as he walked toward the swinging double doors that led into the dining hall.

Life was good, he thought.

Chapter 3

The moment he'd realized that this time Boyd Arnold's discovery wasn't just a figment of his imagination, Wes had firmly sworn Boyd to secrecy. Knowing that Boyd had a tendency to run off at the mouth, words flowing as freely as the creek did in the winter after the first big snowstorm, he'd been forced to threaten the small-time rancher with jail time if he so much as breathed a word to *anyone*.

Boyd had appeared to be properly forewarned, his demeanor unusually solemn.

As for him, despite the fact that the words kept insisting on bubbling up in his throat and on his tongue, desperate for release, Wes hadn't even shared the news with his family. Not yet. He couldn't. He needed to be *absolutely* sure that the man with the partially destroyed face—he supposed the fish in the creek had to survive, too—actually *was* Mark Walsh.

There would be nothing more embarrassing, not to mention that it would also undermine the capabilities of the office of the sheriff, than to have to take back an announcement of this magnitude. After all, Mark Walsh had already been presumed murdered once and his supposed killer had been tried and sentenced. To say, "Oops, we were wrong once, but he's really dead now," wasn't something to be taken lightly.

His reasons for keeping this under wraps were all valid. But that didn't make keeping the secret to himself any easier for Wes. However, he had no choice. Until the county coroner completed his autopsy and managed to match Mark Walsh's dental records with the body that had been fished out of the creek, Wes fully intended to keep a tight lid on the news, no matter how difficult it got for him. Why dental records weren't used properly to identify the victim of the first crime was anybody's guess.

With any luck, he wouldn't have to hold his tongue for much longer. He desperately wanted to start the wheels turning for Damien's release. If the body in the morgue *was* Mark Walsh, then there was no way his older brother had killed the man over fifteen years ago. Not that he, or any of the family, including seven brothers and sisters, had ever believed that Damien was guilty. Some of the Colton men might have hot tempers, but none of them would ever commit murder. He'd stake not just his reputation but his life on that.

Damien was going to be a free man—once all that life-suffocating red tape was gotten through.

Damn, he thought, *finally.*

Deep down in his soul, he'd always known Damien

hadn't killed Mark. Been as sure of it as he was that the sun was going to rise in the east tomorrow morning.

He supposed that was one of the reasons he'd run for sheriff, to look into the case, to wade through the files that dealt with the murder and see if there was anything that could be used to reopen the case.

Now he didn't have to, he thought with a satisfied smile.

And he owed it all to Boyd, at least in a way. Granted, the body would have been there no matter what, but Boyd was the one who'd led him to it.

Who knew, if Boyd hadn't decided to sneak off and go duck-hunting—something that was *not* in season— maybe the fish would have eventually feasted on the rest of Walsh, doing away with the body and effectively annihilating any evidence that would have pointed toward Damien's innocence.

In that case, Damien would have stayed in prison, sinking deeper and deeper into that dark abyss where he'd taken up residence ever since the guilty verdict had been delivered fifteen years ago.

Wes made a mental note to call the county coroner's office later this afternoon to see how the autopsy was coming along—and give the man a nudge if he was dragging his heels. Max Crawford was the only coroner in these parts, but it wasn't as if the doctor was exactly drowning in bodies. Homicide was not a regular occurrence around here.

Smiling broadly, Wes poured himself his second cup of coffee of the morning. He was anxious to set his older brother's mind—if not his body—free. The sooner he told Damien about the discovery at Honey Creek, the sooner Damien would have hope and could begin walking the path that would lead him back home.

That had a nice ring to it, Wes thought, heading back to his desk. A really nice ring.

Miranda James had been an only child with no family. Her mother, Beth, had died two years ago, ironically from the same cancer that had claimed Miranda—and her father had taken off for parts unknown less than a week after Miranda was born, declaring he didn't have what it took to be a father. Because there was no one else to do it, Susan had taken upon herself all the funeral arrangements.

Bonnie Gene had offered to help, but one look at her daughter's determined face told the five foot-six, striking woman that this was something that Susan needed to do herself. Respectful of Susan's feelings, Bonnie Gene had backed away, saying only that if Susan needed her, she knew where to find her.

Susan was rather surprised at this turn of events, since her mother was such a take-charge person, but she was relieved that Bonnie Gene had backed off. It was almost cathartic to handle everything herself. Granted, it wasn't easy, juggling her full-time work schedule and the myriad of details that went into organizing the service and the actual burial at the cemetery, but she wasn't looking for easy. Susan was looking for right. She wanted to do right by her best friend.

Wanted, if Miranda *could* look down from heaven, to have her friend smile at the way the ceremony had come together to honor her all-too-brief life.

So, three days after she'd sunk down on the bench

outside the hospital, crying and trying to come to grips with the devastating loss of her best friend, Susan was standing at Miranda's graveside, listening to the soft-voiced, balding minister saying words that echoed her own feelings: that the good were taken all too quickly from this life, leaving a huge hole that proved to be very difficult to fill.

Only half listening now, Susan ached all over, both inside and out. In the last three days, she'd hardly gotten more than a few hours sleep each night, but she had not only the satisfaction of having made all the funeral arrangements but also of not dropping the ball when it came to the catering end of the family business.

As far as the latter went, her mother had been a little more insistent that she either accept help or back off altogether, but Susan had remained firm. Eventually, it had been Bonnie Gene who had backed off. When she had, there'd been a proud look in her light-brown eyes.

Having her mother proud of her meant the world to Susan. Especially right now.

Susan looked around at the mourners who filled the cemetery. It was, she thought, a nice turnout. All of Miranda's friends were here, including mutual friends, like Mary Walsh. And, not only Susan's parents, Donald and Bonnie Gene, but her four sisters and her brother had come to both the church service and the graveside ceremony.

They'd all come to pay their respects and to mourn the loss of someone so young, so vital. If she were being honest with herself, Susan was just a little surprised that so many people had actually turned up. Surprised and very pleased.

See how many people liked you, Miranda? she asked silently, looking down at the highly polished casket. *Bet you didn't know there were this many.*

Susan glanced around again as the winches and pulleys that had lowered the casket into the grave were released by the men from the funeral parlor. At the last moment, she didn't want to dwell on the sight of the casket being buried. She preferred thinking of Miranda lying quietly asleep in the casket the way she had viewed her friend the night before at the wake.

That way—

Susan's thoughts abruptly melted away as she watched the tall, lean rancher make his way toward her. Or maybe he was making his way toward the cemetery entrance in order to leave.

Unable to contain her curiosity, Susan moved directly into Duke's path just before he passed her parents and her.

"What are you doing here?" she asked.

It was a sunny day, and it was probably his imagination, but the sun seemed to be focusing on Susan's hair, making some of the strands appear almost golden. Duke cleared his throat, wishing he could clear his mind just as easily.

Duke minced no words. He'd never learned how. "Same as you. Paying my last respects to someone who apparently meant a great deal to you. I figure she had to be a really nice person for you to cry as much as you did when she died."

Susan took a deep, fortifying breath before answering him.

"She was," she replied. "A *very* nice person." She watched as the minister withdrew and the crowd began to thin out. The mourners had all been invited to her parents' house for a reception. "It just doesn't seem fair."

Duke thought of his twin brother, of Damien spending the best part of his life behind bars for a crime he *knew* beyond a shadow of a doubt his brother hadn't committed. They were connected, he and Damien. Connected in such a way that made him certain that if Damien had killed Walsh the way everyone said, he would have known. He would have *felt* it somehow.

But he hadn't.

And that meant that Damien hadn't killed anyone. Damien was innocent, and, after all this time, Duke still hadn't come up with a way to prove it. It ate at him.

"Nobody ever said life was fair," he told her in a stoic voice.

Susan didn't have the opportunity to comment on his response. Her mother had suddenly decided to swoop down on them. More specifically, on Duke.

"Duke Colton, what a lovely surprise," Bonnie Gene declared, slipping her arm through the rancher's. "So nice of you to come. Such a shame about poor Miranda." The next moment, she brightened and flashed her thousand-watt smile at him. "You are coming to the reception, aren't you?" she asked as if it was a given, not a question.

Duke had had no intentions of coming to the reception. He still wasn't sure what had prompted him to come to the funeral in the first place. Maybe it had been the expression he'd seen on Susan's face. Maybe, by being here, he'd thought to ease her burden just a little. He really didn't know.

He'd slipped into the last pew in the church, left before the mourners had begun to file out and had stood apart, watching the ceremony at the graveside. Had there been another way out of the cemetery, he would have used that and slipped out as quietly as he had come in.

Just his luck to have bumped into Susan and her family. Especially her mother, who had the gift of gab and seemed intent on sharing that gift with every living human being with ears who crossed her path.

He cleared his throat again, stalling and looking for the right words. "Well, I—"

He got no further than that.

Sensing a negative answer coming, Bonnie Gene headed it off at the pass as only she could: with verve and charm. And fast talk.

"But of course you're coming. My Donald oversaw most of the preparations." She glanced toward her husband, giving him an approving nod. "As a matter of fact, he insisted on it, didn't you, dear?" she asked, turning her smile on her husband as if that was the way to draw out a hint of confirmation from him.

"I—"

Donald Kelley only managed to get out one word less than Duke before Bonnie Gene hijacked the conversation again.

Because of the solemnity of the occasion, Bonnie Gene was wearing her shoulder-length dark-brown hair up. She still retained the deep, rich color without the aid of any enhancements that came out of a box and required rubber gloves and a timer, and she looked approximately fifteen years younger than the sixty-four years that her birth certificate testified she was—and she knew it. Retirement and quilting bees were not even remotely in her future.

Turning her face up to Duke's—separated by a distance of mere inches, she all but purred, "You see why you have to come, don't you, Duke?"

It was as clear as mud to him. "Well, ma'am—not really." Duke made the disclaimer quickly before the woman could shut him down again.

The smile on her lips was gently indulgent as she momentarily directed her attention to her husband. "Donald is his own number-one fan when it comes to his cooking. He's prepared enough food to feed three armies today," she confided, "and whatever the guests don't eat, he will." Detaching herself from Duke for a second, she patted her husband's protruding abdomen affectionately. "I don't want my man getting any bigger than he already is."

Dropping her hand before Donald had a chance to swat it away, she reattached herself to Duke. "So the more people who attend the reception, the better for my husband's health." Bonnie Gene paused, confident that she had won. It was only for form's sake—she knew men liked to feel in control—that she pressed. "You will come, won't you?"

It surprised her that the man seemed to stubbornly hold his ground. "I really—"

She sublimated a frown, keeping her beguiling

smile in place. Bonnie Gene was determined that Duke wasn't going to turn her down. She was convinced she'd seen something in the rancher's eyes in that unguarded moment when she'd caught him looking at her daughter.

Moreover, she'd seen the way Susan came to attention the moment her daughter saw Duke approaching. If that wasn't attraction, then she surely didn't know the meaning of the word.

And if there was attraction between her daughter and this stoic hunk of a man, well, that certainly was good enough for her. This could be the breakthrough she'd been hoping for. Time had a way of flying by and Susan was already twenty-five.

Bonnie Gene was nothing if not an enthusiastic supporter of her children, especially if she saw a chance to dust off her matchmaking skills.

"Oh, I know what the problem is," she declared, as if she'd suddenly been the recipient of tongues of fire and all the world's knowledge had been laid at her feet. "You're not sure of the way to our place." She turned to look at her daughter as if she had just now thought of the idea. "Susan, ride back with Duke so you can give him proper directions."

Looking over her youngest daughter's head, she saw that Linc was heading in their direction and his eyes appeared to be focused on Duke.

Fairly certain that Susan wouldn't welcome the interaction with her overbearing friend right now, Bonnie Gene reacted accordingly. Slipping her arms from around Duke's, she all but thrust Susan into the space she'd vacated.

"Off with you now," Bonnie Gene instructed, putting a hand to both of their backs and pushing them toward the exit. "Don't worry, your father and I will be right behind you," she called out.

Without thinking, Susan went on holding Duke's arm until they left the cemetery.

He made no move to uncouple himself and when she voluntarily withdrew her hold on him, he found that he rather missed the physical connection.

"I'm sorry about that," Susan apologized, falling into step beside him.

He assumed she was apologizing for her mother since there was nothing else he could think of that required an apology.

"Nothing to be sorry for," he replied. "Your mother was just being helpful."

Susan laughed. She had no idea that the straightforward rancher could be so polite. She didn't think he had it in him.

Learn something every day.

"No, she was just being Bonnie Gene. If you're not careful, Mother can railroad you into doing all sorts of things and make you believe it was your idea to begin with." There was a fondness in her voice as she described her mother's flaw. "She thinks it's her duty to take charge of everything and everyone around her. If she'd lived a hundred and fifty years ago, she would have probably made a fantastic Civil War general."

Duke inclined his head as they continued walking. "Your mother's a fine woman."

"No argument there. But my point is," Susan empha-sized, "you have to act fast to get away if you don't want to get shanghaied into doing whatever it is she has planned."

"Eating something your dad's made doesn't exactly sound like a hardship to me." Donald Kelley's reputation as a chef was known throughout the state, not just the town.

Susan didn't want Duke to be disappointed. "Actually, I made a lot of it."

His eyes met hers for a brief moment. She couldn't for the life of her fathom what he was thinking. The man had to be a stunning poker player. "Doesn't sound bad, either."

The simple compliment, delivered without any fanfare, had Susan warming inside and struggling to tamp down what she felt had to be a creeping blush on the outside. Pressing her lips together, she murmured, "Well, I hope you won't be disappointed."

"Don't plan on being," he told her. Duke nodded toward the vehicle he'd left parked at the end of the lot. "Hope you don't mind riding in a truck, seeing as how you're probably used to gallivanting around in those fancy cars."

When it came down to matching dollar for dollar, the Coltons were probably richer than the Kelleys, but despite his distant ties to the present sitting president, Joseph Colton, Darius Colton didn't believe in throwing money away for show. That included buying fancy cars for his sons.

Duke was referring to Linc's sports car, Susan thought. He had to be because her own car was a rather bland sedan with more than a few miles and years on it.

But it was a reliable vehicle that got her where she had to go and that was all that ultimately mattered to her.

"I like trucks," she told him, looking at his. "They're dependable."

In response, Susan thought she saw a small smile flirt with Duke's mouth before disappearing again. And then he shrugged a bit self-consciously.

"If I'd known I'd be heading out to your place, I would've washed it first," he told her.

"Dirt's just a sign left behind by hard work," she said philosophically as she approached the passenger side of the vehicle.

Duke opened the door for her, then helped her up into the cab. She was acutely aware of his hands on her waist, giving her a small boost so that she could avoid any embarrassing mishap, given that she was wearing a black dress and high heels.

A tingle danced through her.

This wasn't the time or place to feel things like that, she chided herself. She'd just buried her best friend. This was a time for mourning, not for reacting to the touch of a man who most likely wasn't even aware that he *had* touched her.

Duke caught himself staring for a second. Staring at the neat little rear that Susan Kelley had. Funerals weren't the time and cemeteries weren't the place to entertain the kind of thoughts that were now going through his head.

But there they were anyway, taking up space, coloring the situation.

Maybe, despite the best of intentions, he shouldn't have shown up at the funeral, he silently told himself.

Too late now, Duke thought as he got into the driver's seat and started up the truck. With any luck, he wouldn't have to stay long at the reception.

Chapter 4

"Take the next turn to the—"

There was no GPS in Duke's truck because he hated the idea of being told where to turn and, essentially, how to drive by some disembodied female voice. He'd been driving around, relying on gut instincts and keen observation, for more years than were legally allowed.

For the last ten minutes he'd patiently listened to Susan issuing instructions and coming very close to mimicking a GPS.

Enough was enough. He could go the rest of the way to the Kelleys' house without having every bend in the road narrated.

"You can stop giving me directions," he told her as politely as he could manage. "I know how to get to your place."

She'd suspected as much, which was why she'd been

surprised when he'd allowed her to come along to guide him to the big house in the first place.

"If you didn't need directions, what am I doing in your truck?" she asked him.

He spared Susan a glance before looking back at the road. "Sitting."

Very funny. But at least this meant he had a sense of humor. Sort of. "Besides that."

Duke shrugged, keeping his eyes on the desolate road ahead of him. "Seemed easier than trying to argue with your mother."

She laughed. The man was obviously a fast learner as well. "You have a point."

Since she agreed with him, Duke saw no reason to comment any further. Several minutes evaporated with no exchange being made between them. The expanding silence embraced them like a tomb.

Finally, Susan couldn't take it any more. "Don't talk much, do you?"

He continued looking straight ahead. The road was desolate but there was no telling when a stray animal could come running out.

"Nope."

Obviously, he was feeling uncomfortable in her company. If her mother, ever the matchmaker, hadn't orchestrated this, he wouldn't even be here, feeling awkward like this, Susan thought. What had her mother been thinking?

"I'm sorry if you're uncomfortable," she apologized to him.

Duke spared her another glance. His brow furrowed,

echoing his confusion. "What makes you think I'm uncomfortable?"

"Because you're not talking." It certainly didn't take a rocket scientist to come to that conclusion, she thought.

Duke made a short, dismissive noise. Discomfort had nothing to do with his silence. He just believed in an economy of words and in not talking unless he had something to say. "I don't do small talk."

She was of the opinion that *everyone* did small talk, but she wasn't about to get into a dispute over it. "Okay," she acknowledged. "Then say something earth-shattering."

For a moment, he said nothing at all. Then, because she was obviously not about to let the subject drop, he asked, "You always chatter like that?"

Blowing out a breath, she gave him an honest answer. "Only when I'm uncomfortable or nervous."

"Which is it?"

Again, she couldn't be anything but honest, even though she knew that if her mother was here right now, Bonnie Gene would be rolling her eyes at the lack of feminine wiles she was displaying. But playing games, especially coy ones, had never been her thing. "Both right now."

Despite the fact that he had asked, her answer surprised him. "I make you nervous?"

He did, but oddly enough, in a good way. Rather than say yes, she gave him half an answer. "Silence makes me nervous."

He nodded toward the dash. "You can turn on the radio."

She didn't feel like hearing music right now. Somehow, after the memorial service, it just didn't seem right. What she wanted was human contact, human interaction.

"I'd rather turn you on—" As her words echoed back at her, Susan's eyes widened with horror. "I mean, if you could be turned on." Mortified, she covered her now-flushed face with her hands. "Oh, God, that didn't come out right, either."

Despite himself, the corners of his mouth curved a little. Susan looked almost adorable, flustered like that.

"That's one of the reasons I don't do small talk." He eyed her for a second before looking back at the road. "I'd stop if I were you."

"Right."

Susan took a breath, trying to regroup and not say anything that would lead to her putting her foot in her mouth again. Even so, she had to say something because the silence really was making her feel restless inside. She reverted back to safe ground: the reason he'd been at the cemetery.

"It was very nice of you to come to the funeral," she said. "Did you know Miranda well?"

He took another turn, swinging to the right. The Kelley mansion wasn't far now. "Didn't know her at all," he told her.

The answer made no sense to her. "Then why did you come?"

"I know you," he replied, as if that somehow explained everything.

She was having a hard time understanding his

reasons. "And because she was my best friend and meant so much to me, you came?" she asked uncertainly. That was the conclusion his last answer led her to, but it still didn't make any sense.

"Something like that."

But she and Duke didn't really know each other, she thought, confused. She knew *of* him, of course. Duke Colton was the twin brother of the town's only murderer. He was one of Darius Colton's boys. Each brother was handsomer than the next. And, of course, there'd been that crush she'd had on him. But she didn't really *know* him. And he didn't know her.

In a town as small as Honey Creek, Montana, spreading gossip was one of the main forms of entertainment and there were plenty of stories to spread about the Coltons, especially since, going back a number of generations, the current president of the United States and Darius Colton were both related to Teddy Colton who'd lived in the early 1900s. To his credit, the distant relationship wasn't something that the already affluent Darius capitalized on or used to up his stock. He was too busy being blustery and riding his sons to get them to give their personal best each and every day. He expected nothing less.

That kind of a demanding, thankless lifestyle might be the reason why Duke preferred keeping to himself, she reasoned.

She felt bad for him.

Following the long, winding driveway up to what could only be termed a mansion, Duke parked his pickup truck off to one side she supposed where it wouldn't be in anyone's way.

Still feeling a bit awkward, Susan announced, "We're here."

He gave her a look she couldn't begin to read. "That's why I stopped driving."

Susan waited for a smile to emerge, but his expression continued to be nondescript. She gave up trying to read his mind.

As she got out of the cab, Susan heard the sound of approaching cars directly behind them. The onslaught had begun.

"We might be first, but not by much," she observed. Within less than a minute, the driveway, large though it was, was overflowing with other vehicles, all jockeying for prime space.

The first to arrive after them were Bonnie Gene and her husband. Bonnie Gene was frowning as she looked around.

"Knew I should have hired a valet service," she reproached herself as she joined Susan and Duke. Donald came trudging up the walk several feet behind her. Since the driveway was at a slight incline, Donald was huffing and puffing from the minor exertion.

"Don't start carrying on, Bonnie Gene. People know how to park their own damn cars. No need to be throwing money away needlessly," he chided in between taking deep breaths.

Turning around to look at her husband, Bonnie Gene frowned. "Don't cuss, Donald," she chided him. "This is a funeral reception."

"I can cuss in my own house if I want to," he informed her, even though, since she'd chastised him, he knew he'd try extra hard to curb his tongue.

Bonnie Gene sighed and shook her head. "See what I have to put up with?" She addressed her question to Duke. Not waiting for a comment, she turned and raised her voice in order to be heard by the guests who had begun arriving. "C'mon everyone, let's go in, loosen our belts and our consciences just a little, and eat today as if it didn't count."

That definitely pleased Donald who laughed expansively. The deep, throaty sound could be heard above the din of voices coming from the crowd. "Now you're talking, Bonnie Gene."

His wife was quick to shoot him down. "That wasn't meant for you, Donald. That was for our guests." Keeping her "public smile" in place, Bonnie Gene uttered her threat through lips that were barely moving. "You eat any more than your allotted portion and there'll be hell to pay, Donald."

"I'm already paying it," Donald mumbled under his breath.

About to walk away, Bonnie Gene stopped abruptly and eyed her husband. "What was that?"

The look on Donald's round face was innocence personified. "Nothing, my love, not a thing."

Duke held his peace until the senior Kelleys had moved on. Once they had disappeared into the crowd filling the house, he lowered his head and asked Susan, "She always boss him around like that?"

"She does it because she loves him," Susan answered, feeling the need to be ever so slightly defensive of her mother's motives. "Mother's convinced that if she doesn't watch over him, Dad'll eat himself to death.

It's because Mother wants him around for a good long time to come that she tends to police him like that."

Duke nodded, saying nothing. Knowing that if it were him being ridden like that, he wouldn't stand for it. But to each his own. He wasn't about to tell another man how to live his life.

They'd moved inside the house by now and Duke looked around absently, noting faces. There were more people inside this room than he normally saw in a month.

He wondered how long he would have to stay before he could leave without being observed. As he was trying to come up with a time frame, his thoughts were abruptly interrupted by a flushed, flustered young woman who accidentally stumbled next to him. About to fall, she grabbed on to the first thing she could—and it was Duke.

Horrified that she'd almost pushed him over, Mary Walsh immediately apologized.

"Oh, I'm so sorry," she cried with feeling. "I didn't mean to bump into you like that." Her face was growing a deep shade of red. "New shoes," she explained, looking down at them accusingly. "I'm still a little wobbly in them."

He'd been ready to dismiss the whole thing at the word *Oh*. "No harm done," he assured her.

Drawn by the voice, Susan was quick to throw her arms around her flustered friend. "Mary, you made it after all! I wasn't sure if you were coming to the reception." She punctuated her declaration with a fierce hug.

"Yes, I made it. Just in time to step all over—" she

paused for a moment, as if searching for a name, then brightened "—Duke Colton."

The next moment Mary made the connection. A sense of awkwardness descended because she wasn't altogether sure how to react. This was Duke Colton, the brother of the man who had been convicted of killing her father. Still, manners were manners and she thoroughly believed in them.

"I really am sorry. I didn't mean to bump into you like that. New shoes," she explained to Susan in case Susan hadn't heard her a moment ago.

"She's wobbly," Duke added, looking ever so slightly amused.

"Who's wobbly?" Bonnie Gene asked, materializing amid them again with the ease of a puff of smoke. She looked from her daughter to her daughter's long-time friend, sweet little Mary Walsh.

The girl should have been married ages ago, Bonnie Gene thought. Maybe, if Mary was married, Susan wouldn't be such a stubborn holdout.

"I am, Mrs. Kelley," Mary explained. "These heels were an impulse purchase and they're too high for me. I really haven't had a chance to break them in yet," she added sheepishly.

"Well, break them in by the buffet table," Bonnie Gene urged. With a grand wave of her hand, she indicated the line that was already forming by the long table that ran along the length of the back wall. Leaning in closer to Mary, she added with enthusiasm, "Right next to that really good-looking young man in the tan jacket. See him?" she wanted to know.

"Mother," Susan cried, struggling to keep her voice low.

"Susan," Bonnie Gene responded in a sing-song voice.

She knew that none of her children appreciated her matchmaking efforts, but that was their problem, not hers. She intended to keep on trying to pair off the young people in her life wherever and whenever she had the opportunity—whether they liked it or not. People belonged in pairs, not drifting through life in single file.

Mary already knew what Susan's mother was like, but Duke undoubtedly hadn't a clue. So Susan turned toward him and said in a soft voice, "I suggest we make our getaway the minute her back is turned. Otherwise, she'll probably have you married off by midnight."

"I don't think so," Duke answered with a finality that told Susan that not only was he not in the market for a wife, he'd deliberately head in the opposite direction should his path ever cross that of a potential mate.

Susan vaguely recalled that there had been some kind of scandal last year involving Duke and an older married woman. She thought she'd heard that the woman, Charlene McWilliams, had committed suicide shortly after Duke broke things off with her.

Something of that nature would definitely have a person backing away from any sort of a relationship, even the hint of a relationship, Susan thought sympathetically.

God knew she backed away from them and she had no scandal involving a man in her past. As a matter of fact, she had nothing in her past. But there was a reason for that. She just wasn't any good at relationships.

Her forte, Susan was convinced, lay elsewhere. She was very good at her job and at raising other people's spirits. For now, she told herself, that was enough. And later would eventually take care of itself.

"There's an open bar over there." Susan pointed it out. There were a number of people, mainly men, clustering around it. She wanted to give him the opportunity to join them if that would make him feel more comfortable. "If you'd rather drink than eat, I'll understand," she added, although she doubted that would make a difference to him one way or the other.

Duke wasn't even mildly tempted. He liked keeping a clear head when he was on someone else's territory. Drinking was for winding down, for kicking back after a long, full day's work. He hadn't put in a full day yet.

"Nothing to understand," he replied. "I'd rather eat."

She couldn't exactly say why his answer had her feeling so happy, but it did.

"So would I," she agreed, flashing a wide smile at him. "Why don't I just go get us a couple of—"

She didn't get a chance to finish her sentence. Linc had swooped down on her like a hungry falcon zeroing in on his prey.

"There you are, Susan," he declared, looking relieved. "I've been looking all over for you. You shouldn't be alone at a time like this."

Oh, please, not now. Don't smother me now. She wanted to remain polite, but she wasn't sure just how long she could be that way. Linc was beginning to wear away the last of her nerves.

"I'm hardly alone, Linc," she informed him. "There're dozens and dozens of people here."

Her answer didn't deter Linc. "You know that old saying about being lonely in a crowd." He slipped his arm around her waist as comfortably as if he'd been doing it forever. At the same time, he looked smugly over at Duke. "I'll take it from here, Colton. Thanks for looking out for my girl."

She had to stop this before it went too far. Linc was being delusional. They'd dated a few times in the past, but it had gone nowhere. She thought they were both agreed on that point. Obviously not.

"I am *not* your girl, Linc," she insisted, lowering her voice so that she wouldn't embarrass him or wind up causing a scene.

She still had feelings for Linc, but they were all of the friendly variety. The romance that Linc apparently had so desperately hoped for had never materialized, although she really had tried to make herself love him the way he obviously wanted to be loved. It just wasn't meant to happen. Linc was handsome, funny and intelligent. But there was no spark, no chemistry between them. At least, she'd never been aware of any.

Apparently, Linc had been the recipient of other signals.

"You're just upset," Linc told her in the kind of soothing voice a parent used with a petulant child. "Once things get back to normal, you'll change your mind. You'll see," he promised.

"There's nothing to see," she informed him tersely,

framing her answer more for Duke's benefit than for Linc's.

But she might as well not have bothered. Linc obviously wasn't listening and Duke, when she turned to look at him, wasn't there to hear.

What is he, part bat? she silently demanded. That was twice that he'd just seemed to disappear on her. Once outside the hospital and now here. Both times, it had been just after Linc had attached himself to her side as if they were tethered by some kind of invisible umbilical chord.

Stop making excuses for him. If Duke had wanted to hang around, he would have, Susan told herself.

Besides, she had more guests to see to than just Duke Colton.

The next moment, she was saying it out loud, at least in part.

"Excuse me, Linc, but I have guests to see to," she told him, walking quickly away before he could make a comment or try to stop her obvious retreat with some inane remark.

When it came to being the perfect hostess, Susan had studied at the knee of a master—her mother. Bonnie Gene Kelley was the consummate hostess, never having been known to run out of anything, and always able to satisfy the needs and requirements of her guests, no matter what it was they wanted.

Like mother, like daughter, at least in this one respect.

Susan wove her way in and out of clusters of people exchanging memories of Miranda along with small talk. She made sure that everyone ate, that everyone drank and, just as importantly, that she didn't find herself alone with Linc again.

And all the while, she kept an eye out for Duke. She spotted him several times, always standing near someone, always seeming to be silent.

And watching her.

Their eyes met a number of times and, unlike with Linc, she felt a spark. There was definitely chemistry or *something* that seemed to come to life and shimmer between them every time she caught his eye or he caught hers.

She would have liked to put that chemistry to the test. Purely for academic purposes, of course, she added quickly.

But there was a room full of people in the way. Maybe that was the whole point, she thought suddenly. The room full of people made her feel safe. Not threatened by the tall, dark and brooding Duke.

Still…

Get a grip and focus, Susan, she upbraided herself. Her best friend was barely cold and she was exploring her options with Duke Colton. What was *wrong* with her?

She had no answer for that. Besides, right now, there was really nothing she could do about exploring any of these racing feelings any further.

And maybe that was a good thing. Everyone needed a little fantasy to spice up their lives and it only remained a fantasy if it wasn't tested and exposed to the light of day.

She was fairly certain that hers never would be. Not if Duke kept perform his disappearing act.

Chapter 5

"If I didn't know any better, I'd say you were trying to avoid me."

Startled, Susan swallowed a gasp as her heart launched into double time. She'd left the reception and come out here to the side veranda to be alone for a moment. She hadn't realized that Linc was anywhere in the immediate vicinity, much less that he'd follow her outside.

She took a deep breath to calm down. Linc was right. She *had* been avoiding him and she felt a little guilty about it. But at the same time, she felt resentful that he was making her feel that way.

Was it wrong not to want to feel hemmed in? And lately, that was the way Linc was making her feel— hemmed in. By avoiding him, she was trying to avoid having to say things she knew would hurt him.

She could see that he was hopeful that they could

"give their relationship another chance." But kissing him was like kissing her brother and that was the way she felt about him, like a sister about a brother. She cared for him, but not in *that* way.

To try to turn that feeling into something more, something sexual between them seemed more than a little icky to her. But there was no graceful way to say that, no way to avoid hurting his feelings and his ego.

So she'd been trying to avoid Linc and avoid the awkwardness that was waiting out in the wings for both of them once she made her feelings—or lack thereof—plain to him.

Susan shrugged, hoping to table the discussion until she felt more up to having it out between them. "I'm not trying to avoid you, Linc, I've just been trying to be a good hostess."

He nodded his head, as if he was willing—for now—to tolerate the excuse she was giving him. "Well, now it's time for you to think about taking care of *you*," Linc said with emphasis.

If someone had asked her about it, Susan had nothing specific to point to as to why alarms were suddenly going off in her head, but they were. Loudly.

Survival instincts had her taking a step back, away from him. She wasn't sure where he was going with this, but it had her uneasy.

"What do you mean?" she asked him.

"I mean," Linc replied patiently, like someone trying to make a mental lightweight understand his point, "that you need someone to wait on you for a change."

As he spoke, he moved in closer and didn't appear to be too happy that she was taking a step back the moment he took a step forward. Pretending not to notice, he continued moving in toward her until the three-foot-high railing that ran along the veranda prevented her from moving back any further. He'd effectively managed to corner her.

"Someone who would put your needs ahead of their own," he continued. With a smile, he slowly threaded his fingers through her hair.

Susan pulled her head back with a quick, less-than-friendly toss. He was so close to her, if she took a deep breath, her chest would be in contact with his. She didn't want to push him back, but he wasn't leaving her much of a choice.

"Linc, don't."

His voice was low, almost hypnotic as he continued talking to her. "You're confused, Susan. Your emotions are all jumbled up. You need someone to take care of you and there's nothing I'd like more than to be that someone," he told her. He bent his head so that his mouth was closer to hers.

But when he brought it down to kiss her, Susan quickly turned her head. He wound up making contact with her hair. "Linc, no."

Despite her reaction, Linc gave no sign that he was about to back off this time, or let her step aside. Instead, he coaxed, "C'mon, Susan. You know I'm the one you should be with."

She moved her head in the opposite direction, awarding him another mouthful of hair. "Linc, no," she insisted more firmly. "I want you to stop."

Her words fell on deaf ears. "Might as well give in

to the inevitable." This time, his voice was a little more forceful.

The next moment, Linc found himself stumbling backward. Someone had grabbed him by the shoulder and yanked him away as if he were nothing more than a big, clumsy rag doll.

"The lady said stop," Duke told him. His voice was deep, as if it was emerging from the bottom of a gigantic cavernous chasm. There was no missing the warning note in it.

Anger, hot and dangerous, flashed in Linc's eyes as he glared at the man who had interrupted his attempted play for Susan.

"This isn't any business of yours, Colton," he snapped at Duke.

Placing his range-toned muscular frame between Hayes and the target of Hayes' assault, Duke hooked his thumbs in his belt and directed a steely glare at the shorter man.

"Man forcing himself on a defenseless woman is everybody's business," Duke said in his steady, inflection-free voice.

Susan's chin shot up. She didn't care if this *was* Duke Colton, she was not about to be perceived as some weak-kneed damsel in distress.

"I am *not* defenseless," she protested with just enough indignation to make Duke believe that that little woman actually believed what she was saying.

She might be spunky, Duke thought, but there was no way that Susan Kelley could hold her own if Hayes decided to force himself on her. Or at least not without a weapon—or a well-aimed kick.

Still, he wasn't about to get drawn into a verbal sparring match with her over this. He'd had every intention of retrieving his truck and leaving, until he'd discovered the vehicle was barricaded in by two other cars that would have to be moved in order for him to get out. He'd been on his way to enlist Bonnie Gene's help in finding the owners of the other two vehicles when he'd seen Hayes crowding Susan.

So he shrugged now in response to Susan's protest. "Have it your way. You're not defenseless."

But Duke gave no indication that he was about to leave, at least, not until Hayes moved his butt and went back inside the house or into the hole he'd initially crawled out of.

Instead, Duke continued to stand there, his thumbs still hooked onto his belt, waiting patiently. The look in his eyes left absolutely no doubt what he was waiting for.

"I'll see you later, Susan," Linc finally bit off and then marched into the house, looking petulant and very annoyed.

Once Linc had retreated, closing the door behind him, Susan took a breath and let it out slowly. She turned toward Duke. "I suppose I should thank you."

A hint of a shrug rumbled across his broad shoulders. "You can do whatever you want to," he told her.

His seemingly indifferent words hung in the air between them as his eyes swept over her slowly. Thoroughly.

It was probably the heat and her own edgy emotional turmoil that caused her temporary foray into insanity. That was the only way she could describe it later.

Insanity.

Why else, she later wondered, would she have done what she did in response to Duke's words? Because she suddenly found herself wanting to do something that she would think in the next moment was outrageous. If she could think.

If nothing else, it was certainly out of character for her.

One minute, she was vacillating between being furious with the male species in general—both Linc and Duke acted as if they thought she was just some empty-headed nitwit who needed to be looked after.

The next minute, something inside her was viewing Duke as her knight in somewhat battered, tarnished armor. A tall, dark, brooding knight to whom she very much wanted to express her gratitude.

So she kissed him.

Without stopping to think, without really realizing what she was about to do, she did it.

On her toes, Susan grabbed onto his rock-hard biceps for leverage and support and then she pressed her lips against his.

It was a kiss steeped in gratitude. But that swiftly peeled away and before she knew it, Susan was caught up in what she'd initiated, no longer the instigator but the one who'd gotten swept up in the consequences.

That was *her* pulse that was racing, *her* breath that had vanished without backup. That was *her* head that was spinning and those were *her* knees that had suddenly gone missing in action.

Had she not had the presence of mind to anchor herself to his arms the way she had, Susan realized she might have further embarrassed herself by sinking to the ground, a mindless, palpitating mass of skin, bone and completely useless parts in between.

God, did he ever pack a wallop.

It wasn't often that Duke was caught by surprise. For the most part, he went through life with a grounded, somewhat jaded premonition of what was to come. Duke had been blessed with an innate intuition that allowed him to see what was coming at least a split second before it actually came.

It wasn't that he was a psychic; he was an observer, a student of life. And because he was a student who never forgot a single lesson he'd learned, very little out here in this small corner of the world managed to catch him by surprise.

But this had.

It had caught him so unprepared that he felt as if he'd just been slammed upside his head with a two-by-four. At least he felt that unsteady. Not only had Susan caught him completely off guard by kissing him, he was even more surprised by the magnitude of his reaction to that very kiss.

Because Charlene McWilliams' suicide over a year ago had left him reeling, he'd stepped back from having any sort of a relationship with the softer sex. Her suicide had affected him deeply, not because he'd loved her but because he felt badly that being involved with him had ultimately driven Charlene to take her own life.

Consequently, practicing mind over matter, Duke had systematically shut down those parts of himself that reacted to a woman on a purely physical level.

Or so he'd believed up until now.

Obviously he hadn't done quite as good a job shutting down as he'd thought, because this little slip of a girl— barely a card-carrying woman—had managed to arouse him to a length and breadth he hadn't been aroused to in a very long time.

Fully intending to separate his lips from hers, Duke took hold of Susan's waist. But somehow, instead of creating a wedge, he wound up pulling her to him, kissing her back.

Kissing her with feeling.

He had to create a chasm before his head spun completely out of control, Duke silently insisted, doing his best to rally.

With effort, his heart hammering like the refrain from "The Anvil Chorus," Duke forced himself to actually push Susan back—even though everything within him vehemently protested the action.

With space between them now, Duke looked at her, still stunned. And speechless.

His mind reeling and a complete blank, Duke turned on his heel and walked away from the veranda and Susan. Quickly.

The warm night breeze surrounding her like sticky gauze, Susan stood there, watching Duke grow smaller until he disappeared around the corner. Shaken, she couldn't move immediately. She wasn't completely sure if she'd just been caught up in some kind of ground-breaking hallucination or if what had just transpired— possibly the greatest kiss of all time—had been real.

What she did know was that she was having trouble breathing and that feelings both of bereavement and absolute, unmitigated joy were square-dancing inside her.

Confusing the hell out of her.

Taking as deep a breath as she could manage, Susan turned around and hurried back into the house. She needed to be able to pull herself together before she ran into her mother. One look from her mother in this present shaken-up condition and she'd be answering questions from now until Christmas.

Maybe longer.

"Where the hell have you been?" Darius Colton wanted to know.

Home to replenish his supply of water before heading back out to the range and his men again, Darius had seen his son's dusty pickup truck on the horizon, on its way to Duke's house. Like several of his other offspring, Duke lived in a house located on the Colton Ranch.

Duke had been conspicuously absent, both this morning and now part of the afternoon. He'd been absent without clearing it with him and Darius didn't like it.

Darius Colton didn't consider himself an unreasonable man, but he needed to know where everyone was and what they were doing at any given hour of the day. It was his right as patriarch of the family.

To him it was the only way to run a ranch and it was the way he'd managed to build his ranch up to what it now was.

Getting on the back of the horse he'd tethered to the rear of his truck, Darius rode up to meet Duke. Within range of the pickup, Darius pinned his son with the sharply voiced question.

When he received no answer, he barked out the question again. "I said, where the hell have you been, boy?"

Stopping the truck, Duke met his father's heated glare without flinching. He'd learned a long time ago that any display of fear would have his father pouncing like a hungry jackal on unsuspecting prey. His father had absolutely no respect for anyone who didn't stand up to him.

The confusing flip side of that was that the person who opposed him incurred his wrath. There was very little winning when it came to his father. For the most part, to get on his father's good side, a person had to display unconditional obedience and constant productivity. Anything less was not tolerated for long—if at all.

"I went to a funeral," Duke told his father, his voice even.

The answer did not please Darius. He wasn't aware of anyone of any import dying. "Well, it's going to be your own funeral you'll be attending if I catch you going anywhere again during working hours without asking me first."

"I didn't tell you because you were busy."

Duke deliberately used the word *tell* rather than *ask,* knowing that his father would pick up on the difference, but it was a matter of pride. He wanted his father to know that he wasn't just a lackey, he was a Colton and that meant he expected to be treated with respect, same as his father, even if the person on the other end of the discussion *was* his father.

His horse beside the driver's side of the truck's cab, Darius looked closely at his son. His eyes narrowed as he stared at Duke's face.

"This a frisky corpse you went to pay your respects to?" he finally asked.

There was no humor in his voice. Before Duke could ask him what he was talking about, Darius leaned in and rubbed his rough thumb over the corner of his son's lower lip.

And then he held it up for Duke's perusal.

There was a streak of pink on his father's thumb. Pink lipstick.

The same shade of lipstick he recalled Susan wearing.

"That didn't come from the corpse" was all that Duke said. And then he preemptively ran his own thumb over his lips to wipe away any further telltale signs that Susan might have left behind.

"Well, that's a relief," Darius said sarcastically. "Wouldn't want the neighbors talking." He drew himself up in the saddle. "You're way behind in your chores, boy," he informed Duke coldly. "Nobody's going to carry your weight for you."

Darius had long made it clear that he expected his offspring to work the ranch every day, putting in the long hours that were necessary. No exceptions.

"Don't expect anyone to," Duke replied. "I just came home to change," he added in case his father found fault with his coming back to his own house rather than heading directly to the range.

"Well, then, be quick about it," Darius barked. He was about to ride his horse back to his own truck parked before the big house, but he stopped for a second. Curiosity had temporarily gotten the better of him. "Whose funeral was it?"

"Miranda James," Duke answered.

Bushy eyebrows met together over a surprisingly small, well-shaped nose. Darius scowled. "Name doesn't mean anything to me."

His father's response didn't surprise him. Darius Colton didn't concern himself with anyone or anything that wasn't directly related to the range or the business of running that ranch.

"Didn't think it would," Duke said more to himself than his father.

Darius snorted, muttered something under his breath about ungrateful whelps being a waste of his time and effort, and then he rode away, leaving a cloud of dust behind in his wake.

Duke shook his head and went into the house to change. Despite the hour, he had a full day's work to catch up on. His father expected—and accepted—nothing less and he didn't want to give the man another reason to go off on him. He wasn't sure how long his own temper would last under fire.

Chapter 6

Admittedly, though it had been close to a year since he was elected sheriff, Wes was still rather new on the job. However, some things just seemed like common sense. According to the unofficial rules of procedure in cases where there was a dead body involved, the next of kin was the first to be notified.

Usually.

But in this particular troubling case, the next of kin had already *been* notified. Fifteen years ago. After getting confirmation from the county medical examiner that the body in the morgue really was Mark Walsh, Wes figured that he could put off notifying Jolene Walsh about her husband's murder for an hour or so, seeing as how this was the second time she would be receiving the news.

Since this turn of events was really disturbing—who would have thought he'd get a genuine, honest-to-God mystery so soon after being elected?—Wes wanted to turn to a sympathetic ear to run the main highlights past. Again, he didn't go the normal route. Since this case did involve his older brother, by rights the family patriarch should be the one he would go to with this.

Should be, but he didn't.

He and Darius had a prickly relationship—the same kind of relationship, when he came right down to it, that his father had with each of his children. Darius Colton, for reasons of his own that no one else was privy to, was *not* the easiest man to talk to or get along with. He never had been.

But someone in his family should be told and since this was Wes's first time notifying anyone about the death of a loved one—or, in Mark Walsh's case, a barely tolerated one—he wanted to practice it before upending Jolene Walsh's world a second time with what amounted to the same news.

So he rode out to his family's ranch and headed toward the section he knew that Duke was assigned to tending.

Wait 'til Duke hears this, Wes thought. If this didn't shake his older brother up, nothing would.

Blessed with excellent vision, Duke saw Wes approaching across the range a good distance away. Just the barest hint of curiosity reared its head as he watched his brother's Jeep grow larger.

Today was his day to mend fences—literally—and he could do with a break, Duke thought. Putting down his hammer and the new wire he was stringing across the posts, Duke left his cracked leather gloves on as he wiped the sweat from his brow with the back of his wrist.

Once he did, that brow was practically the only part of him that wasn't glistening with sweat. His shirt had long since been stripped off and was now tied haphazardly around his waist.

"Slow day in town?" he called out just before Wes pulled up beside him. "If you're tired of playing sheriff and want to do some real work, I've got another hammer around here somewhere." He glanced around to see if he'd taken the second tool out of his battered truck or left it in the flatbed.

Though no one would ever call him laid-back, Duke was considerably more at ease around his siblings, and even his nephew, his sister Maisie's son, than he was around most people. And that included his father, who he viewed as a less-than-benevolent tyrant.

When Wes made no response in return, Duke narrowed his eyes and looked at his brother more closely.

Now that he thought about it, he'd seen Wes look a lot less serious in his time.

"Who died?" he said only half in jest.

Pulling up the hand brake, Wes turned off the ignition and got out. He pulled his hat down a little lower. Out here, on the open range, the sun seemed to beat down almost mercilessly. He'd forgotten how grueling it could be out in the open like this.

"Mark Walsh," Wes answered his brother.

Duke frowned. What kind of game was this? "We already know that, Wes. Damien's in state prison doing time for it."

Wes looked up the two inches that separated him from his brother. "Damien didn't do it."

"Also not a newsflash," Duke countered. He picked up his hammer again. If Wes was out here to play games, he might as well get back to work. "Although the old man hardly lifted a finger to advance that theory." It wasn't easy, keeping a note of bitterness out of his voice. He'd always felt his father could have gotten Damien a better lawyer, brought someone in from the outside to defend his twin instead of keeping out of it the way he had. "But the rest of us know that Damien didn't do it." Bright-green eyes met blue. "Right?"

"Absolutely right," Wes said with feeling. He took a breath, then launched into his narrative. "Boyd Arnold found a body the other day in the creek."

Duke waved his hand in dismissal. He paid little attention to what went on around Honey Creek these days—even less if it involved people like Boyd Arnold.

"Did it have one head or two?" he asked sarcastically. "That lamebrain's always claiming to find these weird things—"

Wes stopped him from going on. "What he found was Mark Walsh's body."

That managed to bring Duke up short. He stared at Wes, trying to make sense out of what his brother had just told him. "Somebody dug Walsh up and then tossed him in the creek?" Nobody had ever really liked the man, but that seemed a little excessive.

Wes shook his head. "No. Whoever's in Mark Walsh's grave isn't Walsh."

Duke went from surprised to completely stunned.

He waited for a punch line. There wasn't any. "You're serious."

"Like the plague," Wes responded. "County coroner just confirmed it from Walsh's dental records. Nobody else knows yet," he cautioned, then added, "except for the coroner and Boyd, of course. Boyd's sworn to secrecy," he explained when he saw the skeptical look that came into Duke's eyes.

"That'll last ten minutes," Duke estimated with a snort. And then he realized something. "You haven't told Jolene yet?" he asked, surprised.

Wes shook his head. "Not yet. I planned to do that next. I wanted to tell you first."

Duke didn't follow his brother's reasoning. They got along all right, but he wasn't any closer to Wes than he was to some of the others. "Why me first?" Duke wanted to know.

Wes gave him an honest answer. "Because telling you is almost like telling Damien." The two weren't identical, but it was close enough. Wes sighed deeply. The guilt he bore for not being able to find something to free his brother earlier weighed heavily on his soul. "I'm going up to the county courthouse after I tell Jolene, get the wheels in motion for Damien's release."

"Why don't you go there first?" Duke suggested. He saw he'd caught Wes's attention. "Seeing how 'fast' those wheels turn, you need to get the process started as soon as possible." He gave Wes an excuse he could use to assuage his conscience. "You won't be telling Jolene anything she hasn't heard before. The only thing that's different is the timeline. She's still going to be a widow when you finish talking to her. There's no hurry to deliver the news."

Wes gave the matter a cursory thought, then nodded, won over. Duke's plan made sense. "I guess you're right."

"'Course I'm right." A small, thin smile curved Duke's lips. "I'm your big brother." And then he rolled the news over in his head as the impact of what this all meant hit. "Hell, Mark Walsh…dead again after all this time." He shook his head. "Don't that beat all? You got any idea who did it?"

Wes didn't have a clue. What he did know was the identity of the one person who didn't do it. "Not Damien."

The thin smile was replaced with a small grin on Duke's lips. "Yeah, not Damien." And that, he thought, a wave of what he assumed had to be elation washing over him, said quite a lot.

Wes checked his watch. "See you," he said, beginning to get back into his vehicle. And then, shading his eyes a little more, he stopped to squint in the direction he'd come from. "Looks like you've got company coming, Duke. This place isn't as desolate as I remember," he commented with a short laugh, getting behind the wheel of his Jeep.

Still stunned by the news Wes had delivered, even though he didn't show it, Duke looked down the road in the direction Wes had pointed.

His green eyes narrowed in slight confusion as he made out the figure behind the wheel of the silver-blue sedan.

Hell, if this kept up, they were going to need a traffic

light all the way out here, Duke thought darkly, watching Susan Kelley's little vehicle approach.

Woman didn't have enough common sense to use a truck or Jeep, he thought in disdain. Cars like hers weren't meant for this kind of road, didn't she know that?

His brother passed Susan's car, pausing a second to exchange words Duke wasn't able to make out at this distance.

He thought he saw Susan blush, but that could have just been a trick of the sunlight. The next minute, she was driving again, getting closer. This was blowing his schedule to hell.

He ran his hand through his hair, trying not to look like a wild man.

Duke wasn't wearing a shirt. She hadn't thought she'd find him like this.

Susan could feel her stomach tightening into a knot. At the same time her palms were growing damper than the weather would have warranted.

God, but he was magnificent.

For the length of a minute, Susan's mind went completely blank as her eyes swept over every inch of the glistening, rock-hard body of the man standing beside the partially completed wire fence. His worn jeans were molded to his hips, dipping down below his navel—she found her breath growing progressively shorter.

Focus, Susan, focus. The man's got other parts you could be looking at. His face, damn it, Susan, look at his face!

But that didn't exactly help, either, because Duke

Colton was as handsome as Lucifer had been reported to be—and most likely, she judged, his soul was probably in the same condition.

No, that wasn't fair, she upbraided herself. The man had come to her aid at the funeral reception. If he hadn't been there, who knew how ugly a scene might have evolved when she tried to push Linc away? She'd loudly proclaimed that she could take care of herself, but Linc outweighed her by a good fifty pounds. He could have overpowered her if he'd really wanted to.

And Duke hadn't been the one to kiss her after Linc had slunk away. She was the one who had made that fateful first move.

Duke waited until Susan was almost right there in front of him before he left the fence and walked over to her vehicle in easy, measured steps.

"Lost?" he asked her, allowing a hint of amusement to show through.

Preoccupied with thoughts that had caught her completely by surprise and made her even warmer than the weather had already rendered her, she hadn't heard him. "What?"

"Lost?" Duke repeated, then put the word into a complete sentence since her confused expression didn't abate. "Are you lost? I've never seen you this far out of town."

There was a reason for that. She'd never been this far out of town before. There hadn't been any need to venture out this way—until now.

Forcing herself to pull her thoughts together, she shook her head. "Oh. No, I'm not lost. I'm looking for you."

Suspicion was never that far away. His eyes held hers. "Why?"

She felt as if he was delving into her mind. "To apologize and to give you this."

This was a gourmet picnic basket. The general concept was something she'd been working on for a while now, attempting to sell her father on the idea of putting out a mail-order catalogue featuring some of their signature meals.

Donald Kelley was still stubbornly holding out. He thought that shipping food through the mail was ridiculous, but her mother saw merit in the idea, so currently, the "official" word was that Kelley's Cookhouse was in "negotiations" over the proposed project. The final verdict, Bonnie Gene insisted in that take charge-way of hers, was not in yet.

Duke eyed the picnic basket for a long moment before finally taking it from her. "What, exactly, are you apologizing for?" he wanted to know.

It wasn't often that she found herself apologizing for anything. The main reason for that was that she never did anything that was out of the ordinary—or exciting. Until now.

"The other afternoon," she told him, lowering her eyes and suddenly becoming fascinated with the dried grass that was beneath her boots.

"The whole afternoon, or something in particular?" Duke asked, his expression giving nothing away as he looked at her.

He was going to make this difficult for her, she thought. She should have known he would. Duke Colton had never been an easygoing man.

"For you feeling as if you had to come to my rescue," she murmured, tripping over her own tongue again. He seemed to have that effect on her, she thought. But she was determined to see this through. "For me putting you on the spot by kissing you."

Pretending to be inspecting the picnic basket, Duke drew back the crisp white-and-red checkered cloth and looked inside. The aroma of spicy barbecued short ribs instantly tantalized his taste buds. It mingled with the scent of fresh apple cinnamon pie and biscuits that were still warm. She must have brought them straight from the oven.

He glanced down at her. "Still haven't heard anything to apologize for," he told her. "I enjoyed taking that little weasel down a couple of pegs. As for you kissing me," his eyes slowly slid over her, "you *definitely* don't have anything to apologize for in that area."

Trying not to grow flustered beneath his scrutiny, Susan tried again. "I didn't mean to make you uncomfortable.…"

Duke cut into her sentence. "You didn't," he told her simply.

Susan cleared her throat. This wasn't going as smoothly as she'd hoped. How was it that he made her feel more tongue-tied every time she tried to talk to him?

"Well, anyway, I just wanted to say thank you for being so nice."

That made him laugh. It was a sound she didn't recall ever hearing coming from him. She caught herself smiling in return.

"Nobody's ever accused me of being that," Duke

responded, more than slightly amused by the label, "but have it your way if it makes you happy."

Susan brushed her hands against the seat of her stone-washed jeans. She couldn't seem to shake the nervous, unsettled feeling that insisted on running rampant through her. The fact that he was still bare-chested, still wearing jeans that dipped precariously low on his hips, didn't help matters any. If anything, they caused her breath to back up in her lungs and practically solidify.

Try as she might, she couldn't seem to ignore his sun-toned muscles or his washboard abs. Her mouth felt as if it was filled with cotton as she tried to speak again. "They told me at the house that I'd find you out here. I asked," she tacked on and then felt like an idiot for stating the obvious.

Duke nodded at the information. "They'd be the ones to know."

She licked her overly dry lips and tried again. She definitely didn't want him thinking of her as a village idiot. She normally sounded a lot brighter than this. "What are you doing out here, working out in the sun like this?"

He was smiling now, enjoying this exchange. Ordinarily, he had no patience with flustered people, but there was something almost…cute about Susan hemming and hawing and searching for words. "Haven't found a way to turn down the sun while I do my work."

She didn't understand why he had to be out here in this heat, doing things that could just as easily be handled by a ranch hand. "Don't you have people to do this?"

One side of his mouth curved more than the other,

giving the resulting smile a sarcastic edge. "My father thinks his sons should learn how to put in a full day's work each day, every day. Besides," he added, "it saves him money if we do the work."

She thought that was awful. "But your father's the richest man in the county." She realized that sounded materialistic, not to mention incredibly callous. "I mean—"

Duke took no offense at her words. He was well aware that his father had amassed a fortune. The fact didn't mean anything to him one way or another. It certainly didn't make him feel as if he was entitled to a special lifestyle or to be regarded as being privileged. He believed in earning his way—and maybe he had his father to thank for that—if he were given to thanking his father.

He saw the blush creeping up her neck. "You do get flustered a lot, don't you?"

She looked embarrassed by the fact. "I'm not a people-person like my mom."

He didn't think she should run herself down like that. The way she was was just fine. "No offense to your mom, but she does come on strong at times. You, on the other hand," he continued in his off-hand manner, "come on just right."

Susan felt her pulse beginning to race.

More.

If she was being honest with herself, her pulse had started racing the instant she saw Duke's naked chest. All sorts of thoughts kept insisting on forming, thoughts she was struggling very hard not to explore.

Right now, she was just barely winning the battle. Emphasis on the word *barely*.

She licked her lips again, fearing that they might stick together in mid sentence if she didn't. "I—um—I've got to be going."

By now he'd reached into the basket and plucked out a short rib. He glanced into the interior. He could probably transfer the rest of the food into the cab of his truck, out of the sun, not that in this heat it would buy him much time.

"Want the basket back?" he offered.

"No!" she heard herself saying a bit too forcefully. *Calm down, Susan.* "I mean, that's yours. A token of my appreciation."

She'd said that already, hadn't she? Or had she? She couldn't remember. It was as if he'd just played jump rope with her brain and absolutely everything was tied up in a huge, tangled knot.

Duke nodded. "It's good," he told her, holding the short rib aloft. "But I considered any debt already paid by your first token of appreciation."

Confused, she was about to ask what token he was talking about when it hit her. He was referring to when she'd kissed him.

Pleased, embarrassed and breathless, she could only smile in response. Widely.

The next moment, she was back in the car and driving away. Quickly. She thought it was definitely safer that way. Otherwise, she ran the risk of ruining the moment by tripping over her own tongue. Again.

Chapter 7

Going to the county seat to officially file Mark Walsh's autopsy report with the court had taken longer than Wes had expected. He didn't mind. There was a certain rush that came from knowing that he could finally—finally—get Damien free, and he savored it.

He'd known all along in his gut that Damien hadn't killed that worthless SOB.

Granted, he could have saved himself a lot of time if he had called the information in over the phone or started the ball rolling via the computer, but Wes had always favored the personal touch. In this highly technical electronic age, he felt that human contact was greatly underestimated. It was easy enough to ignore an e-mail or a phone message, but not so easy to ignore a man standing outside your office door, his hat in his hand. The gun strapped to his thigh didn't exactly hurt, either.

But doing it in person had caused him to be rather late getting back to Honey Creek. He'd been gone the better part of the day and a growling stomach was now plaintively asking him to stop in town for dinner before ultimately heading toward the ranch and the small house where he lived.

The old sheriff, he knew, would have put notifying Jolene Walsh off until some time tomorrow, tending to his own needs first. After all, as Duke had said, it wasn't like telling Jolene that her husband was dead was actually going to be much of a surprise to the woman. And there certainly wasn't anything to mourn over. Everyone in town felt that Mark Walsh had been a nasty-tempered womanizer who'd had an ugly penchant for young girls. Moreover, Walsh made no secret of the fact that he'd treated Jolene more like an indentured servant than a wife throughout their marriage.

There hadn't been a single redeeming quality about the man. He hadn't even been smart, just lucky. Lucky that he had picked the right man to run his company.

His CFO, Craig Warner, was and always had been the real brains behind Walsh Enterprises. It was Warner, not Walsh, who had turned the relatively small brewery located right outside of town into a nationally known brand to be reckoned with.

But somewhere along the line, Walsh must have stumbled across a cache of brains no one else knew he had acquired. How else had he managed to fake his own death and pull it off all these years, hiding somewhere in the vicinity? Someone had finally done away with the man, but it had taken them fifteen years to do it.

But why, Wes couldn't help wondering, had the

original murder been faked to begin with? What was Walsh trying to accomplish?

And what was *he* missing?

Tired, resigned to his duty, Wes brought his vehicle to a stop before the Walsh farmhouse. Jolene had gone on living there after her husband had been murdered. The first time, Wes added silently.

It was late and he was hungry, but it just wouldn't seem right to him if he put this off until morning. She had a right to know about this latest, bizarre twist and the sooner Jolene Walsh was informed of this actual murder of her husband, the sooner she could begin to get over it. Or so he hoped.

There were several lights on in the large, rambling house. Walsh wouldn't have recognized the place if he'd had occasion to stumble into it, Wes mused. Five years after the man's supposed death, Jolene had had some major renovations done to the house, utilizing some of the profits that the business was bringing in.

Jolene had become a different woman since Walsh had vanished from her life, Wes thought. More cheerful and vibrant. She smiled a lot these days and there was a light in her eyes that hadn't been there when Walsh was around. It was good to see her that way.

This was going to knock her and Craig for a loop, Wes thought, wishing he didn't have to be the one to break this to the woman. But he couldn't very well postpone it or shirk his duty.

Standing on the front porch, Wes rang the doorbell. Then rang it again when no one answered.

He was about to try one more time before calling it a night when the door suddenly opened. Mark Walsh's widow—rightfully called that now, he couldn't help thinking—was standing in the doorway, her slender body wrapped in a cream-colored robe that went all the way down to her ankles. Her long hair was free of its confining pins and flowed over her shoulders and down her back like a red sea.

Warm amber eyes looked at him in confusion a beat before fear entered them. She was a mother and thought like one.

"Is it one of the children?" she asked. She had four, the youngest of whom, Jared, was twenty-five and hardly a child, but to Jolene, they would always be her children no matter how many decades they had tucked under their belts. And she would always worry about them.

"No, ma'am," Wes said respectfully, removing his hat. Uncomfortable, he ran the rim through his hands. "I'm afraid I've got some really strange news."

She hesitated for a moment, as if debating the invitation she was about to extend to him, then moved aside from the doorway. "Would you like to come in, Sheriff?"

He didn't plan on staying long. He had no desire to see how this news was going to affect her once the shock of it faded. "Maybe it'd be better if I didn't." He took a short breath. "Mrs. Walsh, your husband's body turned up in the creek the other day."

She stared at him as if the words he was saying were not computing.

"Turned up?" she echoed. "Turned up from where?" Horror entered her expressive eyes. "You don't mean to tell me that someone dug up his body and—"

"No, ma'am, I don't mean to say that. According to

the county coroner, Mark Walsh has only been dead for five days."

Stunned, Jolene's mouth dropped open. "But we buried Mark almost sixteen years ago. He was definitely dead." It had been a closed-casket service. Whoever had killed her husband had done it in a rage, beating him to death and rendering him almost unrecognizable, except for his clothes and the watch on his wrist. The watch that she had given him on their last anniversary. "How is this possible?"

He tried to give her a reassuring smile. "Well, we buried *somebody* sixteen years ago, but it wasn't your husband." Wes made a mental note to have that body exhumed and an identification made—if possible—to see who had been buried there. "I'm really sorry to be the one to have to tell you this," he apologized.

Jolene looked as if the air had been completely siphoned out of her lungs and she couldn't draw enough in to replace it. For a second, he was afraid she was going to pass out. Jolene clung to the doorjamb.

"You're just doing your job," she murmured, her thoughts apparently scattering like buckshot fired at random into the air. "Do you want me to come down to make a positive I.D.?" she asked in a small voice. It was obvious that she really had no desire to take on the ordeal, but would if she had to.

"No, ma'am, there's no need." He was glad he could at least spare her that. "The coroner's already made a positive identification, using your husband's dental records. I just wanted you to hear it from me before word starts spreading in town." She looked at him blankly, as if she couldn't begin to understand what he was telling her. "Boyd Arnold was the one who found the body in the creek," he explained. "And it's only a matter of time before he lets it slip to someone. Boyd's not exactly a man who can keep a secret."

Jolene nodded, seeming not altogether sure what she was nodding about. "Do you have any idea who did it?"

"That's what I aim to find out, ma'am," Wes told her politely.

Horror returned to her expressive eyes as her thought processes finally widened just a little. "Oh, my God, Sheriff, your brother, he's been in prison all this time for killing Mark. We have to—"

He anticipated her next words and appreciated the fact that Jolene could think of Damien's situation when she was still basically in shock over what he'd just told her.

"I've already started the process of getting him released from prison," Wes assured the woman. "Again, I am sorry to have to put you through this."

"It's not your fault, Sheriff." Pale, shaken, Jolene began to close the door, retreating into her home. She felt as if she was in the middle of a bad dream. One that would continue when she woke up. "Thank you for coming to let me know," she murmured.

Shutting the door, she leaned against it, feeling incredibly confused. Incredibly drained.

Jolene shut her eyes as she tried to pull herself together. When she opened them again, she wasn't alone. Craig Warner, the man who had singlehandedly helmed the brewery into becoming a household name and the sole reason she'd become the happy woman she was, was standing beside her.

"That was the sheriff. He came to tell me that Mark wasn't dead before. But he is now." Did that sound as crazy as she thought it did?

Craig nodded. "I heard," he said quietly.

Jolene blew out a breath as she dragged her hand through her long, straight hair. At fifty, she didn't have a single gray hair to her name. Astonishing, considering the trying life she'd led until Mark had been killed—or reportedly killed, she amended silently.

Her eyes met Craig's, searching for strength. "What do I do now?"

Shirtless and wearing only jeans that he'd hastily thrown on when he'd heard the doorbell, Craig padded over to her. Linking his strong, tanned fingers through hers, he gave her hand a light tug toward the staircase.

"Come back to bed," he told her.

She couldn't pull her thoughts together. Was she to have a second funeral? Did she just have the body quietly buried? There were so many questions and she just couldn't focus.

"But, Mark—" she began in protest.

"Is dead and not going anywhere," Craig told her. "He'll still be there in the morning. And he'll still be dead. You've had a shock and you need time to process it, Jo." He kissed her lightly on the temple, then looked down at her face. "Let me help you do that."

Jolene blew out another shaky breath, then smiled a small, hesitant smile reminiscent of the way she'd once been. Craig was right. He was always right.

Without another word, she let him lead her up the

stairs back to her bedroom and the bed that had become the center of her happiness.

"You think he'll stay dead this time?" Bonnie Gene asked her husband the next afternoon. The story was all over town about Mark Walsh's second, and consequently, actual murder.

Donald Kelley was in his favorite place, the state-of-the-art kitchen that he had installed at great cost in his restaurant. Feeling creative, he was experimenting with a new barbecue sauce, trying to find something that was at once familiar yet tantalizingly different to tease the palates of his patrons. Bonnie Gene had come along with him, whether to act as his inspiration or to make sure that he didn't sample too much of his own cooking wasn't clear. But he had his suspicions.

"Who?" Donald asked, distracted. Right now, the hickory flavoring was a little too overpowering, blocking the other ingredients he wanted to come through. The pot he was standing over, stirring, was as huge as his ambitions.

"Mark Walsh," she said with an air of exasperation. Didn't Donald pay attention to anything except what went into his mouth? "That man must really have enemies, to be killed twice."

"He wasn't killed the first time," Donald pointed out, proving that he *was* paying attention. "He had to fake that."

Bonnie Gene was never without an opinion. "Most likely he faked it because he knew that someone was out to get him. And apparently they finally did. Mark Walsh is really dead this time," she told her husband with finality. "Boyd Arnold's running around town volunteering details and basking in his fifteen minutes of fame for having found the body in the creek." She shivered at the mere thought of seeing the ghoulish sight of Mark Walsh's half-decomposed body submerged in the water.

"Found whose body?" Susan asked, walking into the kitchen, order forms for future parties tucked against her chest.

She set the forms down in her section of the room. It was an oversize kitchen, even by restaurant standards, which was just the way her father liked it. The size was not without its merit for her as well. It allowed her to run the catering end of the business without getting in her father's way—or anyone else's for that matter.

Bonnie Gene swung around in her daughter's direction, delighted by Susan's obvious ignorance of the latest turn of events. There weren't all that many people left to surprise with this little tidbit.

Crossing to her, Bonnie Gene placed her arm around her daughter's slender shoulders, paused dramatically and then said, "Mark Walsh."

Susan looked at her mother, confused. "What about Mark Walsh?"

"Boyd Arnold just found his body. Well, not just," Bonnie Gene corrected herself before her husband could. "Boyd found it several days ago."

That cleared up nothing. Susan stared at her mother, trying to make sense of what she was being told. She knew that in New Orleans, whenever the floods covered the various cemeteries in that city, the waters disinterred the bodies that had been laid to rest there, but there'd been no such extreme weather aberrations here.

What was her mother talking about? "But Mr. Walsh's been dead for the last fifteen years," she protested. "His body's buried in the cemetery."

There was nothing that Bonnie Gene liked more than being right. She smiled beatifically now at her daughter. "Obviously not."

Susan jumped from fact to conclusion. "Then Damien Colton is innocent."

Donald sneaked a sample of his new sauce, then covertly slipped the ladle back into the pot and continued stirring. "It would appear so," he agreed.

Susan couldn't help thinking of all the years that Damien had lost, cooling his heels in prison for a crime he hadn't committed. The years in which a man shaped his future, made his reputation, if not his fortune. All lost because a jury had wrongly convicted him.

She looked from her mother to her father. "My God, what kind of a grudge do you think Damien's going to have against the people who put him away for something he didn't do?"

The thought had crossed Bonnie Gene's mind as well. "There's something I could live without finding out," she responded.

Susan's mind went from Damien to Duke, his twin. They said that most twins had an uncanny bond, that they felt each other's pain. That was probably why he'd been so solemn all these years, she thought. How would Duke take the news of his brother's innocence?

Or did he already know?

If he did, Duke had to be filled with mixed feelings.

She knew that he'd never believed that Damien had been the one to kill Mark Walsh and he'd turned out to be right. He had to feel good about that, she reasoned.

But now Mr. Walsh really *was* dead. Who *had* killed the man after all this time? And had someone tried to frame Duke's twin brother for that first murder?

Or maybe whoever had made it look like Mr. Walsh was killed that first time had tried to frame Duke and Damien had mistakenly been accused of the crime.

But wait a minute.

Her thoughts came to an abrupt halt. Mark Walsh *hadn't* been dead at the time and he never came forward. That meant what, that Mark Walsh had been behind all this? That he had been the one who had deliberately tried to frame Damien? Or Duke?

Why?

She had to see Duke, Susan thought suddenly. This was a huge deal. The man was going to need someone to talk to, to be his friend. He'd been there for her, albeit almost silently, but he'd made his presence known. Returning the favor was the least she could do for the man.

She made up her mind. "Mother, I don't have an event to cater today."

Bonnie Gene looked at her, trying to discern where Susan was going with this. "And your point is?" she prodded, waiting.

Susan saw that one of the kitchen staff had cocked her head in her direction, listening. She moved closer to her mother, lowering her voice. "I think I'll see if Duke Colton needs a friendly ear to talk to."

Bonnie Gene nodded. "Or any other body part

that might come into play," she commented with an encouraging smile.

No, no more matchmaking, Mother. Please. "Mother, I just want to be the man's friend if he needs one," Susan protested.

"Nobody can ever have too many friends," Bonnie Gene agreed, doing her best to keep a straight face. She failed rather badly.

Susan rolled her eyes. "Mother, you're incorrigible."

"What did I say?" Bonnie Gene asked, looking at her with the most innocent expression she could muster.

Susan turned to her other parent. "Dad, back me up here."

Her father spared her a quick glance before turning his attention back to the industrial-size pot he was standing over. He chuckled under his breath, most likely happy that someone else was drawing Bonnie Gene's fire for a change.

"This is your mother you're dealing with. You're on your own, kiddo," he told her.

Bonnie Gene raised her hands, as if she was the one surrendering. "I have no idea what you two are inferring," she declared. "But I have guests to mingle with," she told them. And with that, she crossed to the swinging doors that led out into the Cookhouse's dining room. But just as she was about to walk out, she stopped and stepped back into the kitchen.

When she turned to look at Susan, there was a very pleased smile on her lips. "Looks like you won't have to drive out of town to play good Samaritan, honey."

As was the case half the time, Susan had no idea what

her mother was talking about. "What do you mean?" she asked, crossing to her.

Bonnie Gene held one of the swinging doors partially open so that Susan could get a good look into the dining area.

"Well, unless my eyes are playing tricks on me, Duke Colton just took a seat at one of the tables in the main dining room." She let the door slip back into place. "Why don't you go see what he wants?"

That was being a bit too pushy, Susan thought, suddenly feeling nervous. "I can't just go out and play waitress."

"You can if I tell you to," Bonnie Gene countered, then turned toward the lone waitress in the kitchen. The girl was about to go on duty. "Allison here is feeling sick, aren't you, Allison?"

Confusion washed over the woman's broad face. "I'm fine, Mrs. Kelley," Allison protested with feeling.

Bonnie Gene was not about to be deterred. "See how sick she is? She's delirious." Placing both hands to Susan's back, Bonnie Gene gave her a little push out through the swinging doors. "Go, take his order. And follow it to the letter," she added, raising her voice slightly as the doors swung closed again.

"You're shameless, Bonnie Gene," Donald commented with a chuckle, never looking away from the sauce, which now was making small, bubbling noises and projecting tiny arcs of hot red liquid in the air.

"As long as I get to be a grandmother, I don't care what you call me," she told him.

With that, she went to the swinging doors to open them a crack and observe Susan and Duke—and she hoped that she would have something to observe.

Chapter 8

Duke looked up just as Susan reached the two-person booth where he had parked his lean, long frame.

"Duke, I just heard."

She was breathless, although she wasn't certain exactly why. It wasn't as if she'd rushed over to his table and she hadn't been doing anything previous to this that would have stolen the air out of her lungs, but she was definitely breathless.

Subtly, Susan drew in a deep breath to sustain herself and sound more normal.

Duke continued to look at her, arching a brow, as if he was waiting for her to finish her sentence.

So she added, "About Wes finding Mark Walsh's body. I don't know whether to congratulate you or to offer my condolences."

"Why would you feel you had to do either?" Duke

asked her in that slow, rich voice of his that seemed to get under her skin so quickly.

She shifted uncomfortably. Why did he need her to explain? "Well, because this means that Damien didn't do it."

"I already knew that," he told her, his voice deadly calm.

She had no idea how to respond to that, especially since Duke was definitely in the minority when it came to that opinion. Most of the town had thought that Damien was guilty and were quick to point out that there'd been no love lost between Damien and Mark Walsh. Matters had grown worse when Walsh had discovered that Damien was in love with his daughter, Lucy.

Never in danger of being elected Father of the Year, Walsh still wanted to control the lives of all of his offspring. None of his plans included having his oldest daughter marry a Colton and he made that perfectly clear to Damien. He was the one who had broken things up between Lucy and Damien. When Walsh was discovered beaten to death in the apartment he kept expressly for romantic trysts in Bozeman shortly afterward, everyone assumed that Damien had killed Walsh.

"Why condolences?" Duke finally asked when Susan said nothing further but still remained standing there.

She took his question as an invitation to join him. Sliding into the other seat, she faced him and knotted her fingers together before responding. "Because your brother had to spend so much time in prison for a crime he hadn't committed."

Duke lifted one shoulder in a careless shrug. "Yeah, well, that's life."

Susan stared at him, stunned. How could he sit there so calmly? Did the man have ice water in his veins? Or didn't he care? She felt excited about this turn of events and she wasn't even remotely related to Damien. As a matter of fact, she hardly remembered him. She'd been barely ten years old when Damien Colton had been sent off to prison.

"Don't you have any feelings about this?" she questioned.

"Whether I have feelings or don't have feelings about a particular subject is not up for public debate or display," he informed her in the same stony voice.

Well, that certainly put her in her place, Susan thought, stung.

Angry tears rose to her eyes and she silently upbraided herself for it. Tears, to Duke, she was certain, were undoubtedly a sign of weakness. But ever since she was a little girl, tears had always popped up when she was angry, undercutting anything she might have to say in rebuttal.

The tears always spoke louder than her words.

So rather than say anything, Susan abruptly rose and walked away.

Duke opened his mouth to call out after her. He'd caught sight of the tears and felt badly about making her cry, although for the life of him he saw no reason for that kind of a reaction on her part. But then he'd long since decided that not only were women different than men, they were completely unfathomable, their brains operating in what struck him as having to be some kind of an alternate universe.

Still, he did want to apologize if he'd somehow hurt her feelings. That hadn't been his intent. However, Bertha Aldean was sitting with her husband at the table over in the corner. A natural-born gossip, the woman was staring at him with wide, curious eyes. She was obviously hungry for something further to gossip about.

There was no way he was going to give the woman or the town more to talk about.

So he went back to scanning the menu and waited for a waitress to come and take his order. Susan Kelley was just going to have to work out what was going on in her head by herself.

"He's been alive all this time?" Damien's hand tightened on the black telephone receiver he was required to use in order to hear what his brother, Duke, was saying to him.

They were seated at a long, scarred table, soundproof glass running the length of it, separating them the way it did all the prisoners from their visitors. He was surprised at the middle-of-the-week visit from Duke. Weekdays were for doing chores on the ranch according to his father's rigid work ethic.

And he was utterly stunned by the news that Duke had brought. With a minimum of words, his twin had told him about the body that Wes had discovered.

Damien had received the news with fury.

"Yeah," Duke replied to his twin's rhetorical question.

"Until the other day. Now, according to Wes, Walsh is as dead as a doornail."

Duke saw the anger in his brother's eyes and hoped that no one else noticed. He didn't want Damien doing anything to jeopardize his release.

Damien fairly choked on his anger. "That bastard could have come forward any time in the last fifteen years and gotten me released."

"Not likely, since he hated your guts," Duke reminded him in a calm, collected voice. "And more than that," Duke pointed out, "he was afraid."

Dark-brown eyebrows narrowed over darkening green eyes. "Afraid of what? Me?"

"You, maybe," Duke acknowledged. His twin was a formidable man, especially now. He'd used all his free time to work out and build up his already considerable physique. There's always the possibility that Mark framed Damien himself, but that seems like an awful lot of trouble to go to. The victim was wearing Mark's clothing and watch. "More likely, he was afraid of whoever killed that guy they found in his apartment fifteen years ago and mistook for him. He probably figured that the killer thought the same thing, that he'd killed him—Walsh," Duke clarified. "As long as people thought he was dead, Walsh thought he was safe. If that meant that you had to stay in prison, well, Walsh probably saw that as being a bonus."

"Bonus?" Damien echoed incredulously. "What do you mean bonus?"

Duke would have thought that was self-evident. "If you were in prison, you weren't making babies with his daughter."

Damien snorted. "Small chance of that. Lucy hates my guts." She'd made that perfectly clear the last time he'd seen her. But before then…before then it had been another matter. He'd thought they really had something special, something that was meant to last.

"Because she thinks you killed her father," Duke emphasized. "That's the reason she hates you. Since you didn't, there's nothing for her to hate any more."

"It's too late," Damien said quietly. *Too late.* Too much time had been lost.

Damien scrubbed his hand over his face. Joy filtered in to mix with the rage. Impotent rage because there wasn't anyone to direct that rage toward, now that Walsh was dead. Holding the jury—and his father who should have stood up for him—accountable for his being here all these years seemed pointless.

Nonetheless, he had a feeling it was going to take him a long time to work out all these anger issues he had going on inside of him.

"How much longer do I have to stay here?" he wanted to know. "And why isn't Wes here, telling me all this himself?"

"Cut the guy a little slack, Damien," Duke said. "He's been seeing everyone he can, trying to cut through the red tape and get you released. He's always been on your side, right from the start." Duke could see how restless Damien was, so he added, "There are forms to file and procedures to follow. Nothing is ever simple."

"Throwing me into jail was," Damien said bitterly.

Damien told him what they could do with the procedures and the forms. Duke laughed shortly under his breath, then advised, "You better can that kind of talk for a while, Damien. Don't give anyone an excuse to drag their feet about letting you out of here."

The veins in Damien's neck stood out as he gripped the phone more tightly. "They *owe* me."

"No argument," Duke answered, his voice low, soothing. "But you can't start to collect if you do something to get your tail thrown back into prison. You're a free man in name only right now. Hold your peace until the rest of it catches up." His eyes held Damien's, clearly issuing a warning. "Hear me?"

Damien blew out a long, frustrated breath. "I hear you." And then the barest hint of a smile crept across his lips as the reality of it all began to sink in. "I'm really getting out?"

"You're really getting out," Duke assured him, feeling a great deal of relief himself.

"How about that," Damien said more to himself than his brother. And then he looked at his twin. "What's the old man say?"

Darius Colton's expression hadn't changed an iota when Wes had told him about the new development. Instead, he'd merely nodded and then said that he could use the extra set of hands.

Damien stared at his twin. He would have thought, after all this time, that their father would have registered some kind of positive emotion. "That's it?" he pressed.

For Damien's sake, Duke wished that there had been more. But he wasn't going to lie about it. It would only come back to bite him in the end. "That's it. He never was much of a talker," Duke reminded him.

His father hadn't come to see Damien once in all the

years that he'd been confined. "Not much of a father, either," Damien bit off.

Duke shrugged. It was what it was. There wasn't anything he could do or say to change things. "Yeah, but we already knew that."

Oh, God, not again.

The thought echoed in Susan's brain the moment she saw the dead roses on the mat outside the private entrance to her catering business. She'd gotten the wilted flowers before but hadn't thought anything of it. She'd thought it was someone's idea of a bad joke.

Preoccupied with the challenging feat of keeping an ice sculpture frozen and firm in the middle of a July heat wave long enough to look good at a reception, she hadn't seen the bouquet on the ground until she'd stepped on the roses and heard them crunching under her shoes.

Startled, she'd backed up and saw what was left of them. And the envelope lying next to them. It was the type of envelope that was used for greeting cards. But if this was like the two other times, there was no greeting card inside. Instead, there was probably a note. A note written in childish block letters that made no sense to her.

Taking a deep breath, Susan stooped down and picked up the bouquet and the envelope. Steeling herself, she opened the envelope.

Sure enough, there was a folded piece of paper tucked inside it. Taking it out, she unfolded the paper. Uneven block letters spelled out another threat, similar to the one that she'd received yesterday.

DEAD FLOWERS FOR A DEAD WOMAN.

The warning might have been downright scary if it didn't make her so mad. She held the note up to the light. And what do you know, the Coltons' watermark.

It wasn't Linc. As aggressive as he'd become lately, he was too smitten to pull something like this. It wasn't his style. She knew exactly who was behind this. It was just the kind of thing he'd do.

Duke.

But why?

Just what was he trying to pull? Was this his obscure way of saying that he thought she was childish, as childish as the block letters in the message? Or was he trying to get her to back off? But back off from what? From expressing a few feelings about the current state of affairs regarding his brother? She was only trying to be neighborly.

Just what the hell did Duke Colton think he was doing?

The more Susan thought about it, the angrier she became.

While she willingly acknowledged that she might not be the bravest soul God had ever created, she was definitely *not* about to be intimidated by rotting flowers and stupid, enigmatic notes that sounded more deranged than anything else.

It was damn well time to put a stop to this before she found herself knee-deep in dead roses and dried-up thorns.

Still clutching the flowers, she marched to the kitchen's threshold.

Since this was between meals and there was no one else around, she told her father. "I'm going out, Dad."

Donald Kelley had his back to her. He was still experimenting with the new sauce he was determined to create. Currently, he was on his sixth theme and variation of the new recipe, and he barely acknowledged that he'd heard her.

"That's nice. Have fun," Donald muttered. Reaching for the long yellow tablet he'd been making all his notations on, he crossed out an ingredient near the bottom of the list.

Susan doubted that her father had actually heard what she'd said.

But her father wasn't a problem right now. Duke was. Duke Colton was insulting her with these childish notes and bouquets of dead roses. It had to be him. Who else could it be? She had every intention of putting a stop to this behavior—and give him a piece of her mind while she was at it.

The sooner the better, she thought, storming out to her car.

A head full of steam and indignation propelling her, Susan was torn as where to go first in order to locate Duke. As luck would have it, she actually found him in the first place she looked.

Wanting to cover all bases, at the last minute, rather than going to the main house on the ranch, she'd decided to stop at his house first since it was actually closer. She'd stopped her car right in front of the front door, got out and rang his doorbell. She gave him to the count of ten.

He opened the door when she got to six.

Duke's face registered a trace of surprise when he saw her. His sister, Maisie, had said that she might be stopping by and that was who he had expected to see on his doorstep, not a five-foot-ten caterer whose brown eyes were all but shooting lightning at him.

Before he could ask Susan what had brought her out to the Colton ranch for a second time in such a short period of time, she yelled "Here!" and threw what looked like a bouquet of flowers way past their prime at his feet.

Dried petals rained right and left, marking the passage before the bouquet landed.

Duke glanced down at the all but denuded bouquet and then back up at her.

"I don't remember asking for dead flowers," he said in a voice as dry as the flowers.

"Don't try to be funny!" Susan retorted angrily, her arms crossed before her.

"All right, how about confused?" he suggested. What the hell was going on? Susan was acting as crazy, as unstable as his older sister Maisie was. He toed the bouquet. More petals came loose. "Why'd you just throw those things at me?"

Duke was behaving as if he'd actually never seen the bouquet before. Maybe the man should become an actor, she thought sarcastically. "Because you left them on my doorstep."

Her answer only confused things more, not less. "I don't believe in wasting money," he told her. "But if I did decide to give you flowers, trust me, I could afford ones that weren't so damn shriveled up."

She drew herself up indignantly. He was lying to her face, wasn't her?

Or was he?

She began to vacillate ever so slightly. Her eyes on his, she asked, "You're telling me you didn't leave those flowers on my doorstep?"

"I'm telling you I didn't leave those flowers on your doorstep," he echoed.

He saw no reason to plead his case any further. If Susan had half a brain—and he was fairly confident that the youngest of the Kelleys was a very intelligent young woman—she would realize that there was no reason for him to do something so bizarre.

A little of Susan's fire abated. "What about the note?"

"What note?" he challenged.

Digging the last missive she'd received out of her purse, she held it up in front of his face. "This note."

Taking the note out of her hand, Duke held it at the proper distance so that he was able to read it. When he did, he frowned and folded it up, then handed it back to her.

"I didn't write this," he informed her flatly.

She was beginning to believe him, but she couldn't just capitulate and back away. He might be a very good liar. She knew she wasn't experienced enough when it came to men to tell the difference.

"If you didn't write this, then who did?" she challenged.

Outwardly, her bravado remained intact, but inwardly, she knew she was beginning to lose ground. Embarrassment was starting to take hold.

He paused for exactly one second, thinking. "My first guess would be Linc."

"Linc?" she echoed incredulously. "Why would he keep sending me dead flowers?" she asked, not wanting to go there. She and Linc had been friends forever. If he actually was the one sending her these horrid bouquets, that meant that he wasn't the kind of person she thought he was. And that meant that she was completely incapable of judging *anyone's* character.

"Why would I?" Duke countered, then suddenly realized what she'd just said. "This isn't the first time you've gotten dead flowers?"

She shook her head, her straight blond hair swinging back and forth, mimicking the motion. "No. I got a bouquet of rotting roses yesterday, and one the day before that. They each had notes like this one."

Once was a stupid prank. Twice was something more. Three times meant that there was a dangerous person on the other end of those notes. She could very well need protection. "Have you gone to Wes about this?" Duke wanted to know.

She was beginning to get nervous. If Duke wasn't sending the flowers as some kind of nasty prank, then who was? She refused to think it was Linc. She'd just seen him yesterday and aside from seeming a little morose, he was the same old Linc. He *couldn't* be the one sending these notes.

"No, I haven't," she said quietly.

"Maybe you should."

She looked uneasy, he thought. He hadn't meant to scare her, but on the other hand, Susan should be aware that this might be more than just some really stupid joke.

If it did turn out to be that spineless Linc character, he was going to beat the tar out of him.

The chores and his father's obsession with having all his offspring working from sunup to sundown could wait. He felt responsible for the sliver of fear he saw entering her eyes.

After reaching into the house for his hat, he closed the door. "C'mon, I'll go with you."

It was an offer she couldn't refuse.

Chapter 9

Wes had sat quietly, unconsciously rocking ever so slightly in his chair as he listened to what the young woman his brother had brought in to see him had to say.

He could feel the hairs at the back of his head rising. Wes didn't like what he was hearing.

"And this isn't the first time you've found a note like this on your doorstep?" he asked her, indicating the envelope in the center of his desk. Taking a handkerchief, he turned the envelope over, not that he expected to notice anything now that neither he nor the other two people in the room hadn't up until now.

Susan set her mouth grimly before she shook her head. "No."

"She already told you that," Duke reminded his brother impatiently. He'd taken a seat beside Susan in front of Wes's desk, but it was obvious that he would have felt more comfortable standing, as if he had better control over a situation if he was on his feet.

"Just double-checking the facts, Duke," Wes replied mildly. He wondered if there was ever going to be a point where Duke wouldn't think of him as his little brother but as a sheriff first. Probably not. Wes directed his next question to Donald and Bonnie Gene Kelly's youngest offspring. "Do you still have the other notes somewhere?"

Susan knotted her hands in her lap and shook her head. "No. I threw them away along with the flowers." She realized now that she should have hung onto them, just in case. But it had never occurred to her that the person sending this was dangerous. "I thought it was only a stupid prank."

Wes's face remained expressionless but he nodded, taking the information in. "So what changed your mind?"

"I didn't change it," Susan contradicted. "I just got fed up and mad."

Wes continued making notes in the small spiral pad he always kept on his person, replacing it only when he filled one. He wrote in pen so that the notes wouldn't fade away before he needed them.

Eventually, the pad would find its way into a file. A real file rather than a virtual one. Computers were for law-enforcement agents who had to contend with crime in the big cities and had a lot of information to deal with. In comparison to those places, Honey Creek seemed like a hick town.

A hick town with a murderer and a possible stalker, Wes reminded himself. He finished writing down what

Susan was saying and couldn't help wondering what else would crawl out from under the rocks while he was sheriff.

"Any particular reason you thought Duke was the one sending you the notes and flowers?" he wanted to know, sparing his brother a quick, sidelong glance.

Susan drew herself up, like a schoolgirl in a classroom when things like posture and radiating a positive attitude mattered. "Not now, no."

"But before?" he coaxed sympathetically.

Slim shoulders rose and fell beneath the bright pink-and-white-striped tank top. She actually did look more like a girl in high school than the successful head of the catering division of Kelley's Cookhouse.

"I thought it was Duke's way of saying I was acting like a kid," she murmured. Looking back, she realized that her reasoning didn't make any real sense. But admittedly, she wasn't thinking as clearly as she normally did, what with dealing with Miranda's death and viewing life through new, sobered eyes.

"Now that you don't think that it's Duke anymore, do you have any new thoughts about who might be sending you these threats and dried flowers?" Wes asked gently, as if he was trying to coax words out of a witness who had just been intimidated.

Susan began to shake her head because she really couldn't think of anyone this nasty, but Duke interrupted anything she might have to say. "You should check out that Lincoln character," he suggested. There was no uncertainty in his voice.

There was only one person with that first name around the area, but Wes asked anyway, wanting to make sure.

"You mean Lincoln Hayes?" When his brother nodded his response, Wes continued questioning him. "What makes you think that Lincoln Hayes is behind this?"

"It's not Linc," Susan interjected before Duke could respond.

Duke ignored her. The woman was too soft. She probably wouldn't want to think the worst of Satan. Seeing the skeptical look on Wes's face, he gave his brother what he felt was proof. "I caught him trying to force himself on her," he nodded toward Susan, "after the funeral."

Susan waved her hand at the statement, dismissing it. "Linc has this notion that we should give dating another chance. I told him it wasn't going to work. He thought it would." Duke snorted his contempt for the man. She slid forward on her chair and tapped the envelope that she'd brought in to the sheriff. "That's not Linc's handwriting."

"He write you notes in block letters often?" Duke asked her sarcastically.

Why was it that this rancher with the hard body could get to her faster than any other human being on the face of the earth? She'd never met anyone else who could scramble her emotions so quickly, making her run hot then cold within the space of a few moments.

"No, but—"

His point made, Duke looked at his brother. "I'd check it out if I were you," he repeated firmly to Wes. "See if there're any fingerprints on the envelope or the note that belong to Hayes."

Wes raised his eyes to Duke's, his patience stretched

to what he figured was his limit. "I know what to do, Duke."

"Just makin' suggestions," Duke replied.

That was, Wes knew, as close to an apology as he would ever hear from Duke. Rather than comment, he merely nodded, then turned to Susan again.

"Anything else you can think of?" he asked her. "Something Linc or someone else might have said that would make you think that they were the one sending you these threats?"

Coming up empty, Susan shook her head. "Nothing comes to mind."

"That's all right," he told her sympathetically. "Give it some time. And if something *does* come to you, give me a call," Wes instructed. He debated his next words, then said them—just in case. "It's probably harmless—a prank like you said—but for a while," he told her, offering her an encouraging smile, "I wouldn't go anywhere alone if I were you."

Instead of the expected fearfulness, Duke was surprised to see anger entering Susan Kelley's expressive eyes. She tossed her head, once again sending her short, straight blond hair swinging back and forth about her chin.

"Honey Creek is my home, Sheriff. I'm not about to let anyone make me afraid to walk around my home," she declared fiercely.

"I'm not asking you to be afraid, Ms. Kelley, I'm asking you to be sensible. Cautious," he tagged on when she continued looking at him as if she found his choice of words offensive. "There's a lot to be said for 'better safe than sorry,'" Wes told her.

"She'll be sensible," Duke chimed in, solemnly making the promise for her.

Wes nodded. "I'll hang on to this for now," he said, indicating the envelope on his desk.

"Keep it," she replied, her voice rather cool and formal. "I was just going to throw it away anyway."

"I'll get back to you on this," Wes said, then added, "we'll find out who's behind this, Susan."

"Yeah, we will," Duke added his voice to the promise as he strode out of the one-story building that had been the sheriff's office for the last fifty-some years. It was hard to say exactly to whom he was addressing his words, his brother, Susan or some invisible force he meant to vanquish.

Right now, Susan was fit to be tied and would have wanted nothing more than just to walk away from Duke Colton, but she couldn't. She'd left her car parked in front of Duke's house and he was her ride back. She had no choice but to hurry after him.

Oh, she knew she could ask someone at the Cookhouse to drive her to the Colton Ranch so she could get her car, but she really didn't want word getting back to her mother or her father about this. Neither of them knew about the notes and the flowers and she wanted to keep it that way. She didn't want them worrying.

She also didn't want her mother finding out that she'd gone to see Duke for *any* reason. The way her mind worked, her mother would be sending out invitations to her wedding by nightfall if she suspected that there was something going on between them.

Right now, Susan thought as she wordlessly plunked herself down in the passenger seat of Duke's truck, the only thing going on between them was anger. At least there was anger on her part.

She stole a look at Duke's chiseled profile as he turned the ignition on and his truck's engine coughed to life. On Duke's part, she was willing to bet, there was nothing but complete ignorance of the offense he'd just committed.

Typical male, she thought. Her anger continued to smolder and grow, like a prairie fire feeding on shoots of grass and tearing a path through the land.

Pressing her lips together, she stared straight ahead at the road and said nothing.

She'd been quiet the entire trip back to his ranch. Not that he actually minded the quiet, Duke thought, but it seemed somehow unnatural for her. The girl was nothing if not a chatterbox.

Which meant, if he remembered his basic Women 101, that there was probably something wrong. Or at least *she* thought that there was.

Nothing occurred to him.

Duke debated not staying quiet about her silence. The purpose of this trip back was to reunite her with her car. Once that happened, then she'd be on her way. And out of his hair, so to speak.

And it wasn't as if he was given to an all-consuming curiosity. Pretty much most of the time, he couldn't care less if he knew something or not. Rabid curiosity was not one of his shortcomings.

So exactly what was it about this slip of a girl that made things so different? That made *him* behave so differently?

The question ate at him.

Duke saw his house in the distance. They'd been on Colton land for a while now, all traveled in annoying silence.

A couple of more minutes and he'd be home-free, he told himself. He'd pull up his truck beside her prissy little sedan, let her get out and then she'd be gone. And he could get back to his work and anything else he felt like getting back to.

The problem was he didn't feel like getting back to work. He felt like—

Startled, Duke abruptly clamped down his thoughts. There was absolutely no point in letting his imagination go there. He had no business thinking about that. It wasn't going to happen. Moreover, he definitely didn't want it to.

Liar.

Five minutes, just five more minutes and he'd be at the house and she'd be unbuckling. And then—

Oh, hell.

Duke turned toward her. Her face was forward and her features were almost rigid. He stifled an inward sigh. So much for letting sleeping dogs lie.

"Something wrong?" he asked her in a voice that was fairly growling.

She made no answer, which told him that he'd guessed right. Something *was* wrong. He found no triumph in being right, only annoying confusion because he hadn't a clue what was sticking in her craw.

"All right, *what's* wrong?" he demanded, sparing her a second look.

He heard her sigh.

That makes two of us, honey.

Still facing forward, Susan pressed her lips together. It had been eating away at her all the way back to his ranch.

The reason she hadn't said anything was because she knew damn well that it wouldn't do any good. It would be like banging her head against a wall. Men like Duke Colton didn't learn from their mistakes. And the reason they didn't learn from their mistakes was because they didn't believe they *made* mistakes.

He'd probably say something like, she was being too sensitive, or imagining things.

Or—

But if she didn't say anything, she silently countered, she was going to explode. The man *needed* a dressing down.

She shifted in her seat and looked at him. "I don't need you to make promises for me."

Duke silently cursed himself for saying anything. He was better off with her not talking. But now that she had, he had to respond. It was going to be like picking his way across quicksand, he just knew it. "What are you talking about?"

She might have known that he wasn't aware of his transgression. Nobody probably ever challenged him. At least no woman. "You told the sheriff that I'd 'be sensible.'"

He spared her a glance. Funny how her face seemed to glow when she got excited about something. "Well, won't you be?"

Didn't he understand anything? "Whether I will or won't be isn't the point—"

Damn but women should come with some kind of a beginner's manual. Something like *A Guide to Women for the Non-Insane.*

"So what the hell is the point?"

She did have to spell this out for him, didn't she? Susan could feel her temper fraying and growing shorter and shorter.

"The point is you have no right to think you can speak for me. You don't know the first thing about me."

"I've known you all your life," he snapped indignantly.

He actually believed that, didn't he? she thought incredulously.

"No, you've been *here* all my life. In Honey Creek," she pointed out. "But you don't know anything about me, Duke."

This time the sidelong glance was more of a glare. "I know you like picking fights."

"I'm not picking a fight," she cried, exasperated. "I'm making a point." *You big, dumb jerk. Don't you even know the difference?*

Duke snorted. "Seems like the same thing from where I'm standing."

God, but there were times when she hated being right. He *was* being obtuse. "Because you're not paying attention."

"When you say something worth listening to, then, I'll pay attention," Duke told her in his cold, offhand manner.

She suddenly shut her eyes. "What color are my eyes?" she asked him.

Approaching his house, Duke looked at her. Now

what was she doing? "What the hell does that have to do with anything?"

Susan kept her eyes shut. She intended to show Duke how wrong he was in terms that even a thick-headed idiot like him could understand.

"If you 'know' me like you claim, you've got to at least know what color my eyes are. You were just looking at me a second ago. Okay, come on, tell me. What color are they?"

He was really beginning to regret this good deed he'd undertaken. "This is stupid," he told her between gritted teeth.

Susan was not about to back off. "What color?" she demanded again, then laughed. She'd proven her point. "You don't know, do you?"

She heard him huff and half expected a cuss word to follow.

Duke surprised her.

"They're brown," he finally told her. "Chocolate brown. Warm and soft when you look at a man. Warm," he repeated, "like the inside of a pan-baked brownie fresh out of the oven on Christmas morning."

Stunned, Susan slowly opened her eyes to make sure she was still sitting next to Duke Colton and that someone else hadn't slipped into the driver's side in his place.

"Lucky guess." The two words dribbled out of her mouth in slow motion. There was absolutely no conviction to them.

"Like hell it was," he retorted.

Finally home, Duke pulled up the hand brake, put the manual transmission into Park and turned off the ignition. His engine sighed audibly before shutting down. Getting out of the cab, he rounded the hood and came over to the passenger side.

He opened the door for her. Then he took her hand and, rather roughly, "helped" her out of the truck.

To be honest with himself, he wasn't exactly sure who he was angry at. Her for stirring up feelings he wanted no part of, or himself for *having* these feelings in the first place and for not being able to rein them in the way he'd trained himself to.

After that numbing fiasco with Charlene—first the affair and then her suicide—he'd sworn to himself that he wasn't going to get caught up in any kind of a relationship again. Women just weren't worth it. A few minutes of pleasure in the middle of weeks of turmoil and grief was what it usually amounted to. Hell, it just wasn't worth it.

And then she came around, this naive little girl-next-door with the heart-shaped face. Looking at her, he would never have thought that she could get under his skin, but she had.

He still didn't understand how or why. He was ten years older than she was. Ten damn years. She was only seven years old when he'd had his first woman. Seven years old. Just a baby, nothing more.

What was he doing, having feelings for someone who was so young? Yet, there it was. He had feelings for this slip of a thing. Feelings he couldn't seem to cap or harness.

Feelings that threatened to tear him apart if he gave in to them even a little.

Yeah, like he had a choice, Duke silently mocked himself.

He bracketed her arms with his strong, calloused hands. But it was his eyes that pinned her in place, his eyes that held her prisoner.

"I know everything there is to know about you," he told her angrily, biting off each word. "I don't want to, but I do."

Pulling her into his arms, he didn't give her a chance to say anything in reply, whether to challenge him or perhaps, just possibly, to admit to having feelings for him herself, the latter being a long shot in his estimation.

Susan didn't have time to say or do anything except brace herself because, in the next second, Duke's mouth came down on hers and the world, as she knew it, exploded.

It most definitely stopped turning on its axis.

Chapter 10

Duke only meant to kiss her. It was a way of venting his feelings for a moment. Maybe he even meant to scare her away by showing her the intensity of what he was feeling.

If that was his intent, it backfired. Because he wasn't scaring her away. If anything, kissing her like this had the exact opposite effect.

And worse than that, he somehow managed to lose himself completely within his own attempt at a defensive maneuver.

She tasted sweet, like the first ripe strawberries of the summer. More than that, she caused the spark within him to burst into flame, consuming him. Making his head swirl and causing his thought processes to all but disintegrate.

What was going on certainly wasn't logical.

He sure as hell hadn't meant to push this up to the next level.

But he had, and he could feel Susan's willingness to have this happen. Could feel the way she was yielding to him, silently telling him it was all right to press on. Given that, it was impossible for him to stop. Hell, it was hard for him to maintain control, not just to take her out here, with the warm sun as a witness and the hot July breeze caressing her bare skin.

The only thing that *did* stop him was that someone might ride by at the worst time and the last thing he wanted was to embarrass her. Nor did he want to share with that passerby what he felt certain in his heart was a magnificent body.

So, as he continued pressing his lips urgently against hers, drawing his very reason for existing out of the simple act, Duke scooped her up in his arms and took the three steps up to the porch.

He didn't keep the front door locked. It wasn't so much that he trusted people as that he knew he had nothing worth stealing. Someone would have to be a fool to risk coming onto the Colton Ranch solely for the purpose of breaking into his house. There was nothing to be gained by that.

Elbowing open the door, he carried Susan inside, then closed the door with his back. Only then did he allow her feet to touch the floor.

His pulse was racing and he could have sworn that there were all sorts of fireworks, crafted by anticipation, going off inside him. Who would have ever thought—?

Duke drew his head back.

* * *

He'd stopped kissing her. Was it over? Had she done something to make him back away? To suddenly change his mind?

Because she'd thought…

Determined not to come so far only to have it abruptly end, Susan rose on her toes, framed the handsome, chiseled face between her long, slender hands and kissed him.

For a moment, she felt a surge of triumph. He was kissing her back. But then that triumph faded because he drew his head back again. This time he took her hands between his, holding them still.

His eyes delved into hers. Susan struggled to catch her breath.

"You sure?" Duke asked, looking straight into her soul.

Susan didn't want to talk, didn't want to stop. She had never felt like this before and she just wanted that feeling to continue. Wanted it to flower and grow until it reached its natural conclusion. Until he made love with her.

So instead of answering him, she started to kiss Duke again. But for the second time, he took her hands in his. His eyes were deadly serious as they pinned her in place and he repeated his question.

"Are you sure?"

"Yes," she breathed, her pulse doing jumping jacks. "I'm sure."

Well, he wished he was. But he wasn't. Wasn't sure at all that this was the right thing to do. All he knew was that he really *wanted* to be with her, wanted to make love with this fresh-faced young woman and experience that incredible feeling that ultimately defied all description.

He hadn't been with a woman since he had broken things off with Charlene and she had killed herself. Hadn't thought it worth the trouble to get to that point with a woman. Duke didn't believe in paying for sex, and getting sex any other way required putting in time. Setting down groundwork.

He wasn't interested in doing that. Wasn't interested in getting tangled up with another woman.

He really had no idea how this had managed to happen so quickly. And with a woman—a girl—he'd never even thought of in this particular light.

But he was attracted to her, there was no denying that. And he wanted her. There was no denying that, either.

She made his blood rush the way he couldn't remember it rushing in a very long time.

Susan struggled to keep from losing consciousness. She'd never, *ever* felt like this before. Never experienced passion to this level before. Never experienced the desire to go the distance and find out just what there was about this ultimate bond between a man and a woman that was so seductively compelling. An eager curiosity propelled her on.

Her relationship with Linc that brief time when they'd attempted to be more than just friends was the only other time she'd even contemplated being intimate with a man—and the moment that Linc began kissing her, she'd stopped contemplating and wound up pushing him away. There'd been no bright, swirling lights, no surges of heat coupled with all but unmanageable desire.

There had only been the deep, bone-jarring sense of disappointment.

That wasn't what was going on here.

This was a whole brand-new brave world she was entering.

The excitement she felt at every turn was almost unmanageable. It fueled her eagerness. They moved from the front hall into the living room area.

When she felt Duke's strong, sure hands on her, touching her, being familiar, caressing her with a gentleness she hadn't thought he was capable of, it almost completely undid her.

She wanted to know what those hands felt like on her bare skin.

Her own hands were shaking as she began unbuttoning his shirt. She knew what she would find underneath the material and the excitement of that knowledge was making her fumble.

Damn it, he's going to figure out you're a novice before he gets to the last part. She upbraided herself, telling herself to slow down, to be calm.

She couldn't calm down.

One of the buttons got stuck and she tugged at it to no avail, feeling inept.

"Having trouble?"

Was he laughing at her? No, Duke wasn't laughing at her she realized, raising her eyes to his face. He was smiling.

Really smiling.

She couldn't remember if she'd *ever* seen Duke without at least a partial scowl on his face.

Having no experience at lying, she went with the

truth. "I'm not used to doing this," she murmured, feeling somewhat embarrassed at her ineptitude.

The smile on the rugged face deepened. "Good," she thought she heard him say.

The next moment, he helped her take off his shirt, then proceeded to do the same with hers, employing a great deal more ease than she had used.

There was no time for hesitation, no time for thought. No time to contemplate whether she was going to regret this later. The only thing Susan knew was that she didn't regret it now, and now was all that mattered.

When the rest of their clothes were shed, Duke inclined his head toward her again. Her heart was pounding as she felt his lips skim the side of her neck, then her throat. By then, she could hardly breathe. There were all sorts of wondrous, delicious things going on within her, and Susan gave up the effort of trying to catch her breath.

All she could do was fervently hope that she wasn't going to pass out.

Hungry for the taste of him, hungry to explore everything there was about this wondrous, exciting familiarity that was unfolding before her, Susan ran her hands along the hard contours of Duke's body, thrilling to his muscularity.

Thrilling even more to the evidence of his wanting her.

She knew that someone else would have pointed out that he was just having a physical reaction, that it meant nothing.

But it meant something to her.

Because this was Duke Colton and he wanted her.

Wanted her as much as she wanted him. She felt a throbbing sensation within her inner core she'd never experienced before.

As he continued kissing Susan, acquainting himself with every inch of her, Duke found himself both wanting to go slow, to savor every second of this—and to go quickly so that he could experience the ultimate pleasure that tempted him so relentlessly.

Somehow, he managed to continue going slow.

To his surprise, he enjoyed watching her react to him, enjoyed the decidedly innocent way surprise registered on her freshly scrubbed face when he teased a climax from her using his fingertips and then his lips. Enjoyed, too, the urgency with which Susan twisted and bucked against him, seeking to absorb the sensation he'd created for her as she also gasped for air.

The expression of wonder on her face made him think that she hadn't ever—

Duke abruptly stopped what he was doing and looked at her.

Susan felt the change in him immediately. A shadow of fear fell over her and something inside her literally froze.

Her eyes flew open. "What? Why did you stop?" she cried, then immediately questioned, "Did I do something wrong?"

Troubled, Duke sat up and dragged a hand through his hair. It didn't seem possible in this day and age, and yet…

"Susan, are you a virgin?" he asked her quietly.

Susan pressed her lips together. "No," she cried with feeling.

Too much feeling, Duke thought, looking at her face. "Susan," he asked in the same tone he'd just used to inquire after her virginity, "are you lying?"

She closed her eyes for a moment and sighed. She really wasn't any good at this, she thought. Lying came so naturally to other people, why did it have to stick in her throat?

"Yes."

She couldn't read his expression. Was he angry at her? Disgusted?

"Why?" he asked.

For a moment she stared down at the cracked leather sofa they'd tumbled onto. When she raised her eyes again, there was a look of defiance in them. She had as much right to this, to making a choice, as anyone.

"Because I want it to be you," she told him. "I want you to be the first."

He needed to understand her reasoning. He wanted her to make him understand. "Why?"

Why did they have to discuss this now? Why couldn't it just happen? She was fairly certain that other women didn't have to explain themselves before they made love for the first time.

"Because I never felt this way before," she told him truthfully. "Never wanted to make love with anyone before. I promise I won't hold you to anything, won't expect anything. Not even for you to do it again," she added, her voice soft. She touched his arm, silently supplicating. "Just don't turn away from me now. Please."

He looked at her. Never in a million years would he have thought that he'd be trying to talk a woman out of making love with him. But he couldn't just take her innocence from her without trying to make her understand what she was doing.

"Susan, you don't know what you're asking. I'm not any good for you," he insisted.

Susan raised her eyes to his. "That's not for you to decide," she told him simply. "That's my decision—and I've made it."

He should have been able to get up and walk away, Duke thought. The act of lovemaking—of having sex—had never been so all consuming to him that he couldn't think straight, couldn't easily separate himself from his actions. Couldn't just cut it off with no lingering repercussions.

But this time it was different.

This time, there was something about it, about Susan, about the sweetness that she was offering up to him, that robbed him of his free will, of his ability to stop, get up and walk away. He *always* could before.

He couldn't now.

He lightly cupped her cheek with his hand, the tender expression all but foreign to him. "You're going to be sorry," he predicted.

Susan's voice was firm, confident, as she replied, "No, I'm not."

He had nothing left in his arsenal to use in order to push her away. He didn't want to push her away. Every fiber of his being suddenly wanted her, wanted the life-sustaining energy he saw contained within her. Wanted, he knew, to completely wrap himself up in her and lose himself, lose the huge weight he felt pressing down on him.

Making love with Susan made him feel lighter than air and he didn't want to surrender that. Not yet. Not until he had a chance to follow that feeling to its ultimate conclusion.

Taking her into his arms again, Duke lay back down with her. He kissed Susan over and over again until he felt as if he were having an out-of-body experience.

And when he finally couldn't hold back any longer and he entered her, the small gasp of surprise that escaped her lips almost had him pulling back. The last thing he wanted was to cause her pain.

But she wouldn't let him stop. And for a single moment, she was the strong one, not Duke. She took the choice out of his hands.

They became one, rushing to the final, all-fulfilling moment, one of body, one of soul. And when it happened, when the final burst overtook him, Duke realized that he had never felt this complete before.

He had no idea what that meant. But now wasn't the time to explore it.

He held her to him, waiting for his heart to stop pounding so hard.

Maisie Colton didn't realize she was crying until she blinked and a tear slid down her face.

She'd seen them.

Had seen them kissing.

Had seen that two-bit floozy, Susan Kelley, sinking her claws into her little brother. Into Duke. Casting a spell over him.

Five years older and six inches shorter than Duke, Maisie bore a striking resemblance to her brother, except for her dramatic aqua eyes, and she felt closer to Duke than she did to anyone.

She wasn't going to stand for it. Wasn't going to allow that Kelley slut to make off with the only person on the ranch who was her ally. Duke didn't look down his nose at her, didn't judge her the way her father and the others did. Duke understood what it felt like to be a loner. Moreover, he'd never questioned her about her son, Jeremy, never even asked her who the boy's father was. Unlike their own father, Darius, who even now never missed an opportunity to badger her about her "shameless" betrayal of the family honor.

Like her father knew anything about honor, she thought contemptuously.

It was Duke who knew about honor. Like a strong, silent knight in shining armor, Duke had always been there for her. She could actually *talk* to him, tell him how she felt about things and he'd listen to her. Listen without judging.

She'd come to rely on him a great deal.

But if Duke got mixed up with that little whore, then everything would change. She'd lose him, lose the only friend she had around here.

She'd be all alone.

Suddenly feeling cold, Maisie ran her hands up and down her arms.

It wasn't going to happen, she promised herself. Duke wasn't going to take up with that little twerp. Not if she had anything to say about it.

Not even if she had to do something drastic to Susan Kelley to make her back off.

Permanently.

They'd gone inside.

Holding her breath, Maisie made her way slowly toward the house. She had to see what they were up to, had to see if it was as bad as she thought.

Maisie hated the Kelleys, hated the idea of any of her family getting mixed up with them. She couldn't stand the idea of Susan Kelley even *talking* to her brother. If the little bitch was doing anything else, that would be so much worse.

Maisie looked around. The terrain was as flat as the pancakes she'd made for Jeremy for breakfast this morning. If anyone was coming, she'd see them. But there was no one around. No one to see what she was about to do and chastise her for it.

She had a right to protect herself, Maisie silently argued. A right to protect what was hers.

Tiptoeing over to the window beside the front door, Maisie moved in what amounted to slow motion the last foot. And then she peered into the window by degrees to ensure that they didn't see her.

Maybe there was nothing going on.

Maybe he didn't like the way she kissed.

Maisie looked in, hoping.

Praying.

Her heart froze within her chest.

Pressing her lips together to stifle a gasp, she pulled back against the wall, her heart hammering in her shallow chest.

Damn it, it was worse than she thought.

That whore was naked. Stark-naked. So was Duke. How *could* he? He was letting that little whore throw herself at him. Tempt him. Didn't he know that the little bitch was no good for him? Why wasn't he throwing her out? Telling her to leave?

She squeezed her eyes shut as more tears filled them. A sob clawed its way up her throat but she deliberately kept her mouth shut. She couldn't take a chance on them hearing her.

God but she wished she'd thought to bring her gun with her. Just to fire over that bitch's head. Just to scare her a little.

Or maybe a lot.

Susan Kelley had no right to take Duke away from her. No damn right! If her brother abandoned her, if she chose that whore over her, who was she going to talk to?

She had to find a way to scare this little two-bit whore off. And if she couldn't scare Susan off, then she was just going to have to kill her. There'd be no other choice.

The thought made Maisie smile.

Chapter 11

Dragging air into his lungs, Duke sat up on the sofa, watching Susan. Trying to reconcile what he knew about her with what he'd just discovered about her. That she seemed to have the capacity to do the impossible. She had rocked his world.

"You can stay, you know. If you want to," Duke was quick to qualify. That way, the ball was in her court and not his. He wasn't asking her to stay, he was telling her she could if she wanted to. That put the emphasis on her desire, not his.

He was having trouble wrestling with these newfound sensations and emotions and didn't want to make things worse by exposing them to public scrutiny.

Susan was gathering up her clothes from the floor as quickly as she could. Now that the passion and the ensuing euphoria had both faded away, she felt awkward.

Naked was not exactly her normal state of being. Naked made her uncomfortable.

Very uncomfortable.

Not to mention she had this strange feeling she couldn't seem to shake that they had been observed. She could have sworn that when she'd thrown back her head at one point, she'd seen something move by the window. And if there was someone outside, wouldn't they have knocked by now?

A tree branch, it was probably just a tree branch, swaying in the hot breeze, she silently insisted to herself. She was just being jumpy.

Be that as it may, Susan knew she'd feel better once she had her clothes back on. And as for Duke, well, he didn't sound as if he cared one way or another if she stayed or if she left.

So she was determined to leave while there was still a shred of dignity available to her—or for her to pretend that it was available.

"I've got to get back to the restaurant," Susan murmured in response to Duke's cavalier invitation of sorts.

"You do what you have to do," he told her matter-of-factly.

Totally unselfconscious about being stark-naked he fetched his jeans and slid them on.

Even battling embarrassment, Susan had trouble drawing her eyes away from Duke from the moment that he got up.

She couldn't help thinking that Duke Colton was one hell of a specimen of manhood.

Wearing only his jeans, barely zipped and still

unsnapped, consequently dipping precariously low on hips that put the word *sculptured* to shame, Duke turned to her. Very slowly, as if he was drawing out scattered leaves, he ran his fingers through her hair.

His eyes held hers.

She hadn't a clue as to what he was thinking or feeling.

"Sure you have to go?" he asked her.

A very firm yes! hovered on her lips, but somehow couldn't manage to emerge. The lone word was seared into place by the heat of the lightning bolts that insisted on going off inside her all over again. She could hardly even breathe.

One by one, Duke removed the clothes she was clutching against her, never looking at either them or at the bit of her that was uncovered once the clothing was cast aside. Instead, his eyes remained on hers, doing a fantastic job of unraveling her.

She finally found her tongue. It was thick and clumsy—and definitely not cooperating. "I…really… have to…go."

"If you say so," Duke murmured. Tilting her head up toward his, he brought his mouth down to hers again.

And succeeded in keeping her there for yet another go-round, another hour filled with salvos of ecstasy and brand-new peaks that begged to be explored and then went off like rocket flares.

"You know he's only toying with you."

Two days later, lost in her own world, her mind only partially on working out the menu for the next dinner she and her staff were scheduled to cater, Susan looked up, startled by the intrusion of the harsh voice.

She was in her office and although she distinctly remembered leaving her door open, it was closed now. And there was a woman in the office with her. Glaring at her.

It took Susan a moment to realize who the woman was. Maisie Colton, the oldest of eight full- and half-sibling Colton offspring. The woman looked a little wild-eyed. And not a hundred-percent mentally stable.

Susan knew all about the whispers, the rumors. Maisie Colton had borne a love child, fathered by a man she refused to name. Speculation, even now, fourteen years later, ran high and rampant as to who that man might be. But Maisie's lips were sealed.

Guarding her secret so zealously despite her father's unrelenting attempts to uncover the man's identity might be the reason that Maisie seemed to be so off-kilter these days. To everyone who dealt with her, she seemed to be two cards shy of a full deck, if not more. That was the way Susan had heard her father describe Maisie. There'd been pity in his voice when he'd said it.

There were times, like now, when Maisie appeared to be going off the deep end.

"I'm afraid I don't know what you're talking about, Maisie," Susan answered, her tone politely dismissing the woman.

But Maisie wasn't about to be brushed aside that easily. She drew herself up, looming over Susan, "Sure you do," she insisted, then fairly shouted at her. "I'm talking about my brother."

Susan raised her chin. She was *not* about to let herself be chastised.

"You have lots of brothers." Whereas she had only one and she really wished Jake was here right now to rid her of this menace.

The next moment, Susan silently upbraided herself. She was twenty-five years old, running a successful business and had, due to that romantic interlude with Duke, crossed over into the world of womanhood. It was time she stopped looking to others to champion her and took up weapons to fight her own battles.

"Duke, I'm talking about Duke!" Maisie shouted at her impatiently. "He's just toying with you. You don't mean anything to him, so why don't you save yourself a lot of grief and just stop hanging around him?" Maisie fairly spat out.

For a moment, Susan stared at the older woman. Was she guessing, or had Duke actually told her about their afternoon? Had he thought so little of her that he'd broadcast what they had done together for anyone to hear? How many other people knew?

And then, for no apparent reason, it came to her out of the blue. She had her answer. She hadn't imagined that there was someone watching them that day at Duke's house, there *had* been someone watching. Maisie.

She thought she was going to be sick.

But in the next moment, the feeling passed. Instead, Susan became angry. Very, very angry. "You watched us, didn't you?" she demanded, her eyes narrowing into blazing slits.

Taken by surprise by the accusation, Maisie had no ready answer at her disposal.

She stumbled over her own tongue, then tossed her long brown hair over her painfully thin shoulder. "What if I did?" she retorted haughtily.

Susan would have preferred to be friends with the older woman. She liked to think of herself as friendly and outgoing. The kind of woman another woman would have welcomed as a friend.

But by attacking her, Maisie left her no choice. This was *not* her fault.

"There are names for people like you," she informed Duke's unstable sister, making no secret of the disgust she was experiencing.

Nothing Susan could have actually said could have been worse than the names that were running now through Maisie's head. Names her father had flung at her more than once. Wanting to strike out, she doubled up her fists. But rather than hit Susan, Maisie uttered an angry cry and swiped her hand along Susan's desk, sending a vase of daisies crashing to the floor. The vase broke, leaving the flowers homeless.

"You'll be sorry," Maisie predicted furiously, yanking open the office door. "Wait and see, you'll be sorry."

And with that, Duke's sister slammed the door and stormed out.

Susan closed her eyes for a moment, gathering herself together. Part of her wanted to run after Maisie, to pin the thin, fragile woman down and send for the sheriff to file a complaint.

Not a wise move, she pointed out to herself. After all, the sheriff was one of Maisie's brothers.

The other part just felt sorry for Maisie. She knew that the woman had had a hard time of it, being harassed not only by the holier-than-thou people in town, but by her own father. Darius Colton allowed his daughter to live on the Colton ranch—along with her son he had never accepted into the family—but he made her pay for the so-called kindness. Made her pay for any tiny crumb he sent Maisie's way.

It made her eternally grateful for her own set of parents—even if her mother did tend to drive her insane with broad hints about not getting any younger and needing to get started on creating a family *now*, if not yesterday.

Well, if nothing else, the Coltons were certainly not a dull lot, Susan thought. Carefully getting down on her knees, she gingerly began to gather up the shards of glass that had once been a cut-glass vase.

That was the way Duke found her, on her knees, piling up pieces of glass onto a tissue that was spread out on the floor beside her desk. Opening the door in response to her wary "Come in," he took one look at the mess and crouched down to help her.

"What happened?" It was actually meant as a rhetorical question. The answer he received didn't fall into that category.

She took a breath before giving Duke an answer. "Your big sister had a 'run in' with my vase." She grimaced. "The vase lost."

Duke sat back on his heels, looking at her. "My sister?" he repeated, confused. "Maisie?"

"You have any other sisters I don't know about?" Susan asked drolly.

There was his half-sister Joan, a product of one of his father's affairs, but that's clearly not who Susan meant.

Duke frowned. Deeply. This wasn't making any sense. Why would Maisie cause a scene like this? He hadn't even thought that his sister *knew* Susan. "No, but—what was she doing here?"

Susan sighed, reliving the event in her mind. She couldn't quite separate herself from it. It had really bothered her.

"Telling me that you were just toying with me and that I should walk away if I knew what was good for me." She stopped picking up pieces of glass and looked at Duke. He wasn't reacting. "Is she right? Did you send her to warn me off?"

She couldn't fathom his expression as he looked at her. "Is that what you think?"

Susan looked up toward the ceiling, thinking. And not getting anywhere. "I don't know what to think— except that Maisie could be dangerous if she got angry enough."

If he were being honest, Duke would have to admit that there was part of him that agreed with Susan. There were times when he worried that Maisie might do something that couldn't be swept under the rug or just shrugged off. Something that would go badly and backfire on her.

But family loyalty made him feel compelled to dismiss Susan's concerns, so out loud he said, "Maisie's harmless. She's just a little off at times, that's all. But she's been through a lot and the old man hasn't exactly made life easy for her. He rides everyone, especially Maisie and she's a little fragile."

There was merit to his argument, Susan thought. But he was missing a very significant point. He might even be blind to it, she judged. "I think Maisie's afraid I might try to take you away from her."

"That's ridiculous," he scoffed. The shattered vase forgotten, Duke rose to his feet, not a little indignant over what he assumed that Susan was implying. "Why would Maisie think that? She's my sister, not some woman I've been seeing."

Susan quickly stood up and placed her hand on his chest, in part to calm him, in part to keep him from leaving before she explained herself. She hadn't meant to insult him.

"I'm not saying that's how you see her, but I think in Maisie's world, things are a little...confused. She probably looks to you as someone she can trust, someone she can share her thoughts with."

The man might be stoic, but there was a gentleness in his manner when he mentioned his sister's plight with their father. Her guess was that Duke didn't want to see Maisie hurt. She liked him for that, even if Maisie had overtly threatened her.

His eyes were angry as he promised, "I'll have a talk with her."

"Don't yell at her, Duke," Susan cautioned, in case what she'd just told him caused his temper to flare. "I think your sister is really scared." She paused for a moment, debating, then decided that Duke had a right to know what she suspected had happened. "I also think she saw us."

Duke's gaze grew very dark as he stared at her. "Saw us?" he echoed.

Now what was Susan talking about? Women were way too complicated, never coming right out and saying what was on their minds. They had to hint, to skirt around the words until a guy's head got painfully dizzy.

"Yes, *saw us,*" Susan emphasized meaningfully, her eyes on his.

Because his mind didn't work that way, for a moment he didn't know what Susan meant by that cryptic phrase. And then it hit him.

"Oh."

Anger over having his privacy invaded battled with the general compassion he normally felt for his sister. He'd always cut her a lot of slack, especially after Damien had been sent to prison.

"Hell," he sighed, shaking his head, "now I really *am* going to have a talk with her." One hand on the doorknob, he was about to leave when Susan called his name.

"Duke?"

He stopped abruptly, his mind already back at the main house. "What?"

"What are you doing here?" Susan wanted to know. When he looked at her blankly, she became a little more specific. "You don't usually come into town," she pointed out. Was this a casual visit, or was there something more behind it? She knew which way she would have wanted it. She tried not to sound too eager as she asked, "Why did you come by my office?"

"I was in town on an errand." It seemed rather foolish now to say that he'd just wanted to see her. To see if he'd just imagined the whole thing back at the ranch the other day or if the sight of her actually could make his stomach feel as if it was at the center of a Boy Scout knot-tying jamboree. "Thought I'd stop by," he mumbled.

Damn, but this wasn't him, Duke thought in disgust at his own behavior. He was never tongue-tied. He was quiet by choice, not out of necessity to keep from sounding like some kind of babbling idiot. And yet, this bit of a thing had him tripping over his own tongue, badly messing with his thought processes.

What *was* it about her that made him act like a village idiot?

Pushing all thoughts of Maisie aside, Susan smiled at him as she drew closer.

"I'm glad you did," she told him. "Are you hungry?" she asked him, suddenly thinking of it. Glancing over her shoulder at the small refrigerator where she kept all sorts of samples for her catering business, Susan made him an offer. "If you are, I could just whip up something for you to nibble on, take the edge off."

What he found himself wanting to nibble on required no special preparation by Susan. All she had to do was stand there.

Where the hell had that come from?

The next moment, stifling an annoyed sigh, Duke mentally shook his head. It was official. He had become certifiably crazy. And all it had taken was two consecutive rolls in the proverbial hay with the Kelley girl.

Maybe this dropping by wasn't such a good idea. He didn't like discovering that he had these needs knocking around inside him. At least, not to this extent. He'd known he was attracted to her, but he'd figured he could keep it under control.

Time to go. "No thanks," he muttered, begging off. "I'm good."

Yes, you are, Susan thought, then realized that she could probably go straight to hell for what she was thinking right now.

Clearing her throat, she nodded in response to what he'd just said to her. "Well, thanks for stopping by. It was nice seeing you again."

"Yeah, well…" For the second time, he began leaving the office, his hand on the doorknob, ready to pull it shut behind him and make good his escape. He was almost home free when the words seemed to escape of their own volition. "You free tonight?"

Her mother had taught her that it was never a good thing to appear to be too available because that made it seem as if no one else wanted her. But no one else did, other than Linc and there was no way she wanted even to entertain that thought. Besides, her mother was a big one for playing games. Playing games had never held any appeal to her. And to that end, she just wasn't any good at it. Lies had a way of tripping her up.

"I'm free," she told him. "Why?" She crossed her fingers behind her back, hoping that the reason he was asking was because he wanted to see her.

Duke knew he was voluntarily putting a noose around his neck, but he assured himself that he could remove it at any time and would, once he grew tired of Susan. But for now, he was very far from being tired of her. "I was thinking maybe I could come by, pick you up and we could go out to eat."

He liked the way a smile came to her eyes when he asked her out. It was almost as if he could feel the warmth. "Sounds good to me."

He did his best to appear as if he was indifferent to

the actual outcome. It was rather adolescent of him, but this was a brand-new place he found himself traveling through. "So if I come by, you'll be there?"

"That better be 'when,' not 'if,'" she informed him, doing her best to sound serious and not letting him hear the way her heart was pounding, "and yes I'll be there when you come by. Oh, by the way, I'm staying in the guest house behind the main house."

Duke nodded. He understood how that was. There were amenities that were hard to give up, but they weren't worth trading hard-won independence for, either. A compromise was the best way to go. "All the comforts of home without having them underfoot."

She didn't really consider her parents being "underfoot" but it was too early in this budding whatever-it-was to admit that to him outright. He might look down at her for that.

"Something like that," she answered vaguely.

He nodded, not pressing the issue. "Seven o'clock sound all right to you?"

"Seven o'clock sounds fine." Hesitating, Susan knew she'd have no peace about the evening ahead unless she asked. "Maisie won't be coming with you, will she?"

"Don't worry," he assured her. "She'll be staying home tonight. Even if I have to tie her to a chair," he promised.

"You don't have to go to those drastic measures," she told him. But secretly, the thought of knowing that Maisie would be unable to suddenly pop up and ruin their evening was rather appealing, not to mention comforting. "Just make sure she doesn't know where you're going—and with whom."

He looked at her closely. "She really did spook you, didn't she?"

Susan was going to say no, because that sounded braver, but it was also a lie. So she shrugged, trying her best to look casual. "Let's just say I'm not used to being threatened."

"Don't worry, you won't have to get used to it. It won't happen again," he promised.

There was definitely something of the knight in shining armor about the dusty cattle rancher, Susan thought with a smile, watching him leave.

Chapter 12

"Is it true?"

Wes hadn't heard the door to the sheriff's office open, had been too preoccupied working at his desk to even hear anyone come in.

Only in office for a little more than a year and it was already looking as if every unaccounted-for piece of paper in the county had somehow found its way to his desk, presumably to die. A man had to have access to a thirty-hour day—without any sleep—in order to do this job properly and still take care of all this annoying paperwork, he thought darkly.

Right about now, Wes was convinced that he would welcome any distraction to take him away from these damn reports he needed to file. But when he looked up to see his sister standing before his desk, looking every bit like a commercial seeking pledges of money for food for a starving third-world country, he wasn't quite so sure about welcoming *any* distraction.

Maisie, at forty, was his older sister—as well as his only sister—but there were a lot of times when he felt as if he were the older one, not Maisie. These days there was something of the waif about her. Seeing her like that usually brought out his protective instincts.

But dealing with Maisie took a great deal of patience, which in turn meant a great deal of time, and time was something he was rather short on right now. As sheriff of Honey Creek he had a murder with a twist on his hands and the sooner he got to the bottom of it, the sooner life in this small town would go back to normal. Back to people engaging in harmless gossip instead of looking at one another with suspicion and uneasiness. Too many people were heading to the hardware store to buy deadbolts for their doors, something that had been, heretofore, unheard of in Honey Creek.

Maisie's thin but still beautiful face was now a mask of consternation. Wes couldn't even begin to guess why.

His first thought was that whatever had brought her here to him might have something to do with her son, his nephew Jeremy. Or maybe with their father.

And just possibly, both.

His guess turned out to be wrong.

"Is what true?" he finally asked her when she didn't elaborate.

Maisie drew in a shaky breath, as if that would somehow help her push out the next words she needed to say. "Is it true that Mark Walsh came back from the dead?"

That pulled him up short. Where the hell had that come from? There just seemed to be no end to the annoyances this dead man could stir up. "Who told you that?"

Her thin shoulders scratched the air in a hapless shrug. "I heard talk. They said that you found Mark Walsh in the creek." Maisie paused, clearly waiting for him to confirm or deny the statement.

Wes folded his hands on top of the opened report on his desk and looked into his older sister's eyes. "I did."

Maisie stifled a strange, hapless little noise. "Then he did come back from the dead."

She began to tremble visibly, her busy fingers going to her lips as if they could help her find the right words to say next. But only small frightened sounds escaped.

Getting up, Wes abandoned the tiresome work that was spread over the surface of his desk. He considered his sister's peace of mind—or what he was about to coax forward—to be far more important than filing something on time.

Rounding his desk, Wes came over to where Maisie was standing and put his arm around her shoulders in an effort to comfort her. Maisie responded to kind voices and a soft touch.

"No, Maisie, Mark Walsh didn't come back from the dead," he told her in a firm, gentle voice.

But it didn't help. She pulled away from him, her aquamarine eyes wide and frightened. "But we buried him. There was a casket and a body and they were buried," she insisted, her voice bordering on hysteria. "Fifteen years ago, they were buried. I *saw* it."

"It was someone else—" Wes began, still patient. His voice was low, soothing. Damn, he wished Duke was here. Duke always seemed to be able to manage her better than the rest of them could.

"Who?" Maisie wanted to know, almost begging to be convinced she was wrong. If she was wrong, if Mark hadn't come back from the dead to haunt her, then the nightmares she was afraid of wouldn't start again, the way they had when Mark was first buried.

"I don't know," Wes told her wearily, "but it wasn't Walsh." He tried talking to her the way he would to anyone else. To a stable person. "I'm having the first body exhumed to try to see if we can determine who it was." No one else had been reported missing at the time, so for now, he still held to his drifter-in-the-wrong-place-at-the-wrong-time theory.

It was obvious that Maisie was desperately trying to come to terms with what had happened. "But that body you found in the creek, that was Mark?"

"Yes, Maisie, that was Mark Walsh."

Just when he thought he'd made her understand, she suddenly challenged him. "How do you know that was Mark Walsh?"

He supposed it was a fair enough question. He did his best to hang onto his patience. "The county medical examiner matched up Walsh's dental records with the man we fished out of the creek."

Maisie blew out another shaky breath, her eyes never leaving her brother. "And he's really dead?"

Wes tried to give her an encouraging smile. "He's really dead."

She still looked fearful, still unable to believe what he was telling her.

"You're sure?" Clutching at his shirt with her damp fingers, she implored him to convince her. "You're really sure it's him? And that he's dead?"

Very gently, he separated her fingers from his shirt. "Maisie, what's this all about?" An uneasy feeling undulated through him. Could his sister have had something to so with Walsh's death? She did seem unhinged at times and there was no way to gauge what was going on in her head.

She didn't answer his question, she just repeated her own. "Are you sure, Wes?" she pressed, enunciating each word.

"I'm sure. There's no mistake this time. It *is* Mark Walsh and he's dead." Still holding her hands in his, Wes looked into her eyes, trying to make sense out of what was going on. "Maisie, why are you so agitated about this?"

"I don't want the nightmares to start again," she said, more to herself or to someone who wasn't in the room than in response to his question. For a moment, Maisie looked as if she was going to cry, but then she raised her head defiantly, as if issuing a challenge to that same nonexistent person. "Not again."

Wes did what he could to reassure her. He really didn't have time for this. "They won't," he promised her. "Everything's going to be fine, Maisie. Just fine. Look, why don't I take you home? You're too upset right now to be alone."

"All right," she agreed docilely, the agitation leaving her as quickly, as suddenly, as it had come. Subdued, she followed him outside to the street like some obedient pet.

About to open the passenger side of his police vehicle for her, Wes happened to look across the street, to the side entrance of Kelley's Cookhouse. He saw Duke walking out of the restaurant and heading toward his truck.

Wes saw his way out.

"C'mon, Maisie," he urged, "I think I just found you a ride home."

His sister looked at him blankly as he took hold of her arm and propelled her down the street. "I thought you said you were taking me home."

"I was, but then I'd have to come back." But Duke didn't, he thought. Duke was going home.

His brother had already started up his truck. Waving, Wes hurriedly put himself directly in Duke's path. The latter was forced to pick up his hand brake again and turn his engine off.

Now what? Duke wondered.

He stuck his head out through the driver's-side window, looking at Wes. "From what I recollect, they issued you a bulletproof vest when you took this job, not a car-proof vest. You got a death wish, Sheriff?"

Wes came around to Duke's side of the cab. "I need you to get Maisie home."

Duke scowled as he looked at his sister. "Maisie." There was no inflection whatsoever in his voice, no way of telling what he was thinking.

"Yeah, Maisie." And then, because he *was* the sheriff, he had to ask. "Something wrong?"

Maybe Duke knew the reason why Maisie seemed

to be on the verge of hysteria this afternoon. Was it really only about the discovery of Mark Walsh's body—something that was upsetting a lot of people—or was there something else going on? And why was Duke looking at their sister that way? Was he missing something?

Duke suppressed an annoyed sigh. He was not about to tell Wes that their sister had threatened Susan. Even if he wasn't the sheriff, Wes would want to know why Maisie was behaving that way. What was going on—or not going on—between him and Susan was nobody's business but his—and maybe Susan's, he added silently. There was no way he was going to talk about it with anyone.

"No, nothing's wrong," Duke said. His eyes shifted toward his sister who was hanging back. "Get in, Maisie," he told her.

Maisie looked a little hesitant; her initial smile when she'd seen Duke had all but vanished. But when Wes opened the passenger-side door for her, she got into the truck's cab docilely.

Securing the door, Wes crossed back around to Duke's side. Once next to his brother, he lowered his voice and said, "Something about my finding Walsh's body in the creek has her spooked." He paused for a second, debating whether to add the last part. But he decided it couldn't hurt. "Go easy on her."

"I have for the last fifteen years," Duke told his brother.

And maybe that was the problem, Duke thought. Maybe he'd gone too easy on Maisie and that had eventually allowed her to slip into a place where he couldn't readily reach her. Maybe if he'd made her behave a little more responsibly, he'd have done them both a favor.

They were going to have a little talk, he and Maisie, and get things straightened out, Duke promised himself. Once and for all.

Duke started up his truck again and pulled away without saying another word to Wes.

"You don't have to worry about Maisie anymore," Duke told Susan that evening when she opened the door to admit him to her home. A man who believed in getting down to business, he'd skipped a mundane greeting in favor of setting her mind at ease as he walked into the Kelley guest house.

Susan did her best to look composed and nonchalant—not like someone who'd spent the last forty-five minutes two steps away from the front door waiting for Duke to finally arrive.

Duke wasn't late, she was just very early. "Oh?" That came out sounding a little too high, she upbraided herself as she closed the door behind him. He could probably tell she was nervous.

Duke looked around the living room. The house was neat, tidy, with sleek, simple lines. With just enough frills to make him think of her. But then he'd noticed that, lately, a lot of things made him think of her.

"Yeah," he responded. "I had a talk with Maisie." He'd used the time it took him to get his sister back to the main house to his advantage. And Maisie had listened solemnly—and crossed her heart. "She promised not to bother you anymore."

What a woman said was one thing, what she did was another, Susan thought. But she didn't want to spoil the evening by getting into any kind of a discussion about his sister's possible future behavior. So she offered him a bright smile and pretended that she thought everything was going to be just peachy from then on.

"That's good." She knew she should just drop it here, but there was a part of her that was a fighter. That didn't just lie down and wait for the steam roller to come by and finish the job. So she said, "Does that mean she'll stop leaving dead flowers and nasty notes too?"

He looked at her sharply. "You got more?"

She pressed her lips together and nodded. "I got more."

Damn it, who the hell was stalking her? He didn't like thinking that she could be in danger. This was Honey Creek. Things like this didn't happen here—until they did, he thought darkly. Like with Walsh.

"Well, they're not from Maisie," he told her, measuring his words slowly. "I took her home from town and left her sleeping in her room. Jeremy's looking after her," he added.

Though no one would have guessed it, he couldn't help feeling sorry for his nephew. The poor kid had been dealt one hell of a hand. No father, a mother who was only half there mentally and a grandfather whose dislike for the boy was all but tangible whenever the two were in the same room together.

He and his brothers did what they could to make Jeremy feel that he was part of the family, but it wasn't easy when Darius was just as determined to make

Jeremy feel like an outsider subsisting solely on the old man's charity.

"Anyone else in my family you think is sending them?" he asked her archly.

She bristled slightly. "I didn't mean to sound as if I was focusing on your family," she apologized. "But this has me a little shaken up. There's no reason for *anyone* to be sending me dead roses and threatening notes, but they still keep on coming."

He heard the distress in her voice, even though she struggled to hide just how nervous this was making her. Nobody was going to hurt her if he had anything to say about it.

"For my money I still think it's that Hayes character," he told her, then repeated his offer. "You want me to talk to him?"

She shook her head. "It's not Linc. He wouldn't do something like this." She was certain of it. They were friends, good friends. He wouldn't resort to this kind of mental torture.

Duke didn't quite see it that way. "'Fraid you've got a lot more faith in Hayes than I do. Let me take the latest note and the last batch of flowers with me when I leave. I'll bring them over to Wes tomorrow, see if he's gotten anywhere with his investigation."

Susan wondered if he realized the significance of his offer. In case the small detail eluded him, she pointed it out. "That means you'll have to admit to seeing me. Are you ready to do that?"

Duke knew a challenge when he saw one. And Susan, whether she knew it or not, was definitely challenging him. Calling him out.

"Woman, I've been on my own for a lot of years," he told her. "I don't have to ask anyone's permission to do anything I want to do." He left the rest unsaid and let her fill in the blanks.

"What about your father?" she asked. "Don't you have to run things by him?"

She'd heard that the patriarch of the Colton clan could make life a living hell for anyone who crossed him. He was a strict man who demanded allegiance and obedience from the people he dealt with, especially from his own family.

"Only when it comes to things that concern the ranch," he allowed. And there was a reason for that. "The ranch is his. My life is mine. Any other questions or things you'd like to clear up?"

She had to admit she felt a little more at ease. Susan smiled at him. "Can't think of a thing."

"All right, then let's go," he prodded. It was getting late and he'd promised her dinner in town. When she made no move to follow him out the door, Duke raised one eyebrow. "Change your mind?"

"Only about where we're eating," she replied. He raised his eyebrow even higher. "I thought maybe we could eat in. I threw some things together," she explained, then stopped, wondering if maybe she was taking too much for granted or sending out the wrong signals again. This creating a relationship was hard work. Worth it, but hard work.

Duke asked, "Edible things?"

He was teasing her. Susan didn't bother attempting to hide her smile. She considered herself a very good cook, having inherited her father's natural instincts for creating epicurean miracles.

"Very."

That was good enough for him. Duke took his hat off and let it fall onto the cushion of the wide, padded leather sofa to his right.

"Talked me into it," he told her.

His eyes caught hers. He felt something stirring inside him. Anticipation. It surprised him and he savored it for a moment. In so many ways, Charlene had been superior to Susan. Experienced, clever and worldly, she'd been a woman in every sense of the word. And yet, there was something about Susan, something that pulled him to her, that had him looking forward to being with her, more than he'd *ever* looked forward to being with Charlene. Who would have thought—?

"This way," he continued pointedly, "we won't have to go so far or wait so long for dessert."

Dessert. Was that what he was calling it? Or was she reading too much into his words? Too much because she desperately wanted him to mean that he wanted her. Wanted to believe that he had planned the evening around dinner and lovemaking.

Because she'd thought of nothing else since he'd asked her about her plans when he came to her office earlier today.

"Come this way," she invited. Turning on her heel, she led him into her small dining room.

Duke entertained himself by watching the way Susan's trim hips moved as she walked ahead of him. It reminded him of a prize show pony he'd once owned, a gift from his grandfather when he'd been a young boy.

The pony had had the same classy lines, the same proud gait as Susan did now. It had been a thing of beauty to watch when it ran, he recalled.

Just like Susan was a thing of beauty to behold when she was in his arms. Making love with him.

Wow.

He hadn't realized he was even capable of having thoughts like that. Susan was definitely bringing out the best in him, he mused. Making him want to be a better man. For her.

He found himself hoping she hadn't made very much for dinner because whatever was on the table wasn't going to whet his appetite one-tenth as much as the taste of her mouth would.

And that was what he craved right now. Her. But she'd gone to all this trouble, it wasn't right to ask her to skip it because he was having trouble holding back his more basic appetites.

"Sit down," she told him. "This won't take long, I promise."

"Need any help?" he offered, raising his voice so that it would carry into the kitchen.

Her back to him, Susan's mouth curved in pure pleasure. She would never have believed that Duke Colton would actually offer to help out in the kitchen. As a matter of fact, she would have been fairly certain that Duke didn't even know what to do in a kitchen. You just never knew, did you?

"No, everything's fine," she answered, tossing the words over her shoulder. "All you have to do is sit there and enjoy yourself."

Susan's casual instruction brought an actual grin to Duke's lips before he could think to stop it.

He fully intended to, he thought. He fully intended to.

Chapter 13

Susan sighed.

She finally put down her pen and gave up her flimsy pretense that she hadn't noticed the looks Bonnie Gene had been giving her each time the woman walked by the open office door. Which was frequently this morning. Susan had lost count at eleven.

"All right, Mother, what is it?"

Bonnie Gene had already gone by and had to backtrack her steps in order to present herself in the doorway.

"What's what, dear?" her mother asked innocently.

The stage had lost one hell of a performer when her mother had decided not to pursue an acting career, Susan thought.

"You know perfectly well 'what's what,'" Susan insisted. "You must have walked by my office about a dozen times this morning. And each time, you looked in with that self-satisfied smile of yours." When her mother raised a quizzical eyebrow, Susan continued to elaborate. "You know, the one you always wear whenever you place first in the annual pie-baking contest."

"I *always* place first in the pie-baking contest," Bonnie Gene informed her regally. "Unless the judges were being bribed that year or had their taste buds surgically removed."

Susan stopped her mother before she could get carried away. "Don't change the subject."

Another innocent look graced Bonnie Gene's face as she placed a hand delicately against her still very firm bosom. "I thought that was the subject."

Okay, Susan thought, *we could go around like this indefinitely.* She worded her question more precisely. "Mother, why do you keep looking in at me?"

Bonnie Gene crossed the threshold, her smile rivaling the summer sun outside. "Because you're my lovely daughter—"

"Mother!" Susan cried far more sharply than she would have ordinarily, impatience shimmering around the single name. "Come clean. What's going on?"

Bonnie Gene adopted a more serious demeanor. "I should be asking you that."

"You could," Susan allowed, feeling her patience being stripped away. "*If* you explained what you meant by your question."

"Don't play innocent with me, my darling." Bonnie Gene looked at her daughter pointedly, having lingered on the word *innocent* a beat longer than the rest of her sentence. "The time for that is past, thank goodness. All right, all right," she declared, giving up the last shred of pretense as Susan began to get up from her chair. "I can't stand not knowing any longer."

"Not knowing *what?*" Susan cried, completely frustrated. What was it that her mother was carrying on about? It couldn't possibly be about her and—

"How things are going with you and Duke Colton."

Oh, God, it was *about her and Duke.*

In response, Susan turned a lighter shade of pale and sank back down in her chair. She'd been afraid of this.

"What are you talking about?" she finally asked in a small, still, disembodied voice that didn't seem to belong to her.

With a superior air, one hand fisted at her hip, Bonnie Gene tossed her head, sending her hair flying jauntily over her shoulder. "Oh, come now, Susan, you didn't *really* think that you could keep this to yourself, did you?"

In retrospect, Susan supposed that had been pretty stupid of her. Her mother had eyes like a hawk and the sensory perception of a bat; all in all, a pretty frightening combination. Especially since it meant that *nothing* ever seemed to escape her attention.

"I had hopes," Susan murmured, almost to herself. She raised her eyes and blew out a breath, bracing herself for the answer to the question she was about to ask. "Who else knows?"

Bonnie Gene laughed. She staked out a place for herself on the corner of Susan's desk and leaned over to be closer to her youngest.

"An easier question to answer, my love, is who else

doesn't know. I must say though, I've had my work cut out for me."

"Your work?" Susan echoed, really lost this time. What was her mother talking about now?

"Yes." Bonnie Gene looked at Susan as if completely surprised that she didn't understand. "Defending your choice. Defending *Duke*," she finally stressed.

"There is no 'choice,' Mother," Susan informed Bonnie Gene, knowing that she really didn't have a leg to stand on. She *had* chosen Duke. The problem was, as of yet, she had no idea how the man really felt about her. There were no terms of endearment coming from him, no little gifts now that she had ruled out that those awful flowers had been from him.

For all she knew, Duke was just seeing her because he had no one better within easy access at the moment. She knew that making herself available to him if she believed that made her seem like a pathetic woman, but she couldn't help it. She was so very attracted to Duke, she would accept him on almost any terms as long as it meant that the evening would end with them sharing passion. When she was away from him, she was counting off minutes in her head until they were together again.

But that was by no means something she wanted her mother—or anyone else for that matter—to know. At least, not until she knew how Duke felt about her.

And for that matter, maybe it was better that she didn't know how he felt. She was more than a little aware that the truth could be very painful.

"And exactly what do you mean *defending Duke?*"

Susan suddenly asked, replaying her mother's words in her head.

Bonnie Gene rolled her eyes dramatically. "Well, I can't begin to tell you how many people have come up to me, wanting to know what a nice girl like you is doing with a man the likes of Duke Colton. If I hear one more 'concerned' citizen tell me about Charlene's suicide after Duke broke it off with her, I'll scream—if I don't throw up first."

Susan squared her shoulders, indignation shining in her eyes. She resented the gossipmongers having a field day with Duke's past behavior, and they were all missing a very salient point.

"Duke broke it off with Charlene when he found out she was married. He told me that he would have never been involved with her in the first place if he'd known that she wasn't single." In her eyes, he had done the right thing, the honorable thing. Why couldn't anyone else see that?

"Simmer down, Susan, I believe you." Bonnie Gene smiled into her daughter's face, lightly touching the hair that framed it. "As much as I want to see you married, I wouldn't let you throw your life away on someone I didn't think was good enough for you. What kind of a mother would that make me, if all I wanted was just to get you married off?" She looked at her daughter pointedly.

She was right, Susan thought. There were times that she forgot that, at bottom, her mother loved and cared about all of them. Worried about all of them. She'd lost sight of that amid all the less than veiled hints that came trippingly off Bonnie Gene's tongue about time running out.

"Sorry," Susan said quietly.

Bonnie Gene beamed, looking more like her older sister than her mother. "Apology accepted. Now," she drew in closer, her eyes lively and hopeful, "how *is* it going between the two of you?"

Her mother deserved the truth, Susan thought. "I don't know," Susan confessed. "It's a little early to tell. We've only been seeing each other for two weeks," Susan pointed out, using the innocent phrase *seeing each other* as a euphemism for what was really going on: that they had been making pulse-racing, exquisite love for those two weeks.

In truth, she felt as if she was living in a dream. But dreams, Susan knew, had a terrible habit of ending, forcing the dreamer to wake up. She dreaded the thought of that coming to pass and could only hope that it wouldn't happen too soon. She'd never felt like this before, as if she could just fly at will and touch the sky, gathering stars.

"Time isn't a factor. I knew the first time your father kissed me," Bonnie Gene told her with pride. She saw the skeptical expression that descended over the girl's face. "Oh, I know what you're thinking—your father is this overly round man with an unruly gray mane and a gravelly voice, but he didn't always look like that."

Bonnie Gene closed her eyes for a moment, remembering. The sigh that escaped was pregnant with memories.

"When I first met your father, he was beautiful. And what that man could do—" Bonnie Gene stopped abruptly, realizing who she was talking to. Clearing her throat, she waved her hand dismissively. "Well, never mind. The point is, it doesn't take months to know if you want to spend the rest of your life with someone or not. It just takes a magic moment."

That rang true. For her. For Duke, not so much. "Well, as far as I know, Duke hasn't had a magic moment," Susan told her.

Bonnie Gene heard what wasn't being said. "But you have." It wasn't a question.

Susan didn't want to go on record with that. "Mother, if I don't get back to putting together a spectacular menu, Shirley and Bill Nelson are going to let her sister take over cooking for the party," she protested. "And I don't want that to happen."

Bonnie Gene leaned even further over the desk and lightly kissed the top of her daughter's head. "Go, work. Make your father proud. I have what I wanted to know," she assured Susan.

"Mother." There was a note of pleading in Susan's voice.

Bonnie Gene smiled. "My lips are sealed."

Susan sincerely doubted that.

"Only if you get run over by a sewing machine between here and the kitchen," Susan murmured. No one would have ever recruited Bonnie Gene to be a spy whose ability to keep secrets meant the difference between life and death in the free world.

Bonnie Gene stuck her head in one last time. "I heard that."

"Good, you were supposed to."

Susan attempted to get back to work. She really did

need to finish this menu today. *Something exciting that isn't expensive*—those had been Shirley Nelson's instructions. So far, she really hadn't come up with anything outstanding.

Her ability to concentrate was derailed the next moment as she heard her mother all but purr the words, "Oh, how nice to see you again," to someone outside her door, then adding, "Yes, you're in luck. She's in her office."

The next second, Susan heard a quick rap on her doorjamb. She didn't have to ask who it was because he was there, filling up her doorway and her heart at the same time.

And looking far more appealingly rugged and handsome than any man had a legal right to be.

"Hi," Duke said, his deep voice rumbling at her, creating tidal waves inside her stomach and an instant yearning within the rest of her.

"Hi," Susan echoed back.

"I just ran into your mother," Duke told her needlessly.

He was at a loss as to how to initiate a conversation with Susan, even at this point. Coming to see a woman was new for him. Usually, the women would come seeking him out, their agendas clearly mapped out in their eyes. Conversation had very little to do with it. This was virgin territory he was treading—appropriately enough, he added to himself as an afterthought.

The thought hit him again that he had been Susan's first. He couldn't really say that had ever mattered to him before, but this time around was different. He realized that he liked being her first.

Her only, at least for now.

Even though it brought with it a rather heavy sense of responsibility he'd never felt before. A heavy sense of responsibility not because of anything that Susan had said or demanded, but just because he felt it.

"Yes, I heard," Susan answered.

The first few moments were still awkward between them every time they met and she couldn't even explain why. It wasn't as if they hadn't seen each other for a while. Duke had come over just last night. As he had every other night since the first time they had made love. The time they spent pretending that they intended to go somewhere or do something had been growing progressively shorter. They were in each other's arms, enjoying one another, enjoying lovemaking, faster with each day that passed by.

What pleased her almost as much was that he did talk to her once the lovemaking was over. Talked to her about little things, like what he'd done at the ranch that day, or his plans for a herd of his own. It meant the world to her.

Please don't let it end yet. Not yet, she prayed, watching him walk into the room.

Out loud, she asked, "Um, can I get you anything?"

The hint of a wicked little smile touched the corners of his mouth, sending yet another ripple through her stomach.

"Not here," he told her.

To anyone else, it might have sounded like an enigmatic response, but she knew exactly what he was saying to her. And it thrilled her. She had absolutely no idea where any of this was headed, or even if it was headed anywhere, but she knew she was determined to enjoy every moment of this relationship for as long as it lasted.

Susan was well aware that in comparison to the other women Duke had been with, she could be seen as naive and completely unworldly. Consequently, she wasn't about to fool herself into thinking that she and Duke actually had some kind of a future together. Not in this world any way, she thought. He wasn't the marrying kind. Everyone knew that.

She blushed a little at his response and heard Duke laugh as he crooked his finger beneath her chin and raised her head until her eyes met his.

Damn, but there was something about her, something that just kept on pulling him in, he thought, watching the pink hue on her cheeks begin to fade again. Each time he made love with her, he expected that was finally going to be that. That he'd reached the end of the line.

But he hadn't.

He hadn't had his fill of her, wasn't growing tired of her. He wasn't even aching for his freedom the way he normally did whenever something took up his time to this extent.

Maybe it was a bug going round, he reasoned, searching for something to blame, to explain away his odd behavior satisfactorily.

"I just came by to let you know that I'm going to be late coming by your place tonight," he told her. "I'm in town to pick up some extra supplies and what I'm doing's going to take more time than I thought."

Susan nodded, thrilling to his slightest touch. And

to the promise of the evening that was yet to come. She didn't care how late he came, as long as he came.

"I'll keep a candle burning in the window for you," she promised.

Why did the silly little things she said make him want to smile? And why did she seem to fill up so much of his thoughts, even when he should be thinking of something else?

If he didn't watch out, he was going to get sloppy and careless. And then he'd have his father on his back, watching him like a hawk. That was all he needed. He could guarantee that a blow-up would follow.

"You do that," he told Susan.

Still holding his finger beneath her chin, he bent his head and brushed his lips quickly over hers.

Her eyes fluttered shut as she absorbed the fleeting contact and reveled in it. She could feel her pulse accelerating.

When she opened her eyes, she found him looking at her. More than anything, she wished she could read his thoughts.

"Um, listen, since you're here, can I get you something to eat?" she wanted to know. "It's almost lunch time and I'm assuming that your father lets you have time off for good behavior."

The smallest whisper of a smile played along Duke's lips. She ached to kiss him again, but managed to restrain herself.

"Who says I have good behavior?" he asked. His voice sounded almost playful—for Duke. It sent more ripples through her, reinforcing the huge tidal wave that had washed over her when he'd kissed her.

"No, really," she tried to sound more serious. "Aren't you hungry?" She nodded in the general direction of the kitchen. "I could just whip up something quick for you—"

Yes, he was hungry he thought, but the consumption of food had nothing to do with it. He wanted her. A lot. Another first, he realized.

"If I stay to eat," he told her, his eyes holding hers, "I might not leave anytime soon."

They weren't talking about food. Even she knew that. And the idea that she could actually entice someone like Duke Colton thrilled her beyond measure.

"Wouldn't want to do that."

Her words were agreeing with him, her tone was not. Her tone told him that she wanted nothing more than to have him stay and do all those wondrous things to her that he had introduced her to. Just the thought of it stirred his appetite.

He looked at her for a long moment, debating. The door had a lock on it.

"Oh, I don't know about that," he answered speculatively, allowing his voice to trail off.

But the thought of being interrupted by one of the staff, or either of her parents, tipped the scales toward behaving more sensibly. He told himself that passing up a chance to make love with her now meant that there was more to look forward to tonight.

Suppressing a sigh, Duke gathered himself together and crossed to the doorway. He nodded his head. "See you tonight."

"Tonight," she echoed to his retreating back.

Tonight.

The single world throbbed with promise. If she weren't afraid of her mother passing by again and looking in, she would have hugged herself.

Chapter 14

The extra feed he'd come for all loaded up in his truck, Duke got behind the wheel, put his key into the ignition and turned it on.

Then he turned it off again.

He'd never been a man given to impulsive moves. He thought things through before he did them. But he was here, so he took advantage of time and opportunity. Taking the note that Susan had given him, he got out of the truck's cab, secured the door and went to the short, squat building across the street.

Wes's car was parked outside. That meant that Wes was most likely inside or close by. Duke walked into the sheriff's office without bothering to knock. He was a man with a timetable.

"I know you're busy with looking into Mark Walsh's latest murder, but I really need you to look into this for me," he declared, holding the crudely handwritten note out in front of him. "Susan got another one. Along with more dead flowers."

About to leave to grab some lunch, Wes took a step backward in order to allow his older brother to come in. Taking the note that Duke held out to him, he glanced at it quickly. Same block letters, an equally childish threat on the sheet.

"You mean you want me to look into this in my spare time between midnight and 12:04 a.m.?" he asked wryly. He wasn't a man who complained, but venting a little steam wasn't entirely out of order. He'd been hunting for Walsh's killer even before the autopsy had confirmed his identity—and getting nowhere. "I had no idea there were so many people who hated Mark Walsh." Wes walked back to his desk and sat down, placing the note on top of the pile of papers that were there. "Right now, the only ones who I know aren't suspects are Damien and me."

Hooking his thumbs onto his belt, Duke continued to stand, his countenance all but shouting that he was a man with things to do, places to go. "That bad?"

"Pretty much. Hell, the spooked way Maisie's been acting lately, if I didn't know any better, I'd say that she did the guy in herself." Wes rocked back in his chair, glancing again at the note that Duke had brought in. He'd hoped that the previous notes and flowers had been a prank that had played itself out. Obviously not, he thought. "I'm starting to think that maybe getting elected sheriff was not the wisest career move I could have made."

Duke had never seen the appeal of the position, but

he'd backed Wes's choice nonetheless. "Still better than ranching with the old man."

"You do have a point." Straightening up, Wes frowned as he perused the note more closely. "Now, remind me again what is it I'm looking for?" he asked, *other than a little sleep,* he added silently.

"Find out who sent the notes and the flowers," Duke replied simply.

Wes raised a quizzical eyebrow. "This is important to you, isn't it?"

Duke was about to say no, that it was all one and the same to him, but it was upsetting Susan, but that would have been a lie and Wes had a knack of seeing through lies.

Maybe he shouldn't have come here, pushing the issue, Duke thought. He didn't want Wes picking through his business. But then, this wasn't about him, it was about Susan, about her safety. He was beginning to get worried that maybe whoever was sending these notes and the dead flowers wasn't exactly up for the most sane person of the year award. If that person turned out to be dangerous as well…

He shrugged. "She's afraid. I don't like seeing women threatened."

Wes looked at him knowingly. "You seeing Susan Kelley?" It wasn't really so much a question as it was a statement seeking verification.

Duke managed to tamp down his startled surprise. "What makes you say that?" he asked in a toneless voice.

"Because I'm a brilliant detective, because I've got fantastic gut instincts—" and then he gave Duke the

real reason "—and because Maisie complained to me
that you're going to ruin the family line by getting the
Kelley girl pregnant."

Damn it, he thought Maisie and he had settled this.
Apparently he needed to have another talk with her,
Duke thought, annoyed. Out loud, he confirmed Wes's
guess. "Yeah, maybe I'm seeing her."

"Either you are, or you're not," Wes pointed out,
looking at him, waiting for an answer.

"Okay, I am. For now," he qualified, leaving himself
a way out. "Now, are you going to look into this for her
sometime before the turn of the next century?" he asked
irritably. "Someone's been leaving these on her doorstep
the last couple of weeks, along with bunches of dead
flowers," he reiterated, in case Wes had forgotten.

"And you really don't have any idea who's been doing
this?"

Duke looked down at his brother pointedly. "I
wouldn't be talking to you if I did."

"Good point, although I'd rather not have one of my
brothers turn vigilante on me. Especially not now when
we're finally getting Damien out." He figured there was
nothing wrong with issuing a veiled warning to his
brother. If it didn't come out in so many words, there
was more of a chance of Duke complying with it.

A cynical smile touched the corners of Duke's mouth.
"When she first started getting them, Susan really
thought that I was the one sending them."

Wes surprised him by nodding. "I can see why she
might." Duke looked at him sharply. "You're so damn
closed-mouthed, nobody ever knows what's going on in
that head of yours. You're like this big, black cloud on

the horizon. Nobody can make an intelligent guess if it's going to rain or just pass through. And you're always frowning. Hell, when I was a kid, I thought that scowl of yours was set in stone."

Duke blew out an impatient sigh. "I don't have time for memory lane, Wes. Just take a few hours away from the Walsh thing and look into this for me, okay?" He couldn't remember when he'd asked Wes for something, so he took it for granted that Wes's response would be in the affirmative.

He wasn't prepared for the slightly amused grin that curved his brother's mouth.

"What?" Duke demanded.

"You and Susan Kelley, huh?"

Duke's eyes narrowed to small, dark slits. "That is none of your business."

Wes would have been lying if he hadn't admitted that contradicting Duke stirred up more than a small amount of satisfaction. "Well, actually, with my being sheriff, it kinda is if for some reason the two of you being together made someone write these." He nodded at the note on his desk for emphasis. "And if we're talking personal—"

"We're not," Duke quickly bit off.

Wes ignored Duke's disclaimer and continued with his thought. "I think it's great that you've finally moved on and put that whole Charlene McWilliams thing behind you. Susan looks like a really great girl—and she's just what you need."

Duke was not about to admit anything, even if, somewhere in his soul, he secretly agreed with his brother's pronouncement. That was his business, not anyone else's. Just like he felt something lighting up inside of him every time he saw Susan was his business.

"I wasn't aware that I needed anything," Duke said, his voice a monotone.

"That just means that you need it more than the rest of us," Wes told him with a knowing smile. "Not a single one of the Almighty's creatures does better without love than with it."

Annoyed, Duke asked him with more than a small touch of sarcasm, "You thinking of becoming a philosopher now, too?"

Wes took no offense. He hadn't expected Duke to suddenly profess how he felt about the girl. Duke had trouble coming to grips with feelings, they all knew that.

"No, just happy someday, if the right woman crosses my path," Wes qualified.

Duke sighed and shook his head. He was not about to get into a discussion over this. "Just get back to me on that," he instructed, nodding at the note.

Wes rose and walked with his brother to the door. "Don't let that bit about being 'a servant of the people' fool you, big brother. Just so we're clear, I find this guy, *I'll* handle it, not you." There was no negotiation on this point.

Though he wouldn't say it in so many words, Duke gave his younger brother his due. "Whatever," he muttered as he walked out.

"Nice talking to you too, big brother," Wes said to Duke's back.

The phone in Susan's office rang as she got up to walk out for the evening. She looked longingly toward the doorway.

It wasn't like her to ignore a call. Susan was one of those people who felt a compulsion to answer every phone that rang, whenever it rang. But she knew that if she picked up this time, she'd wind up leaving the office and town later than she wanted to.

She didn't want to have to amend her schedule. What she wanted to do was hurry home and get ready for her evening with Duke. Granted there was nothing special planned—just being together was special enough as far as she was concerned—but she wanted to take her time getting ready tonight. That meant actually indulging in a bubble bath for a decadent twenty minutes—fifteen minutes longer than she usually spent in the shower.

And there was this new scent she wanted to try out, something that she had ordered via the Internet and that smelled like sin in a bottle. She was anxious to wear something as different as possible from her usual cologne whose light scent brought fresh roses to mind. After being on the receiving end of all those dead roses, roses were the last thing she wanted wafting around her as she moved about.

Susan had almost made it out of the office when she finally stopped. Guilt got the better of her.

Turning around, she hurried back to her desk and picked up the receiver just as her answering machine clicked on.

"This is Susan," she told the caller, raising her voice above the recorded greeting. "Wait until the tape in the answering machine stops before talking."

But her instructions came too late. Whoever was on the other end of the line had hung up.

Well, she'd tried, she thought, replacing the receiver

into its cradle. At least this way, she told herself silently, she didn't have to feel guilty.

Guilt was the last emotion she wanted lingering around when Duke was with her.

Glancing one last time at the package she was bringing home with her—she'd made beef tenderloin with a green chili and garlic sauce as well as a double serving of grilled vegetables for dinner tonight—she smiled and hurried out.

The dinner's warm, welcoming aroma followed her to her car and then filled up the space around her as she closed the door. Susan started up her car.

Ultimately, this aroma would probably tempt Duke more than the expensive perfume she just bought would, she thought.

But she hoped not.

Reaching home, she parked her car, grabbed her package and raced inside. It struck her, as she closed the door behind her, that she'd left it unlocked again. She was forever forgetting to lock the door when she left in the morning. But this was Honey Creek, she reasoned. Other than Mark Walsh's death—and those stupid notes along with the dead flowers—nothing ever happened here. It was a nice, safe little town.

Hurrying, she took the warming tray out of the cabinet and got it ready to be pressed into service once she finished her bubble bath. She put the package on the counter beside the tray and raced off to the bathroom.

Too excited to come close to relaxing, Susan shaved six minutes off her bubble bath and utilized that extra time fixing her hair and makeup.

She'd decided to show Duke that she wasn't just another fresh-scrubbed face. That she could be pretty—maybe even more than a tad pretty—if she set her mind to it, given the right "tools."

So she carefully applied the mini battalion of shadows, mascara and highlighters she'd amassed and redid her hair three times before she was ultimately satisfied with the woman she saw looking back at her from the mirror.

Throwing on a light-blue, ankle-length robe to protect the shimmery royal-blue dress that only went half way down her shapely thighs, Susan hurried back to the kitchen. She wanted to do a few last-minute things to the dinner so she could put the meal out of her mind until it was time to serve it.

Just as she entered the kitchen, Susan could have sworn she saw something hurry past the large window located over the double sink.

Probably just some stray animal, lost, she decided, and looking to find its way back.

Aren't we all? she mused, grinning.

It wasn't unheard of to catch a glimpse of a stray deer every so often, although now that she thought about it, there'd been fewer sightings in the last couple of years.

That was the price of progress, a trade-off. Two-legged creatures instead of four-legged ones.

Plugging in the warming tray, she froze, listening. She was certain she'd heard a noise coming from the front of the house.

It *wasn't* her imagination. She *had* heard something.

Her parents—even her mother—didn't just come over without either calling first or at the very least, ringing the doorbell to give her half a second's warning before they walked in.

And she *knew* that Duke wouldn't play games like this, making noise to scare her. The man didn't play games at all.

Grabbing a twelve-inch carving knife out of the wooden block that held the set of pearl-handled knives that her mother had given her for her catering business, Susan tightly wrapped her fingers around it.

"Is anyone there?" she called out.

Susan thought of the gun her father had tried to convince her into taking when she had moved in here. She wished now that she hadn't been so stubborn about it. A gun would have made her feel more in control of the situation.

It was probably nothing, she told herself as she inched toward the front of the house. Just the wind causing one of the larger tree branches to bang against the living-room bay window.

It was the last thing to cross her mind before the searing pain exploded at the back of her skull.

The next moment, everything went black.

Susan dreamt she was drowning. She struggled to reach the surface and gulp in air. It took her a beat to realize that she wasn't in the creek, desperately trying to swim for the bank while Mark Walsh tried to pull her back under. She was in her house.

And then she gasped, trying to breathe. Someone

had just thrown water in her face. A lot of water, all at once.

Coughing and gasping, it took her another couple of beats before she became completely aware of her surroundings.

She *was* still in her house, in the kitchen. But instead of standing by the counter, she was sitting on a chair. Not just sitting but sealed onto it. Duct tape all but cocooned her waist and thighs, holding her fast against the wood. Her hands were bound behind her. She couldn't move no matter how hard she pulled against the silvery tape.

Afraid, wild-eyed, Susan looked around, trying to understand what was going on. Her head felt as if it was splitting in half, the pain radiating from the back of her skull to the front.

She couldn't see anyone but she *knew* that there was someone in the house with her. Someone who had hit her from behind and then bound her up like an Egyptian mummy. But who could have done this?

Maisie?

Linc?

And if not either of them, then who? And why?

Her thoughts collided as she struggled to control the hysteria that threatened to overwhelm her.

"Who's there?" she cried. "Why are you doing this? Show yourself," she demanded, doing her best to sound angry and not as afraid as she really was. "Show yourself so we can talk. You don't want to do this."

She heard someone moving behind her and tried to turn her head as far as she could in that direction. But she needn't have bothered. The person who had put her in this position moved into her line of vision.

"Oh, but I do," the thin-framed, weatherbeaten, nondescript man told her. "You can't even *begin* to understand how much I want to do this."

Susan stared at the man. He was maybe as tall as she was, maybe shorter. She didn't know him. His face meant nothing to her and no name came to mind. No frame of reference suggested itself.

Why did he hate her?

"Why?" she managed to ask hoarsely, fear all but closing up her throat. "Why do you want to tie me up like this?"

"I don't want to tie you up," he informed her condescendingly. "That's just a means to an end." He brought his face in close to hers. The man reeked of whiskey. Had he worked himself up, seeking courage in a bottle before going on this rampage? "I want to hurt you," he said, enunciating each word. "I want to make you slowly bleed out your life, just like she did."

This was a mistake. It had to be a mistake. She needed to get this man to talk, to make him see that what he was doing was crazy.

If nothing else, she needed to stall him. To stall him until Duke came to save her from this maniac.

"Like who did?" she asked urgently. "Who are you talking about?"

His face contorted, as if someone had just hit him in the gut and the pain was almost too much to bear. "My wife. My wife killed herself because that worthless scum you're playing whore for walked out on her." Again he stuck his face into hers. "Do you know how that feels?" he demanded. "Do you have *any* idea how it feels to know that your wife would rather kill herself than come back to you?"

He straightened up, reliving the memory in his mind. Staring off into space, he sucked in a long, ragged breath.

"I thought my gut had been ripped out when I had to go and identify her body. They found her in her car, her wrists slashed." There were angry tears shimmering in his eyes. The next second, the tears were replaced with rage. "Well, that's what I want Duke Colton to feel. I want him to feel like he's been gutted when he looks at what I've left behind for him."

Picking up the knife that she had dropped when he'd knocked her unconscious, Hank McWilliams held it for a moment, as if contemplating the would-be weapon's weight and feel.

A strange look came into his eyes as he looked back at her. "Had a notion to become a doctor once. Studied on my own. Didn't matter, though. Never got to be a doctor because there weren't enough money." The smile that slipped across his lips made her blood run cold. "But I know where every vital organ is. And I know how and where to cut a man so that he stays alive for a very long, long time." His smugness increased. "Same goes for a woman," he concluded, delivering the first cut so quickly, she didn't even see it coming.

Susan heard the shrill, bloody scream and realized belatedly that it was coming from her.

The next second she felt the sting of his hand as he slapped her across the face.

"Damn it, whore," he exclaimed, then seemed to

regain control over himself. "My fault," he mumbled under his breath. "Forgot that you'd scream."

Leaving the knife on the floor for a second, McWilliams ripped off an oversize piece of duct tape and clamped it hard over her mouth. He smoothed it down over and over again to make sure it stayed in place.

"That should keep you quiet," he announced, deftly slicing her two more times in her chest and abdomen. As the blood began to flow, he laughed gleefully, his eyes bright and dancing. "This might go quicker than I thought," he told her, his tone as unhurried as if he was timing something in the oven instead of watching her life drain from her.

Susan struggled to stay conscious, trying to focus on what time it was. How long had she been out? Where was Duke?

And then she remembered. He'd said he was going to be late tonight.

Fear wrapped itself around her, making it all but impossible to breathe as the blade of the maniac's knife sliced through her flesh as quickly and easily as if she was only a stick of butter.

The duct tape stifled the scream that tore from her throat, defusing it. Susan still screamed for all she was worth, her head spinning wildly from the effort and from the pain.

She was barely hanging on to consciousness by her fingertips.

He slashed into her flesh again, twisting the knife this time.

Chapter 15

Duke had worked at a quick, steady pace all afternoon, taking no breaks, creating shortcuts when he could. Though he told himself he was only being practical and that working this quickly would get him out of the sun faster—a sun that was beating down on him without mercy—he knew that he was just feeding himself a line of bull. That wasn't the real reason he was working this hard and he knew it.

The real reason had soft brown eyes that could melt a man's soul and even softer lips. Lips that made him forget about everything else. Lips that, for the first time in his life, actually made him glad to be alive instead of just feeling as if he was marking time until something of some sort of import happened.

For him, it already had.

He'd met someone he'd known, more or less, for most

of his life. Certainly for all of hers. Someone who, the more he saw her, the more he *wanted* to see her.

Damn, he didn't even know where all these complicated thoughts were suddenly coming from. What was going on with him anyway, Duke scolded himself as he drove up to Susan's house.

Stopping the truck, he took one last look at himself in the rearview mirror, angling it so that he could see if his hair still looked combed or if the hot breeze had ruffled it too much.

He'd taken a quick shower and changed before coming here but still looked sweaty. It had never bothered him before, but now it mattered that he looked his best.

Though he'd never told her, he liked the way Susan ran her fingers through his hair, liked the way she looked up at him, half innocent, half vixen. And when he came right down to it, he didn't know which half he liked better. Was a time he would have known, would have picked vixen hands down.

Now, though…

Tabling his thoughts, he got out of the truck. Duke walked up to Susan's front door and raised his hand to knock.

The sound of a man's voice, coming from within the house, stopped him. There wasn't another car parked in the driveway to give a clue as to who it may be.

That wasn't her father, he thought. The timbre of the voice was all wrong. Donald Kelley had a raspy, coated voice, the kind that came from decades of sipping whiskey on hot, summer nights. This voice belonged to someone else.

To another man.

Duke glanced at his watch. He was early, at least earlier than he'd told her he'd be. Was she "entertaining" someone else while she waited for him?

Well, why the hell not? It wasn't as if any pledges had been made between them. Hell, there wasn't even any wordless understanding. They were both free to do whatever they wanted with whomever they wanted.

Even so, the thought of Susan being with another man angered him more than he thought it would. More than he'd ever felt before.

He glared at the door. He could hear the man talking again.

The hell with her.

He didn't need this, didn't need the aggravation or the humiliation. Turning on his heel, he started to walk away. He was better off giving the whole breed a wide berth, just as he had before he'd gotten roped in by doe eyes and a shy smile.

Shy his as—

Duke's head whipped around toward the door.

Was that a scream? It sounded awfully muffled if it was. But what he had absolutely no doubt about was the streak of fear he'd heard echoing within the suppressed scream.

Making up his mind to go in, he tried the doorknob and found that it wouldn't give. She'd finally learned to lock her door, he thought.

There it was again. A muffled scream, he'd bet his life on it.

Duke's anger gave way to an acute uneasiness, which in turn gave way to fear, even though he couldn't logically have explained why.

Susan was in trouble. His gut told him so.

Instead of calling out to her, Duke braced his right shoulder, tightened his muscles the way he did whenever he lifted one of the heavier bales of hay on his own and slammed his shoulder hard against the door.

It gave only a little.

With a loud grunt that was 50 percent rage and 50 percent fear, Duke slammed his aching shoulder into the door again. As he braced himself for another go-round, he caught a glimpse of Bonnie Gene and Donald coming out of their house and heading in his direction. There was a puzzled look on Bonnie Gene's face.

Had they heard the strange scream, too? Or were they coming because they'd heard him trying to break down Susan's door?

He had no time to explain what he was doing or why he was doing it. For the same mysterious reason that was making him try to break down her door, his sense of urgency had just multiplied tenfold.

The third meeting of shoulder to door had the door splintering as it separated itself from the doorjamb. What was left of the door instantly slammed into the opposite wall as Duke ran in, bellowing Susan's name at the top of his lungs.

In response he heard that same muffled, strange scream, even more urgent this time than before.

It took him more than half a minute to realize what was going on, the lag due to the fact that it all looked so surreal, literally as if it had been lifted from some bad slasher movie.

Susan had silver tape wrapped around over half her body, sealing her to one of her kitchen chairs. There was blood on her, blood on the floor and a deranged-looking man wielding a knife which he nervously shifted back and forth, holding it to Susan's throat, then aiming it toward Duke to keep him at bay. The man continued to move the knife back and forth in jerky motions, as if he couldn't decide which he wanted to do more—kill Susan or kill Duke.

Duke wasn't about to give the man a chance to make up his mind.

With a guttural yell that was pure animal, Duke sailed through the air and threw himself against Susan's attacker, knocking the man to the floor. The assailant continued to clutch his knife. Duke saw the blood on it.

Susan's blood.

Sick to his stomach, he almost threw up.

And then a surge of adrenaline shot through him. Duke grabbed the man's wrist, forcing him to hold the knife aloft where, he hoped, the sharp blade couldn't do any harm.

Restraining Susan's attacker wasn't easy. The man turned out to be stronger than he looked, or maybe it was desperation that managed somehow to increase his physical strength. Duke didn't know, didn't have the time to try to analyze it and didn't care. All he knew was that he had to save Susan at any cost, even if it meant that he would wind up forfeiting his own life in exchange.

It was at that moment, with adrenaline racing wildly through his veins as he faced down a madman with a knife, that Duke realized that without Susan, he didn't have a life, or at least, not one that he believed was worth living.

It was a hell of an awakening.

"Who the hell are you?" Duke bellowed as he continued to grapple with the man.

"I'm Hank McWilliams, the husband of the woman you killed," he replied angrily, stunning Duke.

McWilliams wrenched his hand free and slashed wildly at Duke's shoulder. He hit his target, piercing Duke's flesh and drawing blood. He also succeeded in enraging Duke further.

The fight for possession of the weapon was intense, but ultimately short if measured in minutes rather than damage. Disarming McWilliams amounted to Duke having to twist his arm back so hard that he wound up snapping one of the man's bones.

Sounding like a gutted animal, McWilliams's shrill scream filled the air.

Duke was aware of the sound of running feet somewhere behind him and cries of dismayed horror. Prepared for anything, he looked up to see Donald and Bonnie Gene charging into the house.

"I need rope to tie this bastard up," he yelled at Bonnie Gene, sucking in air. "Donald, call the sheriff. Tell my brother I caught the guy stalking Susan."

Grabbing a length of cord from one of the upper kitchen cabinets, Bonnie Gene ran back into the living room.

"Someone was stalking Susan?" she cried, alarmed.

Panting, Duke had already allowed Donald to take over holding McWilliams down. Donald had done it wordlessly by planting his considerable bulk on the man, who was lying facedown on the floor. Taking the rope from his wife, he tied McWilliams up as neatly as he'd tied any horizontally sliced tenderloin that had come across his work table.

Not waiting for an answer to her question, Bonnie Gene hurried over to her daughter, who was struggling to remain conscious.

Duke had already begun removing the duct tape from around her. Susan was trying not to whimper but every movement he made, however slight, brought salvos of pain with it.

"I'm sorry," Duke kept saying over and over again as he peeled away the duct tape. "I'm trying to be quick about it."

"It's okay," Susan breathed, struggling to pull air into her oxygen-depleted lungs.

"Oh, my poor baby," Bonnie Gene cried, feeling horribly helpless. A sense of torment echoed through her as she took in her daughter's wounds.

Standing back as Duke worked to remove the rest of the duct tape, Bonnie Gene quickly assessed the number of wounds that Susan had sustained. A cry of anguish ripped from her lips when she reached her total.

Bonnie Gene swung around and kicked McWilliams in the ribs six times, once for each stab wound that her daughter had suffered. As she kicked, Bonnie Gene heaped a number of curses on the man her husband had no idea she knew. Donald looked at her with renewed admiration.

"You're going to be okay, Susan, you're going to be okay. I don't think the bastard hit anything vital," Duke told Susan as he looked over her wounds.

He felt his gut twisting as he assessed each and every

one. As gently as he could, he picked Susan up in his arms and turned toward the door. He almost walked into Bonnie Gene, who was hovering next to him, trying hard not to look as frightened as she probably felt.

"I'm going to take Susan to the hospital," he told her mother.

Bonnie Gene bobbed her head up and down quickly, glad for the moment that someone had taken over.

"We'll use my car," she told him, digging into her pocket for her keys. "It's faster than your truck," she added when he looked at her quizzically.

"I'll get...blood...all over...it," Susan protested haltingly. The fifty-thousand-dollar car was her mother's pride and joy, her baby now that her children were all grown.

"Like I care," Bonnie Gene managed to get out, unshed tears all but strangling her. Getting out in front, she quickly led the way out of the house.

"Don't let him out of your sight until my brother gets here," Duke cautioned Donald just before he left the house with Susan.

"I'm not even going to let him out from under my butt," Donald assured him, raising his voice. "Just get my daughter to the hospital."

But he was talking to an empty doorway.

Looking back later, Duke had no idea how he survived the next few hours.

The moment Bonnie Gene drove them into the hospital's parking lot, he all but leaped out of the vehicle, holding an unconscious Susan in his arms, pressed against his chest. Silently willing her to be all right.

Terrified that she wasn't going to be.

A general surgeon was on call. One look at Susan and Dr. Masters had the nurses whisking her into the operating room to treat the multiple stab wounds on her torso. The surgeon tossed a couple of words in their general direction as he hurried off to get ready himself.

That left Duke and Bonnie Gene waiting in the hall as the minutes, which had flowed away so quickly earlier, now dragged themselves by in slow motion, one chained to another.

There was nothing to do but wait and wait. And then wait some more.

Duke wore a rut in the flat, neutral carpeting in the hallway directly outside the O.R. His brain swerved from one bad scenario to another, leaving him more and more agitated, pessimistic and progressively more devastated with every moment that went by.

Sometime during this suspended sentence in limbo, Donald arrived to ask after his youngest daughter and to tell them what had happened at the guest house after his wife and Duke had left. The sheriff had arrived soon after they drove off for the hospital, and Donald had quickly filled Wes in on what he knew, which wasn't much. After turning McWilliams over to the sheriff, Donald had sped to the hospital.

"She's a strong girl," Donald assured Duke, taking pity on the young man. "She takes after my side of the family."

Bonnie Gene looked up, leaving the dark corridors of her fears. Though she was trying to keep a positive outlook, it was still difficult not to give in to the fears that haunted every mother.

"Susan gets her strength from my side of the family," Bonnie Gene contradicted.

"Right now, she needs all the strength she can beg, borrow or steal from both sides," Duke told the pair impatiently. The last thing he was in the mood for was to listen to any kind of bickering.

Bonnie Gene rose, taking a deep, fortifying breath and doing her best to look cheerful, even as she struggled with the question of how this could have happened to her baby. And right under her nose, too.

She put her hand on Duke's shoulder, giving it a quick squeeze. "She'll pull through, Duke. Susan might not look it, but she's a fighter." Her eyes met Donald's for affirmation. "She always has been."

Duke made no response. He really didn't feel like talking. So, instead, he took a deep breath and just nodded, silently praying that Bonnie Gene was right.

With effort, he maintained rigid control over his mind, refusing to allow himself to think about what might have happened if he hadn't come when he had.

If he'd worked more slowly and arrived an hour later.

There was a definite pain radiating out from his heart. A pain, he was certain, he would have for the rest of his life if Susan didn't pull through.

"She didn't look very strong when they took her into the O.R." Until he heard his own voice, he wasn't even aware of saying the words out loud.

Bonnie Gene pressed her lips together, pushing back an unexpected sob.

"That's my Susan, soft on the outside, tough on the inside. You're not giving her enough credit," she told Duke. "But you'll learn."

The woman said that as if she believed that he and her daughter would be together for a long time, Duke noted. Bonnie Gene had more confidence in the future than he did, he thought sadly.

The next moment, the O.R. doors swung open, startling all three of them. It was hard to say who pounced on the surgeon first, Bonnie Gene, Donald or Duke.

But Duke was the first who made a verbal demand. "Well?"

Untying the top strings of his mask and letting it dangle about his neck, Dr. Masters offered the trio a triumphant, if somewhat weary smile.

"It went well. She's a tough one, luckily," he declared.

"I told you," Bonnie Gene said to Duke. She almost hit his shoulder exuberantly, stopping herself just in time, remembering that McWilliams had sliced him there and he'd had to have it treated and bandaged.

Duke wasn't listening to Bonnie Gene. His attention was completely focused on the surgeon. "Will she be all right?"

Masters looked a bit mystified as he continued filling them in. "Yes. Miraculously enough, none of her vital organs were hit. Don't know how that happened, but she is an extremely lucky young woman." He looked at the trio, glad to be the bearer of good news. "You can see her in a little while. She's resting comfortably right now, still asleep," he added. "A nurse will be out to get you once she's awake."

Duke didn't want to wait until Susan was awake. He just wanted to sit and look at her, to reassure himself that she was breathing. And that she would go on breathing. He slipped away from Susan's parents and went in search of her.

He slipped into Susan's room very quietly, easing the door closed behind him.

She did look as if she was sleeping, he thought. He fought the urge to reach out and touch her, to push a strand of hair away from her face and just let his fingertips trail along her cheek.

She was alive. Susan was alive. She'd come close to death today, but she was still here. Still alive. Still his.

He let out a long, deep breath that had all but clogged his lungs. He never wanted to have to go through anything like that again.

Seizing one of the two chairs in the room, he brought it over to her bed, sat down and proceeded to wait for Susan to wake up.

He didn't care how long it took, he just wanted to be there when she opened her eyes.

Chapter 16

Consciousness came slowly, by long, painfully disjointed degrees. Throughout the overly prolonged process, Susan felt strangely lightheaded, almost disembodied, as if she was floating through space without having her body weighing her down.

Was this what death felt like?

Was she dead?

She didn't think so, but the last thing she remembered was Duke carrying her to the car—her mother's car—and she was bleeding. Bleeding a lot and feeling weaker and weaker.

After that, everything was a blank.

Was heaven blank?

Struggling, Susan tried to push her eyelids up so that she could look around and find out where she was. But she felt as if her eyelids had been glued down. Not only that, but someone had put anvils on each of them for good measure. Otherwise, why couldn't she raise them at will?

She was determined to open her eyes.

Something told her that if she didn't open them, she was going to fade away until there was nothing left of her but dust. Dust that would be blown off to another universe.

She liked *this* universe.

This universe had her parents in it. And her siblings.

And Duke.

Duke.

Duke had saved her. Did that mean that he loved her? Whether he loved her or not, she didn't want to leave Duke, not ever.

With a noise that was half a grunt, half a whimper, she concentrated exclusively on pushing her eyelids up until she finally did it.

She could see.

And what she saw was Duke.

Duke was standing over her, looking worn and worried. More worried than she remembered ever seeing him. His left arm was in a sling, but he was holding her hand with his right hand.

He didn't believe in public displays of affection, she thought. But he was holding her hand. In a public place.

Was she dead?

"Duke?" she said hoarsely.

He'd never cried. Not once, in all his thirty-five years. Not when Damien was convicted of murder and they had taken him out of the courtroom in chains. Not even when that horse had thrown him when he was ten and had come damn near close to stomping him to death, only his father had jumped into the corral and dragged him to safety at the last minute, cursing his "brainless hide" all the way.

He hadn't cried then.

But he felt like crying now. Crying tears of relief to release the huge amount of tension that he felt throbbing all through him.

She was alive.

"Right here," he told Susan, his reply barely audible. Any louder and she'd be able to hear the tears in his throat.

"I know...I can...see...you," she answered, each word requiring a huge effort just to emerge. Her hand tightened urgently on his. "Charlene's...husband...tried to...kill...me."

"He won't hurt you any more," Duke swore. *Not even if I have to kill him with my bare hands,* he promised silently.

"He...didn't want to...hurt...me, he...wanted to... hurt...you," she told Duke, then rested for a second, the effort to talk temporarily draining her.

"Hurt me?" Duke echoed incredulously. Was she still a little muddled, reacting to the anesthetic? She'd been the one to receive all the blows, he thought angrily. Again he promised himself that if by some miracle, Hank McWilliams was ever released from prison, he was going to kill the man. Slowly and painfully, to make him pay for what he'd done to Susan. And even then it wouldn't be enough.

"Yes... By hurting...someone you...loved," she told

him. A weak smile creased her lips. "I…guess…he… wasn't…very…smart."

Duke realized what she was saying. That McWilliams had made a mistake. But the man hadn't. McWilliams had guessed correctly. "No, I guess he's smarter than he looks," he told her pointedly.

Susan's eyes widened. The words were still measured, but were now less labored coming out. "That…would mean…that…you—"

"Love you," he finished the sentence for her. And then he smiled. "Yes, it would. And yes, I do."

This had been the hardest thing he had ever had to say. But today had taught him that not saying this would have taken an even heavier toll on him. Because he would have carried the weight of this lost opportunity around with him for the rest of his life.

Susan passed her hand over her forehead. She was back to wondering if she had indeed died. At the very least, "I…must be…hallucinating."

He smiled. "No, you're not. I'll say it again. I love you."

It was a tad easier the second time, he thought. But not by much. If he was going to say it the way he felt it, it was going to take practice. Lots and lots of practice.

"Maybe I'm…not…hallucinating," she allowed slowly. "Maybe this…is a dream…and if it is…I just won't…let…myself…wake up." Because hearing Duke say he loved her made her supremely happy and ready to take on the whole world—in small increments. "So, if that's…the case…if I'm…asleep…then I don't…have to worry…about sounding…like an idiot…when I…tell you…that I…love you."

"You wouldn't sound like an idiot. You *don't* sound like an idiot," he assured her softly.

So this was how it felt.

Love.

Exciting and peaceful at the same time. Duke grinned to himself. Who knew?

"Ask her to marry you already." Bonnie Gene's disembodied voice ordered impatiently from the hallway. She'd gone to fetch them both coffee and arrived back in time for this exchange. She'd been waiting outside the door for the last ten minutes. "I can't stand outside this door much longer."

Duke laughed, shaking his head. These Kelleys were a hell of a lively bunch. They were going to take some getting used to. In a way, he had to admit he was looking forward to it.

"So don't stand outside the door any longer. Come on in, Bonnie Gene," he urged.

The next moment, Susan's mother, carrying two containers of coffee, one in each hand, eased the door open with her back and came into the room.

"The heat of the coffee was starting to come through the containers," she informed them with a sniff, putting both coffees down on the small table. "I felt like I was standing outside in the hall forever, waiting for you to get around to the important part."

"And what makes you think I was going to get around to the 'important part'?" he asked, wondering if he should be annoyed at the invasion of his privacy, or amused that the woman just assumed that everything was her business. He went with the latter.

Bonnie Gene waved her hand, dismissing his attempt to be vague.

"Oh, please." She rolled her eyes. "You risked getting yourself killed to save my daughter, then, your shoulder bleeding like a stuck pig, you picked her up in your arms and looked like you were ready to carry her all the way to the next town on foot. Besides—" Bonnie looked up into his face and patted his cheek "—one look into your eyes and anyone would know how you feel."

"I didn't," Susan protested, weakly coming to her hero's aid.

"That's because you're still a little out of your head, my darling. You're excused." Taking her container back into her hands, Bonnie Gene removed the lid, then looked up at Duke pointedly. "All right, so when's the wedding?"

"Mother!"

Susan had used up the last of her available breath to shout the name as if it were a recrimination. It was one thing to kid around. It was completely another to put Duke on the spot like this.

In addition to beginning to really hurt like hell, Susan was now also mortified. Didn't her mother take any pity on her?

"As soon as she's well enough to pick out a wedding dress," Duke replied quietly, answering Bonnie Gene's question.

"Mother, please, you can't just—" And then Susan's brain kicked in, echoing the words that Duke had just uttered. Stunned, Susan attempted to collect herself. She had to ask. "Duke, did you just say something about a wedding dress?"

"He did," Bonnie Gene gleefully answered the question before Duke could.

"Whose?" Susan all but whispered. They'd established that she wasn't dead. But maybe she had a concussion.

"Yours," Duke told her, beating Bonnie Gene to the punch this go-round. And then he looked at the older woman who seemed so bent on being involved in all the facets of their lives. "You *are* going to stay home when we go on our honeymoon, aren't you?"

Delighted, Bonnie Gene smiled from ear to ear. "I don't think you two need any help there."

Duke breathed a genuine sigh of relief. For a second, he'd had his doubts. "Good."

"Hey, wait a minute," Susan did her best to call out, feeling completely out of it and ignored. "Haven't you forgotten something?"

With effort, she pushed the button that raised the back of the bed, allowing her to assume the semblance of a sitting position.

Duke thought for a moment, stumped. And then it came to him. "Oh, right." Duke reached for her with his free arm, lowering his head to hers in order to kiss her.

Susan put her hand up in front of her mouth, blocking access. "No, wait. I mean you didn't ask me."

He pulled his head back, looking at her. "Ask you what?"

Either the man had an incredibly short attention span, or she was just not making herself clear. "To marry you."

"Oh."

He had taken her compliance for granted. It hadn't

occurred to him, after what they had just both been through, that she would turn him down. But maybe he was wrong. Maybe she didn't feel about him the way he did about her. Maybe this life-and-death experience had had a different effect on Susan, making her want to run into life full-bore and sample as much of it as she possibly could.

Because Bonnie Gene was looking at him expectantly, he went through the motions. Part of him was dreading the negative answer he might receive at the end. "Susan Kelley, will you marry me?"

"That's better." Pleased, Susan nodded her head in approval. "And yes, I'll marry you," she said with a deceptively casual tone, followed up with a weak grin. The grin grew in strength and size as she added, "Now you can kiss me."

"You going to give me orders all the time?" he asked, amused.

"No, I think you'll get the hang of all this soon enough." She glanced at Bonnie Gene. It was time for her mother to retreat. Far away. "Mother?"

"You want me to kiss him for you?" Bonnie Gene offered whimsically.

"Mother," Susan repeated more firmly this time, using all but the last of her strength.

With a laugh, Bonnie Gene raised her hands in total surrender. "I'm going, I'm going." But she stopped for a moment, growing a little serious. "Treat my daughter well, Duke Colton, or I will hunt you down and make you sorry you were ever born."

To his credit, he managed to keep a straight face. "Yes, ma'am."

Susan pointed toward the door. "Leave, Mother."

"Don't have to tell me twice," Bonnie Gene assured her, backing out of the room.

As the door closed behind her, a broadly grinning Bonnie Gene began to hum to herself.

One down, five to go.

* * * * *

COVERT AGENT'S VIRGIN AFFAIR

BY
LINDA CONRAD

First published in Great Britain 2011
Harlequin Mills & Boon Limited,
Eton House, 18-24 Paradise Road, Richmond, Surrey TW9 1SR

COVERT AGENT'S VIRGIN AFFAIR © Harlequin Books SA 2010

Special thanks and acknowledgment to Linda Conrad for her contribution to
The Coltons of Montana miniseries.

ISBN: 978 0 263 88508 8

46-0211

Harlequin Mills & Boon policy is to use papers that are natural, renewable
and recyclable products and made from wood grown in sustainable forests.
The logging and manufacturing processes conform to the legal environmental
regulations of the country of origin.

Printed and bound in Spain
by Litografia Rosés S.A., Barcelona

Dear Reader,

Once again Intrigue authors are happy to bring you a compelling story from the Colton family. This branch of the Coltons is headquartered in Montana, and we had lots of fun developing the intrigue between three powerful families living in the small town of Honey Creek.

Covert Agent's Virgin Affair is the second story in the series and I really enjoyed writing it. Both my hero and heroine had damaging pasts and I wasn't sure they could ever overcome them in order to find happiness together. But I love my heroine, who has just lost over a hundred pounds and is ready to start a new life. Mary's a special person who deserves a special love, and I think she finds it in the man who is ready to die to save her life. But the trick for Mary is to open her eyes and see who the man she loves really is underneath his shell.

Thanks for coming along on the journey. Hope you enjoy reading the Coltons' stories as much as we enjoyed writing them!

Happy Reading!

Linda Conrad

When asked about her favourite things, **Linda Conrad** lists a longtime love affair with her husband, her sweetheart of a dog named KiKi and a sunny afternoon with nothing to do but read a good book. Inspired by generations of storytellers in her family and pleased to have many happy reader's comments, Linda continues creating her own sensuous and suspenseful stories about compelling characters finding love.

A bestselling author of more than twenty-five books, Linda has received numerous industry awards, among them the National Reader's Choice Award, the Maggie, the Write Touch Readers' Award and the *RT Book Reviews* Reviewers' Choice Award. To contact Linda, read more about her books or to sign up for her newsletter and/or contests, go to her website at www.LindaConrad.com.

To Marie, Jennifer, Cindy, Beth and Karen;
What a pleasure it was to work with you!
Let's do it again!

And to Patience Smith, who came up with the spark
that started it all. You continue to be the editor
extraordinaire!

My many thanks to all of you for making this
a great book and a fun time!

Chapter 1

As the first blow crashed into his right shoulder, FBI special agent Jake Pierson wasn't thinking about self-defense. He'd been deep in his head, preparing and memorizing backstory for his latest undercover assignment.

Standing alone in the delivery zone behind a hotel bar after sundown without backup wasn't the smartest move for a special agent, even one undercover. But Jake was waiting for the contact to let him know when his target had entered the bar.

He'd done his pre-mission checking and considered the medium-size western city of Bozeman, Montana, a safe place after dark. Apparently, he was wrong.

But it didn't take him ten seconds to get back in the game. Jake's body curved backward as the assailant pressed a thumb to his windpipe. If it hadn't been such a surprise, Jake might've laughed at the amateurish attempt at overpowering someone like him, well-trained in martial arts. But the sudden knee to his kidney switched the mood from light to serious in a flash.

Planting his feet, Jake bent at the knees and burst upright with a roar. Power-lifting had been one of his specialties during training at Quantico, and he hadn't tried a move like this in the many years since.

The assailant clung to his neck. Jake easily rolled him over his shoulder and slammed him to the ground.

In seconds the attacker jumped back to his feet. Jake had to hand it to him, the guy was resilient.

Suddenly a knife appeared, and the man was waving it in Jake's face. In the low light it was hard to tell, but Jake figured this was a kid. At least ten to fifteen years younger than his own ancient age of thirty-five.

What was this? A robbery attempt? Or something more?

Jake would have to ask the asshole. As soon as he disarmed him.

The kid's knife hand swung wildly, and when Jake sidestepped, the assailant threw himself off balance. Jake used the opportunity to grab him by the elbow and twist the attacker's whole arm up and behind his back.

"Ow!" The kid screamed like a child on a Ferris wheel and dropped his knife.

Jake whirled him around and slammed the heel of his hand square in the assailant's nose. The blow reverberated back up Jake's arm, but the sickening sound of breaking cartilage told him his attacker would be hurting a lot worse than he was.

"My nose. You broke my frigging nose!" The kid started throwing punches without looking.

Jake sighed, wishing the kid would simply go down easy. He hated having to inflict more damage in order to subdue an obvious nonprofessional.

"Hey, what's going on out here?"

A sudden bright light from the bar's open back door, along with the sound of someone shouting, took Jake's attention away from his assailant. For only an instant. But it was enough time for the kid to get in one last smash at Jake's side and then break away. Jake stumbled to the left while the kid made a mad dash down the side of the building and out of sight.

It took everything Jake had in him not to chase after his attacker. *The mission always comes first.*

The bartender stepped beside Jake. "Are you okay? You want me to call the cops?"

Jake straightened up as he shot the wrinkles out of his lightweight leather jacket. "No need to call anyone. It was a simple misunderstanding."

The last thing he needed was for the Bozeman cops to question him. If this attack had come twenty miles south in the little town of Honey Creek where Jake's main assignment would be taking place, talking to the sheriff wouldn't be a problem. The sheriff there knew the FBI would be in his town conducting an undercover operation. But here? Not worth all the effort.

"Well, if you're sure." The bartender shrugged. "Oh, yeah. The reason I stepped out here is that woman you were asking about is in the bar. She came in with several friends, but they're gone now. She's sitting at a small table all alone. Is that what you wanted?"

"Good work." Jake shoved a few bills into the

bartender's hand. "Remember not to tell anyone I was asking. Right?"

"Yes, sir." The bartender grinned and put his fingertip to his lips.

Annoyed that he hadn't been able to question his attacker, Jake tried to tell himself that it must have been a simple robbery attempt. But his gut told him that wasn't true. It would've been a huge coincidence, and Jake had never believed in coincidences.

Foul-ups on this job had started from the get-go. The man he was supposed to meet in Honey Creek had turned up dead a few days ago—before he could tell Jake anything. That put a giant kink in the FBI's information stream.

Jake had frantically put together a fall-back plan with the help of Jim Willis, his partner back in Seattle. He'd spent most of the past twenty-four hours memorizing facts and backgrounds that Jim had supplied.

Following the bartender inside, Jake rubbed at the knuckles on his right hand, absently opening and closing the fingers. He stopped to stand in the shadows behind the bar, taking time to study his new target and running over what he knew of her in his head.

Late twenties with shoulder-length bright red hair, she was one of his original informant's two daughters. The other daughter reportedly kept nearly constant company with a new boyfriend, whereas this one, a single, quiet librarian, seemed like a much easier mark. In addition, the *other* daughter also had more involvement in the secondary aspects of this case. For one thing, she'd had at least one good reason to want to see her father dead.

When Jake finally spotted his target in a far corner,

the sudden kick of attention from his libido surprised the hell out of him. Where had that come from? He hadn't taken much interest in the opposite sex beyond a few brief liaisons in the past ten years. And it would not have been his choice to start noticing again in the middle of an undercover mission. The timing was inopportune at the very least.

Then again… He reconsidered the idea as he continued studying the woman who was sipping wine and flirting casually with the bartender. Maybe his own…uh…interest would add a layer of reality to the mission. He and his partner Jim had devised a plan calling for Jake to pretend a romantic relationship with this target. The idea was to insinuate himself with her first. Then she would introduce him to the rest of her family and the others in Honey Creek while he took his time gathering information.

Jake suddenly thought *pretending* a romantic relationship might not be such a hardship. *The mission always comes first.*

Mary Walsh fidgeted in her seat and sneaked a glance around the bar. Maybe she was being foolish. Coming to a librarians' conference and expecting to find a wonderful stranger who would introduce her to the joys of womanhood seemed a bit incongruent. Probably there wouldn't be one real man in this whole hotel.

But Mary was determined to find out in the little time she had left at the conference. Her life was already changing, enough, in fact, that she could scarcely keep up. For one thing, her father, the one who had supposedly died fifteen years ago, had suddenly turned up dead—again! She had barely managed to put all her baggage behind her and now she was facing memories of her childhood one more time. Damn him anyway.

Mary took a sip of her wine and tried to calm down. Then, staring absently at the remaining rose-colored liquid, she winced. Her therapist would have his own breakdown if he knew she was using alcohol as a substitute for food. He expected her to go for a nice long run instead.

But, well, screw him. *He* wasn't the one who'd had to fight hard to change his whole life. And after coming this close to her ultimate goal, *she* was the one who'd been smacked in the face with the same old problems she'd thought were far behind her, not her therapist.

After all, who else in the entire world but the Walsh family would have a father who'd died not once but twice, for pity's sake?

She raised her hand and signaled to the bartender for another wine. A new start. That was what she needed. She was all done preparing for life. This latest mess her father had brought down upon the family had clinched it for her.

Mary was ready to start living.

"Hey. This seat taken?" The deep male voice brought her head up and she stared into the most wonderful pair of ice-blue eyes.

Wasn't that what Nora Roberts, her favorite romance author, once wrote about heroes who had stark blue-colored eyes like this? As much as Mary had memorized nearly every word in her favorite novels, right this moment she could barely remember her own name for sure, let alone any particular quotations.

"Um. Is that a pick-up line?" Now why was that

the first thing out of her mouth? She would scare him away.

"Maybe. But can I sit anyway?"

Oh. This guy was cool. "Sure. I might not mind being picked up tonight."

He raised his eyebrows and the corners of his mouth curved in the most interesting version of a smile that Mary had ever seen. She noticed his rugged chin then, and the even craggier jawline. His eyes were cold, deep pools. Deep and full of secrets. *Icy* was certainly the right word for them.

His black jeans and black leather jacket added to the picture of a hard man. And wasn't that a scar running from his eye to his temple?

She realized she might've been wrong. Nothing about him seemed heroic. Fascinating and handsome, maybe. But he was not a romance hero.

He reminded her of the newest actor to play James Bond. Yes, definitely. This guy looked like a secret agent.

"The name's Jake," he said as he turned to signal the waitress. "Jake Pierson."

He sat down and stuck out his hand. "And you are?"

"Mary Walsh." She took his hand and a shock wave ran up her arm.

Pulling back, she tried to look calm and pleasant instead of making a wisecrack. Wow. They had electricity between them. Just like in one of her novels. This guy was going to be *it*. For sure. She promised not to mess things up for herself.

The waitress brought Mary's wine and asked Jake for his order.

"Whatever you have on tap will be good." He gestured to Mary's wine. "And put that on my tab."

The waitress nodded and left.

"Did you just buy me a drink?" Mary's nerves were jangling with anticipation.

"That okay with you?"

"Better than okay. Thanks!" The first time a stranger had ever bought her a drink. Things were looking up.

"Tell me about yourself, Mary. What do you do and where are you from?"

"I'm a librarian in Honey Creek—unfortunately."

He chuckled and the sound warmed her down to the pit of her stomach. "Why unfortunately? I think it's great. I recently moved to Honey Creek myself."

"You did?" A man like this in her backwoods small town? Whoo boy. "Why?"

This time when he laughed out loud, the warmth flashed all the way through her body. It heated up parts of her that she'd barely known she had.

"I'm in commercial real estate. There're a couple of new projects near Honey Creek that I want to pursue."

"Really?" The possibilities for a longer-term relationship with this man danced in her mind.

She suddenly remembered that her best friend forever, Susan Kelley, had mentioned meeting a handsome new real estate agent in town. Jake must be that guy. He was sure handsome enough.

Susan had found her own true love over the past few weeks. She even had the ring to prove it. Wouldn't it be something if Mary could find someone, too?

"I don't want to talk about business." He gave her a look that seemed to be full of meaning, but she had no idea what that meaning might be. "You're not married or engaged or anything are you?"

Ohhh. *That.* "Me?" The giggle erupted before she could order it back. "Not at all."

"What's funny?"

The waitress arrived with their drink order, giving Mary a chance to think over a response. Here she was, at yet another crossroads in her life. She considered telling a white lie. Or maybe giving him a nice easy line that would avoid her having to answer. But then she remembered her father. The world's biggest liar. And she decided she hated liars and everything that went along with them. No, she had no choice but to tell Jake the truth.

If that meant that he would do a quick disappearing act—so be it.

Jake wasn't sure what he expected her to say in answer to his question. The woman acted much younger than her twenty-nine years. Perhaps she would say something about being more interested in intellectual pursuits. Or something about her current strange family circumstances.

A father who'd turned up newly dead, after having already been declared dead fifteen years ago, would probably wreak serious havoc on anyone's social life.

Whatever she would eventually say, Jake was sure enjoying the play of emotions across Mary's face while he waited. Her gorgeous eyes sidetracked him. That wondrous color hadn't shown up particularly well in the photos his partner had faxed along with her file. What hue were they exactly? What color could she possibly list for them on her driver's license?

Eyes: the color of fine aged whiskey.

Or maybe…

Eyes: deepest amber, the color of clover honey.

"For most of my life I've been at least a hundred pounds overweight," Mary finally answered flatly, with no emotion in her voice—despite what he could only describe as fear in her eyes. "I've recently taken off the weight and reached my goal…more or less."

She lowered her chin, and stared into her glass of white zinfandel before continuing, "Being the 'fat one' in every crowd tends to put people off."

"You can't be serious," he cracked, before he thought about what he was saying.

When her head came up too fast, he tried to recover. "People shouldn't judge others by their outward appearance. You're sure beautiful now. I would never have guessed you haven't always looked the same as you do now. How'd you lose the weight?"

"Are you asking if I had weight-loss surgery?" She shook her head but was watching him closely. "Too chicken. I did it the old-fashioned way—by letting a psychologist take my brain out and replace it with one a hundred pounds lighter and supposedly more sane."

A tentative chuckle leaked from her mouth, but Jake was having a hard time joining her in laughing over her little joke.

"That's phenomenal. Your willpower must be amazing." He reached over his untouched beer and took her by the hand, anxious to get even that much closer to her. "I'm impressed."

"Don't be." She tugged at her hand halfheartedly. But when he didn't let go, she stilled.

"Food was prime in my life." She reached for the wineglass with her other hand. "Dr. Fortunata helped me see the truth. For years I used food to numb and distract myself."

"Numb yourself? To what? Why would a sweet girl from a nice small town need to feel numb?"

Mary didn't want to answer him. Couldn't find the way. She made a big show of sipping wine instead.

In the meantime, familiar words kept circling through her mind. *You're no damned good, Mary Walsh. No one could ever love you. God only knows what I did to deserve a child like you. You'll always be worthless and ugly. Get out of my sight.*

"Okay," Jake said in a hoarse whisper as he rubbed his thumb across her knuckles. "Maybe that question's too personal for our very first conversation. But I like you a lot and I want to know more about you. Tell me about your family. I vaguely remember hearing something about a Walsh in the past few days… Was it on TV? A relation of yours?"

"My father." Oh, boy. If Jake hadn't run off screaming after learning she'd been a tubby all her life, finding out about her father was sure to do it.

"What happened to him?"

"They found his body. Someone murdered him." Funny, but over the years she'd gotten used to saying that word. *Murdered.* It had taken almost fifteen years, but the sound of it no longer seemed nearly as horrific as it once did.

"How awful for you. Were you two close?"

What could she say that wouldn't chase him off? Again, she had little choice but tell the truth. He was bound to find out sooner or later anyway.

"Not at all. In fact, I...everyone...thought that he'd died already. There's a fellow in the state prison doing time for murdering him fifteen years ago."

Jake sat back, but stayed in his seat. "That's...uh... unusual. Where's your father been all this time?"

She rolled her eyes and shrugged one shoulder. "Your guess would be as good as anyone's. And before you ask, I don't have a clue why he would pretend to be dead."

Probably because he was a lying playboy bastard, she thought grimly, but refused to say so. No doubt quite a few women would've been happy to see him suffer and die. Running from any of those women might've been an excellent reason for her father pretending to be dead.

Mary took a huge slug and finished off the wine. Jake motioned to the waitress again.

"I shouldn't have any more. I'm still dieting and didn't eat much today. I'm here at the librarians' conference and we've been in meetings all day." Not to mention that she normally didn't drink.

Tonight would be the first for many things, she hoped.

Jake sat back and studied her while he played with his beer mug. "You're embarrassed about your father being a murder victim. Don't be. Not unless you killed him."

"Me? I can't even step on a spider." Not that she hadn't dreamed about killing her father many times over the years. Even after she felt convinced he was already dead.

The waitress brought her another glass of wine and

Mary only stared at it as though it was a bug. Finally, she shook her head to break through her fog and picked it up. This was the start of her new life. What twenty-nine-year-old woman couldn't manage a few glasses of wine?

"My old man embarrassed the hell out of me, too, while I was growing up," Jake said, and Mary felt the tension between them easing. "He was an overbearing bastard. Bound and determined his son would grow up to be just like him—despite knowing damned well that I didn't want any part of who he was."

Mary reached out and laid a gentle hand on Jake's arm. "I'm sorry. That's hard. Who was he?"

"A survivalist. One of those crazed individuals who lives in the backwoods and stockpiles weapons, waiting for the day when the big, bad government will arrive for a showdown."

"Oh, my gosh. Sounds like an awful way to grow up." Mary's heart turned a somersault in sympathy.

"He did teach me how to handle weapons. And I can survive on my own without the trappings of civilization." Jake sounded as if he thought those things weren't any big deal.

"But that wasn't what you wanted. Was it?"

He took a swallow of what had to be by now warm beer, and then gazed at her as if she was the only person on the planet who mattered.

"Not me." With a hollow-sounding laugh, he added, "I wanted to be involved in one of civilization's biggest accomplishments—electronics. I wanted to learn how things work. How computers run. Why cell phones sometimes get signals and sometimes don't. I thought engineering was magic and I was desperate to learn all those kinds of tricks."

"Whoo boy. I bet your father hated that." Their stories weren't the same, but Mary was feeling connected to this man. A connection through their overbearing fathers.

"Yeah, he did. I got out from under his control at the first opportunity."

She took a slow sip from her glass while trying to clear her head. "So, why are you in real estate and not electronics?"

Had she slurred a couple of those words? Maybe it was time for her to give up the wine. She set the glass back down on the table and tried to focus her eyes on Jake.

He wiped his hand across his forehead and then put his palm out as if he was unable to explain himself.

After a moment he said, "Commercial real estate is more lucrative. Electronics makes a better hobby."

He'd opted for the money. Of course. She could certainly understand that. She was considering a change of jobs for the very same reason.

"You're not married?" Jeez. She must be drunk.

"I've never had the pleasure." His whole expression changed and he smiled as if she'd just handed him the moon—or a new BlackBerry. "So far, I haven't found anyone who could love me."

Think of that. They were like two nuts off the same branch. Mary felt as if she'd known him all her life.

The waitress arrived at the table. "Sorry. It's closing time. The bartender says you can have one more round. But you'll need to drink up."

Jake turned to Mary and inclined his head as though it were totally up to her.

"No, thanks. I think I've had my limit."

After the waitress took Jake's money and left, Mary began to rise from her seat and said, "I can't believe it's 1:00 a.m. already. I…wish we had more time to talk."

Talking wasn't what she wanted, but she didn't have the foggiest notion of how to ask him back to her room.

Jake jumped up from the table and helped her to her feet. "Let's take our time going back to your room. We can talk on the way."

Trying her best to keep the wide-eyed look of wonder off her face, she knew she was failing miserably. But she couldn't help it. Everything she had ever wanted—ever dreamed about—was right here beside her.

And he was walking her back to her room.

Chapter 2

Jake's mission couldn't have been going any better if he'd written his target's lines himself. After a couple of hours and several glasses of wine, he'd already piqued Mary's interest enough that she'd allowed him to walk her back to her room. This night would be a great start to his plan—of becoming Mary's boyfriend.

When she weaved from side to side down the hall, he slid his arm around her shoulders. She trembled slightly under the weight of his arm. Taking a deep breath, he caught the sweet smell of strawberries coming from her hair. A perfect scent for her. Like a field full of summer sunshine.

It made him want to pull her closer. Take her in his arms and kiss her until they both lost track of their senses. Until the smell of strawberries surrounded them in a cloud of lust.

Ahem. *The mission always comes first.*

Straightening up, he went over the things bothering him about this assignment—in addition to his unusual physical reactions to the target. The target—Mary. He'd never met anyone quite as guileless as she seemed. Like a naive teen, she appeared incapable of holding back or fudging the truth. Was it all an act? To his trained lawman's eye she looked about as old as the twenty-nine that was listed as her age. Those minor laugh wrinkles at the corners of her eyes gave her away.

If she was putting on a gullible act for some reason, she sure as hell had him suckered in. But he was supposed to be a pro. This was his twelfth mission in ten years. Not his first.

Still, this mission marked the first time that he had actually given out his own background during an undercover operation. Not a smart move. Once a covert agent started mixing up his cover story with his own life history, the whole backstory he'd constructed might come crumbling down around him. He understood that well.

But she had been completely open with him about her relationship to her father. Open and embarrassed about letting him see that the murdered man was not someone she was sorry to see dead. Mark Walsh must've been difficult for her to deal with during their years together.

Jake thought about how a good covert agent twisted with the wind. Went with the flow. The truth about his own father had come tumbling from his lips in an effort to gain her sympathy. Then he'd had a hell of a time recovering when she'd asked him why he'd chosen to go into real estate.

Real estate. Why had he ever allowed Jim to talk him into that crazy cover? Yeah, yeah. Jake understood how real estate would be the perfect occupation, allowing a man on a mission to gain information. Real estate gave him plenty of excuses for snooping around. *Just looking for potential property acquisitions.*

But now, hell…

"We're almost there."

They were. A few more doors down the hall. And they had yet to say two words to each other on the way here.

Jake checked over his shoulder, still concerned that the earlier attack on him had some connection to his mission. But the hotel hallway was quiet. Not one soul in sight. His gut told him they were as isolated out in the hall as they would be inside her room.

Mary pulled the key card from her purse and stopped. She turned to him with the most hopeful expression on her face.

"This is it."

She was beautiful. Her eyes sparkled with youthful anticipation. Her long, full hair dared him to run his hands through it—to lose himself in the satiny texture and heavenly scent. But could he stoop to taking improper advantage of her inebriated state? It wouldn't be fair.

The mission always comes first.

It had been eons since she'd let a man kiss her, and in Mary's memory those previous times had been… stressful. She'd wondered why she had ever thought to give it a second try.

But wasn't that why she'd come to Bozeman in the first place?

She gazed up into Jake's piercing blue eyes and saw a sizzle in them that made her all antsy and suddenly filled with unbearable longing. *Oh, yeah.* She was going to try kissing a man again. Now. Right now.

He bent his head, came within a whisper of her mouth and hesitated. It seemed as if he was giving her a chance to back out. Not a prayer of that happening.

Mary closed the gap between them and fell into heaven. Instead of his mouth being mashed to hers as had happened in her previous experiences, Jake toyed with her lips. He nipped at them, then licked his tongue across her bottom lip to soothe any small pain. The tip of his tongue touched the middle of her closed mouth tentatively as if he wanted her to open up for him.

She parted her lips, let his tongue enter and experienced pure bliss. He dug his fingers through her thick hair and pulled her closer. All of a sudden, the languourousness that had begun in her chest and tummy widened to encompass her limbs. Her fingers grew warm and limp. Her legs became weak and shaky.

As he tightened his hold she felt every inch of his hard body pressed against her softness. His erection pushed into her belly. A jolt zapped through her when she came to the amazing realization that she was the one making him hot. Outstanding.

Their tongues tangled again and the sensual awareness inside her grew to impossible heights. Her whole body began tingling. This was how a kiss was supposed to be. She'd read all about kisses and knew that at least some people liked the feelings that went along with a really good kiss. But she'd never imagined it could be like this.

Letting herself revel in the sensations, she noted the changes in her body's temperature. From somewhere in the back of her mind she knew that sweat was starting to form at her temples. Her palms were becoming damp. Her panties were getting wet between her thighs.

The key card slipped from her fingers and hit the carpet.

"Oh." She pulled her head back and then bent to pick up the key, but her knees refused to hold her up. "Oh."

Crumbling to the floor, she felt flushed with embarrassment and regret. Surely no other woman had ever collapsed after their very best kiss ever and before they'd even made it to the bed. How ridiculous that she could be this much of a newbie at her age.

"You okay?" He reached out his hand to help her up.

"Um. I guess so." If *okay* meant having the most amazing kiss of her whole life.

She tried to stand, but found her legs wouldn't hold her up. "I can't... I can't..." Down she went again, landing on her backside.

When she began to laugh and cry at the same time, Jake took pity on her and reached down to haul her up in his arms. After all, it was his fault that she'd had too much to drink. He'd wanted her talking and in a good mood—not too drunk to stand up.

But he would never in a million years regret that kiss.

"The key card," she said through giggles and tears.

His knees were almost too old for this kind of move,

but he managed to hang on to her and at the same time bend to pick up the card.

"I've got it." He opened the door and brushed them both inside.

Once inside he was at a loss for what to do with her. He didn't figure she was in any shape to stand on her own two feet again. Her room was small. One queen-size bed. One nightstand and one dresser with a TV sitting on top. The lone chair in the room was shoved into a far corner under a minuscule desk. Straight-backed with no cushions, he couldn't figure a way to place her upright in that chair without her sliding back to the floor.

Sighing, Jake walked to the bed and lowered her gently to a sitting position on the mattress. Steadying her, he stepped back and watched, making sure she didn't hit the floor again.

She popped straight up like a Whac-A-Mole. He pushed at her shoulders until she went down on the bed again. She came right back up.

"Hey, aren't you going to kiss me again?" She took a shaky step in his direction.

He took another step backward toward the door. "I think I'd better be going."

"Not just yet." She grinned at him and his whole body went rock-hard. "Um…um… Stay long enough to help me."

He would be a lot better off simply making a run for the door; instead, Jake made the fatal mistake of asking, "Help you with what?"

Rocking uneasily on her feet, she reached for the hem of her sparkly orange, long-sleeved top and pulled it up and over her head in one move. Pitching the top into a corner, she turned back to him wearing nothing above the waist but a silky lace bra and a big smile. She tilted her head and stared at him as if to say, *Help me and yourself, big boy.*

"Do you know what you're doing?" His voice was too steely and harsh for the situation. But he was at a loss as to how to change things.

She shook her head. "What am I doing?"

"Making it hotter than hell in here." His mind was on a dangerous edge as he fought with dueling impulses.

He needed an out. Fast. Or an excuse to change the subject.

Fortunately, he'd spotted something to talk about while she'd had her back turned. It gave him a momentary reprieve and would be something to occupy her mind, he hoped.

"You have a tattoo on your shoulder." He slid a little farther away and pointed. "What is that? A mermaid?"

"That's Disney's Ariel. I had her done last week. I think she's kinda sexy. Do you like her?"

The mermaid tattoo did look like a kid's cartoon character. It was sweet, but not the least bit sexy.

"She looks like you," he managed. "With the red hair and all. But why her?"

"The tattoo was an effort to change. To become a new person."

That sounded like just so much psycho babble to him. "And did you? Become a new person?"

Mary's face flushed bright red. "Not yet. But Ariel is helping me on my journey to find the real me. I was hoping…" Her words stopped as her face paled.

Reaching a shaking hand toward him, she clutched

her stomach with the other hand. "I was hoping you would help me, too."

With that, whatever she'd eaten for the past twenty-four hours came back up her throat and spewed from her mouth. If he'd been a step closer, it would've gone all over him. As it was, the goo covered her pants and got on her shoes.

She started to cry in earnest. "I'm sooo sorry. Look at me. I'm a mess."

"Don't worry. I'll help." He couldn't stop himself. He could no more leave her like this than he could play the violin. It wasn't in him.

He took great care in carrying Mary into the bathroom and cleaning her up. After using a washcloth on her face, he splashed water into her mouth and let her swish toothpaste to rinse. When he was done, he helped her out of her shoes and pants and pitched them into the tub. He found a couple of aspirin in her bag on the back of the toilet and got them down her with a big glass of water. Then he carted her to the bed, threw the covers back and slid her between the sheets.

"Thank you. I'm grateful. But my head is still spinning." She beamed up at him. "Are you going to join me?"

He shook his head and saw the shadow of disappointment cross her face. "Uh, I'd better clean up some more before I do anything else."

"Don't leave me, Jake. Please."

"I won't go far," he promised. "You're going to be fine. Don't worry. Rest is what you need most."

It took him ten minutes to wet a couple of towels and clean up the carpeting. He threw the towels into the tub and filled it up with hot water to let everything soak.

When he arrived back beside the bed, Mary was sound asleep. He headed for the door. With his hand on the knob, he remembered his promise not to leave.

But she would be all right. He could sneak out and she would never notice he'd left until morning.

Then he made the mistake of turning back to look at her.

She looked peaceful now, but what if she had alcohol poisoning or something? Perhaps she could get sick again and choke to death before ever waking up.

He walked to the desk and dragged the tiny chair over beside the bed. Figuring he could sit here for a while, he decided he had nothing better to do tonight.

As Jake stared down into Mary's sweet face, he remembered their kiss. He'd kissed a lot of women over the years. In fact, for five whole years of his life he had looked forward to sharing his wife's kisses on a daily basis. But Tina had been gone for ten years, and at this point he couldn't quite bring the memory of his dead wife's kisses to mind anymore.

Was that disloyal? Jake couldn't stand thinking about that possibility, or about Tina right now.

He couldn't concentrate on anything but the way Mary clung to him. The way her body had melded to his as if the two of them were destined to be together. As if they had been made for each other right from the beginning of time.

A stray curl of soft red hair had fallen over her cheek, and he reached over to push it behind her ear. Running his knuckles over ivory skin, Jake remembered how open she'd been. From the very beginning in the bar, she'd been willing to tell him anything.

She'd also been wide-open to his kisses. Gave him

everything he asked for—and more. She was a hell of a good kisser, making him wonder who had taught her so well. Her file hadn't listed a boyfriend or fiancé, but Jake felt sure that by the age of twenty-nine there must've been someone.

The thought of her file reminded Jake of his mission. He wouldn't leave her for long, but he was overdue to check in with his partner.

Forcing his fingers away from her soft, smooth skin, Jake pulled the sheet up over her shoulders and tucked her in. He'd covered up the mermaid, but he didn't think she would mind.

Smiling, he pocketed her key card and slipped out of the room. Seconds later he was down the outside stairs and in the parking lot, looking for a quiet place to make his call.

"What do you mean your assailant—the *kid*—got away?" His partner Jim was chuckling so loudly over the phone that Jake was afraid someone in the hotel might be able to hear him. "You can't mean you've suddenly grown into such an old man."

Stepping farther under a tall ponderosa pine, Jake gritted his teeth and backed into the shadows. "Ha. Ha. Very funny. What are you? All of two years younger than I am? Or maybe you've regressed to your teenage years while I've been away. At least I got in a clean shot at the kid. Broke his nose for sure."

"If he was someone from Honey Creek, a broken nose won't be hard to spot." Jim's silent grin shouted right through the receiver, even though he made every effort to hide it by clearing his throat. "How about the target? Mary Walsh. How'd your first contact go?"

Jake had to bite his tongue. No way would he tell his partner how unprofessional he'd been.

"Fine," he said in a calm voice. "The new plan is going to work out great. In a couple of days I should be meeting everyone in town through her."

Before Jim could ask anything else about Mary, Jake sent the conversation off in a slightly different direction. "I know the sheriff in Honey Creek is your old navy SEAL buddy, but are you sure he is definitely in the clear on the murder of our informant?"

"Wes Colton is so straight you could mistake him for a ruler." Jim took a deep breath through his nose and Jake could imagine him tempering his irritation over the insolent question. "Wes isn't involved in our money-laundering investigation. You and I already came to that conclusion. He's provided us with solid information."

Jake tsked at his partner's lame excuses. "We're talking about the murder of our main informant. You do remember that we've discussed the fact that Mark Walsh had a lot of enemies? His death could've been a crime of passion and not connected to our investigation at all. There're several kinds of passion. Revenge, for one. Wes Colton's brother has been sitting in the Montana State Prison for the past fifteen years for a crime he obviously did not commit. Sounds like a possible motive for murder to me."

Jim grunted through the phone. "I've already checked on Wes's whereabouts around the time of Mark Walsh's murder, smart-ass. He was at Quantico, taking one of the Bureau's weekend classes for local enforcement. He was back in time to haul the body out of the creek. But as a suspect? Nope, he's not a possibility. Check the sheriff off your list."

This time it was Jake who was holding back the chuckle. "Got it. Anything else?"

"Dead ends and false leads so far. But I'm working every detail. Keep me informed of how you're doing in Honey Creek."

Jake hung up and pocketed his phone. Taking one more exploratory trip around the hotel grounds, he checked for anything suspicious and came up empty.

He headed back to Mary's room, hoping she hadn't awakened while he'd been gone. After he'd slipped inside and checked to make sure she was still breathing, he emptied the bathtub and wrung out the towels. Mary's clothes looked like a lost cause. He dumped them in a pile on the floor.

Then Jake took up residence in the straight-backed desk chair. One of the most uncomfortable places to sit in his memory.

But he kicked off his shoes and settled down to wait anyway. He wanted to watch her until the morning to assure himself that she was okay.

While he watched her sleeping, Jake vowed that he would use these hours to his best advantage. He would work to convince himself that the two of them *could* indeed have a romantic relationship without becoming intimate. He vowed to use her only up to a point. After all, a few things in life went far beyond his job description.

"No. No. No. Don't make me."

Jake practically jumped out of his seat and scanned the room for intruders. Early-morning light peeked around the edges of the curtains. No intruders.

Another noise drew his attention toward the bed.

Mary was whimpering and flailing her arms in her sleep. Tears streamed down her cheeks, and she cried out with unintelligible words.

"I hate you. Hate you!" Those words had been clear enough. He relaxed slightly, realizing she was having a nightmare.

In the next moment she twisted in her sheets and kicked fiercely. She screamed and he began to worry that she was becoming hysterical and might hurt herself. Mary then uttered words that drove a chill up Jake's spine and sent him stumbling to her side.

"I wish you were dead. I swear I'll kill you!"

Chapter 3

Strong arms closed around her, bringing Mary out of her nightmare with a start. *Where was she? And who could be jumping her while she slept?*

"Easy there. Everything's okay. I've got you. It was only a bad dream."

Jake. The cobwebs in her mind disappeared in a flash and she pasted herself to his body. If it had been possible to crawl right inside him, she would not have hesitated.

He cocooned her. Wrapped her in warmth and tenderness.

"Relax," he whispered into her hair. "You're safe."

Swallowing down the night's terrors, Mary reached out toward his face to assure herself that this was no dream. She used her forefinger to trace his features, drawing a line from his high forehead down his Roman nose. Her fingers fanned across the strength in his jaw and in and out of the tiny cleft in his chin. She wanted to memorize every dip and ridge, every nuance.

The reality of being in bed with a sexy man was so much better than anything she had ever read in the pages of a book. She molded herself to him—tried to align their legs in perfect union.

His breathing became rough, uneven. She heard and it turned her to mush. She fisted her hands in his shirt and breathed in his exotic smell. All man. Masculine and exhilarating.

Jake eased back and gently rubbed his thumbs across her wet cheeks. "Okay? No more dream bad guys?"

More than okay, she felt totally wonderful. As though someone had poured a vat of warm chocolate over her. This was what she had been waiting for her whole entire lifetime.

He bent his head and placed his lips against her forehead. Nuh-uh. Not what she wanted from him at all.

Digging her hands in his hair, she pulled his head back and put his lips where she wanted them. On hers. Her tongue slid inside his mouth. The all-consuming flames instantly sprang between them, as she'd expected—as she'd hoped.

Sensation after sensation raged through her. Rainbows of bright colors. Textures and shapes, a tapestry of passion.

Frantic to touch him—everywhere—Mary kept half her brain concentrating on the taste of his mouth and on worrying his lips between her own. And with the other half of her fuzzy mind, she fought to open the buttons on his shirt. A button popped. Then something ripped. But the sounds only served to spur her on.

At last she reached her goal, warm skin and chest hair. The sensation of wiry hair against her fingertips was erotic. She wanted to plant her lips there, replacing her fingers. She needed a taste of him. Of all of him. The pulse right below the surface at the base of his neck would be a great place to start. His salty skin and all those fascinating hidden ridges and creases came next.

"You're killing me here." He dragged his mouth from hers, panting hard.

Through his sensual haze, Jake knew his breathing wasn't the only thing growing hard. She was too close. He couldn't think. Couldn't remember why they shouldn't be doing this.

"Am I hurting you?"

Exasperated, Jake pried her fingers off his shirt and placed her hand against the hard ridge lying under the zipper of his pants. "What do you think?"

"Oh." Her voice was deep, flirty. "Then don't stop now."

Before he could stop her, she began lowering his zipper. The sound mesmerized him. Like someone scratching their way out of a dilemma. His every sense went on alert. The feel of her luxurious hair against his skin. The sound of her breathing coming from her mouth in small pants. When she looked up into his eyes, he saw fire.

He felt something inside him clutch, then give way. He'd seen her willingness. Her longing. Through her sensitive touch he'd found she not only had gentleness and passion, but empathy as well.

It had been a long damned time since he'd wanted anything—anyone this badly.

His erection popped free. Mary sighed deeply and took him in hand. Her obvious pleasure at touching him was contagious. He rolled her to her back and ran his hands down her rib cage and up to cup her breasts.

Her mouth brushed over his briefly, setting fires where she kissed. Just enough to burn through any of his remaining boundaries. He covered her mouth and kissed her back relentlessly. Her lips and tongue stoked the flames of his desire and burned any questions or regrets away like so many cinders blowing in the wind.

"Mary." A single word. A single breath.

And he was lost.

The blood coursed through his veins, leaving his brain and rushing to his extremities. He was out of control. Defenseless against his own needs.

Desperate, he slid her arms free of the bra, pulled it to her waist and then filled his hands with her lush flesh. Her breasts were firm and as soft as rose petals. As he thumbed over the nubby tips, her chest rose and fell. She moaned through pursed lips. His fingers had found perfection, but his mouth hungered for its turn.

He lowered his head to take what he wanted. When his mouth closed over the hard and pebbled peak of one breast, she arched upward with a gasp. Pulling her deeper into his mouth, he laved his tongue back and forth over her nipple. It grew harder—and so did he.

Ignoring the growing ache in his groin, he kept his attention focused on Mary, on her reactions to his moves. As he moved to the other breast, she whimpered and moved restlessly under him. He took a nip of the tip, just a tiny bite. She jumped but made it clear she liked what he was doing, digging her fingernails into his shoulders and holding him right where she wanted. Blowing air over her to both soothe and stir, he kissed and suckled her breasts until she begged.

"Jake, *please*. I want…I want…"

Yes, Jake knew what she wanted and was determined to please them both. Why he shouldn't seemed lost in a haze of need and desire.

He flattened the palm of his hand on her belly and felt her muscles quivering under his touch. Inching his fingers beneath her panties, he soon reached his goal— all that glorious heat in the lush curls at the center of her thighs. He brushed aside any silky material standing in his path. With her help he pulled the undergarment down and off, frantic that nothing should stand between them.

He shoved his own slacks out of the way with one hand while he used the other to stroke and torture. Her thighs fell open and she lifted her hips off the bed. Finding her already wet and hot, he bent his head and dipped his tongue into her sweetness.

Mary groaned, struggled and urged him back up her body. He obliged her, blazing kisses over her belly and across the valleys and curves of her body. Then she reached down and gripped him with both her hands, using a gentle touch that drove him wild.

He jerked and went rigid. Her touch ruled his moves. But he didn't want gentle from her. His whole body felt like molten lava and Jake knew he couldn't last much longer. He grabbed her wrists and pulled her hands up over her head.

Looking into her face, he found her glazed eyes fixed

on him. "Now, Jake," she said through a sob. "I beg you. Hurry."

She lifted her hips, inviting him inside. With a last bit of clarity, he reached into his pants pocket for his wallet. He found the silver-wrapped condom and had it freed and installed within seconds.

Moving over her again, he let the tip of his erection nudge her swollen flesh. She writhed. Whimpered. He leaned his hips forward, brushing his length against her for a second time while she cried out her pleasure.

The sound enflamed him, engulfed him, as blood pulsed and pooled in the part of him begging for quick release. His own ragged breathing blocked the tiny niggles of guilt already building deep inside his chest.

When he brushed her entrance for a third time, she bucked upward. Her whole body pleaded for him as she rubbed herself against his length and called out his name. Every inch of her wept with wanting, and she begged him to hurry.

With amazing self-control, Jake gently pressed his hard length inside her entrance. Testing. He needed this to be good for her. Better for her than for him.

Her internal opening surrounded him with tiny tremors. Like welcome-home hugs. Hearing her making explicit noises of pleasure, he pressed a little deeper into the shock waves. But he wanted her to be just as wild with need as he was. With some regret he made a slow withdrawal, only seconds later to inch forward again.

She tensed but murmured encouragement. Her body was like a warm, welcoming paradise, tight and wet. The greatest gift he'd ever been offered. He pushed deeper, trying not to rush.

Feeling her body start to contract around him, he slid himself farther toward ecstasy. So hot. Slick. Tight.

Just before he succumbed to the madness, it hit him. *Too tight.* There might not be any barrier, but no one had ever come this way before. He suddenly knew for certain that he was the first.

Her first? Was it possible?

He used the last bit of his resolve to lean up on his elbows and look down at her. Her face was the picture of abandon. Her hair a wild carpet spread out across the pillows.

This was too big a gift for him to take without words. "Mary."

Not sure he could stop if she asked him to, he still felt he had to try. Had to say something.

She'd closed her eyes and arched her neck, pushing her engorged breasts up invitingly. He tried not to look. Fought to forget their sweet taste.

"Mary, listen to me." Desperation colored his efforts.

"Please. Please. Please." She undulated her hips and threw her legs over his thighs, bringing him closer to the edge.

"Mary, look at me."

Her head swung back and forth. Her arms went around his back, trying to urge him down into her. He wanted what she seemed to want. To slam his body into hers and bring them to the quick ending they both craved. Why did he hesitate? It was a hell of time for another attack of conscience, but he was already up to his ears in guilt. He had to keep trying to make her listen.

Jake fisted his hands in her hair and forced her

attention. "Are you sure? Sure it's me you want? You don't even know me."

She stared up at him with heavy-lidded eyes, her lips slightly parted and her chest heaving. His mouth went dry as she bit on her bottom lip and tried to smile.

"Time doesn't matter. I know you," she managed on a hoarse laugh. "I chose you because you're a good person. A kind and careful soul who cares about being somebody's first."

Jake started to shake his head, to deny what she'd said. He was far removed from anyone who resembled such a description. But she didn't know it. Couldn't know it.

Her internal canal began convulsing around him, milking him and seducing him to complete the lesson. "Mary. Damn it. I can't do this."

"Shush. Jake, please. I'm so close to something and I know it's going to be spectacular. Please…"

She didn't have time to complete her plea because Jake gave in to the temptation jolting through him. Dripping with sweat, he thrust hard into her and embedded himself to the hilt. He couldn't think. Could only let go.

Could only cry out when he felt the contractions take her and she screamed his name in pleasure. He pumped hard into each one of her rolling earthquakes.

Faster and faster. Higher and higher. Until they were each a sobbing, shouting explosion.

As one, they shuddered and fell over the edge. Together in body—if not in mind.

Amazing.

Sprawled over the bed, tangled in Jake's arms and

legs, Mary waited for her heart rate to slow. She couldn't move. Didn't want to.

Unbelievable. Utterly unbelievable.

Why hadn't she known about this before? But then again, she hadn't met Jake before now. Grateful. Yes, totally grateful that she'd waited for him, she turned her head to make sure he was all right. His skin was damp, glistening with sweat. And his breathing was as erratic as her own.

"Thank God," she murmured.

Jake opened his eyes and rolled to look at her. "For what?"

"Thank God you were the first."

He shifted to one side, pulled her snugly against him and pressed a kiss to her hair. "You could've told me."

She laid a palm on his chest, felt the pulse beat of his heart. "What? That I was a twenty-nine-year-old virgin? And how long would you have stuck around after hearing that?"

His chuckle rumbled up through her hand. "Maybe you're right. And I would've hated missing what just happened here."

"See? I have a lot of strikes against me. And I wanted you. Badly."

"I wanted you from the first moment I laid eyes on you." He kissed the tip of her nose, then raised her hand to his lips and kissed her fingertips. "I saw you in that sparkly orange top and nearly swallowed my tongue."

"It's burnt umber, not orange. Red-haired women aren't supposed to wear orange." But this red-haired woman was going to wear that top as much as possible from now on.

She started to turn over but winced with the discovery that lots of interesting places on her body ached.

Jake's mouth pressed into a hard line. "I didn't even manage to get your bra all the way off. Hell of a way for a first time to go."

He rolled out of bed, ripped off his own rumpled shirt and then reached back and undid her bra. She started to follow him to her feet, but he put his hand down and held her still.

"Hold on. I know what you need right now." He slid his hands under her body and lifted her into his arms. "Let me take care of you."

Feeling like a princess, like her little mermaid, Mary grinned into his shoulder as she threw her arms around his neck and hung on.

He carried her into the bathroom and stepped with her into the bathtub. Then he turned on the shower tap, thankfully warm. The spray covered them in a shower of liquid calm.

Slowly, Jake lowered her down his body to stand on her own shaky legs. "Hang there a second." He kept one arm tightly around her and reached for the soap. "You're going to find out that good sex is always messy, Miss Mary Ariel."

"I like the sound of that. I wish my parents had called me Ariel. Maybe I'll change my name." Along with her whole life—starting tonight.

He placed a wet kiss on the mermaid's face and Mary laughed, feeling careless and coy.

The bar of soap rubbing across her breasts made her nipples tighten. Did he notice? Jake never changed the motion. His knuckles brushed the soft undersides of her breasts. He ran his hands down her spine and around her backside. He seemed intent on smoothing soap bubbles over her skin and she wasn't sure he was paying attention.

Until…he reached between her legs. His touch was as light as a cloud, and he bent his head to place gentle lips against her wet temple.

An electric buzz rushed through her veins like a warm wind. Desire, close to the surface since their first kiss, kicked off her pulse again. Her heart pounded with the need, the heat.

"Jake…" The word was only a whisper of sound. A plea. A question.

But it didn't have the desired effect.

He pulled his hand away and stepped back, studying her under the spray. Suddenly she felt more embarrassed than she had in her whole life and raised both palms to cover her breasts. No man had ever seen her stark naked before. It was one thing to have sex in bed—in the dark. It was quite another to be faced with full-frontal nudity under the bathroom's fluorescent light.

Jake's eyes clouded over and instead of ice blue, they looked gray and unfocused. "That's it." He handed her the soap, turned his back and pushed aside the shower curtain ready to step out of the tub.

"Is it me?" she asked quietly. "Now that you've seen me in the light are you regretting what we did?"

He shook his head, then turned back and reached for her. "Maybe I have some guilt. But I'll never regret one moment of what we did. Don't ever think that. You are a gorgeous woman. And if I had a choice…"

Pulling her close, he lasered a kiss across her lips. A kiss that spoke of need and desperation. A kiss that spoke of *tomorrow*.

By the time he let her go, his breathing was coming in hard pants and his erection was poking her in the stomach. "You're going to be sore for a couple of days. You have lots of time left in your future to experience everything. Let's take things slow for now."

She sighed but nodded her acceptance of his decision. It wasn't her first choice but if he could wait, so could she.

Jake stepped from the tub. "Take your time. When you get out we'll have breakfast before we each head back to Honey Creek."

He put a towel over the bar for her to use after the shower. "This is the only dry cloth left in the room, and it's all yours. I'll air-dry. Oh, and when you get out of the shower, you might want to make a decision about your clothes."

"My...?"

He grinned and pointed to the pile by the sink.

"My new silk pants? And my brand-new heels? They look ruined." The pants would probably be easy to replace, though she regretted the heels.

"Sorry you picked last night to wear your new clothes."

"*All* my clothes are new." Hmm. That sounded a little too sharp and full of self-pity and it wasn't how she truly felt. "Besides, those clothes were lucky for me."

"I told you never to call me here."

At the same time as Mary was stepping from the shower, Truman was making lame excuses.

"But, boss, I'm using a pay phone outside the Bozeman hospital E.R. No one will find out."

The boss tried to keep sudden anger and frustration

from spilling over through the phone. "I'm not paying you to get your nose broken. I wanted you to follow that new guy around for a while and report back on his behavior. What's the idea of jumping him?"

Groaning, Truman raced to explain, "He looked like he was spying on somebody. I only wanted to scare him off. Make him regret he came to our part of the country."

"Yeah? And that worked out so well, didn't it?"

"It's not my fault." Truman's whining voice set nerves to jangling. "He's gotta be some kind of pro."

The idea wasn't a novel one. "I'm beginning to believe you're right. I thought at first he was a private investigator and I wanted to know who hired him. I'm more convinced now that he's probably a fed. DEA or FBI maybe. Makes me think I'd better bring in a pro myself."

Truman issued a laugh, but the sound rang hollow and too loud across the line. "You get him, boss. What do you want me to do next?"

"Go on vacation."

"But, boss…"

"Get out of the area. Go to Florida for a while. I don't want to see your face around here until your nose heals. Is that clear?"

If it wasn't clear, the boss figured the pro he hired could take care of Truman the same way as he would take care of the undercover agent in their midst.

Permanently.

Chapter 4

"Ow!" Mary rammed her hip into the book cart for the third time this morning.

Darn it. Why couldn't she watch where she was going? After all, she'd been employed as the assistant librarian here at the Honey Creek library for the past eight years. Certainly by now she should know where everything was located.

Absolutely nothing had been going right. Not since she and Jake had parted ways last Saturday morning in the parking lot of the Bozeman hotel. That morning had been so hopeful—so full of promise. They'd exchanged cell phone numbers and had stolen a few public kisses.

He'd said he would call. But her friend Susan told her that was what they all said.

Not in romance novels. In her favorite books the

couples might have their troubles, but things always worked out in the end. If a hero said he would do something, he did it. The heroic characters she'd read about in romance novels were what had given her the idea that a man could be trusted.

Not that she'd had many examples of that in real life.

Nothing her father had ever said was the truth. He'd cheated on her mother. He'd probably cheated his business partners and friends. He'd even cheated about his own death.

Jake was not like her father. Yet Jake had said he would call, and here it was a rainy Tuesday morning and no word yet.

Why couldn't she get over what had happened between them? Yes, he'd been her first lover and she knew a woman's first was supposedly a big deal. But this yearning to make love to him all over again seemed to have put her under a spell. A strong and unyielding spell. Was that natural? Being reckless wasn't like her. Or at least not like the person she used to be.

If she could just see him again… Maybe she would discover that he wasn't everything she remembered. Maybe…

A squeal of delight coming from the children's book section caught Mary's attention. She started walking that way to find out which book had enthralled the little girl.

One of the biggest changes Mary wanted to make in her life was having kids. She wanted one, or maybe two—or three. Now that she'd lost the weight and it was possible to think about such things, it seemed children were on her mind a lot.

As she passed by the computer stations, empty at this hour, she fought the urge to stop and look up Jake Pierson. To check up on his background. But she would never do that without telling him first. It seemed dishonest.

"Mary, may I speak to you a moment?" Mrs. Banks, the head librarian, motioned from her office.

Mary changed course and headed her way. She'd been meaning to have a serious conversation with her boss for the past couple of days. Ever since she'd decided to change her whole life. But, well, the time had never seemed quite right.

Mrs. Banks ushered her into the tiny office and shut the door behind them. "Have a seat, Mary. I'd like to tell you something. My husband has decided to retire from his job and he wants us to move to Arizona. He likes the weather there."

"No kidding?" Mary couldn't imagine living anywhere else but Honey Creek. This was home. All her family and friends were here, along with everything else she knew and loved.

Mrs. Banks put her hand up as if she was about to say something profound. "I gave three weeks' notice to the Library Board last night. They asked me to suggest my replacement."

Mary began shaking her head before her boss even finished her thought.

Mrs. Banks must've noticed the denial in Mary's expression because she gave her the cordial smile of a long-time business comrade. "I know you don't have the credentials, Mary. But if you really want the job, I'll go to bat for you."

Mary's boss had been her mentor from the beginning,

and Mrs. Banks must've assumed Mary wanted what she wanted. She did not.

"You could always get your master's degree in Library Science while you worked," Mrs. Banks added. "It'll be difficult to accomplish both at the same time in this small town, but it's possible."

"Thanks." Mary's mouth rushed to say something else, but her mind was lagging as she fought to find the right words. "But…I… I've been meaning to tell you… I've been thinking about quitting myself."

Mrs. Banks raised eyebrows expressed what she thought of that idea. "You don't want to work at the library anymore? What will you do?"

Good question. One Mary had been mulling over for weeks. "I have a few ideas. But I was hoping for a little time to check things out."

"Does this have anything to do with the authorities finding your father's body last week?"

"No." And that was the truth. Her father had nothing whatever to do with her wanting to make some changes. After all, she'd lost over a hundred pounds on her own—before his body had been found for the second time.

"I see. Then I can tell the board to look for someone else?"

Mary nodded, but bowed her head rather than face the disappointment in Mrs. Banks's eyes.

"Okay then. A young woman who used to live in Honey Creek recently contacted me about a job." Mrs. Banks's expression was thoughtful. "I'll check on her qualifications. In the meantime, Mary, if you need a few days off, the best time would be during the next couple of weeks. While I'm still here and can watch over a temp."

Mary agreed to take time off, starting tomorrow, and then she left her boss's office as quickly as possible. Now she'd done it. Big changes would be coming at her fast. Whether she was ready for them or not.

Outside the Honey Creek library at 5:00 p.m. on a drizzly Tuesday evening, Jake leaned against his rental SUV and waited for Mary to get off work.

Torn between duty and his awakening feelings for Mary, Jake had spent the better part of four days secretly meeting with the Honey Creek sheriff and assuring himself that Mary had absolutely nothing to do with Wes's current murder investigation. Somewhere along the line, Jake had found himself hoping he'd been totally wrong about Mary and that she was the murderer. That notion would be infinitely better than the idea of her as an innocent bystander that he was using for his investigation.

But no. Mary was exactly what she seemed.

Sweet. Naive. Trusting. And no longer a virgin, due to his asinine lack of self-control.

A trickle of cold summer rain eased down the back of Jake's neck, but he shook it off. He deserved to stand in a frozen hell for what he'd done to Mary—for what he intended to do.

His head came up when he spotted her at the library's front door. She was opening an umbrella and making her way down the stairs past the building's wide white columns.

Damn, but she was pretty. Even wet and dressed in a plain gray dress that seemed suitable only for a librarian. The sight of her made things twist inside him, and that hadn't happened in a very long time.

Folding his arms over his chest, he waited for her to come closer. It was starting to register in his idiot's mind that Mary might be in real danger. Honey Creek had at least one murderer lurking about. And Jake's gut was telling him that whether or not Mark Walsh's death and his own money-laundering investigation were linked, one murder could easily become two.

He'd been trying to narrow down the possible suspects, but found it difficult without knowing the people involved. He'd come to the conclusion that the best plan was to meet the various townsfolk. Maybe he could gain access to a couple of their personal computers and files.

And what better way to accomplish those goals than in the company of a beautiful, sexy woman—who might be in need of a protector?

But he swore there would be no more intimate nights. No more erotic touches and starry-eyed kisses. His conscience couldn't take it.

"Jake?" Mary stood a few feet away in the rain, staring up at him. "What are you doing here?" Her eyes were the color of a pale ale today and clouded with questions.

He wished he could give them to her. "Waiting for you. And hoping you'll come to dinner with me."

"That would be nice. But where have you—"

Gathering her in his arms, he rushed her around the car and seated her in the passenger seat before she could change her mind—or ask any difficult questions. He didn't want to give her a chance to think too much. Not about dinner. And especially not about him.

By the time he'd slipped behind the driver's wheel,

she was buckling up and placing her wet umbrella on the floor mats under her feet.

He turned the ignition key and brought the car to life. "I thought we'd go to Kelley's Cookhouse for barbecue. That okay with you?"

Out of the corner of his eye, he caught her rolling her eyes before she asked, "You sure that's where you want to go? My best friend's family owns the place and we're likely to run into everyone in town I know."

He'd already started the car, but now he put it into neutral and stepped on the brake. "Mary…Ariel…" He reached over, captured her hand and tried a sincere smile. "I want to meet your friends and family. I want us to learn everything there is to know about each other. Give me a chance?"

Mary's flip-flopping heart had landed back in her chest by the time they'd driven the three blocks to Kelley's. The rain was easing up, but her fascination with Jake grew greater with every passing moment.

Of course, she would give them a chance to get better acquainted. He didn't even need to ask. Otherwise, how would she ever know for sure if he was *the one* or not?

After he was introduced to all her crazy family and friends, she would find out if he still wanted to stick around. Or…if by then he was ready to run away—either laughing himself sick or screaming in terror. It would be a good test.

Unbuckling her seat belt, she watched him closely. She was having some trouble believing he was for real. The moment she'd spotted him outside the library, she'd begun pinching herself to be sure she wasn't dreaming. He was almost too good to be true.

After they climbed out of his SUV and headed toward the restaurant's front door, Mary's sister Lucy appeared on her way out. Lucy's arms were loaded down with take-out food packages.

Mary gave Lucy a peck on the cheek. "Jake Pierson, I want you to meet my sister Lucy Walsh."

"Hey, good to meet Mary's sister. Need some help carrying those things?" Jake opened his arms and grinned like a Boy Scout.

"I guess so…Jake, was it?" Lucy gave her sister a raised-eyebrow look, as if to say, *Where'd you hook this one?*

Jake took the packages and then waited for Lucy to show the way to her car. Lucy didn't seem to be in any hurry to leave now that her arms were free, and Mary couldn't figure out how to give her sister the hint.

"I was sorry to hear about your father," Jake told her. "It must be hard having to wonder where he'd been all those years."

Lucy nodded sharply at Jake but turned to Mary without making a reply. "You're not coming to quilting club tonight? We haven't seen you in a while."

"That group is a bunch of gossips," Mary complained—before she realized that Jake was listening closely. "I'm in the process of changing my life, Lucy. Quilting doesn't fit the image in my head of the new me."

Mary turned to Jake and nearly batted her eyelashes at him before she could catch herself. "My sister owns the knitting store in town." And Mary had been a little jealous of her pretty older sister ever since they'd been in their teens.

She held her breath and waited for Lucy or Jake to make a comment. If Jake liked Lucy more, it might kill her.

Immediately Mary felt guilty. Lucy's life had been no better than Mary's, despite the fact that Lucy looked like every man's fantasy of the girl next door.

Mary understood what her sister had been through. What they'd both been through. No one else on earth had any idea but the two of them. At one time Mary had thought that would keep them close, but now she knew better. Lucy wasn't too crazy about hanging around the one person who shared all her secrets.

In addition to that, Lucy was already engaged to be married. Mary was truly happy for her sister. Truly.

Lucy turned to Jake. "Are you visiting someone in Honey Creek?"

Jake's bright eyes blazed at Lucy as he shifted to the other foot. "I'm in the process of moving to town for business. Just leased a house, in fact. Big old place out in the country."

Mary perked up at the idea of him settling into Honey Creek. "Which house?"

Turning to gaze at her with a look that made her itchy, Jake said, "It's south of town, where Main Street runs under the highway. The agent told me it's known as the old Jenkins place."

"Oh, I've always loved that house," Mary told him. And meant it. "But it's huge. Do you need all that space?"

Jake took his sweet time in giving her an answer and it made her wonder what he had in mind. "Maybe." He twisted back to talk to Lucy. "I'm in commercial real estate and I need an office at home. And I have a…uh… hobby or two. Plus, that place was the only available property anywhere nearby."

Lucy threw him a look, using her patented saccharin grin and all those sparkling white teeth. Mary felt her sister's grin in the pit of her stomach. "We won't keep you, Lucy."

"Mary, can I speak to you…um…in private for a minute?"

"I'll just put these bags in your car if you'll point me in the right direction and give me the key." Jake was smiling like a blue-eyed, broad-shouldered Boy Scout again.

And making Mary wish they could be somewhere— anywhere else—alone.

"Sure. Thanks." Lucy handed him her key and indicated her ancient truck parked at the far end of the lot. "Put them in the front, please."

When Jake was out of earshot, Lucy dragged her sister away from the restaurant's door and off to the side. "Where did you ever find him?"

"We ran into each other in Bozeman. Stunning, isn't he?"

Lucy looked as though she would like to say something else, but checked over her shoulder instead. "Mom tells me you're thinking of taking time off from work this week. Is that true?"

"Uh…yeah." This wasn't what Mary thought her sister wanted to talk about. Confused, she went along. "Why?"

Lucy lowered her voice. "Would you do me a huge favor, sis? I can't do it myself. I can't leave the shop during the day. And besides…if I did this, everyone in town would start gossiping about me again."

"Tell me what you need. I'll try."

"Go see Damien Colton." Lucy twisted her head, looking behind them. "See if he's okay and if he needs anything. Please?"

"All the way over to Montana State Prison?" The idea of entering a place with hundreds of male prisoners made Mary sweat with apprehension. "That's a hundred miles away. Why can't you simply wait until he gets out and comes home? That shouldn't take too much longer, should it?"

Lucy took her hand and Mary felt her sister trembling. "I can't speak to Damien directly. You know people will talk. As it is, they either think I hate Damien or secretly still love him. I wouldn't want Steve finding out."

"Your fiancé has to know what happened back then. Why would it…?"

"Mary, please. I don't want to talk to Damien in person. I don't want to plant any ideas in his head about me still caring for him."

"But you want me to ride all the way over there by myself to check on him?" Mary shook her head. "Don't you think he might get the wrong idea about that?"

Tears leaked from the corners of Lucy's eyes. "Can't you just do this one thing for me without making a big deal? I feel terribly guilty about him being in that prison all these years. If it hadn't been for me…"

"Okay, okay, take it easy." Mary felt cornered, as she always did around Lucy. "I'll go."

Lucy threw her arms around Mary and hugged her as though she might not ever have another chance. "Thanks, sis. You're the best."

Jake walked back to the two of them. "You're all set, Lucy."

Thanking him and thanking Mary again, Lucy took back her keys and finally left.

Jake slid his arm around Mary's waist. "What was that all about?"

"Nothing much." But Mary couldn't help thinking of her sister.

Mark Walsh had wreaked havoc on both his daughter's lives, but Mary was determined to take control of her own life. What about Lucy? Could her sister have taken things into her own hands—and killed their father for revenge?

Jake took her hand and walked them toward the front door. "You sure she wasn't concerned about you and me?"

"We didn't talk about you." Not much. But that gave Mary an idea. "I agreed to do Lucy a favor and I'm hoping you'll be willing to help out, too."

"Maybe. What did Lucy need?"

Sighing, Mary would've liked some way to get out of telling him the whole truth, but now she had no choice. "It's a long story. Can we talk about it over supper?"

"Sure." Jake bent to kiss her cheek as he pulled on the front-door handle. "I'm starving."

The touch of his lips sent an immediate and staggering jolt down Mary's spine. She was hungry, too. But not for food.

Chapter 5

Jake leaned back in his chair after the waitress took their orders. He looked around at the many empty tables. He'd eaten here a time or two before as there weren't many restaurants located in the town of Honey Creek. Tonight he'd hoped Kelley's would be packed with locals.

At the moment, though, only a few patrons were at the bar and just two other tables had customers seated for dinner. Something didn't feel right here. The hair on his arms stood straight up. Was someone watching? Who? When he casually glanced up again, pretending to look for their waitress, he couldn't spot anyone or any reason for this odd feeling.

He shook it off as another tangible sign of his guilt. Paranoia. Typical of covert agents. In this case, apparently he and Mary had arrived early for the dinner hour. Disappointed about not having access to lots of Mary's friends, but not ready to give up, Jake decided to take his time and see what information he could obtain while they ate.

"Your sister's a beautiful woman," he began casually. "I'm not sure I would've pegged you two as related though."

Mary's eyes narrowed at him. "Yes, she's always been the pretty one."

That was *not* what he'd meant. "If anyone ever said such a thing, they were wrong." He found himself reaching across the table for her hands. "You are infinitely better-looking than Lucy."

On top of that, Lucy was still someone he suspected in the murder of her father. If Mark Walsh's murder was a crime of passion instead of being connected to an international money-laundering scheme, Lucy could well have done the crime. Something in her eyes screamed *secrets*.

Mary was still staring at him but her gaze had softened. Amber points of light in her eyes danced in the low illumination coming from a wall sconce above her head. In his opinion, she was most definitely the prettier of the two sisters.

Gorgeous. With long, silky red hair lying seductively against her back. With her lush full breasts tempting him as they pushed against the material of her dress. And with her perfectly rounded hips and those erotic thighs—hiding now from his view.

Jake closed his eyes for a second and wished to hell he had never seen her naked.

"I have to explain what took place fifteen years ago so you'll understand why Lucy wants my help." Mary took a sip of water and looked around the room before she continued. "You need to know Lucy's story. And the truth about my father." She made a face with that remark as if she'd suddenly remembered that what had happened fifteen years ago was all her father's fault.

"But mostly it's the story of a man named Damien Colton, who was very young at that time. Barely twenty."

Jake nodded. "Is he related to the sheriff, Wes Colton?"

"Yes. His brother." Mary lowered her voice to a whisper and he had to lean in to hear her words.

"If this is too hard for you…" Jake reached over and touched her arm. He needed to keep her talking. Making her believe that he didn't care one way or the other whether she continued was one excellent method of manipulating her into doing the opposite.

Part of the covert agent's training manual.

Mary shook her head. "You have to hear this. If not from me, then someone else will tell you. You see, my father was a difficult man to live with." Hesitating, she put her fingers to her mouth. "Sorry, I guess I already mentioned that. But back to my sister. She was sixteen then and thought she was madly in love with Damien, a kid whose family still today owns a huge ranch with lots of acreage near Honey Creek."

Mary's eyes took on a hazy cast as she seemed lost in the past. "My father threatened to run Damien out of town if he didn't leave my sister alone."

"He didn't want her dating a rich kid?"

Mary's eyes came back to focus on him. "My family is fairly well off, about as rich as the Coltons. But that isn't the point. I think my father didn't like the idea of

Lucy dating someone four years older. Damien was a good kid, but I guess he looked a little too rough around the edges."

Jake knew Mary and Lucy came from first-generation family wealth. It was one of the things that had put him off about pretending a relationship with Mary before they'd met. And he had already read this whole story while digging into the FBI files on Mark Walsh. But he needed to encourage Mary to get it all out. Maybe he would learn something new.

"What happened?" he asked casually, taking a sip of water.

"My father's body was found…or at least everyone thought it was his body. And Damien was accused of killing him because my father had threatened him."

"Pretty slim motive."

"I agree." Mary picked up her water glass, too, but only stared at it as though she could see back to that time long ago. "They tried and convicted Damien despite the lack of evidence. Sentenced him to a life prison term for a murder he obviously didn't commit."

"At the time you didn't believe he'd done it?"

Mary shook her head and set the water glass down without drinking. "But most people did."

"Including Lucy?"

"She seemed bitter and angry back then. I thought it was over Damien. But now, I'm not so sure." Mary absently began rubbing her hands together. A sure sign of distress.

"What's the favor Lucy wants?" Jake wanted her to come fully back to the present. To stay with him.

Mary's nose turned up and her mouth twisted as if she'd just tasted something sour. "She wants me to drive over to the Montana State Prison and see Damien. So far no release date has been set and she wants to find out if he needs anything."

Jake could easily guess the truth. "She wants *you* to tell him she's sorry for what happened?"

Mary looked toward him and took a deep breath. "I suppose that's what she wants, yes."

"And you don't want to go?"

"Not alone. That's quite a drive. And…and…"

"I'll go with you." He took her hand again and gazed into her troubled eyes. "If you're planning to do this favor for your sister, just tell me when and I'll make time to go with you."

A meeting with the prisoner might mean a breakthrough in his case. Talking to Damien Colton could bring fresh leads.

"Thank you. Oh, thank you, Jake. I can't tell you how much I appreciate it." Mary released a big breath, as though she'd been holding it awaiting his decision.

Jake would never let her make the trip to the prison alone. He couldn't. She seemed to be dreading it, and he couldn't stand seeing her in anguish.

It wasn't that he thought of her as fragile. He didn't. And she wasn't one of those needy, clingy women who annoyed him. Mary was definitely one of a kind: strong and soft at the same time.

Sensual? Oh, yeah. Intelligent? Definitely. But he couldn't quite put his finger on why he thought she was special. As he considered all her good qualities, his conscience broke in and kicked him in the butt once more for using her the way he had. The way he continued to do.

Then the waitress arrived with armloads of food, giving Jake the perfect excuse to bury his guilt—yet again.

Mary finished her grilled chicken salad slowly. She even left some of it untouched on the plate. Both those actions, eating slowly and leaving part of the food behind, were things she had never done in her previous life. But she now knew both would help keep the weight off.

Being with Jake was apparently going a long way toward turning her life around. She still had a craving for the gooey chocolate cake that was a favorite at Kelley's Cookhouse, but she ordered coffee along with Jake instead of dessert.

Proud of herself, she relaxed back in her chair and watched him. The man had no idea how sensual, passionate and exciting he was. Something deep inside her yearned for him. It was more than the sex—though she thought that part had been great. Better than great—for a first time. And she suspected it would only become more intense with practice.

She'd always had a knack for picking up nuances and hints from people, and Jake gave off terrific vibes. Well, okay, he obviously had a few secrets that he hadn't shared. Didn't everyone?

But he was clearly a good man. An honest man. Her heart fluttered, actually fluttered, when he caught her watching him and grinned.

"You've always lived in Honey Creek?" he asked.

"My whole life except for a couple of years at college. It's my home."

"That must be nice. I don't have any place I can really call a home."

She wanted to tell him that he could make a home right here—with her. But she knew it was too early in their relationship to talk about a future. They still didn't know enough about each other, despite the fact that they'd seen each other naked.

The idea of them naked made her blush. She dropped her gaze to the tabletop, letting her hair cover her face so he couldn't see her embarrassment. Why had she insisted on them making love on the very first night they'd met? It had been risky, but she didn't regret it for one second. Even if it meant they could never get past that one night and form a real relationship.

"What are you thinking about?" he asked gently. "You're too quiet."

"I was just wondering if you had any brothers or sisters. Is your mother still alive? Where is your father?"

"Whoa. Lots of questions there." He took a last sip of coffee and studied her from across the table for a moment. "My mother died when I was about ten. No brothers or sisters—that I know of. And I have no idea whether my father is alive or dead. When I finally broke free of his influence, I never looked back."

Mary understood immediately. Jake didn't have anyone or anyplace to call his.

When she didn't make any comments about what he'd told her, he asked his own question. "I know about your father's death, and I've met your sister Lucy, but what about other sisters and brothers? What about your mother?"

"My mom is going strong." As Mary thought about

her mother, it made her warm and smiley all over. "She lives on the hobby farm where I grew up—where I still live. Right north of town. And she runs the family businesses that my father left her. With a lot of help from her boyfriend, that is."

"Your mother has a boyfriend?"

That idea made her smile, too. "Craig Warner. An extremely nice man. I couldn't have picked a better guy for my mom. He was my father's accountant for years before he became CFO of the family's company."

"Craig knew your father?"

"Sure. They were in business together before my father faked his own death." The nasty memory of her father's betrayal brought another thought into her mind. "I can't help wondering where my father really was all those years. Isn't it curious?"

Jake's eyes turned steely gray. Instead of answering, he asked a question of his own. "Do you think Craig Warner knew where your father was? I mean, maybe he did, considering they were partners."

"No way." That was one question she didn't need to ask. "Craig would never have done that to my mother. Or to us kids. You can't imagine how difficult life was for all of us after my father's...uh...first murder. Craig helped us through it."

Jake put his hands out, palms down, as though he was trying to gentle a horse. "I didn't mean anything by asking. I only wanted to know what goes into making you who you are. How you think. That's all."

Mary realized her back had straightened impossibly and her shoulders were high and tight. She shook them down and sat back in the chair, taking a last sip of cool coffee to hide her nerves behind the oversize mug.

"Do you have other brothers and sisters?" Jake leaned on his elbows and tilted his head to watch her. "You said 'us kids.' How many are there?"

"There's four of us. Two boys and two girls. Me and Lucy. And our brothers Peter and Jared."

Jake nodded and gave her a wicked grin. "Exactly the right size of family. Do all of you live in Honey Creek? Still on the family farm?"

Mary felt the flush creeping up her neck again, but she fought it down. "I'm the only one still at home." Yeah, and at twenty-nine wasn't that extremely attractive?

She raced to shine a light on a different subject. "Right now Lucy is living above her store—until she and her fiancé get married. And my brothers have both been gone from home a long time.

"Peter is a single dad and lives with his son in a nice house near downtown." Mary kept talking, desperate to use anything to keep the conversation off herself. "My baby brother Jared is far away—getting started in a finance career. I'm not exactly sure where he's living at the moment. He was in New York, but I think he's been taking special training at his company's Washington, D.C., home office for the past few months."

Jake knew a lot about Jared—probably more than Mary knew. But he was under orders not to reveal anything about the youngest Walsh brother.

Instead he refocused the conversation on the other brother. "What does Peter do for a living?"

Mary's whole face dimpled. "My brother is a private investigator. He has a terrific business, but mostly he works outside of Honey Creek. Not much going on around here for him to investigate. This town is what you might call quiet."

Jake almost laughed, but kept his face in a neutral position. Honey Creek was absolutely seething with crime and suppressed passions. The place was anything but quiet.

Her brother, Peter Walsh, had not been involved in the murder. No motive and no opportunity. But the idea of Mary's mother, Jolene, having a romantic relationship with her dead husband's partner had tweaked Jake's lawman's antenna.

Something for him to consider. To pick apart and inspect for hidden motives. In fact, Jake needed to wrangle an introduction to both Jolene and Craig Warner real soon.

Reaching out, he took Mary's hand across the table again and winked at her. He had to swallow back the bubbling guilt, an emotion that was becoming a constant irritant. But while ignoring it and everything else churning in his gut, he leaned in for a quick kiss. After all, what could be wrong with wanting to meet his new girlfriend's family?

It took a couple of days to arrange their visit with Damien in prison, but they were finally on their way. Jake had taken care of the details. Meanwhile, Mary spent most of that time sweeping up her old life and packing it away in boxes.

At one point yesterday her mother saw her leaving the house carrying her *fat* clothes to the car for donation. "What's going on with you?" her mother had asked. "First the vacation from work and now cleaning out your closets. If I didn't know better, I would say you were in love. Is this about that new man in town Lucy says she met?"

Mary murmured something under her breath to indicate her life was on a new track. She wasn't quite ready to tell her mother how she felt about Jake—since Mary barely knew her own feelings on the subject.

Glancing over at Jake now in the driver's seat, she couldn't help wondering why, after over a week, they'd yet to have a repeat performance of their first night. Sure, he'd given her a peck on the cheek a few times. And once or twice he'd surprised her with a deep, warm kiss. But all their encounters were short-lived and fairly chaste. No secret touches. No glassy-eyed looks that promised remarkable things to come.

Mary couldn't quite put it all together in her mind. But then, maybe all newbies felt as lost at first as she did. She wished this was something she could comfortably ask her mother. Or talk over with her BFF Susan. But she couldn't. Talking would mean actually admitting that she'd been twenty-nine before her first sexual encounter.

Every time she thought of it in those terms the whole thing sounded more and more outrageous.

"You're awfully quiet again this afternoon." Jake glanced over at her and opened his hands on the steering wheel. "Have I done something wrong?"

"Not at all. You've been perfect." Too damned perfect. What the hell was wrong with him? "I was just thinking."

"Thinking about what?"

"How pretty it is in this part of the state."

Ever since they'd passed through Butte, traveling on Interstate 90, the mountains had gotten higher and the trees more lush. As she looked out the windshield now, she spotted Elk Park Pass on their right and Mount

Haggin to the left. They'd been dropping down into a wide valley ripe with bunch-grass prairie.

"See the silky lupine and those blanket flowers? Aren't they colorful?"

"All I see are miles and miles of cattle and fences. What are you talking about?"

"Purple and yellow wildflowers. Beautiful this time of year. The mountains off in the distance always look like a picture postcard during August, too."

Jake grinned as he looked out the window. "If you like the mountains in August, maybe we should take Highway 12 over the pass on the way back. It's a little out of the way, but this is a terrific time of year for sightseeing. What do you think?"

"Maybe."

A highway sign announcing their imminent approach to Deer Lodge and to the prison sent a sudden chill down Mary's spine even in the bright sunshine of the warm day. The idea of prisoners—of a prison with no escape—landed heavily in Mary's gut.

That does it. You know where fat, ugly little girls belong. Go! Echoes of curses spoken long ago rang in Mary's head. *No. No. Please don't lock me in there.*

Mary covered her face and breathed in and out of her mouth trying to slow her speeding pulse.

"What's wrong? Are you okay?"

"I'm…" She lifted her head and tried to find somewhere else to focus her attention—anywhere instead of the looming prison.

"I'm fine. Maybe a little tired of riding." She stared out her window and gazed into the outside rearview mirror, desperate for something else to see—to say.

"Hey, they're not back there anymore," she said

without thinking. "I figured for sure they must be going to the prison, too."

"Huh? Who's not where?" Jake checked his mirror and then glanced over to her with the question in his eyes.

"Oh, nobody, I guess. It's just that I noticed a fancy four-wheel-drive truck following us out of Honey Creek, and I've seen them behind us several times since."

Jake suddenly pulled his SUV off to the side of the Interstate and put his foot on the brake. "What did the truck look like exactly?" His eyes were tight. His mouth a narrow line.

"Jeez, Jake, I don't know. It was black. Big. Shiny. With loads of chrome. I've never seen it before around town."

He started up the SUV again and pulled back on the highway. "If you ever see that truck again…or any vehicle that seems to be following us, I want to know right away. Understand?"

Wow. What the heck was that all about?

Chapter 6

Jake stood behind Mary's chair with his arms folded over his chest and his mind racing behind what he hoped was a stoic expression. She'd been acting as if coming to this prison was a death sentence.

He'd asked her twice if something was going on. But she wouldn't discuss it. Only said she was a little tired and nervous about seeing Damien.

Whatever was affecting her head, he must've caught it, too. He couldn't imagine what was wrong with him that he hadn't noticed a truck following them. In ten years of undercover work, he had never been this sloppy.

"You have twenty minutes." The guard ushered Damien into the visitors' room and left to stand at the door.

Jake paid close attention to Mary's expression and

body movements. He'd figured she'd been lying about something having to do with Damien and that was why she'd been jumpy. But as the prisoner sat down across from her, she never flinched and actually smiled at the guy.

"Do you remember me, Damien?"

The prisoner was big—and threatening—at around six foot four. His dark brown shaggy hair hung down around his collar. He had muscles on top of muscles. No question they came from prison workouts. Physical training was a typical way for prisoners to pass their long days.

"The guard told me Mary Walsh was here to see me," Damien said with a sneer. "But if he hadn't told me I wouldn't have known. You look different, kid. You've turned into a real babe."

Jake fisted his hands at his sides and fought the urge to force those words back down Damien Colton's throat. Prison hadn't done much for this jerk's attitude. Whatever he might have been at twenty had obviously been beaten out of him in here. Now he was nothing more than an ordinary head-up-his-ass con.

"I… Thanks," Mary told the bastard. "My friend Jake came with me." She waved her hand toward him standing behind her. "Lucy asked me to come."

"Why?" The bitterness suddenly rolled off Damien like sheets of rain. "Why now? I haven't heard one word from her in fifteen long years. Lucy couldn't even be bothered to come to my trial. And after fifteen years she has something to say now? Now, when I'm finally done with this hell and about to be released?"

Damien spewed out a string of curses, making Jake wonder if Mary should still be sitting there listening to him vent his anger. This wasn't even her fight. She was only the messenger.

Jake took a step closer to Mary, but she spoke up before he reached her. "I agree with you, Damien. Lucy tends to think of only herself. But it's not one hundred percent her fault. You remember what she went through?"

"Bull." Damien pounded his fist on the table. "She went through nothing compared to what I went through with that bastard. Whatever Lucy wants from me at this point, tell her it's too damned late."

"She's engaged to be married, Damien. I'm sure she doesn't want anything from you. Finding out that our father was actually alive all those years has been a big shock for us. I think…I think she just wants you to know she's sorry."

Jake watched defeat pour into Damien's eyes. "Yeah? Well, her sorry can't even buy me an extra minute of freedom. Tell her I don't need it, and I sure as hell don't want it."

Mary sighed and rose from her chair. "I'll tell her. Is there anything else I can do for you? Any other messages you want me to take back to Honey Creek before you get out?"

Damien hung his head as though he was ashamed of his behavior toward Mary, a woman who had never harmed him and had always believed in his innocence. "No. I'll carry my own messages."

Mary grimaced and sighed again. "Okay. Bye, Damien."

Before she could turn away, Damien said, "You shouldn't have come, Mary. I'm…sorry."

The corners of her mouth turned up in a weak version of a smile. "Goodbye." She turned and left the room.

Jake stood where he was for another second. "Are you planning on coming back to Honey Creek?"

Damien looked up at him from where he remained seated. "You're some kind of cop, aren't you?"

Crap. "No. I'm in real estate."

"Liar. I've spent the bulk of my adult life learning to spot narcs. What do you want from me?"

Jake looked Damien straight in the eyes. "I came here for Mary. She's fiercely loyal to her sister, so she came all the way out here for her—and for you. She cares about you as an old friend, Colton."

The prisoner stared at him with absolute misery in his eyes. Jake's few words didn't seem like enough of an explanation.

"Give Mary time," Jake added. "She'll come around and accept your apology."

Jake took one of the biggest risks of his entire covert career and pulled a blank card from his pocket. "When you get out, if there's anything you want to…say. Or anything you need help with, call this number."

He scribbled down the FBI field office number on the back of the card and laid it on the table. Jake wondered if he wasn't coming out of cover to one of the bad guys. But his gut told him that Damien Colton was not the murdering type. He didn't even seem like the criminal type. Not to mention, this Colton was probably too young when he went to prison to be involved in any money-laundering schemes.

Turning his back, Jake sent up a quiet prayer for

the man's soul. Damien had been wronged. Terribly wronged. And he might never be able to recover from it.

Damien fingered the card for the tenth time as he waited for his phone call to go through. He'd almost torn the thing up twice, but something had made him hold on to it. Finally, he'd stuck the paper card down into his shoe, deciding to tear it up later. He looked around to find out if anyone was watching.

Seeing no one, he breathed deeply just as his call was answered. "Hello, Darius?"

"Ah. The black sheep calls. What do you want from me, Damien?" Darius Colton sounded as distant and cold as ever.

Damien bit his tongue to keep from begging his father for help. "My court-appointed attorney isn't returning my phone calls. I want to know why it's taking so long to clear up the paper work for my release."

"Not my problem, son. I told you fifteen years ago that I'd spent my last penny on your defense."

Yes, Damien remembered it distinctly. As devastating as being convicted of murder had been, learning that a few family members believed in his guilt was enough to drive any remaining love for them away for good.

"But now that you know I'm innocent can't you at least make a phone call or two?"

Darius Colton mumbled something under his breath. Then he said, "The system will let you out of prison eventually. Wait your turn. No one remembers or cares about you anymore."

"That's not true, Dad. People do remember me. Mary Walsh came to see me today."

"The librarian? Mark Walsh's fat kid? I don't believe she came all that way by herself."

Damien blew out another breath and counted to five. "She's not fat now. And she came with a friend. Not anyone I remember from Honey Creek."

"Sure she did. Who?"

The question was abrupt and it took Damien aback. This was getting him nowhere. He should never have contacted his father for help.

"Just skip it," he said. "I'll wait. Don't…"

"I'll contact your brother Wes." Darius's interruption was another shock. "Maybe the sheriff can do something to speed things along. But that's the best I can do."

"Sure," Damien said as he let the sarcasm drip from his words. "Wouldn't want to put you out."

"What are your plans for after the release?"

Damien couldn't help himself, the opportunity to dig at his father was too good to pass up. "Thought I would come back and live off you, Dad. The Colton ranch can be a good life."

Actually, ranch life was exactly what Damien had in mind for his future. Not the Colton ranch, of course. But it would have to be a jumping-off point. He needed time to get his feet on the ground.

Darius was quiet for a long moment until at last he said, "Your mother wants you back on the ranch. You can come home—for a while. But I'll expect you to work while you're here."

Sighing, Damien gave up. He had never been able to figure his father out beyond his womanizing and secretive business deals. And it didn't sound as if fifteen years had done anything to make the man more transparent.

"Right, Darius. Well, I guess I'll see you when I see you then."

Hanging up and cursing his father under his breath, Damien swore to put all of Honey Creek in his rearview mirror as soon as possible.

"If you don't still want to do this, we can turn around and head back to Honey Creek the more direct way." Mary looked over at Jake's profile and could see his jaw twitching.

"I promised you the ride," he muttered. "And it will work out fine. It's only that it's getting late. I'm afraid your pretty views will turn to darkness before we reach the top of the mountains. Not much sightseeing to do after dark."

As their SUV put distance between them and the state prison, Mary felt herself relaxing more and more. She'd done it. Walked in and out of a prison with her head held high and with hardly any discernable shaking at all. Now she could breathe easy and enjoy the rest of the day.

Not so for Jake. With each passing mile, he seemed to become more tense. He kept checking the rearview mirror and shifting in his seat.

She decided to turn the tables on him. "You're the one that's quiet now. What are you thinking about?"

Maybe he was disappointed in her. Mary had so hoped he would trust her to know what she was doing. She couldn't bear to explain why it had been so important for her to see Damien and to help her sister. But she wasn't sorry they'd come.

"Seeing Colton back there reminded me that your father was recently murdered." Jake didn't take his eyes off the road ahead as they began their ascent up the grade. "Have you given any thought to who might've wanted him dead?"

The idea was laughable, but she chose not to admit it by frowning. "I would imagine there might be tens of people out there in the world—maybe hundreds of people—who could've killed him. At the risk of repeating myself…"

Jake did the laughing for her, but he didn't sound amused. "Yeah, I know. *He was a difficult man.* But seriously, you must have thought about it."

She wasn't going to talk to him about the members of her family and their many reasons to want Mark Walsh dead. Instead she began with the rest of the community.

"My father's name was linked with several women. Women who might've had hot-tempered boyfriends or could've been a little unbalanced themselves. Any one of them would've been happy to see my father dead."

"You think it was a crime of passion?"

"Sure. What else?"

Jake shrugged and shook his head. "How about business associates? I hear your father first got rich in the liquor trade. The Walsh breweries are legendary. That's not an easy business. Brewing is rumored to have mob connections. Maybe he stepped on toes and paid for it."

Mary was pleased she and Jake were talking over the past—sort of. She liked that he cared and was curious. But she wasn't entirely sure that digging up the past was a smart thing to do.

Deciding to go with being happy about his attention, she said, "My father had a lot of help in the early days of the business. My mother and Craig did most of the real work putting that business on the map. And there's a story that Darius Colton, Damien's dad, lent my father some money just when he needed it the most. I simply can't believe that the mob would do business with my dad. He was…"

"Difficult." Jake's chuckle was for real this time. He glanced over at her and winked. "I know. But I think it's interesting to sort through all the suspects who might've done the crime. Like a murder mystery."

Mary laughed out loud. "Well, it would be a lot more fun if it wasn't my father we were talking about. But yes, we could do that. You'd need to meet the people involved, though. Maybe you could come to one of my mother's famous barbecues. Would you like that?"

Jake reached over and touched her hand. "Sounds good. I want to meet your friends. But don't you think we should check with your mother?"

"Sure, but Mom…" Mary stopped talking and gasped. "Oh, look at that."

They'd rounded a hairpin turn and caught the tail end of a spectacular sunset. Jake pulled the SUV out onto a lookout point and put the transmission in Park, idling the engine and watching the sun going down through the windshield.

This was why she'd wanted to come the long way. This sight. Even though the sun was setting behind their backs, the road they were traveling had enough twists and turns to afford terrific views of both the mountains and the sky.

Streaks of copper, peppered with raspberry points, spread out to the indigo heavens from a cheddar-colored base of sun. Beautiful sunsets never lasted long in the mountains. But as this one eased over the bumpy horizon, it shimmered with colors reminiscent of the best rainbow she'd ever seen.

Mary sighed. "This trip was definitely worth the extra time. Thank you, Jake."

When she looked toward him, he was already watching her.

"Definitely worth it." He leaned in and surprised her with a sensual kiss. Warm and tender, but also full of longing and promise.

As he pulled away and sat back, he whispered, "You are every bit as beautiful as that sunset, Mary. Damned straight it was worth the…"

Mary felt the jolt before she heard the screech of tires. "Jake!" Someone had hit them from behind—hard.

"I'm on it! Hang on."

The SUV roared to life as Jake threw it into gear and took off. He stepped on the gas and sped around the rest of the curve, barreling toward the crest of the mountain.

"What are you doing? You can't leave the scene of an accident. What if someone was hurt?"

"That was no accident. Tighten your seat belt."

What? Not an accident? Then that had to mean someone deliberately ran into them. But why?

As she tugged at her seat belt, Mary looked into the side mirror but saw nothing. Nothing but the blackness of after-dusk in the mountains. Turning to Jake, she started to question what he'd said.

But before she could open her mouth, he thundered out another order. "Brace yourself. They're closing in."

She didn't need to flick another glance in the mirror

to notice bright headlights suddenly close behind them. Too close.

And too bright. The whole inside of their SUV lit up like a sunshine-filled morning.

"Jake!"

He didn't answer as he fought the wheel and stepped down harder on the gas. In the glare of their own headlights, Mary could see one more hairpin turn coming up ahead. If they got hit from behind there, it was a five-hundred-foot drop over the side.

Mary held her breath while Jake urged the SUV to go faster down the hill toward the turn. She noticed the headlights behind them growing slightly dimmer as they raced on in the dark. No one could take these turns at high speeds. It was insane.

But Jake never slowed as he entered the next turn. Mary closed her eyes and put her hands over her mouth to keep from screaming. She heard the brakes, felt the tires skidding sideways and waited for the worst.

Next, her body righted and she noticed the SUV was coming out of its skid. Suddenly it took what felt like a quick ninety-degree right turn. Into the mountain side?

Then they stopped. The engine quit roaring and began to purr.

Mary's eyes popped open, but everything around her was black. Their headlights and dashboard lights were off. She glanced in Jake's direction and opened her mouth to ask what had happened. All she could manage was one squeak.

"Shush," he whispered. "One more moment and…"

From behind them she heard another engine whining and brakes squealing. She shifted all the way around in her seat and looked out the back. As she watched, a big truck flew by on the highway about twenty feet behind their SUV.

Realizing she was still holding her breath, she exhaled and said, "Do you think they spotted us?"

"Hope not. But they'll figure it out when they hit a flat stretch a few miles ahead."

"Where are we?"

"According to the GPS, on a fire road. Good thing I noticed it coming up."

"Does the fire road go anywhere?"

Jake took in a gulp of air, as if to calm himself, and checked his screen. "It meanders around through the highest peaks and eventually comes out on the Interstate right north of Butte. Or at least it's supposed to. I'm not crazy about driving it in the dark, but I don't think we've got a lot of choices."

She sat back in her seat and fought the tears. "You saved us. Where did you learn how to drive like that?"

Turning the headlights back on, Jake put the SUV in gear and eased on the gas. "One of my many hobbies. I once took a defensive driving course."

Mary found it hard to believe anyone could learn how to do what he'd done in driving school. But she wasn't going to question her good fortune at having Jake at the wheel.

There were other questions running through her shaky brain, however. "Why did they come after us? Why would anybody want to hurt us?"

Through the dim light, glowing off dashboard, she saw Jake grinding his teeth.

It took him a moment or two more to answer. "I have

no idea. I would hope it doesn't have anything to do with our seeing Damien Colton in prison."

"No way. Couldn't be." But the next thing to occur to Mary's mind was a far less logical supposition. "Do you think it might be connected to my father's murder?"

"I hope not." Jake cleared his throat and concentrated his gaze straight ahead. "But we can talk about it more when we get back to my house."

"Am I going to your house?" Though her whole body was still trembling from their ordeal, the idea of going home with him made her hot.

"Absolutely," Jake told her. "If that truck had hit us a little harder or it had been a more direct hit, we would be at the bottom of a canyon by now. I nearly lost you—and I'm not letting you out of my sight tonight."

Chapter 7

Mary walked in his footsteps with her fingers stuck through his belt loops in the back. She was close enough that Jake could even feel her erratic breathing on his neck.

He stood still for a moment and whispered to her, "What are you doing? Keep a step or two behind me."

"You said to stay close." Her whispered remark sounded jumpy—nervous.

"Not that close." He eased her back a couple of feet.

It was bad enough that he'd had to sweep his rental house for intruders without benefit of a weapon at the ready. But how would he go about explaining a Glock 9 mm to a woman who thought his job was in real estate? He'd left that weapon under the seat of his SUV. And though he'd stashed several other weapons around the house, he wanted to stay undercover—for the time being.

However, Jake couldn't hope to do a thorough security check as long as Mary's body heat kept seeping through his shirt, mixing with his blood and driving him wild.

"This house is huge." Mary apparently changed her mind and found his intruder check boring.

She wandered off into the open-concept kitchen, where he'd left a soft light burning over the range. "Why would you need a professional chef's kitchen?"

"To cook food."

She swung back to look at him as he closed the storage closet door. "You? You cook?"

"Sure. Give me a few minutes to check all the doors and windows and I'll make you a late supper."

Mary went back to opening refrigerator and pantry doors, exclaiming how well-supplied and neat everything was. Meanwhile Jake made sure every downstairs door and window was secure, each one locked up as tight as he'd left it.

Mentally chastising himself, he took the stairs two at a time to secure the second story, leaving Mary to ooh and ahh over the furnishings in the dining room/ kitchen combination. Yes, he had a well-stocked kitchen and expensive decorator furniture, but he hadn't taken the damned time to ask the Bureau to alarm the house. What an idiot. Now he would have to phone in and plead for emergency service to set up a security system ASAP. Turkey that he was.

But this house was just for show. Or rather it had started out that way when he'd begun this mission a few weeks ago. He'd never planned on using it as a safe house. All he did was sleep here once in a while.

At the thought of sleep and beds, he wondered how the sleeping arrangements would go for him and Mary tonight. He didn't want her going back to the Walsh farm—not until he got a better handle on who had attacked them and found help protecting her.

But he had made a vow not to touch her again after their one crazy and erotic night. He'd already listed a hundred reasons in his head why they shouldn't have slept together in the first place—and why they should never do it again.

But making love to her again had become all he could think about. Day and night. It didn't matter whether she was with him for real or if he was only dreaming about her. He was consumed with thoughts of her.

Rolling his eyes at his own ridiculous notions, he thanked heaven this house was big. Lots of bedrooms.

Hmm. But lots of bedrooms might not be enough to keep him out of her bed.

Finishing his security check, Jake headed down the front stairs with his mind racing. How could he arrange things to make it easy for him to keep his hands off her?

Walking through the two-story open family room, Jake had the only idea that made any sense. He would send her upstairs and he would sleep down here in front of the fire.

That should do it.

He hoped. Unless he started walking in his sleep.

"Hi," she said when she spotted him turning on lights. "Everything okay?"

God, he hoped it would be. "The house is secure. Now let's see what we've got for supper."

"You have *everything* in your kitchen. All the

ingredients and utensils for any meal you could possibly want."

"Don't count on that." The only meal he wanted to eat was standing right before him. "I was top chef in a San Francisco restaurant in another life. I have a repertoire of recipes."

"Cool. Then you decide what you want to cook. Me? I'm a top eater."

They both laughed and Jake actually began to relax. This might not be so tough. He only had to get through one night of protecting her alone before he could call in reinforcements.

How hard could that be?

A couple of hours later Jake was finding out exactly how *hard* things could get. He'd fisted his hands to keep from reaching for Mary enough times that his nails had caused permanent damage to the skin on his palms.

"That was a terrific meal." Mary stood to carry her plates to the kitchen.

"Thanks. It's my healthy take on eggs Benedict. The sauce is made from low-fat yogurt, lemon juice and lemon zest instead of the usual hollandaise."

"You're hired," Mary said with a chuckle as she reached the sink. "You can be my personal chef from now on."

Jake didn't figure either his palms or his groin could stand the strain. "Leave the dishes. Let's have coffee and the flan in the family room in the other wing. I think it's chilly enough to light the fire."

"Okay." She turned slowly and brushed past him to move out of his way.

He caught a whiff of her hair—strawberries—and his knees went weak. Standing by the sink, he grabbed hold of the countertop edge with both hands and counted to ten.

This was going to be one hell of a long night.

Minutes later, Jake carried the coffee and dessert in on a silver tray. Mary was kneeling by the hearth, lighting the kindling.

When she saw him, she grinned. "It's odd to think of it being cold enough in August for a fire. But the nights have been particularly chilly this year. Down to the mid-thirties last night. Although they can withstand much cooler, the farmhands covered the chicken coop to keep the birds warm."

"I forgot you live on a farm."

Mary stood and dusted off her hands while the kindling crackled behind her back. "It's not as much of a farm as it used to be. Everyone in my family has a busy life and no time to mess with farming or the animals anymore." She closed one eye and thought about what she was saying. "Well, no one has time except for me. But I've never been involved much with the farm. Not even as a kid. I was always more into books."

Jake set the tray on the coffee table and pulled the table away from the sofa so they could lounge in front of the fire and also reach the cups and plates at the same time. "Come sit down and let's talk more about who had a motive to kill your father."

She plopped down into the overstuffed sofa and sighed. "This is nice. The kindling has caught. We should have a lovely roaring fire soon. You go first."

He poured the coffee. "I don't know any of the people involved—except for you and Lucy. And I don't think either of you would have a motive. You have to start with a suspect and I'll offer my opinion."

She accepted a mug of coffee and looked up at him across the rim. "I don't like thinking about the people I know having a motive for murder."

Jake reached over and touched her cheek. "This is only to pass the time. But if you'd rather not—"

Mary closed her eyes and bit her lip until he stopped stroking her skin. He understood. His own mind had wandered dangerously while the warmth from her flesh moved through his fingers.

"Um." She cleared her throat and tensed her shoulders. "What if whoever killed my father is also trying to kill me? Someone tried to run us off the road, remember."

He could scarcely forget. "Would your father's murderer have reason to kill you, too?"

"No." She shook her head once, then hedged. "I don't know. I don't think so. But they might think I know something or someone that I don't."

When she looked up at him again, her eyes filled with fear. "Oh, Jake. I might be in trouble and not even know why."

He couldn't stand it. Taking the mug from her hand, he put it aside and scooted in close to put his arms around her. Her whole body quivered.

"That's why you're staying with me tonight." His confident remark sounded cocky, but he couldn't help saying whatever it took to make her feel safe. "You'll be okay here."

She must've believed him because in a moment, she slipped off her shoes and sat back. Sighing, she flexed her feet in front of the fire.

Toeing off his own boots, he noted his heartbeat

kicking into overdrive. Beneath Mary's normally calm exterior he'd sensed a constant sizzle of desire whenever they touched—even when passing a dish or exchanging mugs. He could feel a sort of sensual vibration within her that excited and inflamed him.

"Mary…"

She reached over, touching a finger to his lips. "Shush." Stroking each lip, she used her fingertips as though they were her most sensitive body part.

Capturing her hand in both of his, he kissed each finger. Then he turned his attention to the inside of her arm, kissing his way up to the sensitive skin at the elbow and taking a quick nip.

Mary sucked in a breath, jerked and tugged at her arm. But he held her steady.

Smiling, he blew a warm breath against her flesh. "Are you saying you don't want a repeat performance of the other night?"

He hoped to hell she would say no, but his instincts told him her first answer would be yes. As if of its own volition, his hand moved to her waist, and he flattened a palm against her rib cage, letting his knuckles brush the soft underside of her breast.

A corner of her mouth curved up. "I keep forgetting what kind of things we did. Guess I was sort of out of it that night. It might help if you could remind me…"

He brought his mouth down on hers with hungry enthusiasm. As his skin prickled with an erotic flush, he felt the extra blood pounding into his extremities.

Jake couldn't remember when he'd ever met a woman with such a love of life, such honesty, such passion. A woman who laughed heartily, blushed easily and trusted with abandon.

Yet underneath the wide-eyed, trusting librarian he'd glimpsed a strong, decisive woman. Someone he could spend a lifetime getting to know.

Some other lifetime, he reminded himself. After his assignment was over. But after finishing with this life, he would have to move on to the next. And then the next.

Mary squirmed beneath him and his hands were suddenly fondling her ripe breasts. Just where he'd wanted them in the first place.

To hell with the next life. To hell with his assignment. What he wanted—needed—was right here begging him to give and take extraordinary pleasure.

"Make love to me, Jake." Her whisper seemed to hang in the air like heavy perfume.

Claiming her mouth again in a kiss that could be illegal in ten states, he growled his agreement with what she wanted. The sound she made deep in her throat fed his desperation. He tangled his tongue with hers and sucked at her bottom lip.

His lips moved to her jawline as he began kissing his way down her vulnerable neck. Then he discovered his talented fingers had already unbuttoned her blouse and unsnapped her bra. When was the last time he'd used those moves on a woman? He couldn't remember. Too long ago. But all of a sudden he was truly grateful for his body's automatic responses.

As foggy as his mind seemed, he was determined not to have an exact repeat of the other night. This time he would get the bra all the way off.

He urged her arms out of the shirt's sleeves as he kissed his way across her shoulder. "Hello, Ariel," he murmured when the tattoo came under his lips. "Long time no see."

Mary giggled and slipped out of her bra all on her own. Her hands went to his shirt and he suddenly decided they were both too well-dressed for the occasion. Besides, the heat from the fire had become too intense for clothes.

They stripped as he felt droplets of sweat crisscrossing his forehead. Fire fed the hunger, consuming his brain. He took her mouth again and let his hands roam free.

She shuddered and dug her fingers through his hair, arching into his caresses. One last time he desperately tried to fight her effect on him. But it was then he realized his hands had already moved ahead without him. Giving in with no real regret, he replaced his fingers with his mouth, sucking her nipple hard.

"Please, Jake!" Her hands went to his shoulders, frantically trying to hold on while her nails dug into his flesh.

Yes, he would please her again. But this time he had no intention of rushing. He moved to the other breast and her body bowed, the urgent sense of desire rushing through them both. She pressed against him and suddenly he found his erection cradled at the juncture of her thighs.

It took everything in him not to push inside her. To claim her again. Hard and fast. He'd been her first. He wanted to be her only.

Instead of demanding what he wanted, he scooped her up in his arms and carefully placed her on the sofa. He gazed down into her dreamy eyes as she reached out, arms begging for him to come to her.

Going to his knees before her on the soft hearth rug,

he spread her legs and edged between them. He bent his head to steal a quick taste of her lips again. She tasted of coffee and sugar—and of a unique spice that must be one of her own. Running his hands up along the insides of her thighs, he felt her skin quaking under his touch. When his fingers slipped into her wet and warm spot, she went wild.

It took every ounce of his willpower to keep from savaging her. But he was hanging on to sanity by the slenderest of wires.

Moving closer, he rocked his erection against her most tender flesh. Parting her with his fingers, he widened the path for himself.

"Jake!" Her voice was drenched in white heat.

"I like it when you call my name." He slipped inside her and she threw her legs around his waist to hold him in place.

Kissing her forehead, her nose and finally her lips, he gave her gentleness despite what his body desired. He kept his kisses soft, slow and undemanding. When her breathing at last came easier and she opened her lids to look up at him, he found the firelight had jumped into her amber eyes. They were bright with passion.

He started rocking again. Slow. Sure. Her eyes fluttered shut as a sheen of sweat appeared on her skin. He drew her higher, until he heard her breathing turn to labored pants. In that moment he forced himself to stop again, deliberately slowing things down and not taking her too fast—too rough.

She clung to him and gasped for air. He kissed her earlobe, her hair. He wanted her to acknowledge the sensual nature he knew was buried deep within her. For that, he needed her complete trust and realized the only way to get it was to let her set the pace.

If...waiting didn't drive him mad in the meantime.

Mary urged him to begin their sexual dance once more, using a combination of moans and roaming hands. But he gritted his teeth and held on. Then—at last—she began rocking against him.

"Yes," he murmured. He bent to her breast and took one of her nipples into his mouth.

He sucked and she rocked harder. Faster and higher. When he ground his hips against her pushes and then reached between them to flick his thumb across her sensitive nub, she screamed out.

Feeling the pleasure begin to ripple through her, Jake lost all rational thought. He pounded violently, rejoicing as she met him thrust for thrust. In moments, he felt her shudder and let himself go. Driving deep one last time, he saw stars behind his eyelids as they raced over the edge together.

Outside the large country house at that moment, a man named Vanos Papandreou sat in the brush with a pair of infrared glasses trained on the downstairs windows. Known only as the Pro to clients and competitors, he had no trouble waiting for targets to move—even if that meant sitting in a cold drizzle for hours on end. But it appeared that this man and woman were in for the night.

Vanos's orders had come down from his employer. He was not to make any kind of direct assault. No, this client wanted tactics that were only designed to frighten. To scare off a perceived threat from this man. Or failing that, the client wanted every overt move to appear to be an accident.

The Pro's mess-up on the mountain road earlier tonight had only been a slight miscalculation. He'd intended to push the target's SUV off the cliff and then make it look like an unfortunate accident. It had been a perfect setup, too perfect to pass up. Vanos figured he would be due a bonus for quick work. But when his truck didn't hit the SUV squarely, Vanos was surprised at his target's superior driving skills.

His employer had said the target might be in law enforcement. Vanos could now confirm that assessment.

But it didn't matter. Over the years Vanos's targets had ranged from Secret Service agents to a twelve-year-old boy and everywhere in between. The boy had bothered him—for a while—but the money had been excellent on that job, coming from a stepbrother who wanted the kid's inheritance. Those kinds of major payoffs went a long way toward easing a wayward conscience.

Vanos was known as the Pro for good reason. A professional in every sense, he never missed.

The client in this case wanted scare tactics and accidents. And despite the fact that Vanos was a master marksmen who could hit a moving target at over a hundred yards, what the client wanted was what the client received.

Stashing his night glasses and falling back to his newly rented sedan, Vanos began conjuring up various methods to throw a scare into the man. Perhaps the best idea would be to target the woman?

Perhaps. But whatever methods he decided to use,

Vanos figured he would turn this job into a game. To scare instead of kill.

Yes, this one could be fun.

Chapter 8

Mary awoke when sun came streaming through the blinds and hit her in the eyes. They hadn't slept a whole lot last night. After their spectacular lovemaking session on the sofa in front of the fire, she and Jake had climbed the stairs to his bed—and the party had continued.

A silly grin broke out on her face as she thought of how Jake had reached for her again and again all night long. He'd made her feel needed—special. Mary was feeling much more of everything than she had ever felt. She would never forget the night—or Jake.

Stretching like a lazy cat, she reveled in the odd but sweet aches and the overall languorous feeling she was experiencing. If they decided to stay right here in bed for the rest of the day, she wouldn't care. Actually, they could stay here for the rest of the week.

Rolling over, she reached for Jake, ready to snuggle

up for however long he wanted. But his side of the bed was cold and empty.

She sat straight up and looked around to find herself alone in the bedroom. Listening for running water in the shower, she was disappointed to hear nothing but silence.

Where was Jake?

Deciding he must be downstairs fixing breakfast, she grumbled as she forced herself out of the bed and onto her feet. Food wasn't that important. Not anymore. Mary had found something much better to take her mind off eating.

As she headed for the gigantic master bathroom she considered how, despite its imposing look both from the outside and within some of the rooms, Jake's house seemed warm and inviting. Now she could imagine what Jane Eyre must have felt when she'd first come to Thornfield.

As if she belonged. For maybe the first time in her life.

Hugging herself around the waist, Mary grinned like a fool while walking into the bathroom. She wished for the ability to whistle so that the whole world could see how happy she was. But not a chance. Jolene was the whistler in the family.

After turning on the water for her shower, Mary took a moment to glance around the room. Expecting to see a mess, towels on the floor and water everywhere, she was surprised to see that Jake must have straightened up after both of them last night and after himself this morning.

The man was neat, and the most tender and exciting lover imaginable—and he could cook.

Jake was too good to be true. But that thought stopped her cold. Hadn't Jane Eyre also felt the same about Rochester, her true love and the hero of the book?

But Jane Eyre's love story had been rocky and miserable. She'd found out that her hero was secretly married.

Mary stepped under the shower spray, absently mulling over what her gut instincts had been telling her where Jake was concerned. She had so little experience in the man department that she feared being hasty.

She sensed that Jake was good. Deep-down good. Unlike some of the men in her life up to now. But there was *something*...

As if he were two people, Mary decided as she ran the bar of soap along her chest and belly. Yes, the wonderful-lover-and-good-man side to him had certainly captured her heart. She was far enough gone over that part of him that she almost couldn't remember what had been nagging at her subconscious about his other side.

But then it came to her. Most of the time when Jake looked at her, it was with a combination of heat and tenderness. But on occasion she spotted some emotion in his eyes that didn't match either his words or his actions. Wishing she had enough experience to figure out what that emotion was, Mary finished her shower and dried off, still considering it.

She had seen that look somewhere else besides in his eyes, on someone else—a long time ago. But where? Traipsing back through the bedroom and searching for her clothes, Mary kept sifting through her memories. That look—it was familiar. But...

She suddenly remembered. Her big sister Lucy's eyes had carried that exact same look whenever she'd been feeling guilty about something. As a kid, Lucy was always doing one thing or another that she'd ended up regretting in the end. Stealing Mary's toys when they were little. Stealing a boy Mary had her eye on in junior high. Lying to their mother and father about seeing Damien in high school.

Now that Mary thought it over, the expression was definitely guilt. But Mary didn't have a clue what Jake could be feeling guilty about. Hmm. That wasn't totally true. It could be he was feeling a little guilt over being her first lover. But guilt about taking her virginity was nonsense. She'd begged him. Wanted him to be the one.

Mary hoped with all her heart that wasn't his reason for feeling guilt. But *if* it wasn't, the other possibilities seemed scary. What if he was lying to her about not being married?

A shudder ran along her spine as she finished buttoning up her blouse. She hated the idea, but maybe when she returned to work, she should look him up on the Internet despite her earlier reservations about being sneaky.

Just to prove that he was telling the truth, mind you.

Sitting in a rocker on the house's wide veranda, Jake hung up his secure SAT phone and took a sip from his coffee mug. Grateful the coffee was still warm in the chilled morning air, he looked out at the tangle of pines, Douglas firs and shrub brush surrounding the house.

The entire area encompassing the house had been landscaped with native plantings, making the place look like a mountain ski resort. But at the moment he would've preferred a rolling grass lawn where one could easily see out to every inch of ground. A moment ago he'd finished speaking to his partner Jim about the incident on the road last night and was told that a security alarm team would have to be sent from the Denver field office. It could take days, if not a full week, to free up a team.

Jake knew how alarm systems worked and probably would've been able to install a system himself, but he didn't have the necessary equipment. Frustrated, he wondered how long he could go on like this. Undercover life was no kind of life anymore. He felt as if he'd been living in purgatory for the past few years—neither in heaven nor hell. Just living.

Mary came to mind and Jake tried to will away her image. His guilt on her account had become debilitating. His mind would barely focus on the investigation. What good was a covert agent who couldn't keep his head in the game?

Last night with Mary had shaken him. Consumed him. Not only the sex—past his compulsion where Mary was concerned and way beyond the guilt, he'd glimpsed heaven in her bed.

How was he supposed to walk away from that and go back to purgatory? The need to possess her—to be possessed—had transported him right out of the realm of murderers and money-laundering schemes. He had even ignored whatever rules he'd vowed to follow as a covert government agent. Mary dominated him, mind and body, as she'd begged him to take her again and again.

She had given him the biggest gift of his life—hope. Hope that he could actually love another woman. For ten long years, he'd been positive that for him love was only in the past. That Tina had been it for him.

Tina was the love of his life. She'd brought him out of his shell and turned him into a man who could be charming and make friends. She was his partner, his lover, his coach and his most ardent cheerleader.

When she'd died in that car wreck, Jake had thought his life was over. He'd buried himself in his new job as a covert operative—living other people's lives.

Now…now, Mary's sharp intelligence and loving ways had brought him back to life. Back to giving a damn about what he did and whom he hurt.

And what would come of all this life and hope he was feeling? In the end, he would be forced to walk away from her. If for no other reason than that when Mary discovered the truth about his lies, she would never speak to him again. He couldn't blame her, but it would kill him just the same.

"Jake?" Mary stuck her head out of the front door and spied him sitting at the far end of the long veranda. "There you are. I thought I'd lost you."

As she smiled and walked toward him, Jake's heart knew the truth. He loved her—desperately. If all things were equal, he would tell her the truth right now and take his punishment. But things weren't equal in this case. Mary's life was on the line.

He'd already arranged for someone to keep an eye on her when he couldn't. But despite his assignment, he wanted to be the only one who was her protector. No one could do the job the way he could. He would never recover if any disaster befell Mary. With Tina, it had taken years. This time he knew it was worse for him.

Knowing that, he could not. Would not. Let anything happen.

"Breakfast is on the stove," he said as she came close. "You're getting a late start on the morning. What do you have in mind for today?"

Her bottom lip stuck out slightly and it made him chuckle to see her looking petulant. "I would've liked another hour or two in bed—with you."

Standing, he took her into his arms. The kiss he gave her was slow, warm, with a definite promise of things to come. He wanted her to feel what he felt. Wanted to pour out his love through his kiss—his touch. But he knew she needed words. Words he could not give her.

When he let her go and set her back from him, she looked up with glassy eyes. "That's not helping. It only makes me want to go back to bed all the more."

"Ah, but it's going to be a beautiful day." He forced the covert agent inside him to regain control of the situation. "No rain for a change and temperatures will be more like summer. Let's go to town. I want to talk to the sheriff about that attempt on our lives last night."

"It's not Wes's jurisdiction. That cliff was nearly a hundred miles north."

"Yes, I know. But I believe the driver was someone from Honey Creek, don't you? I find it too coincidental that a perfect stranger would want to shove us off the side of a cliff. The assault on us must be connected somehow to your father's murder and the sheriff should know about it."

Mary was shaking her head. "But why? I've thought and thought and I can't come up with a reason why anyone would want me…us dead. It's almost as if someone heard us talking about suspects. But that's not possible."

Jake ran with it. "Maybe it is possible. I don't remember every place where we talked about the murder. We could've accidently mentioned it in public."

Mary was quiet for what seemed like a long time. "I'm hungry. Let's eat and then you can take me home. I want to change clothes."

"After that, will you come with me to see Wes?"

Mary touched his chin as though she was fascinated with his stubble—with him. "Of course. But only if you shave first. I don't want everyone in town to think I have a scruffy boyfriend."

His eyebrows shot up at her use of the quaint term. "Am I your boyfriend?"

Grabbing his hand, she dragged him inside toward the kitchen. "That's exactly what you are."

No. No he wasn't. He was a liar on a mission. And it was a frigging disaster that he couldn't tell her the damned truth.

"Too bad your mother wasn't at the farm while we were there this morning. I would've liked to meet her."

Not that Jake thought for one moment that Jolene Walsh would arrange to kill her own daughter. But she could very well be up to her neck in the money-laundering scheme. And, after all, that was what his investigation was all about.

Keeping his eyes on the road ahead, he waited for Mary's reply. He had several people in mind as potential suspects for involvement in the international money-laundering operation he'd been sent to Honey Creek to investigate. Jolene was only one of them.

Mary sat straight up in her seat. "You would like to meet my mom?" He could feel her grinning all the way across the front seats of his SUV. "I want you two to meet. But Mom usually works at the family business office in the mornings. In the afternoon, she takes care of Patrick, my brother Peter's little boy, after school. Maybe we can catch her at one place or the other later."

Jake nodded. He had a great interest in gaining access to the Walsh business offices. All he needed was a few minutes alone with one of their computers.

Pulling the SUV into the lot belonging to the sheriff's office, Jake noted that the small redbrick building, situated on the frontage road, was typical of small-town sheriffs' offices throughout the West.

"Are we sure Wes will be in?" Mary undid her seat belt and hesitated with her hand on the door handle.

"Yeah. I called his office while you were changing. The secretary…or dispatcher, whoever answered the phone, said he would be in the office doing paperwork all morning."

Mary opened her door, but Jake spoke before she could step out. "Wait there," he demanded.

She turned her head to look at him but he was already heading around the front of the truck. "It's the boyfriend's job to help his girlfriend out of the vehicle."

Mary laughed and the sound tingled inside his chest. "Vehicle? You sound like a cop. But I like the general idea."

He fitted his hands around her waist and lifted her to

the ground. Golden sunshine sparked in her hair on this cloudless day and made him think of burnished copper pans. The mere sight of her many ripe colors glowing in the sunlight made his gut tremble.

"Thank you," she told him demurely. "I've been on my own a long time. It may take me a while to get used to considering someone else."

"I'm not worried. We've got time." And he would burn in hell for that statement along with all the other lies.

Jake took her by the hand and marched toward Wes Colton's office. Somehow he was going to finish this investigation in record time, and Colton had best find his murderer in record time, too.

When Jake was ready to leave town and disappear back into covert life, he wanted no chance of Mary being hurt by some panicked murderer with nothing to lose. Everything had to be wrapped up here before he left.

Yeah? And how was he supposed to wrap up his love for her then? Not such a simple thing. Nearly impossible, in fact. Sighing inwardly, he supposed he wouldn't even bother to try. He'd better get used to the idea of living without her.

"I'll be back in a few minutes, Jake. I want to step outside and call my mother. I need to ask where we can meet her today."

Mary hesitated at the door to Wes Colton's office. She'd given him her statement. But she couldn't add much to what Jake had already told him. Neither of them had seen the driver of the truck or gotten a glimpse of the plates. Jake said the truck was probably long gone by now and Wes agreed.

Still, the idea that someone had tried to kill them occupied too much of her thoughts. Mary would much rather be thinking of Jake and trying to decide if they had a future together. She wished she could be like her sister and her best friend, holding back and not jumping ahead into a relationship too fast. But Jake kept spinning her head around with his kisses and those longing looks.

"That's fine, Mary." The reply came from Wes. "I have a couple more things to ask Jake anyway. But don't wander too far away from the front door."

"You think someone might try to hurt me here? Right in front of the sheriff's office?" She was aghast.

Wes opened his mouth, but Jake answered first. "No one knows. That's the whole point. When I'm not around, you watch out for yourself. Keep your eyes open, and try not to be alone for any longer than is necessary. I don't want anything happening to you."

She nodded at him and turned away. But his words made her feel stupidly happy as she stepped out into the brilliant, sunshine-filled day.

"So you believe your cover is blown?" Wes leaned back in his desk chair with a thoughtful look on his face.

The sheriff was taller and broader than Jake, and maybe a couple of years younger. But Jake's instincts told him Wes would turn out to be a good ally.

"Not necessarily," Jake hedged. "It's possible the assault was not about me, but it could've been someone who wants to harm Mary. I'm trying to get her to confide in me. Maybe somewhere in her subconscious she has information that could be dangerous to her."

Wes wiped his hand across his mouth as though his next words would be distasteful. "I'm not comfortable with you using Mary Walsh this way. It's obvious she's infatuated with you. You can see it in her eyes. And she…has no experience to fall back on.

"I've always liked Mary," Wes added. "I don't want to see her hurt."

"I like Mary, too," Jake told the sheriff truthfully. "A lot. I was deadly serious when I said I didn't want anything happening to her."

With elbows on his knees, Jake hung his head for a moment, trying to decide how much to tell Wes about his true feelings. "I've got a big problem with Mary, Colton. I care for her. I didn't mean to, but I…

"Well, let's just say she's special," he finished. "But I believe she is in real danger. I'm not sure whether I brought the trouble down on her or not." Like hell. He knew his presence in Honey Creek had contributed to Mary's troubles.

Wes shook his head; he wasn't as positive as Jake. "What's the problem? Tell her who you are and what you're doing in Honey Creek. You know she's not involved with either the murder or the money-laundering scheme. Maybe if you were truthful with her, she might be willing to help you."

"Believe me…" Jake pursed his lips to keep from shouting out his frustration at the situation.

He counted to ten and then said, "I've thought of that a thousand times over the past couple of days. But even if I broke cover for her, I know enough about Mary now to know she could never forgive the lies. I started out on the wrong foot with her—lying to her and keeping her in dark. And now I'm paying for it."

Wes took a deep breath. "I see. You do care for her and you're in a hard place right now. But when this assignment is over… What then?"

"Tell her the truth and beg her to forgive me." Jake opened his hands, palms up as though he needed forgiveness from the whole world. Maybe he did.

"She won't," he continued. "But at least I have to try. And in the meantime, I intend to protect her with my life."

"Yeah, that's a damned hard rock you're sitting on." The expression on Wes's face was sympathetic. "Can I do anything to help?"

"Find the murderer, Colton. I have a feeling he or she is the one also targeting Mary."

"You have any suggestions along that vein?"

Jake started to shake his head, but then he said, "It's occurred to me that if Mark Walsh was such a playboy, there might be a couple of spurned women out there who would gladly have taken his life."

"Yeah?" Wes made a note on the legal pad sitting on his desk. "Well, there're a few women right here in Honey Creek that had both a motive and the means."

Jake cleared his throat, knowing this one was going to be tough. "Have you considered Jolene Walsh as a murder suspect? I mean, talk about a woman spurned. Not to mention that she might be very glad to get rid of her supposedly dead husband in order to take up with his best friend."

Nodding, Wes said. "She's right on top of the list. But you haven't met her yet, have you?"

"Not yet."

"She's one of the least threatening people I've ever known." Wes chopped the air with his hand as if that was a pure truth. "Look, some members of my family have been pissed at her and Craig Warner for fifteen long years because of my brother Damien's incarceration. But I'm absolutely positive she had nothing to do with that one."

Wes tilted his head for a second as though he was considering his next words. "My gut says she didn't do the crime this time, either. But I intend to eliminate her as a suspect the right way. With facts. For your sake, I hope I'm right."

"For my sake?"

"I can't imagine how hard that would be—watching the woman you love find out her mother is a murderer."

Love. Jake had never mentioned the word but somehow Wes had known.

Wes was right. Seeing Mary's faith in her mother dissolve would be tough. Just as tough as if he proved Mary's mother was involved in racketeering and money-laundering.

Jake swallowed the truth down hard, and found himself wishing he was anywhere else but in the middle of this mission. It might cause the death of him yet.

Chapter 9

"I'm sorry, Mare." Craig Warner sat behind a desk piled high with work and looked up at Mary through reading glasses. "Your mother had to run a couple of errands and couldn't wait for you."

"But I talked to her on the phone a little while ago." Mary heard a whine in her voice and fought it. "And she said for us to meet her here at the office."

Disappointed, Mary sat against the armrest of a leather office chair and waited for Craig's explanation. Craig looked especially good today. His crisp navy-blue suit went well with his salt-and-pepper hair and chestnut-brown eyes. But he was such a dear that she thought it could be his warm goodwill making him look so handsome.

Mary wasn't sure what she would've done without Craig Warner after her father had supposedly died the first time. He'd stepped up and became a father figure to all the Walsh kids. If only he'd been her real father, her whole life would've been much different.

Craig folded his hands on the desk and looked over the rim of his glasses. "Your mom won't be too long. But she wanted to know if you and your…friend…would like to join us for lunch today. We're both eager to meet him." Craig looked behind her toward the open door. "Where is he?"

"Jake's waiting in Mom's office. I didn't want to miss her in case she was only across the way at the brewery and would be right back. I figured we'd catch her one place or the other."

Craig nodded. "Listen, it's almost noon. Why don't the three of us ride out to the farm together to meet your mother? Your friend Susan should be delivering a catered lunch for all of us about now."

"Oh, yum. I love Susan's cooking." Things were definitely looking up. "Will she still be there when we arrive?"

"No, sorry again. Susan said she had a million things to do today. You'll have to settle for your mother and me."

Mary chuckled, glad that she had so many people in her life that loved her. Her mother, Craig, Susan…and now Jake?

He had not said a word about love. But perhaps that was one of those *man* things she still didn't understand. Of course, she hadn't told him she loved him, either. Mary felt unsure of herself—of him.

Well, she tried to think on the bright side, he was here now. If it didn't last, she would be okay. She hoped. But meanwhile, she intended to take advantage of him—every chance she got.

Jake barely had the time to replace the back of the computer before Mary and Craig came to get him for lunch. He'd managed to plant a wireless transmitter that could access all the computers in the office. His partner could capture not only everything now on the computer's hard drive, but also everything placed on it at a later date.

This part of his mission had taken a court order, but Jake had no intention of announcing that fact to the potential suspects. He also had another court order in his pocket for planting a transmitter in a different office in another part of Honey Creek. But he wasn't even close to figuring out how to access that one yet.

"It's really nice to meet you, son." Craig Warner gave him a curt smile and shook his hand. "I'm sorry Jolene isn't here, but she can't wait to meet you. Are you ready for a fantastic lunch?"

"I'm always ready to eat, sir. Is Mary's mother a good cook?" He took a deep breath and smelled the pervasive odor of hops coming from the brewery. That sweet molasseslike smell was hard to miss.

Both Mary and Craig laughed at his question and he noted both their eyes crinkled at the corners in the same way. They didn't look like father and daughter, but many of their mannerisms were the same.

"My mother can barely boil water," Mary told him. "But she has other good qualities."

Jake chuckled along with them, trying to match his demeanor to theirs. "Well, then, who's cooking the meal?" He hoped it wouldn't be him. He needed the time to do a little covert snooping and for asking pointed questions.

"Come on," Mary said as she took his arm. "We'll tell you all about it on the way."

Sitting across the table from Craig and Jolene, Jake paid close attention to them for any deception cues. But so far, neither had showed any of the usual signs. He wasn't a world-class detector of liars like those on TV, but he'd been trained by the best of them. With these two suspects, he hadn't noticed even one sweaty palm nor had either touched their forehead tentatively. They never even looked down into their plates. Not once, through the entire long lunch and conversation afterward. They'd both been all smiles and appeared to be trying to please their daughter's new lover. If one or both of them was a liar, they were damned good at it.

Jake kept the conversation steered in the direction of Mark Walsh's murder. Everyone at the table had an opinion to share on the subject of Mark Walsh. But Craig and Jolene were not as gracious as Mary had been on the subject of the dead man. Still, neither of them seemed to hate the man enough to murder him.

The longer he sat with Craig and Jolene and enjoyed their company, the more he was coming to believe Wes Colton's declaration. Jolene Walsh possessed a nonthreatening personality. In some ways she reminded him of Mary. Sweet. Unassuming. Intelligent. But without her daughter's biting wit and sure mind.

He could easily picture Mark Walsh or someone else just as strong manipulating her into assisting with a money-laundering scheme.

As he studied her, he noted that Jolene also had the

same coloring as her daughter. Mary's earnest amber eyes and long red hair were mirrored in the woman sitting across the table. But unlike Mary's, Jolene's beauty was delicate. Almost vulnerable.

On the other hand, Craig seemed happy enough with Jolene. Every once in a while in the middle of the conversation, Craig's hand would sneak over and give Jolene's hand a tender squeeze.

Jake was about to come to the conclusion that if anyone in this room could've been a murderer, it was Craig. Passion swam in Craig's eyes whenever he looked at Jolene. And Jake knew extreme passion could sometimes be a precursor to violence.

Despairing of ever learning anything helpful to his mission from this couple, he said, "It's been a terrific lunch. But don't you two have to return to work?"

"I'm due to babysit my grandson this afternoon after school." Jolene beamed as though the idea itself was as grand as the boy. "I'll drop Craig off at the office on my way into town."

Jolene scooted her chair back and stood before either Craig or himself could assist her. "Mary, before I leave," she said, "I'd like to show you a couple of outfits that I bought for you today. Can you come with me to your bedroom?"

Mary raised her eyebrows as though the idea of new clothes was a surprise, but she followed her mother down the hall.

"I'm glad we have a moment alone, Jake." Craig stood next to the table beckoning Jake to follow him into the family room.

Jake figured this was going to be yet another lecture

about not hurting Mary similar to the one Wes had given. He was ready for it. Deserved it.

Craig sat on the sofa and Jake sat in the lone armchair across from him.

"Mary's mother and I are pleased by your attention to her daughter," Craig began as he leaned forward. "It's time Mary found someone. Jolene once imagined her youngest daughter might never find anyone who would appreciate how special she is. Your appearance at this critical time is almost too good to be true."

Jake nodded but could hear the *but* in Craig's voice and knew what was coming next. "Yes, sir. Mary has grown to mean a lot to me in the short time I've known her."

"Yes, I'm seeing that in your eyes whenever you look at her. That's why I think you should know something about her past that she might not be willing to share."

Uh-oh, this lecture was going to start with the our-daughter-is-a-virgin speech.

Jake tried to head it off. "It's not necessary. But thanks for the thought anyway. I believe it would be better if Mary tells me whatever she wants me to know." That sounded like something a loyal boyfriend would say, didn't it?

"In most cases I would agree with you, son. But Mary may not even be admitting this to herself. You see, Mark Walsh was…"

Jake held his tongue and waited for the *a difficult man* comment. But he didn't get it.

"A bastard. And a terrible father. Especially to the two girls. When they were young, before he disappeared, Mark would take every opportunity to belittle them in public. Make them look small and appear to be selfish brats when they were anything but. And I'm fairly positive he also terrorized them at home."

"He was abusive?"

Craig shook his head softly. "I could never prove any physical abuse. Mary and Lucy never showed any marks and neither ever spoke up. But I'm sure he emotionally stunted both of them."

"Did Jolene ever mention problems at home? Why didn't she do something to stop it?"

"I don't think Jolene actually knew what was going on when she wasn't around. She always worked long hours at the brewery and I believe she may have closed her eyes to what her husband was doing. Both inside and outside the house.

"It's Mary that I have always worried about the most," Craig continued. "Puberty is hard enough to live through without having the person who you most want to love you chipping away at your self-esteem day after day. Mary took it the hardest. She withdrew into her books and found comfort in food. And I…"

Craig hesitated, took a deep breath of air. "I couldn't save her. By the time Mark disappeared it was too late for Mary. By then, none of us could reach inside her shell."

Jake was taken aback for the moment, then it began to make sense. "She said she went to a shrink for help losing weight. Did she go for more than that?"

"I'm sure she did. She's changed a lot in the past few years. Gotten stronger, more self-assured. I hardly ever see that frightened look in her eyes anymore."

Shaken, Jake didn't want to consider what Mary's secret background could mean for his mission. Or what his mission might mean to Mary's well-being when it was over—and he was long gone.

He stood on shaky legs but managed to speak in a strong voice. "Thank you. I'll keep what you said to myself, but I appreciate the heads-up."

"I love Mary, Jake. I love all the Welsh siblings as if they were my own children. But Mary has always been the most emotionally fragile. She seems happy for the first time that I can remember and I don't want any big surprises to come between you."

If Craig only knew, Jake thought sullenly. The biggest surprise of all was yet to come. A terrible storm cloud brewed on their horizon. And there was not a single thing he could think of to stop it.

Mary tilted her head to look at Jake's profile as he drove the SUV back home. She was so pleased with how the afternoon had turned out that she wanted to shout it to the world. Her mother and Craig had gone out of their way to make Jake feel at home and welcome.

The only small glitch in her day had come when her mother had reminded her to go slow with Jake. Jolene told the story of her own first love affair, and how that had been a whirlwind romance, too. It was how she'd ended up with Mark Walsh.

Yes, that none-too-subtle reminder had definitely rained on Mary's good mood. But she'd already been thinking along those same lines. The only problem with going slow was that when she and Jake were together, her mind seemed to take a nap. From there, her body jumped ahead and did all the racing.

As she stared over at him now, she realized that Jake didn't look pleased at all. He clenched and unclenched his jaw. A vein stood out at his temple. Was he mad at her for some reason? Mary felt a shudder of panic, wondering if Craig had said something while she'd been out of the room.

"Are you okay?" she asked, not knowing how else to start.

"What?" He slipped her a glance. "Oh, sure. I'm concerned about an alarm system for the house, is all. I called and they can't send anyone out here right away."

She heaved a relieved sigh. "I suppose you could stay at the farm until the system is installed—if you want. I'm sure my mom wouldn't mind." Mary hoped Jake would say no, but she'd needed to make the offer.

A chuckle rumbled up in his throat. "And you would be staying in your bedroom and I could stay in the guest room? Is that what you want?"

She shook her head vigorously enough that it nearly flew off her neck. "No!"

He removed one hand from the wheel and intertwined his fingers with hers. "Thank God."

After that, his expression lightened. The lines across his forehead relaxed and the corners of his mouth curved up in one of his charming smiles.

Mary would've dearly loved to lean over and plant a kiss on each of those corners. And on a lot of other places as well. It was a good thing they were almost at Jake's house.

Clearing her throat, she forced herself to think about another subject in the meantime. "Remember when I was talking about you coming to one of Mom's parties? Well, guess what? Mom came up with the same idea. I didn't even have to mention it to her."

Jake nodded absently. "That sounds nice. When would it be?"

"Tomorrow night. She wants to throw a big barbecue out in the farmyard and invite most of the town to meet you. You don't mind, do you?"

"Not at all. I'm one of the best grilling chefs you'll ever meet. Barbecue is one of my specialties."

He hesitated for a second as he maneuvered the SUV into his long driveway. Then he added, "That also means I have you all to myself for tonight—and nothing could make me happier."

The look in his eyes as he'd made that comment was unmistakable. Heat ran along her nerve endings and nearly boiled the blood in her veins.

Okay, she thought as she jumped out of the SUV and headed for the front of the house. Now she really couldn't wait to get inside.

Still conflicted about his role in Mary's life, Jake barricaded them inside the house and fought his hormones. All afternoon and through the early evening he distracted them both in the kitchen with talk of the upcoming barbecue and with testing good grilling sauces and rubs.

All that time, Mary kept making it very clear what she would rather be doing. He was right there with her in spirit, but he wasn't sure his conscience could take much more.

Then a little while ago, Mary had disappeared. At first he hadn't been too worried. But he'd only now noticed she was being too quiet and started to worry. She'd better not have left the house. In his gut he could feel the danger lurking outside in the dark woods.

After checking the doors and both wings of the house for any sign of her, Jake reluctantly climbed the stairs. How could he ever hope to resist her? There was no hope.

Deep in his psyche, he knew what was right and what was wrong. And he'd been wrong since the very first night they had ever made love. To keep on making the same mistake over and over seemed insane.

But that was just it. He'd lost his mind where Mary was concerned. In the middle of a mission he'd begun to wish he was in another occupation. Anything else. Covert work had long ago lost its appeal. Now he couldn't wait to forget the Bureau and everything it had come to represent. If only he had changed jobs before he'd met Mary.

Knowing he was thinking crazy thoughts, Jake hit the top of the stairs trying to find some logical excuse for not sleeping in the same bed with her. His hands fisted at the mere thought.

After peeking into a couple of spare bedrooms, he found them as empty as he'd imagined. At last, he lightly pushed open the master bedroom door and prayed he would find her fast asleep on the king-size bed.

The sheets had been turned down, but Mary was nowhere in sight. Then he heard the shower running. He frowned at the bathroom door and his mind drifted into some kind of trance.

He walked toward heaven, shedding his clothes as he went. It was too late for him. Now that he'd tasted her, he couldn't stay away. No other woman had ever made him this hungry. This desperate.

Naked, he eased open the bathroom door. "Mary?" When he got no response, he walked over to the shower, pulled back the curtain and stepped in beside her.

"Jake! You scared me. Is anything wro—?"

He cut off her words by taking hold of her shoulders and lasering a kiss across her lips. Startled, she squeaked under his demanding moves. Almost immediately though, her body turned to soft, warm butter and she threw her arms around his neck.

Yes, he thought. They needed each other tonight. Why keep fighting it?

Deepening the kiss, he felt his heart racing as he turned his back to the warm spray and hugged her closer. Her skin was smooth. Wet. Hot. When she flattened her breasts against his chest and curled one long leg around one of his, Jake's body went impossibly hard.

Dragging her mouth from his, she looked at him with burning, bright eyes. "Help me. I don't know what to do."

He folded his hands under her bottom and backed them both up to the tile. "Wrap your legs around my waist, I'll do the rest."

As he entered her in one swift move, her moans echoed off the bathroom walls. Her head fell back and she tightened her legs around him, making the taut, sweet sensation of being inside her nearly unbearable.

He nipped at her neck, feeling the fire race under his skin. Her fingernails bit into his shoulders as he thrust once. And again. And again.

Too close to hold off any longer, Jake was grateful when her shudder rolled through him and her body pulsated around him. With a groan, he followed her over with one last thrust.

Gasping for air, he let her loose to slide down his

body and find her footing on the porcelain tub. But he kept his arms tightly around her as she sagged against him.

Reaching through the steamy spray, he turned off the water, but held her close for one more beat of his heart. Then he gathered her up in his arms and took her to his bed.

Outside in the dark, under a canopy of pines, the man known as the Pro trained his night-vision goggles on the second floor. Piece of cake.

His efforts of earlier this morning were about to pay off big. No one inside had any inkling of the danger they were in.

The new little game he was playing with them had turned out to be fun after all. Scaring a lawman off would take more than a couple of attempts. But this attempt would be a masterpiece.

Another couple of hours to wait. To be sure they were fast asleep.

Fingering the special cell phone he carried in his pocket, the Pro could hardly wait to place the call. The target would never know what had hit him. All of a sudden hell would surround the two of them in a wall of flames.

Maybe the guy would escape. Or maybe he wouldn't. The Pro didn't much care one way or the other.

Chapter 10

Jake watched as Mary crept down the stairs in front of him. It was late and they'd deliberately left off all the lights. He would've much preferred to still be in their warm bed. But not Mary.

"Come on," she whispered with a giggle. "I'm starving. We forgot to eat dinner."

"Late-night snacking isn't good for you." It was a half-baked attempt at coaxing her back to bed, but he knew it wouldn't work.

"You're as bad as my therapist. All right, I'll eat celery and run an extra mile tomorrow. I just need something in my stomach or I won't sleep." She wrapped his terry robe tighter around her waist and went up on tiptoes to dance down the stairs.

"We could turn on the lights," he grumbled.

"This way is more fun. I guess you've never been to a slumber party."

Yes, he had. Every time they slept together was a party. He was becoming more and more addicted to it every day.

Grateful that he'd stopped upstairs long enough to put on a pair of jeans, Jake wished he'd also taken the time to slip into a pullover sweater. It was damned cold in here.

Mary was nearing the bottom of the stairs when she stopped dead. "I smell…"

In the glow coming from the kitchen nightlights, Jake saw Mary turning back to him. "It smells like smoke in here," she whispered.

"Maybe it's coming from outside. Sometimes the wind shifts and the scent of a neighbor's chimney smoke seeps in late at night."

"No…" Mary tentatively stepped down on the wood-planked floor.

She looked to the right, toward the kitchen and the western wing of the house. Then, she turned left.

"Jake, something's on fire! I see smoke in the family room."

She'd already taken two steps toward the family room before it hit him and he pulled her backward. "Don't go any farther. Run back upstairs, get your cell phone and call the fire department."

"We have 911 service," she said without hesitation. "I'll call."

As she passed him on the way up the stairs, he made a few more demands. "Put on your shoes and grab your purse. Come back downstairs in less than three minutes. It's important."

"But I don't see any flames."

"Just do it."

She nodded and flew up the stairs. Before she was even out of sight, Jake was on his way to the kitchen to retrieve the weapon he had secreted in a floor safe under the stove. He would rather Mary not see where and how he'd hidden the .38, but knew he needed to be armed.

After taking the weapon in hand, he hurriedly checked the chambers. Before his next breath, a small explosion rocked the house. *Mary!* Shoving the .38 into his waistband, he ran toward the sound, praying the explosion had not been on the second floor.

"Jake!"

He saw Mary, stopped on the staircase and staring wide-eyed toward the floor below her. Flames shot outward from the family room toward the stairs and front door. Rivers of fire licked at the bottom of the stairs where she stood.

He opened his mouth to tell her to stay where she was and he would come for her, but she turned and ran back up the stairs before he could get the words out. "Mary, no!" he called after her.

Jake tried to follow her, but blasts of heat and a rain of cinders threatened to sear his clothing. Turning on his heels, he dashed back into the kitchen, put a wet rag to his nose and pulled a ten-pound bag of flour out of the pantry. Back at the stairs, he began pouring the flour on each stair, dousing flames as he went. He tried to keep from succumbing to panic, worrying about Mary upstairs on her own. He had to get to her.

As he began making a dent in the blaze on the lower stairs, Mary appeared right above him. She was covered head to toe by a wet blanket and held another in her hands.

"Here." She bunched up the blanket and threw it down the stairs toward him. Then she covered her face and made a dash for it.

In the distance, Jake could hear a siren. Another soon joined the screeching sounds of the first.

Mary's shoes hit the floor at the bottom of the stairs as she grabbed him by the arm. "Cover up and let's get out of here," she shouted.

Like dozens of tiny fireflies, sparks from the inferno in the family room swirled around in a breeze that had to be coming from an open window. But he hadn't left any windows open or unlocked.

Sounds of the holocaust grew deafening in his ears. Snapping and popping, flames raced along the floorboards and up the walls in fiery ribbons. Smoke curls glided through the air, floating into other rooms and heading up the stairs like living, breathing intruders.

Mary tugged at his arm. "Come on." She started for the front door, but Jake dug in his heels.

She swung on him and a muffled cry reached his ears from under her blanket. "What's the matter with you?"

Wrapping the blanket around his shoulders, he withdrew his .38. "We can't run straight out the front door," he yelled. "It could be an ambush."

"What?" Her eyes opened wide at the sight of the .38. "No way."

He pulled her close, tucked her under the cover of his arm, and headed for the kitchen door. When they reached it, he dragged Mary along with him, flattening them both to the protection of the wall beside the door.

Then he chanced a look outside, searching the grounds nearby. This section of the land had once been used as a kitchen garden and an old six-foot fence protected the entire area. From what he could see in the dark, no one was lying in wait for them within the garden fence.

Clear air prevailed on this side of the house, too. His gut told him the fire must be contained to the family room and the eastern wing of the house. Meanwhile, sirens wailed through the starry night, growing closer by the second. The sounds gave him hope of making it outside without a sniper picking them off.

Tugging Mary along with him, Jake chanced it and dashed for the garden gate. By the time he had unlatched the gate and hidden the weapon under his shirt, blue and white strobe lights were lighting up the entire night sky. Honey Creek's volunteer fire department vehicles and sheriff's cars were already on the scene.

Jake finally relaxed enough to let go of Mary and the two of them ran out to meet the firemen. Fire trucks had already been set up and the firemen were preparing to roll out the hose from one of the pumper trucks.

A pretty blonde woman in a heavy fireman's jacket and hard hat greeted them in the front yard. "Are you hurt? Is anyone else in the house?"

"We were alone and I think we're both okay, Melissa." Mary swiveled to Jake. "You're not burned, are you?"

He coughed and felt his lungs screaming in protest.

"Come with me," the blonde told him. "A little oxygen should help that cough."

"I don't need oxygen. I want to help with the fire."

"Me, too," Mary chimed in. "What can we do?"

The blonde woman studied him up and down and

seemed to come to a decision. "Let's go check with the chief. He's manning the com system."

Within two hours, the fire chief was sifting through ashes inside the still-smoldering remains of the family room. Accompanied by the sheriff, Jake stepped carefully through charred ruins to join him.

Glancing over his shoulder, Jake checked on Mary. She sat on the back of one of the fire trucks with a Mylar blanket over her shoulders, while someone poured her a hot drink from a thermos. The blonde, Melissa Kelley, stood beside her. It turned out that Melissa was a volunteer paramedic for the Honey Creek fire department and the sister of Mary's best friend Susan.

Jake's mind flashed back a couple of hours to Mary, her image reflected by the raging blaze, as she'd used a garden hose to wet down the perimeter of the house. Hot and grimy, Mary had been absolutely spectacular in her borrowed equipment as she'd fought to keep the blaze from spreading.

She was sure something. Not once during the entire emergency had she complained or been too scared to help. An impressive strength of spirit came shining through her otherwise timid and studious demeanor. Jake was impressed by her actions and by her bravery in the face of danger.

He'd thought before that he was falling in love, but now he was hopeless. He had never met anyone like her and doubted he ever would.

"What do you think, little brother?" Wes asked the fire chief when they came close enough to speak.

"Arson. No question." The chief turned to Jake, removed his glove and shook his hand. "Name's Perry

Colton. Wes tells me you and Mary Walsh just made it out with your lives."

Another Colton brother. Jake sifted through his memories of the family's facts. He recollected six Colton brothers altogether. Most of them were not under suspicion, and like Wes, Perry Colton was definitely one of the Coltons he'd put in the cleared column.

"I wanted to thank you for your help manning one of the fire hoses," Perry continued. "It's summer and a few of our volunteers are out of town on vacation. We're a little short-handed and it was a blessing that you stepped in."

"No problem." Jake looked around at the charred walls. "How bad was it?"

Perry turned, scanning the scene. "The bulk of the damage was confined to the family room. The blaze was set by someone who knew what they were doing. But whoever did it wasn't aiming to take down the entire house."

Rubbing the back of his neck, Perry continued speaking over his shoulder. "The upstairs is relatively untouched. Not even much smoke damage. The kitchen doesn't smell wonderful, but it should be easy enough to clean up once the rest of the house is secured. Looks to me like someone was only trying to make a point."

Twisting back, Perry confronted Jake. "You have any idea what that point might've been?"

Wes stepped in between them and his tone of voice became more professional than the one he had been using. "Are you personally going to collect the arson evidence? Or are you planning on calling in the state investigators?"

Perry stared at his brother with speculation raging

in his eyes. "You know something about this you're not saying, Wes?"

Wes's fists went to his hips. "Listen, Perry, just do your…"

Jake put his hand on Wes's chest to keep him from saying anything more, then turned back to address Perry. "There'll be a special investigation team coming in later this morning to secure the rest of the house and clean up the mess. It would be helpful if you could keep the entire area clear of sightseers until then."

The understanding expression on Wes's face and the way he backed up half a step meant he would defer to the FBI in talking to the fire chief. On the other hand, Perry wasn't ready to concede anything.

"Special investigation team?" Perry's eyes narrowed. "This team gonna have some kind of identification they can give me? Who are you anyway?"

"No one who matters," Jake said in the friendliest tone he could manage. "The team will carry ID—for your eyes only. But nothing they can show for general public consumption. Meanwhile, the sheriff will vouch for me and I would take it as a personal favor if you could keep the team's work here quiet. They'll arrive looking like a regular damage cleanup and alarm-system crew.

"It would also be great," Jake tacked on. "If you could tell the media that on first glance this fire looks accidental."

"We don't have a big media presence here," Perry told him. "Just the Honey Creek *Gazette*. And I think I can hold off the editor for the time being."

"I'd appreciate it." Jake started to walk away but turned back first. "Thanks for everything, chief. Fire-fighting is one hell of an occupation. Thank God there are volunteers in the world like you."

Jake shook Perry's hand again, nodded to Wes and headed off to check on Mary. He could imagine the sort of questions he would be facing from her. But the biggest problem remained. What answers would he, could he, give?

"You're sure your mother doesn't mind if I change clothes at the farm? I'm pretty grungy." Jake drove down the long driveway toward the farm as the sun broke through the clouds at midmorning.

"*You're* grungy?" Mary tried not to touch anything inside Jake's SUV. "Look at me. I have twigs and knots in my hair that may never come out. My clothes and shoes are hopeless and will have to be pitched. And I smell like the inside of a chimney. If she finds out, Mom shouldn't care which of us makes the biggest mess."

She'd tried to convince Jake to let someone else drive her home, but he wouldn't hear of it. Ever since the fire had broken out last night, he'd been keeping her in sight constantly.

Mary wanted to believe his motives were pure. That he had been disturbed by the fire and by his fear of her being killed, and he'd needed to keep her nearby in order to assure himself of her safety.

She wanted to believe that.

But then she remembered how he'd magically produced a gun last night and had looked very much like someone who knew how to use it. Curiosity sneaked into her mind at odd moments and caused her extreme anxiety. Why hadn't he told her about the gun before?

Mary tried to talk to him about it earlier. But he'd put her off, saying he didn't want to talk around strangers.

So, she tried again. "You never explained where the gun came from last night. And where is it now? Did you leave it back in the house?"

Jake set his jaw for a moment and she was afraid he wouldn't talk to her. Finally he said, "I keep a gun for protection. It's fairly isolated out there where I live."

"It's isolated here at the farm, too," she argued as he pulled up in the front yard. "But we don't have any guns.

"Well, I have to take that back," she said as she remembered the facts. "We do have a couple of shotguns that the boys used to scare foxes away from the chickens. But I keep forgetting about those. I haven't seen them in years."

He parked the SUV and turned off the engine. As she opened her mouth to ask something else, he hopped out and came around the front to her side.

When he opened her door, she asked point-blank, "Jake, where is the gun now?"

"In the duffel I packed before we left the house."

"Here? You brought a gun along with us? But why?"

"It's for protection, Mary. And I didn't want to explain it to the firemen or anyone else who might be digging around inside the house today."

Shaking her head in disbelief, she slid out of the seat and headed toward her front door. Something was just not right about what he'd said. She could tell he was leaving something out—something big.

Mary needed time alone to think things over. They'd been through a lot together. She didn't want to believe

Jake was doing something wrong. But the truth was, he could be involved in anything. He could be a criminal for all she knew.

A shiver went through her as she unlocked the door and let them inside. By the time they reached the living room, she was already praying that she was wrong. If he wasn't exactly who he said he was, then he had to be lying. Maybe about a lot of things.

And she couldn't stand that idea. Please, no. Not Jake.

A short while after she got him situated in the guest bathroom with towels and soap, Mary stripped and stood under a cold shower spray in her own bathroom. She didn't want to think about Jake, but that seemed to be the only thing on her mind.

What was she going to do about him? How did she really feel about him?

Unfortunately, her heart formed a loud and clear answer. She was falling in love with him, despite all her heroic efforts not to rush. She probably had been in love with him from that very first night and had been lying to herself about it all along.

But right from the beginning she had also known he was keeping something from her. She'd thought it might be because he was already married. Making love to a married man would've been disastrous enough. Now she had to wonder if the man could be a criminal of some sort. Perhaps a murderer?

Rubbing shampoo through her hair, Mary considered all she knew of Jake. Her facts were slim. But the feelings…the warm feelings in her heart could be counted in the billions.

She knew it didn't matter as much about the gun.

Jake was a good man deep inside. She couldn't be in love with a criminal. No way.

Mary rinsed off, still trying to make sense of her emotions. She didn't want to fall for a man she didn't really know. It wasn't smart. She could be left hurt and humiliated in the end.

Grabbing a towel and wrapping her wet hair, she came to the conclusion that she needed advice. From her friends. And from her family. She simply wasn't thinking clearly.

"You've got to be kidding," Jake said with a chuckle. "Your mother still plans on throwing us a barbecue tonight? Haven't we had enough of smoke to last us for a while?"

She planted her hands on her hips. "Ha. We have to eat, don't we? And you said your kitchen won't be back in shape for cooking until tomorrow. I don't think Mom heard about the fire, but still, it was nice of her to offer."

Jake needed time alone. He'd been badly shaken by the fire and didn't want anyone to know it. He'd hoped to leave Mary safely with her family tonight while he went back to work on the house. The FBI security team out of Denver was already there, gathering evidence and securing the undamaged parts of the house. He wanted to help with the boarding-up of windows and doors. To clean up the soot. To be alone with his thoughts and daydream about kicking an imaginary arsonist in the balls.

Mary was in far too much danger while she was with him. And she was beginning to ask difficult questions.

He'd reached a point where he needed a few moments of time-out to consider what to do about her.

What he preferred to do was to love her. Protect her. Keep her with him forever. But none of that was going to happen.

Still, he could not keep putting her into the line of fire. Even if that meant telling her the truth, breaking his cover and forfeiting his mission. He knew the truth would likely mean the end of their relationship. Mary would never accept his lies. Not even if they had been told as part of the job.

Jake had much to consider.

"I guess a barbecue will be okay," he hedged. "What'll we have to do to prepare?"

"Not a thing. My mom, Craig and Susan will handle everything. Mom'll be arriving soon to get started."

Jake couldn't think of any good reason to leave Mary here while he went off to think. "Uh. You look tired. Maybe you should catch a nap this afternoon. We didn't get much sleep."

"I'm not tired. But I do need a favor. My hair is an impossible mess. Can you drive me into town to get my hair done?"

"Sure. How long will that take?"

Mary ran her fingers through her hair and frowned down at the fringy ends. "Days. Maybe weeks." Then she laughed. "Just joking. Don't look so horrified. But I will be at the salon for several hours. Do you mind finding something else to do on your own?"

"Not at all." Perfect, he thought.

The two of them were in absolute sync. When

he'd needed time, she needed time. Two hearts magically beating as one? Naw. Too poetic for an undercover agent.

Chapter 11

Mary couldn't wait to close the door to Salon Allegra behind her. Eve Kelley had been cutting her hair for as long as she could remember. But all of a sudden Mary wasn't comfortable in the woman's shop anymore.

It seemed as though Mary wasn't comfortable in her own skin anymore. She'd begun scrutinizing every person she met in the course of her daily life. It was as if everyone in town, everyone she had known her whole life, could be lying.

Whenever she saw anyone, the first thing she did was wonder what they might know about the fire at Jake's. Or—whether they'd been in on her father's murder.

Drawing in a deep breath, Mary let the warmth of a late-afternoon sun temporarily melt away all her suspicions. She turned, but stopped before she could take the first step. Jake was waiting there, leaning casually against a light pole about five feet down the sidewalk.

"You look beautiful," he said without moving. "How do you feel?"

She felt like a woman in love who had reason to stop trusting her man. To stop trusting everybody. That was how she felt.

But she wasn't ready to say anything about it. "I'm okay. How about you? Any aftereffects from the smoke?"

Jake closed the gap between them and took her by the shoulders. "I don't know. I haven't been breathing all day—not until just now. Having you back in my arms has restarted my heart."

He bent his head, touching his lips to hers. His kiss wasn't passionate or as desperate as many of their kisses. But it was so tender and so meaningful that when he finally pulled away and gazed down at her, Mary's eyes were overflowing with unshed tears and her heart was overflowing, too.

Here was something she could trust. Whatever hidden agendas might lie between them, their need for each other seemed sincere and strong. The two of them had no problems in the bedroom—or the family room, or the kitchen—or wherever they could find a quiet place to be alone together.

So why was she ready to tell him goodbye? It seemed crazy. But on occasion she could swear Jake's eyes held the very same message that filled her heart. That the two of them were only together on borrowed time.

Sighing, she took a shaky step back and broke the spell. Just in time.

"Yoo-hoo. Is that you, Mary Walsh?"

Talk about being a little crazy. Maisie Colton appeared out of nowhere and headed straight down the sidewalk toward them. Caught between Jake and the town's weirdest citizen, Mary felt as if she were drowning in quicksand.

Shifting to the other foot, she mentally prepared for the upcoming blast of nuttiness.

"I thought that must be you," Maisie said as she came within striking distance. "But I could hardly believe my eyes. The formerly chubby little Mary Walsh kissing a strange man in public—and in broad daylight, no less. Who would've thought it? Strange happenings keep on coming in this town."

Mary closed her eyes and wished she could fly away.

"The name's Jake Pierson, ma'am." Jake's mellow voice punctured Maisie's screeching and worked like a salve on Mary's nerves. "And it was me who was kissing the gorgeous Miss Walsh, not the other way around," he finished.

Mary's eyes popped open when she heard Jake's words. He stepped in close to her side and folded her arm around his elbow as though they belonged together.

"How very gallant of you, Jake. And I'm Maisie Colton. Of *the* Coltons, you know?"

"Uh-huh. I've already met several of your brothers."

"Oh, them. Bo-o-o-ring." Maisie waved away any more talk of her family. "I was hoping to run into you two. I need your help."

Mary's mouth dropped open. She didn't even like guessing what Maisie might want from them. Eleven years older than Mary, Maisie Colton had meant trouble for as long as Mary could remember. Though she was certainly beautiful, tall, thin, and with startling aqua eyes, in a way, Maisie reminded Mary of one of the witches from the book *The Witches of Eastwick*. Beautiful but deadly.

"I heard about your house burning last night, Jake. Too bad. What—or who—do you suppose could've started it?"

Jake's eyes narrowed slightly as he regarded her. "The fire started in the family room near the fireplace. Fireplaces are known to be an accident waiting to happen."

Mary heard the hedge in Jake's words and wondered if Maisie noticed it, too.

"Right," Maisie said as she flipped her hair. "Well, I called the *Dr. Sophie* TV show again this morning because I figured arson would be the thing that would tip the scales in favor of them doing a piece on Honey Creek for a national audience."

Yep. Maisie had noted Jake's equivocation.

No one else might've caught it, but Mary saw that Jake was having a strange reaction to Maisie's ravings. He straightened up, the corners of his mouth tensed and he took a step back. Jake wasn't happy.

"Did the show seem interested *this* time, Maisie?" Mary wanted Jake to understand that the nutty woman had contacted the show many times in the past with her wild stories. "The last time you called, didn't they ask you not to contact them anymore?"

Maisie's shoulders slumped. "They said the same thing this time. But one of these days they will pay attention to me. Honey Creek is a hotbed of drama. I mean, really. First a murder, then that attack on your friend Susan a few weeks ago, last night's fire and now the town's former wild child has come back to town. We need something like the *Dr. Sophie* show to open things up around here and make people notice."

"What wild child?" Mary was stumped. "What on earth are you talking about?"

"Why, Mary, you should know. The library has supposedly hired Lily Masterson to be your new boss. Can you imagine? Lily Masterson, of all people. I thought we'd seen the last of her years ago."

Jake took Mary's arm and spun them in the other direction on the sidewalk. "Nice meeting you, Maisie. Mary and I are late. We'll see you around."

He whispered in Mary's ear. "Hope you don't mind me being rude to her, but…"

Mary chuckled. "Don't worry about it. Everyone in town knows she's a little unhinged. She's a single mother, and I pity her son. Poor kid is growing up way too soon, what with trying to compensate for his mother."

"How old is he?"

"Around fourteen. Kinda gawky for a teenager, but he's a really nice kid."

Jake made a couple of mental connections and since they were out of earshot, said, "Do you think it's possible she's just crazy enough to kill your father?"

"Definitely. The woman can be downright spooky. I would have to put her up at the top of any possible list of suspects."

Jake wouldn't go that far. He didn't consider Maisie a serious suspect. In his experience, being a little eccentric was not a prerequisite for a murderer. And inviting the media in to inspect your life usually meant you had nothing serious to hide.

But you never knew with nuts who craved publicity.

As they reached his SUV, Jake asked, "What was she saying about your friend being attacked a few weeks ago?"

Mary climbed into the passenger seat. "Susan was attacked by some weirdo. It turned out some man had been stalking her. She ended up in the hospital." Mary shook her head sadly as she buckled up. "The creep was apparently looking for revenge against Susan's new fiancé and put Susan in the middle."

"But she's okay? The stalker was caught, wasn't he?"

Mary nodded. "And everything is back to normal for Susan. Except now she's engaged to be married."

Jake climbed into the driver's seat and buckled in. He didn't want to keep talking about the town's domestic problems. He didn't want to talk about any sort of problems with Mary right now. She had unanswered questions in her mind about him carrying the weapon and warning her about a sniper while they tried to escape from a house fire. Too much discussion about other things might remind her of her doubts.

"I have good news," he said as he gave her a gentle look. "The house should be secured and cleaned up enough for us to stay there tonight. And your mother told me that her plans are all set for the barbecue. We're just going to make it back to the farm in time for last-minute preparations."

He'd been considering what to do about Mary all afternoon while working with the security-alarm team from Denver. But he hadn't yet come up with any specific plan.

Still, he knew things would soon be coming to a head. He'd even called his partner Jim and told him to stay close and be ready for anything.

Jake knew his cover had cracks as wide as the Grand Canyon, and things were closer than ever to the explosion point. More than anything, he needed to protect Mary from the fallout.

"You care about him. I can tell." Susan stood in the farm's kitchen, putting last-minute preparations together for the barbecue while she talked to Mary.

"Yeah, I do. I think I'm falling in love."

"But…" Susan's head shook and strands of her chin-length dark blond hair swung across her face. "What do you know of him? Wes said his background was okay, but what about the man's family?" She used her wrist to move the hair back.

"Jake told me his mother died when he was a kid and that he and his father are estranged. He said he doesn't have any brothers or sisters."

"How about ex-wives? Kids?"

Mary didn't like facing her worst fears. "He told me there weren't any ex-wives or kids, either."

"And you believe him? Guys can say whatever they want."

"How am I supposed to know for sure? He doesn't act like a liar." At least, not really. Mary could feel the tears threatening.

Susan stopped what she was doing and laid a hand on Mary's shoulder. "I don't mean to upset you right before your party, hon. Enjoy yourself and be happy. But tomorrow you and I need to get busy on the computer. We'll find out about his past. If we can't, we can always ask your brother Peter for help with a full investigation."

Mary sniffed and nodded her head. "Thanks. You're such a good friend. I didn't want to involve Peter, or you for that matter. But I don't know what else to do. Mom and Craig and Wes all seem to like Jake a lot. But…"

"I know. Here." Susan handed her a dish full of chicken pieces covered over with a film of clear plastic. "Help carry the meats out to the firepit. And try to forget about your worries at least for tonight. Tomorrow we'll find your answers about his personal life."

Mary nodded and headed for the door, but she couldn't forget. She couldn't forget anything when it came to Jake. Not the way he held her in his arms when the two of them made love. Nor the way he sometimes looked at her as though she had just made all his dreams come true. And she sure as heck couldn't get past the way his eyes sometimes brimmed over with secret pain.

Feeling a nasty ache of suspicion rising once more in her chest, Mary swallowed it down and stepped out into the late-afternoon sunlight. She hoped her fears would be put to rest tomorrow with a few simple strokes of the computer keys. But her gut told her not one thing about the man she loved was ever going to go down easy.

Jake manned one of the grills and kept an open can of beer at hand, trying to look casual. Every person in the entire crowd but one had been over to speak with him as the party carried on into the night. That should've been exactly the way he wanted it. But the one person missing was the only one he considered important. Mary.

She had been avoiding him all evening. Frustration at the impossible situation he'd created for himself quickly turned to outright panic at the thought of leaving her without protection. He couldn't let her simply walk away from him. Not until she understood the whole truth and could accept a bodyguard.

"Hi, Jake. Need any help?" Craig Warner ambled over wearing a barbecue chef's apron.

"No, thanks. Most of the cooking is over. I'll be looking for help with grill-cleaning duty pretty soon."

"I'll see if I can round someone up for you." Craig chuckled and rolled his eyes. "Have you managed to stay out of the way of all the gossip while cooking?"

Jake laughed. "Nope. I've spent most of the night listening to fantastic tales concerning both Maisie Colton and Lily Masterson, who I gather are unwed mothers with secret pasts. But I never would've imagined that a single difficult fact about a person's past would make them interesting enough to talk about for the rest of their lives."

"It shouldn't, but that's the way with small towns."

Jake threw Craig a quick look, then glanced absently back down at the burgers, blackening slowly on the grill. "Want to talk about something else for a change?" Without waiting for an answer, Jake went on, "A few of the people here tonight have hazarded a guess about who killed Mark Walsh. I think that's a question more interesting than gossiping about unwed mothers. Do you have any thoughts on the subject?"

"On who might've killed Mark? It's kind of amusing, actually." But Craig did not seem amused. "I probably have the strongest motives of anyone when you come to think of it."

"What motives are those?"

Craig shrugged a shoulder and looked around to see

if anyone else was close by. "Well, for one, I'm madly in love with his widow—and have been from the moment I first met her over thirty years ago."

"Yeah, I would consider that a good motive."

"You bet she is." Craig set his cup down and began ticking off reasons on his fingers. "For another thing, I could've killed Mark with my bare hands for the way he treated his daughters. Someone should've strung him up by the fingernails long ago.

"And then," Craig rushed on without even taking a breath, "there's the fact that I care a lot about what happens to Walsh Enterprises. Jolene is a hell of a lot better at running the business than Mark ever was. Together, she and I have probably added ten times more value to the outfit than he ever could've. I think the man might've been stealing from his own company. I could've killed him for that alone."

"Those are all good reasons for wanting someone dead but…" Jake eased around to study Craig's expression while the man bad-mouthed his old partner.

"I'm not even getting started yet." Craig lifted his eyes to Jake's and there was no mistaking the hatred. "Mark Walsh couldn't keep his dick in his pants. He humiliated his wife and kids. Stole the youth and joy from a couple of sweet young girls who didn't know any better. And he allowed a man to go to prison because of some perverted scheme he dreamed up for disappearing."

Craig finally wound down. "I could go on, but you get the picture. I'm glad he's dead. I only wish I *was* the one who ended his life."

"Yes, I can see that." Jake could see something else in Craig's eyes, too. An odd kind of weakness.

Up to that moment, he had thought of Craig as a

tough middle-aged man with fire in his belly. Passionate for his woman. Passionate about his business and for the kids he thought of as his own.

Now the spark was missing. A tiny flick of something painful in Craig's eyes said the man was suddenly feeling weak. Interesting, but none of Jake's business.

"Well, I'd better go see if Jolene needs my help," Craig told him. "It's been real nice talking to you, son. I hope you and Mary can make a go of things."

Jake had very little hope in that direction, but he lied again. "Thank you, sir. I hope so, too."

As he watched Craig leave, Jake mentally checked his name off his list of suspects. Not that Jake intended to stop looking into Craig's business records. But as far as murder was concerned, he didn't believe Craig Warner could have hurt anyone—not even a mosquito.

"I guess that takes care of everything," Mary told him an hour later. "All the guests have gone home. Did you have a chance to meet everyone?"

Jake could feel her withdrawal like a knife in the back. She hadn't said anything yet, but he had a feeling Mary would soon be telling him that she needed time to think.

He loved her enough to give her all the time in the world. But he didn't dare. Without protection, without truly understanding the threat, her life could be in grave danger. He had to find a way to convince her to come back to the house with him tonight. Not only had he made sure a state-of-the-art security alarm was installed in the house, but he'd also made arrangements with Jim to help keep an eye on them tonight. Mary was much safer there than she would be here at the farm.

Deep down, Jake had an ulterior motive for wanting her with him. Even beyond the sex. He planned on telling her the truth about himself first thing tomorrow morning when they could plan for her future safety. He had a feeling he knew how Mary would react to the news. But he kept on hoping he was wrong.

At least with the whole truth, she could make her own judgments about how best to stay safe. With help from the FBI. Perhaps she would ultimately decide to take a vacation until the investigation was over. He hoped she would. But it was killing him knowing they couldn't go together.

"Uh, Jake, I've been thinking," she began. "About tonight…"

No. He had to do something. He reached out, took her in his arms and planted a kiss on her mouth that nearly took him to his knees. God, they were good together.

After they both were thoroughly out of breath, he didn't want to let her go. But he finally needed to come up for air.

He quickly said, "Come home with me, Mary. Come home and let me show you how much I love you. I don't think I can adequately explain it in words. But…"

"You…love…me?" Her eyes were wide. Her lips wet and swollen by his kisses.

At this moment, he had never loved anyone more.

"Of course, I love you, my darling. Beyond words. Beyond reason. Please give me a chance to show you."

Confusion swam in her eyes and she bit her lip to make it stop trembling. "All right," she said shakily. "Then let's go on home."

Chapter 12

The professional assassin known as the Pro melded his body to the tree behind him. He was beginning to recognize every twig, branch and rock in these woods. Stationing himself here in the pines for most of the day, he'd watched the comings and goings at the target's fire-bombed house. Not one of the feds swarming the area had been any the wiser to his existence.

All it took to outsmart them was a little luck and a lot of persistence. It so happened that Honey Creek's only part-time plumber lived in the closest neighboring house to the target's. The plumber and his family had gone off to visit in-laws. But when the feds made their usual neighborhood check after the fire, they had not bothered to interview any of the townspeople about the plumber's current whereabouts. The Pro had simply become the plumber. He was even using the plumber's van as a temporary surveillance headquarters.

Watching this house was easy, and what he'd seen instructive. After the firemen left, a team of federal agents showed up to wire the house with alarms and put new security features in place. Meanwhile another unit cleaned up the mess left by the Pro's firebomb. He had catalogued it all from his safe perch.

He hadn't needed to go in search of his targets. He'd known by all the fuss that they were coming back here tonight.

Good thing, he thought as he remembered the last few bits of torn paper in his pocket. He'd received written confirmation that half the final payment for this job had already been wired to his bank account. When he was through here tonight and had received confirmation of the second payment, everything, including paper, phones and weapons, would go up in another puff of smoke. No traces would be left to incriminate either himself or his employer.

This job was fast coming to a close. His employer had at last okayed the kill. The one part of his job that the Pro enjoyed more than any other.

The Pro heard a twig snapping in the forest nearby and turned his head to the sound. Someone else was also sneaking through these woods tonight? But who would dare sneak around the house where a federal agent was staying? No one, with the possible exception of another fed stationed outside to safeguard the inhabitants.

The Pro smiled wryly to himself in the darkness. Oh, good. A new game. Or at least a slightly changed game. Cat and mouse.

Searching through the shadows with his night-vision

goggles, the Pro spotted his unwary competitor as the anonymous fed scoured the woods looking for anything out of place. But the hapless fellow was not about to spot the Pro in time to save himself. Nor the trap headed his way.

Tonight the rules of the game were all in the Pro's favor.

As they slipped into the house through the kitchen door, Mary and Jake could not seem to keep their hands off each other. Mary's heart was fairly bursting with love.

She had never felt this way about any other person. Not even close. Willing to give up anything if that was what he asked, Mary clung to Jake, nestling against his side as he set the new alarm system.

Jake kept one arm around her waist while he used the other to punch in the security code. "Hang on, love. We have all night."

That was what he'd said, but then he tilted his chin and placed a kiss against her temple. A kiss that was gentle, tender. But she felt the pull between them as strong as ever when he lingered, breathing in the scent of her shampoo.

She suppressed a chuckle of pleasure, knowing what was coming next. Longing for it. She was dying to show him how much she loved him.

Jake stopped in the kitchen only long enough to grab a couple of cold drinks and put together a platter of sandwiches her mother had supplied. "We're not making any trips downstairs this time. Tonight I'm keeping you in my bed."

Her whole body sank into his as arm in arm they

headed up the stairs, each carrying refreshments in one hand. Mary refused to look at the ugly, unpainted boards covering the burned-out shell of the family room. The two of them had made body-melting memories in that room and she hated knowing it would never look the same.

But just maybe, she thought brightly, they would have a chance to put it back together and make new memories. Wouldn't that be fun? Remodeling the house so it represented both of them?

Earlier Jake had hinted he had something important to tell her, but that he wanted to wait until tomorrow morning to talk. A secret thrill shot up her arms as she considered what he might say. Would he ask her to move in with him permanently? Or would he come right out and ask her to marry him? That was what two people who loved each other did, wasn't it?

Mary had a strong suspicion they would be talking about one of those things in the morning. In fact, as she'd packed a little bag to leave the farm tonight, she'd told her mother not to expect her back for at least a few days. Her mother apparently guessed the potential of the situation immediately, and Mary had spotted tears welling in Jolene's eyes. Her mother must've realized she was finally about to see her lonely little girl truly happy for the first time.

Mary couldn't wait for the future. Couldn't wait for tomorrow and all the rest of her tomorrows. Big changes in her life loomed directly ahead. Drawing in a breath, she tried to calm down as the excitement shimmered off her shoulders and bounced around the walls of their love nest.

This was going to be the best night of her entire life.

After they entered the master bedroom and set their burdens of food and drinks down on a side table, Mary immediately reached for the hem of her blouse. Ready to dispense with all her clothes so she could really get close to Jake, she was disappointed when he stayed her hands.

"Don't," he said softly. His gaze raked her body head to toe and fire landed everywhere he looked. "Let me do that for you."

Oh, yeah. The best night ever.

He slipped off his shoes, dumped the contents of his pockets on the dresser and reached for the buttons of his own shirt. But as he shrugged out of the sleeves, he drew in a breath and wrinkled his nose.

"Man, do I ever stink. Would you believe that after four or five showers today I still smell like smoke? And like sweat. Damn. Standing over a hot charcoal grill all night hasn't done a lot for my manly scent, has it?"

"I like your scent just fine." She reached for him but he backed away.

"Hold that thought. Give me a few minutes to clean up, love. I'll jump in the shower and…" He ran a flattened palm over his jaw. "Shave. And be back before you miss me."

"I miss you already."

Jake grinned and leaned in for a quick kiss. "Me, too. Don't move." Swinging around, he started for the bathroom before turning back. "And don't take anything else off. That's my job."

She laughed out loud this time and wrapped her arms around her middle, reveling in the warm love blanketing the room. What a difference a few weeks could make in someone's life. Not that long ago she'd been sure she would never find anyone to love. That she was destined to live as someone's daughter, sister and aunt but would never have a family of her own. She'd been absolutely convinced that the only families she would ever know were the ones found inside books.

But now look where she was. Completely in love and in her mind already building houses, marriages and maybe even children into a future so full of promise it was making her head swim.

Feeling light-headed, Mary plopped down on the bed and kicked off her shoes. Her whole body hummed in anticipation.

She listened to the water running in the bathroom and fidgeted for a moment. Wanting to join him in the shower, it was everything she could do to keep all her clothes on and stay seated on the bed. There would be time enough tonight for another shower or maybe two. Time enough to have tons of showers for the rest of their lives, in fact.

Trying to distract herself, Mary used her forefinger to push the change from Jake's pocket across the shiny flat surface of the nightstand. Quarters and dimes. She lined them up like a little row of tin soldiers.

Her gaze landed on his wallet next and she couldn't resist picking it up. Soft and supple, the dark red leather felt warm in her hand. And when she breathed in its smell, reminiscent of men's dens and lodges, the wallet seemed to come alive.

As she stroked along the stitched edges, she began to think about how a wallet contained a person's whole life story. She knew hers held identification, money to buy whatever she needed or wanted, and pictures of loved ones to remind her of who she was. A wallet could be considered a microcosm of someone's life.

Mary lifted her head when the shower stopped running in the bathroom. But then another faucet went on and she figured Jake was shaving. Maybe she could take a tiny peek inside his wallet before he finished and came back to bed.

What harm would it do? After their talk tomorrow morning, she would belong with him. The two of them would be a couple. They wouldn't keep any secrets from each other ever again.

Using just a fingernail, Mary flipped open the wallet. The first thing she saw was his driver's license. Jake Pierson. Age: 35. Height: six feet. Weight: 185. Eyes: blue. Hair: dark blond.

Staring down at his picture, Mary started to daydream the way she never had as a teen. Mary Pierson. Mrs. Jake Pierson. Mary Walsh Pierson. Wife. Mother. Lover.

Sighing, she flipped through the rest of the cards in his wallet. She found a credit card, social security card and a real estate license for the state of Montana. But no pictures.

Not one picture. She looked in the folding money section and found a few bills but nothing else. About to give up and put the wallet back down, she noticed the tiny edge of a paper sticking out from one side pocket.

Imagining it was some kind of receipt for his work, she slipped her fingers down into the pocket and rescued the folded paper. It turned out to be a piece of yellowed newspaper.

A newspaper clipping? For a man who refused to

carry around even one photo except on his driver's license, Jake had saved an old clipping? How strange.

Carefully, Mary unfolded the paper and smoothed it out on the top of the nightstand under the light. The headline read: Young Woman and Unborn Child Killed in Tragic Car Accident.

Mary quickly scanned the top of the page. The banner announcement came from the Santa Bertha, California, *Herald* and was datelined ten years ago last June. The first paragraph of the story recounted a horrific tale of a young pregnant woman struck in a head-on collision with an over-the-road truck not five miles from her own home.

With her hands shaking, Mary picked up the paper and held it closer to the light. A picture had been included at the bottom of the article. A smiling picture of a pretty blonde woman, wearing a wedding dress and standing beside her handsome new husband in his tuxedo.

No captions appeared under the picture, but Mary could not mistake the man's face. Even ten years younger, the man in a tuxedo had to be Jake.

She ran her finger down the article, searching for names. The first paragraph referred to the woman as Tina Summers. And then as Mrs. Jacob Summers further down in the article.

Oh, my God.

Jake had been married once. He'd lied to her.

And what was with the name? Summers? Had he changed his name? Was he hiding from something? Or someone?

What if he was one of those men who lived secret lives? With wives in two or three different states?

Her pulse rate kicked into high gear, and Mary's overactive imagination jumped to several different conclusions at the same time.

He could be a bigamist. He could be a fraud, wanting to marry her for her family's money. He could be wanted by the police. He could be a...murderer.

That last idea forced her to her feet. What was she doing here with a man she'd only met a few short weeks ago? All she knew about him for sure was that he was a liar. He could be anything.

Mary heard the water in the bathroom stop running. With her stomach in her throat, she couldn't catch her breath and her mind blanked. She had to get out of here.

Now.

Grabbing her purse, she tore open the bedroom door and banged down the hall in the dark toward the front stairs. She raced to leave the house before Jake could stop her.

Her heart pounded crazily inside her chest as she hit the top of the stairs.

"Mary?"

Oh, my God. Jake was out of the bathroom and had already discovered she was gone.

Mary picked up her speed and sprinted down the staircase, taking two stairs at a time. She had to get free to call for help.

Reaching out with both hands, she made a grab for the front-door handle. But when she tugged, nothing happened.

She remembered the new security measures Jake had mentioned. But what about emergencies?

Frantically, she worked on the door locks. Twisting and tugging.

"Mary? Where the hell…" He was at the top of the stairs!

At last, the handle turned and the door came free. But it opened with an alarm blast so loud the sound nearly knocked her down. The outside spotlights automatically came on and sirens screeched into the night as she dashed out the door.

"Damn it, Mary! Don't…"

Jake's words were lost in the chaos while she ran across the wide front porch. No. No. No. She couldn't let him catch her.

The same terrible truth kept repeating in her mind. She didn't even know his real name. Who was he really?

How could she have been this stupid?

Down the front steps she flew, checking over her shoulder to make sure he was not right behind her. What if… What if…

When she hit the ground, she headed down the sidewalk going toward the driveway. If she could make it out to the street, her cell phone should work and she could call for someone to come pick her up.

As she ran past the family room, the smell of charred wood reached her nose. She turned her head to look at the burned-out hulk of the room, but she wasn't about to slow down to look closer.

Mary let loose a loud scream as she tripped over something and took a header into a shrub.

What the heck could've been lying across the sidewalk in the middle of the night? No lights were on in the burned-out section of the house and it was blacker than pitch here beside it. Mary came up on her hands and knees and felt around in the dark, looking for her purse.

Her hand hit something solid. Big. Slightly warm.

Gingerly touching the object, Mary's wildest imagination raged free. She patted and brushed over the form until her hand hit something sticky. Pulling back, she shrieked again. Louder this time.

Even in the dark she could tell this object was a man's body. And she'd read enough murder mysteries to know the sticky substance had to be blood.

Panicked and nearing hysteria, Mary jumped to her feet. Purse or no purse, she was out of here.

But she was all turned around in the dark. Taking two big steps, she realized she was heading back toward the house. Twirling, she blindly dashed off in the opposite direction.

"That's far enough." Strong arms reached out and grabbed her by the shoulders.

But that wasn't Jake's voice. She had never heard this male voice before in her life. Big hands dug painfully into her shoulders and a whiskered jaw scraped her cheek.

"You may have to give it one more scream, girl," the man whispered in her ear. "Your lover has exactly two seconds to show up or it'll be too late to say goodbye."

What? What did he say?

Mary tried to twist out of his grip, but it was useless. Finally she kicked back at his shins and connected.

"Damn it, bitch."

Out of the total darkness came a swift blow to the side of her head. She screamed again.

"That's more like it. Call him to you so you can die together, you stupid whore."

At that moment, more yard lights came on and the entire area was lit up like a used-car lot.

"Jake! No! Stay back! He's going to…"

Another blow to the temple turned the bright lights off again for Mary—as everything in her world went completely black.

Chapter 13

When he heard the first scream, a burst of adrenaline drove Jake down the front stairs running after Mary. But after hearing her scream for the second time, a shot of good sense and extreme caution kept him from chasing her outside.

One scream from her could've meant surprise at finding Jim outside guarding the house. But a second scream worried Jake and made him stop long enough to think. He swung around in mid-stride and headed into the kitchen to retrieve his weapon, thanking God that he'd thought to pull on his jeans before dashing from the bathroom.

By the time he had the gun in hand and sprinted out through the kitchen door and past the gate, the shrieking alarm had shut off by itself. Probably on a timer. More concerned than ever in the silence, Jake rounded the corner of the house. He stopped long enough to flip on a second set of outside floodlights.

Moving on, Jake experienced a sudden flood of fear and panic, too reminiscent of long ago. Ten excruciating long years ago to be exact. The woman he'd loved then was struck down in a startling flash of pain and blood. Killed too young—due to his foolish actions. He'd been young and full of himself, and the person he'd loved died because he was thoughtless and selfish.

Afterward, Jake had been convinced that he would never be capable of loving again. Once was all he got in his lifetime. He'd devoted his life to his work. And in all the years since, no one else had moved him the way his wife had. No one else had managed to open him up. No one else ever bothered to dig under his pain.

Not until now. Not until Mary.

With yet another scream from her, Jake came to his senses, jogging in place on the pine needle–covered sidewalk. The situation must be worse than he'd imagined. She had to be in trouble. Crouching low, he peered through the charred remnants of the family room, hoping to spy movement.

What he saw at the front of the house sent a zing of dread through his veins. Through the stealthy shadows, a bulky figure of a man raised one arm and struck Mary in the temple with what seemed to be a Ruger .44. A frigging big weapon, outfitted with a heavy crimson trace. Mary's knees gave out under the blow and her attacker grabbed her around the waist, pulling her closer to his body in order to keep her upright.

Jake's hands fisted. Fear and fury blinded him for the moment. But after gulping in air, he soon channeled the rage, drawing on his training. He forced any unprofessional thoughts of Mary as the woman he loved into a dark recess of his mind.

Tactics. Remember the breathing. Assess all the possibilities.

While Jake's brain tried to process the scene, their assailant seemed to be assessing possibilities, too. With Mary under one arm, the man backed up to the blackened ruins of the family room—directly in front of Jake's position. Meanwhile, the guy's gun arm arched out, sighting a point of red laser light to both the right and the left.

The gunman must've been hoping for a head-on confrontation. But since Jake had not raced right into his trap after Mary's scream, the assailant was finding his own caution.

An outright confrontation would get both Jake and Mary killed without a fight. And Jake didn't have a clean shot. Not without taking far too great a chance on hitting Mary. An alternative had to be found—and quickly. The assailant might be a pro, but he had misjudged both Jake's determination and his skill.

Jake carefully began picking his way through the part of charred family room that wasn't covered by boards and headed straight for the target. The only chance of surprise in this situation was to sneak between the downed timbers and charcoaled floorboards without making any sound and attack the man from behind. Jake had spent all afternoon in these ruins and figured he could maneuver here with his eyes closed.

Sliding sideways through the blackened timbers, Jake floated along like a ghost shadow. He kept his peripheral vision trained on the target, hoping to do nothing that might alert the assailant to the threat sneaking up behind his back.

As he closed in, Jake heard Mary moaning. Then she moved. Infinitesimally at first, but soon she was squirming in her attacker's grip.

Grateful for small but significant favors, Jake breathed more evenly. Obviously, her injuries were not immediately life-threatening. She was alive. And—she was becoming a major distraction to their assailant at the best moment possible.

Come on. Easy now. Don't anyone make any sudden moves. Let me get a little closer.

Two more steps.

"Show yourself, Pierson! Your woman needs you. Come out and we'll talk." The man jammed his weapon to Mary's temple.

The screech of sirens ringing in the distance suddenly captured the assailant's attention. For only an instant. The security alarm had apparently done its work, summoning help to the fray.

With her assailant's momentary distraction, Mary took the opportunity and planted her feet, spinning free of his grip. The assailant whipped his gun around, putting her directly in his sights.

Jake didn't hesitate. He launched his body through the last three feet of burned-out building, taking the other man to the ground right at the exact moment the weapon fired.

Mary. Jake wanted to check on her welfare, but could not lose his focus. Not yet.

He pinned the assailant's gun hand. The man arched his body, trying to buck Jake off. But Jake hung on, slamming the hand with the weapon into the sidewalk. Once. And again. Over and over until the .44 flew free.

Then Jake's hands went to the man's throat. He squeezed, putting pressure against the gunman's windpipe. Deep down Jake wanted to kill the bastard for hurting Mary. It was all he could do not to squeeze too hard.

The assailant panicked, twisting and kicking until Jake's grip loosened. Out of nowhere, the son of a bitch freed a hand and caught him in the chin with an uppercut. But Jake wasn't about to let the asshole squirm totally free. He pummeled him—in the nose and in the gut.

"Stop! Or…or I'll shoot." Mary stood about ten feet away with her attacker's bulky weapon in both her hands. "Get up."

The assailant stopped fighting immediately. Jake jumped to his feet, dragging the man up with him.

"You won't shoot me," the assailant told Mary with a sneer. "You don't have it in you, librarian."

Jake feared the SOB was probably right, but he wouldn't show any weakness or lack of faith in the woman he loved. Sirens, still screaming through the chilled night air, were coming closer. All he and Mary needed were a few more minutes and their stand-off would be over.

"Who are you and why have you been stalking us? Why try to kill us?" Jake demanded.

Needing a momentary distraction, Jake tried to tempt their assailant into talking instead of acting in panic. Jake also wanted a reason. A name behind the attacks.

Their assailant shrugged, then grinned. "All in a day's work, pal."

In a surprise move, the man ripped his arms free of Jake's grip and spun, heading straight for Mary. She raised the heavy weapon in both hands and took aim. Her whole body shook so badly that Jake worried she might shoot him instead.

As the assailant overtook her, she managed to discharge the gun. But her shot went wild.

However, Jake's shot did not. Their assailant was dead before he ever hit the ground.

It was over that fast.

"Jake! Are you okay?" Mary flew at him, landing against his chest and throwing her arms around his neck. She covered his face in kisses.

He eased both his own weapon and Mary's to the ground and then closed his arms around her, reveling in the feel of her warm body. She was alive and breathing. And Jake felt nearly faint with relief.

Mary eased back in his arms and gazed into his eyes. "Was it my shot that killed him? I was so afraid for you."

Spectacular. "No, my love. You're no killer. But without your actions, we might not have made it."

Jake would never love her any more than he did right this minute. The woman was beyond strong, both emotionally and physically. It thrilled him to see the way she'd been fierce in her determination both to live and to save his life. Determined, because she still had no idea about his lies.

For the moment.

A little later, Jake sat back on his heels beside the body of his partner with memories flooding his mind.

Memories of missions won and lost. Of a decade of years, some with near misses and many with clear victories. Years of being there to watch each other's back and to give assistance when things got rough.

Scraping a hand across his eyes, Jake murmured, "How could this happen? You…taking one for me? If anyone should've died here, partner, it should've been me. I'm a miserable nothing and you had it all. This was my show. My…mistake."

Jake heard heavy footsteps behind his back, but he didn't move. What for?

"I just got off the phone with your boss, Pierson." The voice belonged to the sheriff. "SAC Benton is en route. Should be here within an hour and a half. He'll be bringing a forensics team with him but he wants us to secure the scene and do our best to keep a lid on things."

Jake didn't turn. His eyes weren't focusing and his brain wasn't fully engaged.

"Uh…" Wes cleared his throat. "He also asked me to take charge of your weapons. Only for the time being, you understand."

Jake waved a hand toward the two weapons, lying not far away on the ground. "One is my personal weapon. The other belongs to the unsub. There's also my 10 mm service pistol in a duffel in the master bedroom closet."

He wasn't ready to mention the Glock 9 mm hidden in the SUV. That one would stay hidden for a while.

"Jake…" Wes put a hand on his shoulder. "The county coroner is on his way out to make the pronouncements. Let me cover Jim's body until he arrives. He was my friend from our SEAL days, too, remember."

Jake got to his feet, closed his eyes for an instant then turned to face the sheriff. "Do it."

After Wes spread a Mylar blanket over his partner's body, Jake finally felt able to take his first deep breath since the shooting. "How's Mary?"

"She's with the paramedic. Looks and sounds a little shaky to me, but a lot calmer than most civilians after going through what she did. I can hardly believe Mary actually took a shot at the assailant and then witnessed him die. Most women would be hysterical."

"I know. But Mary's pretty tough." Somehow Jake wasn't the least surprised by the revelation.

"Melissa doesn't believe Mary's in shock, but she wants to take her to the Bozeman hospital for an evaluation and a CT scan. She says Mary's got a hell of a goose egg on her head."

Jake nodded. "Bozeman would be good. Anywhere out of Honey Creek. When is she going?"

"Mary claims she won't leave until she talks to you."

Ah, hell. Jake fisted his hands but knew it was time to man up. Mary deserved answers.

"And Melissa is insisting," Wes went on, "that your cuts and scrapes need to be cleaned and your feet checked before she's free to take Mary anywhere."

"My feet?" Jake looked down and realized for the first time that he was barefoot. "I'm fine. Tell the paramedic not to concern herself."

Wes didn't reply but turned and made his way over to the body of the unsub. "This bastard had been stalking you and Mary."

"I know. That's why I asked Jim to keep an eye on us from outside the alarm perimeter tonight."

Wes screwed up his mouth and nodded before bending to inspect the attacker's corpse. "We found a tree perch in the woods that the stalker must've been using," he said over his shoulder. "And my men located a sniper rifle that was probably the one that took out your partner."

Jake walked over to where Wes was bending over to pat down the unsub. He stood beside the sheriff, gazing down at the man he'd killed and feeling nothing. Absolutely nothing.

Wes had another question for him. "You have any idea why this character would've suddenly decided to kill you instead of sticking with the games he'd been playing?" Wes was gingerly checking the dead man's pockets.

"The bastard was a pro. He was only taking orders." And maybe that was why Jake didn't harbor any guilt for killing the man. He felt as if he'd stopped a robot, a machine aimed at hurting Mary.

Wes turned his head to look up at Jake. "Orders from whom?"

"Exactly. But it's not my investigation. Not anymore."

"Yeah?" Wes's eyes narrowed and he went back to checking the unsub's body. "Well, I've got two more dead bodies on my hands. I know the Bureau will want to investigate the death of one of their own, but I don't much like the idea of having a murder spree in my town. Especially not one involving the murder of a friend."

Wes pulled a few tiny slips of paper from the dead man's pants pocket. "What have we here?" He removed his flashlight from its place at his belt and studied the papers in brighter lighting.

After a moment Wes said, "It looks like part of an execution order—on you. Written by hand on some pretty fancy-looking stationary." Wes tried to piece together two of the tiny scraps of paper. "But why would anyone keep incriminating evidence like this on their person?"

Jake shrugged. "Insurance, maybe. You know, in case he was caught and needed to make a deal."

"Maybe. But the signature is missing. Almost everything needed to identify the writer is missing, actually."

"Have SAC Benton's team do a full forensic workup and then copy you the results."

Wes nodded, but folded the smallest scrap of paper and placed it in his breast pocket. "I'll turn it over. But this expensive stationary is rather rare for our part of the country. I have an idea or two that need following up."

Jake nodded, too. He understood taking tiny shortcuts in order to stay a step ahead of an investigation. And in this case, nothing major would be lost by the sheriff holding on to a nonessential part of the evidence.

Jake didn't consider falling in love a shortcut—not exactly. But everything major in his world had been lost due to his stepping away from procedure. And the idea was killing him.

"I'm going over to talk to Mary." Jake turned, started to walk away from Wes but twisted around to add, "Can one of your guys bring me a pair of boots from upstairs?"

Wes nodded and Jake kept walking. It felt as if he was marching straight into the depths of hell—to the one thing he had been dreading the most.

But it had to be done. His investigation had put Mary in danger and she needed to accept close personal protection from now on, with or without him around, and it was up to Jake to see that she understood why.

"But I don't understand what happened here." Mary could hear her tone of voice rising a couple of octaves but it was beyond her to stop. "No one will tell me anything. Who was that man and why did he try to kill us?"

Her hands had stopped shaking, but her head was starting to pound. Still, she refused to leave or lie down or take any medication until she talked to Jake.

Jake turned to Melissa, who had finished dabbing antiseptic to the cuts on his hands and face. "Can you give us a few moments?" he asked her.

"Sure. I'll go notify the Bozeman hospital we're coming in." She turned to study Mary for a second. "Be back in a few."

Jake stood, leaving Mary the only one still sitting on the back of the paramedic's truck. He watched Melissa walk away, then he turned to Mary and took her by the hand.

"This is all my fault. But I…but I…" He hung his head and dropped her hand.

"Jake, what is it? Why would any of this be your fault? You saved us." It was then she noticed the blood spattered all over his clothing. Suddenly chilled, she rubbed up and down her arms trying to find warmth.

He looked her straight in the eye and stopped hedging. "I've been lying to you. Right from the start. I'm sorry. I should've told you what was going on—who I really am—long ago. But I knew if I did you wouldn't…you would…"

"Lying?" The word filled her mind with the terrible images that she had thought she'd conquered. "About what? About being in love with me? About being married?" She wasn't sure she could stand to hear what he had to say.

Her forehead broke out in a cold sweat.

"I do love you." The plea in his voice for her to understand almost cut through the pain in her heart. Almost.

"But that's about the only thing that wasn't a lie. I'm an undercover agent for the FBI, Mary. My partner and I have been working a covert operation on a Racketeer Influenced and Corrupt Organizations case. We're here trying to open up an international money-laundering scheme—originating in Honey Creek."

"What?" Confused, Mary put a hand to her temple, wanting to make the throbbing in her head subside. "You're not in real estate?"

He kept his eyes trained on her face, watching her closely. "I'm an FBI special agent. My partner Jim…" Jake's face blanched when he mentioned his partner's name.

Sudden images of the two men lying on the ground, bloody and not breathing, caused Mary's stomach to roll. Oh, God, she was going to be sick.

"Jim is the man you found. The dead man you tripped over." Jake's eyes closed for an instant before he began again. "It all started when your father contacted one of our foreign offices while he was in Costa Rica. He wanted to…"

"My father? Costa Rica? What on earth are you saying?"

Mary felt light-headed. And cold. She wanted to lie down. She wanted to run away and hide. Hide from the death. Hide from the blood. Hide from the truth.

None of this conversation made sense and the only subjects that interested her right now were how Jake was handling the shooting and what he wanted to say. But she could feel him pulling away from her.

Was her connection with Jake going to be yet one more thing her father had destroyed in her life?

Chapter 14

"It's a long story and I don't have time right now to tell you everything." Jake's face took on a slightly green cast as if he felt sick, too. "Only that your father had been living in Costa Rica. But he wanted to come back to the States. He contacted the U.S. State Department who put him in touch with the Bureau, and they made him a deal."

Jake stopped speaking for a moment and picked up her hands. "You're cold." His eyes were full of concern… and something else she couldn't name.

But concern wasn't what she wanted from him. She pulled away and folded her hands in her lap. "I'm okay. Go on."

"Mark Walsh was supposed to provide us with the details of an international money-laundering operation, on the condition that the State Department would allow him back into the country and grant him immunity from prosecution."

"Let me get this straight. You're here because you were supposed to get information from my father?" Mary's head whirled in a state of confusion. This wasn't what she'd expected to hear.

Jake blinked, reaching for her again. Then he suddenly dropped his hands back to his sides. "I was supposed to interview him here in Honey Creek and follow up on his information. His body was found the day before our meeting was to take place."

Mary wrapped her arms around her waist, growing colder. "Okay. Okay. You were undercover. But…" She looked up at his beloved face. "Why me? Why did you make…friends…with me? To get information? But I don't know anything. I didn't even know my father was still alive."

The ache in her chest was becoming much worse than the ache in her head. She rubbed over it with one palm.

Jake's face contorted, as though he, too, felt great pain. "I needed an intro to the community. Someone who was familiar with the Walsh family and could get me inside. That was you."

Oh, God. Mary wanted to run, but Jake was standing close. Too close. She couldn't breathe.

"Then everything you said—all the things you told me were lies?"

"Listen to me," he said, his voice hoarse and breathless. "The stories about my past were true—most of them. I wanted to tell you the rest. The complete truth. But when I realized you weren't involved in anything illegal, it was too late. By then I knew you would never tolerate a liar."

In a much quieter voice, Jake added, "And by then I didn't want to lose you. I was already in too deep."

Sudden, intense anger snapped up and out of her mouth without warning. "You bastard! You used me. I almost died a couple of times and I would've never known why."

"I planned on telling you. First thing in the morning. Remember that I had something to say?"

"You were planning on telling me…about this? About your mission?" A red rage blinded her, making her say things before she thought them through. "I hate you. Go away."

"There's something else we have to discuss first. I need a few more minutes."

She jumped up, raised her arm and smacked him hard across the cheek. Damn. Mary had never hit anyone before in her life and the minute she had, she felt completely devastated.

Jake never flinched. He just stood there looking as though he deserved everything she could do to him.

Pulling the yellowed newspaper clipping from her pocket, she confronted him with it—swiping it under his nose. "I don't want to hear anything you have to say. Not unless it's about your dead wife. You remember, the one you never had?"

"You found that. You went snooping in my wallet?" Jake rubbed a hand over his jaw. "I shouldn't have been carrying that clipping. It was my first breach of protocol. I have never done anything this dangerous to the mission before in my entire career."

Mary threw it at him and turned away. "Never mind.

I won't believe anything you have to say, anyway. You're worse than my father ever was."

"Wait." Jake put a hand on her shoulder, his touch so light and gentle it nearly brought her to tears.

She stopped, but had to wage a battle with herself not to turn into his arms.

"Mary, you may hate me. I don't blame you. But I didn't lie about loving you. Never doubt that. You are a very special woman. After my wife died, I was positive there couldn't be anyone else for me. Not ever.

"But then I met you and everything changed. You touched me. Worked your way into my heart without me noticing until it was too late. Now I would gladly give up everything—my job and my whole life—for your sake. I would take a bullet for you without giving it a second thought."

Mary heard the tremor in his voice but refused to turn around.

"But I know you won't let me give you what you need most right now. You need protection, my love, twenty-four seven. Whoever hired our stalker may try again. Wes and the Bureau will do everything in their power to get the word out that you don't know anything. That there's no reason to come after you. But still…"

She turned and lifted her chin. "I don't need anything."

"Yes, I'm afraid you do. You need a guard. At least for a while. And the Bureau will insist you take their help."

"But not help from you." She wanted him gone. Out of her sight. She had to be alone to scream and cry out her pain.

"Not if you don't want me."

"I don't want you. I don't love you. I've never loved you and I don't believe anything you have to say."

Tears threatened to leak from the corners of her eyes and make a liar out of her. She bit her tongue to force them back inside. "Just leave me alone, Jake. I'm done. I've had all the lies from you I can stand.

"I thought I knew you," she added sadly. "But I was wrong. You are exactly like my father. The world's biggest liar. I never want to see you again. Stay away from me."

As dawn broke over Honey Creek, the lavender dew covered both sidewalks and pines. Jake was impervious to the beauty around him while he sat quietly on the front steps of the rental house. Resting his chin on his fists, he waited for his boss to finish up on the SAT phone.

An image of Mary, looking fragile and broken as he'd trampled her dreams, kept intruding upon his thoughts. She hadn't been aware of his pain, but every word she'd uttered in response to his *truths* would forever be engraved in his memory. Each syllable, each dagger of her rage, had sliced him into raw pieces, until at the end of her tirade, he was sure the jigsaw puzzle that used to be Jake Pierson would never be solved again.

He'd been concerned about her going into shock. She'd exhibited all the signs. Seeing a man shot right in front of her eyes and almost dying herself must have affected her more deeply than she'd let on. So he had let her rant.

He'd deserved her rage. He deserved much worse. If he could take back everything that had happened between them he would—except for falling in love with her. Loving her was the only spark of decent behavior he had exhibited through his entire mission.

He was grateful to Melissa for taking Mary to the Bozeman hospital several hours ago. Wes had just received word that, though she was not in immediate danger, the doctors wanted to keep Mary there under observation until tomorrow.

Not a bad thing. Mary would be safe in Bozeman. Wes said he would leave men to guard her while she was in the hospital.

Jake took the sheriff's word as gospel. He had all the respect in the world for Wes. At odd moments in the past few hours, the two of them had silently bonded over the loss of their friend Jim. His partner's death was a shared link between them—a devastating and excruciating tie.

Now Jake sat waiting to talk to his boss about what would happen to Mary after she was released from the hospital. The Bureau needed a fresh plan for her as well as for the rest of the mission, but Jake's brain was too fried to be of much help in devising any schemes for the future. He could barely decide what to do for the rest of the day.

Looking up through the tidy chaos that arose around the FBI's team of forensic investigators, Jake saw SAC Gerald Benton heading in his direction.

"You sure you don't need medical attention?" the SAC asked when he came close.

Ripping off the bandage Jake had allowed the paramedic to tape over one of his cuts last night, he found no fresh blood. "All healed." At least physically.

"I don't think you've had a chance to meet the special agent who's due to arrive momentarily, Pierson. He's newly assigned to the investigation here in Honey Creek. You two will need to spend time together."

"Ah… About that…"

SAC Benton waved away any objections. "I know. You're off the mission. But the information you've already collected will be invaluable. After your critical-incident debriefing, I expect you to give the new man all the time he needs."

Jake shook his head slowly. "I'll write a wrap-up report. Then I'm done. You can have my badge and gun. America will have to get by rounding up bad guys without me. I quit."

His boss regarded him carefully then sat down on the step beside him. "The FBI lost a good man when they lost Jim Willis. And you lost one hell of a partner. But Jim wouldn't want you to make any hasty decisions. You're a damned good undercover operative. Take some time off. You've earned it. Don't throw away a stellar career."

A stellar career? Not so much. A career full of psychotic disassociation was more like it. Years of dropping out of your own personality in order to become someone else wasn't exactly Jake's idea of the most heroic choice in occupations.

"My decision isn't hasty, Benton. I've been thinking about quitting for several years. For Jim's sake, I only wish I had gotten out before it was too late."

"You have to take a mandatory psych eval after your debriefing on the shooting. Talk to the psychologists about your partner's death. Give them and yourself time."

Jake stared at the ground, trying to dredge up some loyalty to the Bureau or some emotion over having had to kill a man. But all he felt was empty. His partner was gone. The love of his life had walked away for good. Any residual feeling about the job couldn't compete.

"I don't need therapy. Sorry, Benton. I'm just finished with the FBI for good."

SAC Benton threw up his hands and walked away, muttering something else about more time. But within fifteen minutes his boss was back with the new special agent assigned to the Honey Creek case.

"Pierson, this is Ethan Ross. Talk to him."

Jake looked up and nodded, but he didn't bother to stand or shake hands. It wasn't his fight anymore.

"I'm sorry about your partner, Special Agent Pierson."

"Me, too." Jake finally came to his feet. "There isn't much I can tell you about Honey Creek or the people here that you can't read in my reports, Ross. It's a nice little town for the most part."

"I've been going over the transcripts of that computer tap you managed at Walsh Enterprises," Special Agent Ross told him. "Nice work, but I'm afraid there's nothing there to help the investigation. We did get a lucky break in the case, though."

"Yeah?" Jake didn't care. He was having trouble caring about anything but Mary's safety.

"Damned right." Agent Ross nodded and went on with his explanation. "There's suddenly no real need to replace you with an undercover operative in Honey Creek. We've come up with a new informant. A volunteer. Someone with better access than you had. This person is already a part of the community."

Confused, Jake shook his head in denial. "Nearly everyone in this town is a suspect—if not for our RICO

investigation then in one of the murder investigations."
He searched through his mental notes for who the
volunteer informant might be but came up empty.

"Our new informant has already been vetted and
is definitely not under suspicion." Ross spoke with a
deliberate but friendly air, almost as if this investigation
was just a walk in the park. "Having someone like this
informant on our team will be exactly what we need to
break the case."

"Good for you." But Jake didn't give a damn.

Sure, he wanted a name for the person who'd put out
the order for his execution—the name of the unsub's
boss. But he wanted that info only in order to be assured
of Mary's safety. Jake had a gut feeling Wes's murder
investigations might turn up persons of interest a hell
of a lot faster than the Bureau's RICO investigation
would.

Jake agreed to write up his report as fast as possible
and send it on to Special Agent Ross within the next
twenty-four hours—along with his formal resignation. He
couldn't wait to wash his hands of this investigation—or
of the entire FBI for that matter. They didn't interest
him.

Nothing did. Not without Mary.

When he finally had the time to do a serious inventory
of what mattered to him now, Jake wasn't sure he could
find anything to take her place. Maybe he never would.
At the moment, the only spark of interest he could find
buried under all his emotional and mental baggage was
a nagging worry about Mary's safety.

He clung to the tiny but real emotion like a lifeline,
and went off to plead with SAC Benton for long-term
protection for her.

* * *

"You did what?" Wes was staring at him as though he'd announced he was taking up cannibalism.

"I quit the Bureau. Once I debrief, go through the regular internal investigation on the clean shooting and write my report, I'm gone."

The forensics team had finished up hours ago. The bodies had been removed. And SAC Benton and Special Agent Ross had taken off for the field office. A special cleanup crew would be sent in to complete the rebuilding on the leased house. Then it would be returned to its out-of-state owner's possession. Everything else was supposed to go back to normal in and around Honey Creek, allowing the FBI's investigation to continue unimpeded.

But Jake was having trouble moving away from this spot, these woods, and vaguely understood he couldn't seem to find much enthusiasm for leaving town.

"I see," Wes said quietly. "What do you plan on doing next?"

Jake shrugged a shoulder and looked toward the woods, at the pines and firs that were beginning to get under his skin. He breathed in the heady scent of sage and that woodsy musk peculiar to this valley and regretted having to leave at all. On the other hand, everything here reminded him too much of Mary. Was too intimately connected to her in his mind.

"No clue yet," he finally replied. "The only thing I seem to care about is making sure Mary stays safe."

Wes scowled. "I've already said I would see to that. She's one of mine. As long as she's in this town, she will be safe. No need for you to concern yourself over her."

Shoving his hands in his pockets, Jake leaned back on his heels and lowered his voice. "Mary is my only concern."

"Ah… I get it. Have you told her that? Does she know?"

"I'm not sure what she knows. She was pretty hot when she left. Said she never wants to hear from me again."

"Give her some time. There's too many new concepts for her to absorb them all at once." Wes folded his arms and shifted his stance. "You have a hometown somewhere with people anxious for you to come home?"

"No place…no people at all."

"How about money? Will you need to move fast to find a job to pay the bills?"

Jake shook his head. "Undercover work pays fairly well and I haven't had much in the way of a real life for years. Don't own anything and don't owe anyone. I'll have enough saved up along with enough back pay to get by for quite a while."

"Hmm. Well, I may have an idea or two for you when you're ready to hear about them."

"I'm not looking for a deputy sheriff's job, pal. Law enforcement has lost all its appeal. Along with everything else."

Wes's smile crinkled the corners of his eyes as he tilted his chin in thought. "Didn't I hear you claim a second ago that there was at least one thing you still cared about?"

"Mary's safety."

"Right." Wes gave him a friendly punch in the

shoulder. "Then let's go find us a cup of coffee and toss around a few ideas."

Someone was following her. Mary's heart pounded out a staccato rhythm. Oh, lordy, not again.

Racing her car down the back roads, she headed toward the farm. Why now? She hadn't even had a chance to go home since the shooting. Who would still want to cause her harm?

Suddenly it occurred to her that she couldn't lead whoever it was straight to her family. Slowing, she decided to face the danger head-on. But when she stopped the car and turned around to look, no one was there.

Exhaling, she waited for her pulse to calm. She wondered if the person following her might have been one of the sheriff's men. When Wes had come to check on her at the Bozeman hospital several days ago, he'd told her that he planned on having someone keep an eye on her when she got back to Honey Creek.

She'd almost forgotten because she hadn't come right home after being released from the hospital. The FBI had wanted her to come in to their field office in Bozeman for an interview and that had taken a couple of days. But staying off the farm, away from her family and Honey Creek, hadn't been any imposition.

Mary had needed those hours and days to think—to cry—and to let her body heal. The bruises were almost gone, but the clear thinking and the crying seemed only to be beginning. She'd been caught up in a kind of dreamland ever since the first instant she'd seen Jake. And coming down to earth was a big jolt of reality.

A reality that seemed to come with an ocean of tears.

The *affair,* for lack of a better word, with Jake *had* changed her. Changed her in many different ways. Her life would never be quite the same again.

Finally navigating up the driveway to the farm, Mary swore her new life would begin as soon as possible. Stopping the car in front of the farmhouse, she turned off her engine but didn't make a move to get out. She sat motionless, gazing out the windshield at the familiar surroundings.

She had grown up in this house. But it did not hold happy memories for her.

She had begun her journey to a new life in this house. But her journey would not be finished here.

This place was no longer hers. She'd changed and didn't feel at home here. She didn't feel at home anywhere.

She was lost. Completely rudderless with no one to talk to. Her friends and her family cared, but all had their own lives. None of them knew what she'd been through.

Oh, man, how Mary wished she and Jake could've remained on friendly terms. She could use a real friend about now.

Chapter 15

With her emotions raging, Mary eased out from the car and headed inside to find her mother. She needed to tell Jolene of her many life-changing decisions.

"There you are." Jolene came toward her daughter as soon as she walked through the front door. "I wish you would've let me pick you up and drive you home. I've been worried about you since you called."

"I'm fine, Mother." Four solid days of crying had left her red-eyed and weak, but Mary straightened her shoulders and faced her mother.

"Good. Where have you been anyway? It's so unlike you to just disappear with only a phone call. Were you with Jake? There's been a few rumors around town about strange things going on out at his house."

At the mention of his name, Mary's heart began to pound. Her palms began to sweat and the tears backed up in her eyes and throat yet again. But the FBI had made it clear she could not tell anyone what had taken place at Jake's. Or who Jake was under his guise as a real estate agent. Or what had happened to her. To them.

She couldn't even tell her family. Especially not her family.

And she did not dare allow herself to dwell on how much her heart still hurt without him—or her mother might see the truth too easily.

So Mary opened her mouth and for the first time in her life told her mother a deliberate lie. "You probably know about the little fire in one of the rooms of Jake's house. It wasn't anything major. The main thing is that Jake and I broke up. I needed a few days by myself to think. No big deal."

"Oh, honey, I'm sorry. I liked Jake. Are you okay? You've never gone off by yourself like that before."

Man, she hated lying to her mother, but she couldn't dwell on it because the time had come to share more important news.

She exhaled and said, "Mom, I'm moving out. I need to find a place of my own."

Instead of looking unhappy or confused, her mother nodded. "I agree. You need a new start, and I would love to help you find a place if you'd like. I know I haven't always been there for you like a mother should. I was so busy with the business and with making sure your father had everything he needed that I..." Jolene stopped talking and her eyes widened. "You're not planning on leaving Honey Creek, are you?"

"No, of course not. Honey Creek is my home." Not that the town had done such great things for her in the past. "I have family and friends here and I don't want to leave them behind. Besides, I can't think of anyplace else that is half as beautiful. I love this part of the country. Where else would I go?"

Jolene gave her a quick hug. "Good. I don't want to lose you before we can actually find time for a real relationship."

"It's okay, Mom. I know you're in love with Craig and your life is terribly busy. But I'll be around. We'll make time for each other from now on. Uh, look, I'm going to be packing up while I try to find a new place."

Then Mary thought of something else. "I need to run into town and turn in my final resignation before I do anything else. I've decided I can't continue working at the library."

"No?" Her mother didn't seem surprised at the news. "But what will you do? Do you want to come to work for Walsh Enterprises? We'd love to have you."

The idea was preposterous, but her mother was being thoughtful and that made Mary actually smile for the first time in days. "I don't know what I want to do exactly. But I can't work for Walsh Enterprises. There's too many unhappy memories there. I've been giving some thought to starting my own business."

"I've always believed you'd be great as a business owner, sweetheart. Like all the rest of us in the family. It's in the blood. But what kind of business?"

Mary shrugged and tilted her head, thinking. "That's the problem. I'm not sure. At first I thought maybe a bookstore, but there's not enough traffic for even a small bookstore in Honey Creek."

Jolene patted her on the shoulder. "Something will come to you. Don't worry. You're a bright young woman. I know you'll find the right thing."

Mary gave her mother a soft nod, but inside she wished she had the same confidence. She'd been so sure she had found the right thing with Jake. And look how well that had turned out.

Mary dabbed at her eyes as she walked out of the library's wide front doors and headed down the steps. She could hardly believe that after all these years she would never again have to come to work at the library. The idea was a little scary but thrilling at the same time.

She just wished Jake was here. She wanted to talk and share her feelings.

Not paying any attention to where she was going, Mary bumped headlong into two women coming up the stairs. "Oh, excuse me."

When she looked up, she realized it wasn't two women at all, but one woman in her late thirties or early forties and a teenager who was her spitting image.

Both had black hair and pretty blue eyes. Mary was taken by how nice they looked together, like a cozy family unit. She stood there gawking.

"I'd bet you're Mary Walsh," the woman said after she smoothed out a wrinkle in her dress. "You look a lot like your mother with all that red hair and those lovely amber eyes. I'm Lily Masterson, the new head librarian. And this is my daughter May."

Mary nodded and found her smile, the disguise she sometimes used in an effort to keep from being exposed. "You two are the ones that look alike. No one would ever miss guessing you're related."

"That's a wonderful compliment. For both of us.

Thank you." Lily laughed, the sound so pleasant that Mary's spirit felt a bit lighter.

"I vaguely remember you as a rather…uh…gawky teenager when I left town fifteen years ago." Lily seemed in no hurry to go inside. "You've changed since then. You're a beautiful woman, Mary. I was sorry to hear we won't be working together."

Mary managed another tentative smile. Then she suddenly remembered the many rumors that spread around town about Lily Masterson years ago, and she couldn't help but steal a quick glance at May. The young teenager was adorable, with her alabaster skin and dimpled smile. But Mary was positive she could not be related to the Walsh family. No possible way. She didn't look like any of them.

A secret pregnancy had been the rampant rumor of the day about Lily, of course. Supposedly, wild-child Lily had been having an affair with Mark Walsh before he'd disappeared.

Now Mary came to the conclusion that those rumors had to have been bogus. In fact, she was having some trouble with the whole concept of Lily as being wild at all. The librarian looked very much like a professional career woman and single mother. Someone that Mary would like to know.

Young May grinned over at her. "Mom says you've worked at the library for a number of years. What are you going to do now?"

"May," Lily scolded. "That's rude. We don't know…"

"No, it's okay." Mary's smile was completely genuine this time. "I'm not sure what I want to do. I have a lot of plans whirling in my head, but first I need to find a new place to live."

"Mom and I are living with my grandfather. He's getting older and doesn't feel well."

"I'm sorry to hear that. But it's nice that you can all be together."

May looked at her through thoughtful eyes that seemed older than her years. "Don't you have family here you can live with?"

"May…" Lily's face flushed as she glared at her daughter.

But Mary only chuckled and said, "I've been living with my mother, but I think it's time I found my own place. I'm all grown up now."

"Well, if I was old enough to go out on my own I would find me a big old house either in the woods or in the mountains. Anyplace outside of this town would be awesome. The town itself isn't much."

An idea sneaked up on Mary, jolting her in the head without warning. She loved the countryside and woods around Honey Creek, too. And as it happened, she knew of a house, only slightly damaged, that was probably available to buy.

"You've given me a thought, May. Thanks."

"Very nice meeting you," Lily said after she threw her daughter a quick look. "But we'd better go inside now." Then she stopped for one more thought. "When you get settled, can I twist your arm into considering volunteer work with the library? I'm trying to talk May into helping out with the children's section after school and we could use all the volunteer help we can find."

"That's a terrific idea. I would love to volunteer.

Especially with the children. I'll stop in the first chance I get."

May gave Mary a quick hug before they split up. Then Mary headed down the stairs toward her car alone. What a darling girl May Masterson was, so warm and full of smiles.

The girl seemed to be aged about fourteen. The same age Mary had been when her father had supposedly died. The stark differences between May and the child Mary had been at that age were stunning.

But when Mary thought it over, the contrast between who she was now and who she had been not too long ago was every bit as amazing. Walking toward her car, Mary considered how her life could have come so far so fast.

Yes, she alone had first decided to make changes in her life. No one had talked her into it. She remembered feeling as if the years were passing her by and that she was sick of feeling depressed all the time.

She'd found the therapist, who'd definitely helped her. And she'd lost over a hundred pounds by sheer willpower—and lots of exercise. But those didn't seem like such huge accomplishments anymore.

As she reached her car and grabbed for the door handle, Mary experienced a sudden gut feeling that someone was watching. The sun was hot this afternoon, but shivers ran down her arms.

Was this Wes's doing again? She looked around, but saw no one. Wes's office would have to be her next stop. Being followed was too creepy. She had enough problems without worrying for her safety in her own hometown. Wes needed to know that he'd gone too far.

The same way Jake had taken his act too far. *Jake*.

Yes, it was true. The biggest changes in her had come from falling in love. Jake had made her face her old fears in a way that no one else had. Too bad their relationship had been doomed from the start. It had all been a fraud. The same as most of her life had been up to now.

Were the newest changes she'd decided to make to her life also likely to be false? She didn't think so. She felt stronger than she ever had, except for all these tears. And there hadn't been any flashbacks or dreams of her childhood terrors in weeks.

As Mary sank down in the driver's seat, she tried to shake off her current depression, wishing for the pain in her heart to stop. This heavy aching in her chest was plain crazy. Even though she'd changed for the better because of loving Jake, a lasting love was not meant for someone like her. Her childhood had left her far too damaged to be loved and wanted for herself. Not for real.

In the end, she was still who she had always been. The little girl who wasn't good enough banished to the closet.

Mary found Wes in the sheriff's front office, talking to a dispatcher and a deputy. She waited for him to break free.

"Do you still have men following me around?" she demanded when the others went back to their desks.

Wes studied her carefully. "Someone has been keeping an eye on you off and on. Why do you ask?"

"I don't need protection anymore. It's feels creepy, Wes. Cut it out."

"As a matter of fact, I tend to agree with you. I don't think you need anyone following you around, either."

"Then you'll stop?"

Wes set aside the clipboard he'd been holding. "Tell me what's going on in your life. Are you back at home for good? Going back to work? I heard a rumor that you were quitting."

"Not that it's any of your business, but…"

He put his big hand on her shoulder. "I care about you, Mary. I'm asking because we're old friends and I want what's best for you."

Mary heaved a heavy sigh. She wasn't mad at Wes for wanting to protect her. He was a good man. A man of honor—not unlike Jake—except when Jake was lying. Shaking her head as the tears filled her eyes again, Mary willed away any thoughts of the man she loved. That relationship was over and done. Still, none of her pain was Wes's fault, and she could use all the friends she could get.

"I did quit my job," she told him quietly. "I'm not sure what I want to do next. Something more exciting than the library, though."

"The excitement of the past month wasn't enough for you?"

"Well, maybe not quite that exciting." She relaxed enough to chuckle at Wes's good humor and he smiled at her in return. "I'm thinking of starting my own business. I want the challenge, but I'm not sure what kind of business yet."

Wes nodded thoughtfully. "I'll keep that in mind. Maybe something will come to me." He rubbed at his chin. "Still living at home? Back on the Walsh farm?"

"Temporarily. But I'm looking to move out on my own. Maybe you could keep that in mind, too."

"I will. Every now and then I hear about a house for sale or someone looking for a roommate."

It was Mary's turn to nod thoughtfully. Wes had never given an answer about stopping her surveillance. And now he looked as though he had something more he wanted to say.

She waited for it.

"You ever give any thought to Jake these days?"

Oh, God. Not that. Could she talk about Jake without breaking down?

For Wes's sake, for the sake of keeping him as a friend, she decided to try. "Yeah. I do. A lot, actually. But…but…I'm trying to get over it."

"Why? Don't you care what he's doing? I thought you two had something going on there for a while."

She nearly choked on the sudden pain, but swallowed past the hurt. "Um, Wes, I hate to be rude. But this one is really none of your business."

"So you do still care?"

The tears welled up again and she was forced to look somewhere else for a second to push them away. "Please. Why are you doing this?"

Wes's eyebrows rose. "I thought you might want to know that Jake has left the FBI. Last time I talked to him he was in pretty sad shape. Having trouble getting over you, is my guess."

Jake quit undercover work? "I…I can't hear about him right now. I don't care—not that much."

"Hmm? And why not? Because he's basically a bad person? You and I both know he is far from that. Or maybe because he lied as part of his job? And I suppose you have never told a single lie in your entire life."

A lone tear trickled out of the corner of her eye and she brushed it away. If Wes had asked her that a few days ago, she might've had a different answer. Telling Jake she didn't love him had been her first big lie.

No. All of a sudden she realized even that wasn't the whole truth. Mary was lying to herself right now, in fact. She'd been hedging around the truth for most of her life. Her mother and brothers and Craig had never known the whole truth of how Mark Walsh had treated her and Lucy. If nothing else, that had been a lie by omission. And earlier today, she'd outright told her mother a huge untruth in order to protect Jake.

But sometimes there were good reasons for lying.

What? Did she really believe that?

"I have to g-go," she stammered. "Wes, please stop following me. I can't take it anymore."

Mary turned, walking as fast as she could without running toward the front door. All the other people in the office surreptitiously followed her with their eyes.

As she put her hand on the door handle, Wes said something very odd. "I'll try, Mary. But I can't promise anything."

"I just heard an interesting rumor, boss." Truman had finally returned to Honey Creek from his forced exile after the beating he'd taken in Bozeman a month ago. He'd been trying to get back in the boss's good graces ever since.

"I hope it's good news. I could use some about now."

"I think you'll like this one." Truman could only

hope. "You remember that fellow you were having me follow before I went on…uh…vacation? Well, my buddy in the sheriff's office told me the dude was actually an FBI agent, but that he'd quit and isn't working in law enforcement at all now. You don't still have someone tailing him, do you?"

A soft curse whooshed from the boss's lips. "That fed's already cost me plenty. No, I don't have anyone following him around anymore. Why toss good money after bad? You sure you heard this rumor right?"

Proud of himself for bringing a smile to his boss's face, Truman stood up a little taller. "Absolutely. But I can confirm it for you if you want."

"No, drop it. There's a plenty of other things you could be doing that would be more cost-effective."

"Sure. Okay. How about the Walsh girl? The one that used to be a fatty? You done with her, too?"

"Mary was never important. The only reason she was included before was that she could've identified the stalker I hired. Now that's no longer a problem and she's off the radar."

"Right." Truman bid his boss goodbye and backed out of the office feeling on top of the world.

His life was finally in order in Honey Creek. And he couldn't wait to get back to his regular job. As long as nobody ever found out what his boss had been doing in secret all these years, everything would be golden.

Chapter 16

Mary clamped her lips down on a soda cracker and used both hands to turn the steering wheel. She drove her car down the long driveway leading to the house in the woods that Jake had rented. The house where they'd been so happy. For a short time.

She'd tried to put in an offer to buy the place several times in the past couple of days. But this morning she'd finally reached a real estate agent who told her the house had already been sold.

Mary's stomach rolled. Again. But being nauseous had nothing to do with the house. She chewed on the cracker, swallowed and prayed that it would stay down.

Must be a flu bug. Perfect. Just what she needed. It was bad enough that she couldn't seem to stem the tears. Rivers of the salty liquid welled up at the worst possible moments. Her emotions had been on a real roller-coaster ride ever since she'd come back to Honey Creek. She couldn't sleep and didn't feel like eating.

Jake's image appeared everywhere she went.

Yes, she was still heartbroken over him. Maybe she always would be. After her discussion about Jake with Wes, Mary had taken the time to review everything they'd been through. Jake had used her for his assignment, true. But he'd also had real feelings for her. Mary's experience with men was extremely limited. Actually, her experience with any relationships seemed almost nonexistent. But everything inside her told her Jake had cared for her. Just not enough to make it last.

Sighing, she wished she could talk to him one more time. Tell him she wasn't mad anymore. That she understood what he'd had to do for his job. Mary had tried reaching him through the FBI, but they refused to give her his forwarding address or number. She'd only wanted to talk to him—not stalk him. But upon second—or maybe third—thought, she'd come to the conclusion that seeing him wouldn't have been smart anyway.

What could she say? That she'd been wrong? Yes, she would do so gladly. That she loved him? Well, it was true. But she wouldn't be able to bear it if he sent her away after she'd laid her heart open. And he would've. Sent her away. She wasn't the kind of woman that men yearned over forever.

Their relationship had been fast and furious. And though Jake meant the world to her, she had done something unforgivable. Called him a liar when he'd only been doing his job. She'd said terrible things, and she didn't deserve his forgiveness or his friendship.

That was part of the reason why buying this house in the woods had become important to her. It reminded her of him. Of how happy they had been during their time here.

Earlier today the agent told her that the new owner was working on remodeling the house. Mary supposed whoever it was wanted to fix up the scorched family room. She hoped they were making the place as wonderful and cozy as it had once been—and that they then would consider selling it to her for a profit.

As she pulled up in front of the house, Mary saw a small group of workmen standing around smoking cigarettes and drinking hot drinks from thermos caps. Several cars and trucks were parked along the driveway. After she slipped her sedan in behind the others and stepped out, she noticed one of the cars belonged to Wes. His sheriff's cruiser.

What was Wes doing here?

She found the sheriff standing near the cluster of other men, with his hands on his hips and his eyes trained on the part of the house under construction. When she came closer, she could hear the most god-awful-sounding racket coming from inside.

She came up beside Wes and raised her voice. "What's going on?"

He turned and his eyes widened. "Hey, I've been trying to reach you. But your cell kept going straight to voice mail."

Mary pulled the cell out of her purse. "No bars." She had to yell to be heard over the noise. "Why did you want to talk to me?"

Wes waved a hand toward the house. "That."

"What is *that?*" She turned to look at the workmen. "What're they doing?"

"They're hoping to go back to work. The commotion you hear is Jake. He says he's dismantling the house. That he wants to take it to the ground."

"Jake? My Ja— I mean, Jake Pierson?" Mary almost shook her head to clear it, ready to believe she was having a nightmare. "I don't understand. What does the new owner have to say about all of this?"

"Jake *is* the new owner. If he wants to tear the place down, I guess there's no law against it."

Now she was sure this was a dream. "Wes, please start from the beginning. What in the world is going on?"

Wes took her arm and pulled her a few feet down the driveway where they could talk in lower tones. "Jake bought the house right after he retired from the FBI. He's been fixing it up. Even hired a remodeling company to do the heavy work." Wes gestured toward the workmen.

"Meanwhile, I've been trying to talk him into starting up a new personal security and alarm business right here in Honey Creek. Thought I was making some headway with him, too, until this morning."

Crazy talk. Jake had been here in Honey Creek all along? "What happened this morning?"

Wes looked down at her with sympathetic eyes. "I drove out today to give it one more try. I told him it was time for him to stop trailing you around and start doing something productive. I even made that mandatory."

"Jake? Jake is the one who's been following me? Why?"

"I'm no psychologist, Mary. But my gut says he's

obsessing over your safety. Not entirely sure what's
behind that, though."

Oh, Jake.

"When I told him he had to stop, he kind of fell apart.
Ordered me and the workmen to get off his property."
Wes screwed up his mouth in a scowl. "You need to
talk to him. He won't listen to anyone else. That's why
I've been trying to reach you. If this gets much worse, I
may have to temporarily commit him to the psych ward
at the Bozeman hospital. He's becoming a danger, both
to others and to himself."

Mary didn't hesitate, or take the time to discuss it
further. She started running toward the front door.

By the time she reached the porch steps, uncertainty
about whether she'd be able to get inside slowed her
down. To her astonishment, the door opened easily. She
closed and locked it behind her with a quiet snick.

Turning toward the room under construction, she
faced a man she barely recognized. Dear Lord, he
must be having a breakdown of some sort. Jake had
a chainsaw in one hand and a sledge hammer in the
other, and he was ripping up newly put up drywall with
a vengeance.

Construction debris, sawdust and scraps of wood flew
everywhere. She blinked a couple of times and realized
Jake had already demolished the back wall. Now he was
moving over to attack a new stone fireplace as tears ran
down his face. Tears. On the strongest male she had ever
known.

Stunned, she just stared at him. He looked twenty
years older than the last time she'd seen him. His
shoulders slumped. His eyes were crazed with emotions
she couldn't name.

Suddenly she didn't know what to do. What to say to get through to him.

But she had to get through. He couldn't keep carrying on like this. It would kill him.

While he hammered at the stone like a wild man, she calmly walked up behind him, crooning his name. Not in the least afraid, she wrapped her arms around his waist and leaned her cheek against his sweat-soaked back.

"Easy does it, Jake. Talk to me."

Stiffening in her arms, his heart pounded out a violent beat under her cheek. She could feel his whole body trembling.

But he didn't pull away. He dropped the sledge hammer and seemed to collapse in upon himself. It was as if she'd popped a balloon and all the air was slowly leaking out until nothing was left. She hung on as they eased to their knees on the floor.

"Leave me alone." His voice was tight, as though at any moment he would inflate again and explode all over the room.

"This isn't like you, Jake. Please tell me…"

He jerked out of her embrace. "You don't know what I'm like. Nobody does. I'm the liar, remember?"

Mary flinched. He couldn't have hurt her any worse if he'd slapped her in the face.

"Jake, tell me what…"

"You want to know all of it?" He laughed, and the sound sent a chill down her neck. "Fine. Why not? You already hate me. It shouldn't make much difference one way or the other if you find out I killed my wife."

Mary put her fist to her mouth to keep from making any sound that would show her surprise. But she *was* surprised. Having trouble with words, she didn't know what to say to him.

"Speechless? You should be. You—everybody— thought I was some noble man of the law. Undercover in order to fight crime. Bull! It was merely the best place for a monster to hide."

Her mumbled words spilled from her lips in double time. "You're no monster, Jake. I don't care what…"

He reached over and took her by the shoulders. "Listen to me. Listen to me tell the truth—for once in my worthless life.

"My wife was a saint." He was shaking with unspent furor. "She took me in and made me a man when nobody else would give the child of a demented survivalist the time of day. And how did I repay her?"

Jake's eyes grew crazed. Manic.

Mary wasn't frightened *of* him but *for* him. She didn't know what to say. How to calm him down. All she could do was hang on and listen.

"Tina told me we were going to have a baby. Great, right? That very night, selfish bastard that I was, I stopped thinking and became completely full of myself. Big man, I gave her my brand-new Porsche. She was thrilled and looked happier than I'd ever seen her. Said she wanted to drive it everywhere."

Mary had to break in before he exploded in grief. "She died in a car accident, Jake. It happens. That wasn't your fault." Mary worked to keep her own tears from spilling out. They weren't what Jake needed right now.

He laughed, nearing hysteria. Dug his fingers into her shoulders.

"Accident, my ass. I was a chock-full-of-myself FBI

agent who had just put one really bad dude in prison. A bastard that I'd been after for a long time. He swore to get even with me. Swore that I would pay with my life."

Jake suddenly released her and choked out a curse. "Well, I paid all right. But not with my life. My wife and unborn child took the punishment for me—dying in my car when the hit came down."

"Oh, Jake. No…" She cowered away from him, her heart torn by grief and sympathy.

"Yes," he hissed. "And what does yours truly do the very next time he falls in love? Once again, without thinking it through, I selfishly put the life of the woman I love on the line. I led the snake right to your door, Mary, and I wasn't even man enough to make you stay away from me where you would be safe."

Mary tried to speak but couldn't. Her lungs refused to breathe.

What could she do about him? With him? She was positive he wouldn't let her help him. He was so determined to be the bad guy in all of this that he would never listen to her or anyone. Shaking, she got to her feet. Crouching in a corner was the coward's way out.

She reached out her hand to help him up, still hoping to make him hear. He swatted her away and came up by himself, hands clenched, tears flowing freely down his cheeks. He was glaring at her, and his breath came in short bursts.

He was going to turn away from her. She could see it clearly in the way he stood. He wasn't going to get over this and let her in. His love for her had obviously died somewhere inside all his pain. Holding a tight rein on the sobs threatening to spill out, she almost laughed.

Of course his love had died. She wasn't the kind of woman who could keep a man. She'd never even been the sort who got what she wanted in the end. Happily-ever-afters were not meant for somebody like her.

It was all she could do not to pull him into her arms and beg. He needed help. And she wanted badly to be the one he needed. But she knew he wouldn't let her. Not now. Their time together was already over.

"Why are you here?" he finally asked.

"Wes asked me to talk to you. He's worried about you. I'm worried, too."

"Both of you need to leave me the hell alone. I'm not worth your time."

"You need to talk to a therapist, Jake." If he wouldn't let her be the one, then he had to find a professional. "Let *someone* help you."

He was trying to focus his eyes on her face. "Why aren't you running the other way?"

Because she loved him.

"You don't strike me as a masochist, Mary." He waved his arm as if shooing her away. "Stay close to me and sooner or later you'll pay with your life."

"You planning on hurting me?"

He narrowed his eyes and scowled. "No."

"You planning on hurting yourself?"

It was then that he looked around and saw the destruction that he'd wrought. "No."

Mary was exhausted. She could barely see straight. But Jake needed her to make good sense. Maybe not forever, but for now.

"You're tired, Jake. Go upstairs and lie down. Things will look better after you've rested."

"Walk away."

She heard the fear in his voice. He didn't want to be alone. She couldn't say that she blamed him.

Reaching out with compassion, she took him by the hand and together they climbed the stairs the way they had done many times in the past. Only this time, when they lay down on the bed, they were fully clothed.

Within minutes Jake fell into a deep, profound sleep. And Mary cradled him in her arms while he did.

Later, she slipped out of the bed and dragged herself down the stairs. She didn't want to be here when he woke up. Not if he wouldn't let her help him. Love him.

She had to get on with her life. Wes would help him. Maybe better than she could.

So tired she wasn't sure she could make it out to her car, all Mary wanted was to curl up in bed until she was over the flu. Then she would find a place to live that wouldn't remind her of Jake.

He needed professional help. Mary only hoped that he would get it soon. But she would probably never know whether he had or not.

Silent tears formed again in her eyes, and she frantically shoved them aside. Mary needed to keep all that hurt locked up inside so no one else ever guessed. But she'd done that kind of thing before.

Mary reminded herself that for once in her life, she had been lucky enough to fall in love with someone who had loved her back. Maybe their relationship had only been temporary. But many women never even got that lucky. She'd been blessed by having this experience.

And she would always have her memories.

Jake thanked Mary's sister Lucy and then headed up the stairs from her shop to the apartment above. It had taken him days to steel himself, but he was on his way to talk to Mary at last. She'd moved off the farm and was living here at her sister's place.

They needed to talk. How could he have let her walk away without at least thanking her for listening to his confession? She'd been right. Despite his misgivings, it had been important for him to talk to a therapist. He'd finally seen one. And he would continue. He needed to thank her for that, too.

Mary Walsh had been right about everything from the start. She was a lifesaver and had given him much more than he could've imagined: compassion, love, tenderness. And, damn him, he'd been so totally absorbed with his own pain that he had let her walk away without a word.

It fascinated him how different Mary's personality was from Tina's. Mary was much stronger and smarter about a lot of things. But she didn't have the self-assurance and knowledge of her own worth that his wife had possessed. Life had conspired against Mary. She'd never felt safe enough or certain enough of her abilities to explore.

But Jake felt absolutely certain. She was worth the world to him. He missed her so badly that he could barely breathe until he had her back in his arms again.

Saying a silent prayer that she would be willing to take a chance on a man only half done finding out what mattered the most, he straightened his shoulders and approached her door.

Breathing in, Jake held his breath and knocked. When Mary answered, she looked stunningly beautiful. And all the air blew right back out of him.

Her skin glowed as she looked up at him. "Jake?"

Like the fool he was, he choked on his own anxiety before he could speak. "Can we talk?"

"Come in." She looked confused. Scared.

Jake didn't like seeing either expression in her eyes. He wanted to see only love when she looked at him. She'd had love in her eyes once. Now it was up to him to put it back.

But he needed to deserve her love.

"How have you been?" He studied her face for a clue as to how she was feeling about him.

"I've missed you." They both said the words at the same time and then smiled tentatively.

Still standing just inside the closed door, they looked at each other. Jake's fingers ached to touch her, but he fisted his hands at his sides instead.

"What brought you here, Jake?" Was that hope that he heard in her voice?

His own hope bubbled up, threatening to spill all over the room. "I came to...uh...say a couple of things."

Her eyes narrowed, and she looked more uncertain than ever. "Why are you really here? Have you heard something about me being sick?"

His turn to be confused. "I haven't heard anything. You don't look sick. Are you?"

She shook her head, turned and waved her hand to convey that she wanted him to continue with his explanation.

"I came to apologize for being such an ass and for spilling my guts to you the way I did." He tried softening his tone. "I came to thank you for listening and to tell you I've been seeing a psychologist."

She blinked up at him. "Sometimes burdens seem

better when they're shared by two people. I'm only glad I could help."

He couldn't stand it. She looked so unsure of herself.

Reaching out, he stroked her cheek, still wishing he could take her in his arms. "You're right again. You have a bad habit of doing that, you know. I'm here asking if you'd be willing to share a couple of more burdens with me."

"What kind of burdens?"

"Well, for one thing, I own a huge house that badly needs redecorating. I've come to the conclusion that it needs a woman's special touch. Your touch.

"And for another thing," he added quickly. "I'm starting up a business and have discovered I'm terrible at administration—all those details. I thought you might consider becoming my partner."

"Oh." The hope grew brighter in her eyes. "Why?"

"Because I love you. And I thought that you…"

"I love you, too." She jumped into his arms and snuggled into his embrace.

Thank God.

He held her close and whispered, "I can't live without you. If you can accept that deep down I'm a selfish bastard, but one who is trying to change, give us a chance. Love me. Marry me. Teach me how to give."

She looked up at him. Her eyes were bright and full of love. It would be too easy to lose himself there.

"I have a burden of my own to share first," she said with a whimsical, lopsided smile. "After I tell you, ask me again."

He held his breath once more and waited.

"I'm pregnant. You and I are going to be parents."

"What?" Jake was having trouble processing the words. This couldn't be happening. Not again. Pure panic spiked his pulse.

"Jake?" Mary pulled out of his arms and put her hands on her hips. "Listen to me. I'm not going to die. Our baby won't die. It isn't happening again. I'm healthy and the baby is healthy. And under no circumstances will I accept any kind of gifts from you. I promise. We'll live long and happy lives. Now, will you marry me?"

Trying to smile, he opened his mouth to form the word but it wouldn't come. Tears built up behind his eyes as he nodded and reached for her.

The tears were a surprise. He'd thought he was all done with them. But the crazy happiness felt familiar.

The most wonderful woman in the whole world would be teaching him how to give. And he would give her anything in return. Tears included. Anything that made her happy.

Then he did something not surprising at all. He kissed her. A simple, I-do kind of kiss. Reminding her of who loved her. Of who was willing to share her burdens from now on.

They would live long and happy lives. Giving and loving and sharing. Together. Forever.

Epilogue

"How thrilling, honey. When do you two plan on being married? I hope we'll have enough time to throw a huge bash." Jolene took a sip of wine and relaxed back next to Craig on Mary and Jake's brand-new sofa.

Mary was so pleased with herself that all she wanted to do was laugh. This was their first real dinner party. Well, it couldn't be called a real party. But it was the first time they'd invited family over. Everything felt just perfect. How good could one life be?

"Yes, Mom, we'll have enough time. I've always wanted a winter wedding. After the holidays. January maybe."

Jake cleared his throat and squeezed her arm lightly. "Can you give me a hand in the kitchen?"

She nodded and stood. "Excuse us. Craig, do you need another drink?"

When Craig looked her way and shook his head, she noticed the corners of his eyes were crinkled and tight. As though he were in pain.

Jake didn't give her time to think; he hustled them both into the kitchen. Once there, he drew her into his arms and kissed her. Another of his fantastic toe-curling kisses that pledged more to come later.

After they split apart to draw in air, she laughed at his urgent desperation, but she felt it, too. "Jolene and Craig won't be here much longer. We're already on the after-dinner drinks. Save some of those kisses for when we're alone, please."

"There's lots more where that came from, woman." Jake looked down at her in his arms as though he was ready to have her for dessert. She knew exactly how he felt.

When she turned to get the coffee, he pulled her back against his chest. "How are you feeling? You look spectacular tonight."

"Thank you, kind sir. I'm feeling well. Being sick to my stomach only seems to come in the mornings now. And I've been extra good tonight, too. No alcohol, of course. And not a lot of empty calories. You should be proud of me."

Jake rubbed his hand along her spine and the temperature soared between them. "Oh, I am. Except for the part where you haven't told your mother and Craig about the baby yet. Shouldn't they know?"

Mary sighed. "I wanted to leave it between us for a little longer. I'll tell them soon."

She wasn't used to sharing. Or being the center of attention. But she was working up to it. She hoped she wouldn't show for a few more months, and she was savoring every precious moment of building a relationship with Jake before the baby came into the picture.

A child would change their relationship once again. And though she couldn't wait to be a mother, she wanted to hold on for a while to the feeling of being loved as a woman and a wife first.

"Did you notice Craig looks like he's in pain?" Mary turned to face the coffeemaker and talked to Jake over her shoulder.

She could hear the shrug in his voice. "Not sure."

Mary grimaced. "Well, for Mom's sake I hope it isn't anything real bad, like his heart. The two of them are only just now admitting how much they love each other. It's their turn to be happy."

Jake put his arms around Mary's waist and kissed the back of the neck. "It's our turn, too, sweetheart. I never thought I could be this lucky—to get a second chance at love."

He snuggled her close and she reveled in the wondrous experience of having someone care. "And I do love you, Mary. I won't ever stop telling you. You are my heart and my life. My nights and my mornings. Give me your burdens and take mine for as long as we both live."

Mary leaned her head back on his shoulder and smiled to herself, loving the feel of his body against hers. And loving the heartfelt words of the very special man who loved her that much.

It occurred to her then that she had never read any words more wonderful, not in any book. Jake's love was better than a bestseller.

* * * * *

INTRIGUE..

0211/46a

INTRIGUE...

0211_BOTM

MILLS & BOON®

are proud to present our...

Book of the Month

Walk on the Wild Side
by Natalie Anderson

from Mills & Boon® RIVA™

Jack Greene has Kelsi throwing caution to the wind
—it's hard to stay grounded with a man who turns
your world upside down! Until they crash with
a bump—of the baby kind...

Available 4th February

Something to say about our Book of the Month?
Tell us what you think!

millsandboon.co.uk/community
facebook.com/romancehq
twitter.com/millsandboonuk

Sometimes love is stronger than death…

For Agent Dante Moran, finding Tessa Westbrook's missing daughter becomes personal when he sees the teenager's resemblance to his murdered girlfriend.

Tessa needs to know who told her daughter the terrifying story of her conception. And it soon becomes clear to Dante that the truth is dangerous—but is it worth dying for?

www.mirabooks.co.uk

Her only hope of survival was her worst enemy

Private security agent Lucie Evans jumps at the offer of escape to South America to become a billionaire heiress's bodyguard. Then her nightmare begins.

With Lucie's life at stake, her ex-boss Sawyer has to ignore their rocky past and forget his contempt for her before it's too late. Lucie's captor will not rest until she is silenced…once and for all.

www.mirabooks.co.uk

No, please don't.

Nashville homicide lieutenant Taylor Jackson is pursuing a serial killer who leaves the prior victim's severed hand at each crime scene.

TV reporter Whitney Connolly has a scoop that could break the case, but has no idea how close to this story she really is.

As the killer spirals out of control, everyone must face a horrible truth: that the purest evil is born of secrets and lies.

www.mirabooks.co.uk

Thriller 2

Stories You Just Can't Put Down

Edited by the grand master of adventure,
Clive Cussler, *Thriller 2* is packed with over
twenty all-new stories from some of the biggest
names in fiction, including Jeffery Deaver,
David Hewson and R.L. Stine

www.mirabooks.co.uk

HENRY PARKER MUST UNCOVER THE MOST DEVASTATING SECRET OF ALL – *HIS OWN*

The brother I never knew is dead – shot point-blank in a rat-hole apartment, wasted by hunger and heroin. A man with whom I shared nothing…except a father.

This stranger came to me for help. Now I'm forced to question everything I ever knew to figure out why he was murdered in cold blood.

All I can do now is uncover the whole, hard truth.

The fourth novel in the thrilling
Henry Parker series

www.mirabooks.co.uk

Discover Pure Reading Pleasure with

Visit the Mills & Boon website for all the latest in romance

🌹 **Buy** all the latest releases, backlist and eBooks

🌹 **Find out** more about our authors and their books

🌹 **Join** our community and chat to authors and other readers

🌹 **Free** online reads from your favourite authors

🌹 **Win** with our fantastic online competitions

🌹 **Sign** up for our free monthly eNewsletter

🌹 **Tell us** what you think by signing up to our reader panel

🌹 **Rate** and review books with our star system

www.millsandboon.co.uk

Follow us at twitter.com/millsandboonuk

Become a fan at facebook.com/romancehq

2 FREE BOOKS
AND A SURPRISE GIFT

We would like to take this opportunity to thank you for reading this Mills & Boon® book by offering you the chance to take TWO more specially selected books from the Intrigue series absolutely FREE! We're also making this offer to introduce you to the benefits of the Mills & Boon® Book Club™—

- **FREE home delivery**
- **FREE gifts and competitions**
- **FREE monthly Newsletter**
- **Exclusive Mills & Boon Book Club offers**
- **Books available before they're in the shops**

Accepting these FREE books and gift places you under no obligation to buy, you may cancel at any time, even after receiving your free books. Simply complete your details below and return the entire page to the address below. You don't even need a stamp!

YES Please send me 2 free Intrigue books and a surprise gift. I understand that unless you hear from me, I will receive 5 superb new stories every month, including two 2-in-1 books priced at £5.30 each and a single book priced at £3.30, postage and packing free. I am under no obligation to purchase any books and may cancel my subscription at any time. The free books and gift will be mine to keep in any case.

Ms/Mrs/Miss/Mr _____ Initials _____

Surname _____

Address _____

_____

_____ Postcode _____

E-mail _____

Send this whole page to: Mills & Boon Book Club, Free Book Offer, FREEPOST NAT 10298, Richmond, TW9 1BR